Praise for Benatar novels reissued by Welbeck

WISH HER SAFE AT HOME

'A masterpiece...matchlessly clever...wholly original.'
John Carey

'With this marvellous book, character and poetry return to the
English novel... Rachel is one of the great English female
characters, like the Wife of Bath or Flora Finching: both an
individual and a species.'
Times Literary Supplement

RECOVERY

'A haunting and highly enjoyable love story.'
Prunella Scales

'A beguiling masterclass in modern fiction. Tension inexorably
builds toward a gripping conclusion...the sort of book you start
reading especially slowly as the final pages arrive.'
James O'Brien, LBC Radio

THE MAN ON THE BRIDGE

'Great understanding and depth of feeling.'
New Statesman

'Handles tricky material with conviction and assurance.'
Guardian

LETTERS FOR A SPY

'A thrilling romantic adventure, with superior characterization and an acute eye for detail.'
Henry Fitzherbert, Sunday Express

WHEN I WAS OTHERWISE

'An intriguing, funny, sometimes exciting and, finally, sad story; the elegant idiosyncrasy of the author's viewpoint, which made *Wish Her Safe at Home* so enjoyably inventive without discarding a carefully controlled narrative, here creates a moving story from what might first appear to be the elements of a black farce.'
Christopher Hawtree, Literary Review

'This book is remarkably convincing... One's first reaction on finishing the novel is "Goodness, how sad!" One's second is "Goodness, how funny!"
Francis King, Spectator

'Sparkling social comedy... the comparisons that come to mind are Ayckbourn's plays and Austen's minor characters.'
Gillian Carey

*

Two other reissues in the pipeline:

Father of the Man
The Golden Voyage of Samson Groves

About the Author

Stephen Benatar was born in 1937, to Jewish parents, in Baker Street, London.

Although he started writing when he was only eight, 'The Man on the Bridge' wasn't published until he was forty-four – and even then, if it hadn't been for the kindness and concern of Pamela Hansford Johnson, the novelist wife of C. P. Snow, this might never have happened.

Since then, however, there have been seven novels – one published by a borough council, the first and only time a council has produced a work of fiction. In 1983 he was awarded a £7000 bursary by the Arts Council; and Boston University in Massachusetts is now the repository for all his papers and manuscripts.

He was married for twenty-nine years to Eileen, with whom he had two sons and two daughters; has taught English at the University of Bordeaux, lived in Southern California, been a school teacher, an umbrella salesman, hotel porter, employee of the Forestry Commission; and at long last, in his retirement, has become a fulltime writer.

Having finally moved back to London, he now lives in West Hampstead – until recently, with his partner of seven years, John.

Stephen Benatar

Such Men Are Dangerous

and

Swimming with William
a play in two acts

Welbeck Modern Classics

This book was written with the financial assistance of the Arts
Council of Great Britain and with the unstinting help of the
Reverend Gordon Sleight, one-time vicar in Scunthorpe. To him
and his wife Lesley – wherever they are now – I should like
again to express my gratitude. I wish them and their children
great happiness.

First published in1985, by Scunthorpe Borough Council.

New edition – © Stephen Benatar, 2010 – reissued by:

Welbeck Press
4 Parsifal Road
London NW6 1UH
Telephone: 020 7433 8084

ISBN: 978-0-9554757-7-1

Cover design: John Murphy

Printed by:
Broadfield Press Limited
Eley Road, London N18 3BB
Telephone: 020 8887 9555

For Gill Carey, in deepest gratitude.

INTRODUCTION

New readers should be aware this Introduction reveals key elements of the plot.

Readers familiar with Stephen Benatar's work will be aware that he has a certain fondness for unusual subject matter: a woman's descent into madness as witnessed from her own perspective in *Wish Her Safe at Home*; the discovery of the corpses of two elderly, isolated women, one a full year following her death, in *When I Was Otherwise*; a serious study of a pact with a time-travelling Lucifer in *The Return of Ethan Hart* (the companion piece to *Recovery*); and a gay relationship, published at a time when gays were less commonly accepted, in *The Man on the Bridge*. Little surprise, then, there is no sign of Benatar taking the easy option in this present novel.

But one rather wonders, on opening *Such Men Are Dangerous*, whether he has not this time surpassed himself. Is he intentionally making life – his own, his readers' – difficult by choosing the most awkward or unfashionable ideas he can think of?

A godly, single-minded vicar of the Church of England as a protagonist.

The steel town of Scunthorpe, South Humberside, as a setting.

Thatcherite 1980's as a period.

Unemployment as a backdrop.

The sighting of an angel as a subject.

And when we say angel we are not talking of a vague, mystical, spiritual, new-world otherness but of a good, old-fashioned, true-to-God, white clad (although no wings) biblical angel with a good old-fashioned message for humanity. Sighted on the parking lot behind the local disco by two schoolboy

I

brothers, William and Michael, one of whom subsequently, miraculously, washes clean his face of acne with his tears.

Needless to say, this is quite a premise to ask the reader to swallow, as indeed it is to ask of the characters in the book. All of them, other than the two boys themselves and their mother, 'Devotional Dawn' who "got religion" in the wake of marital disaster, are initially sceptical. The novel, ambitious and questioning, unfolds around the gradual acceptance of the angel as a true and timely vision before leading the reader smack bang into the huge implications of such an acceptance.

The protagonist of *Such Men Are Dangerous* is Simon Madison, a handsome, thirty-three-year-old C of E vicar who, after interviewing the boys, heading discussion meetings with parishioners and a certain amount of soul-searching, self-questioning and generally turning the matter round and round in his own head (thoughts to which we are privy), reaches the conclusion that the boys are telling the truth and that the apparition of a message-delivering angel really has taken place behind Tiffany's Nitespot.

Cynical, non-believing Josh, father of William and Michael, husband of Dawn (and he remembers the days when his wife's biblical quotes ran no further than "Adam and Eve and Pinch-Me went down to the river to bathe...") turns, with an eye to commercial gain, the angelic visitation into a media circus, headlining broadsheets and tabloids, making appearances on the national news and the Russell Harty Show...and asking the reader (this reader) to suspend disbelief still further.

But just when one is beginning to worry that one's willingness to suspend disbelief is not going to stretch any further, Stephen Benatar pulls off a minor miracle himself. He places the demands of *Such Men Are Dangerous* into perspective. A perspective encompassing two thousand years of the history of western civilization which reminds us that the sighting of angels is one of the basic tenets of Christianity and one which, as a people, we have accepted for an awfully long time.

II

Simon is writing a *Life of Christ* in his 'spare' time; for, as one of his parishioners so rightly comments, "most such existing works are either turgid or sentimental, when you would think our Saviour's life would be the most dramatic and exciting on record," and it is with a certain element of shock that we are taken from Simon's angsting about his capacity to pray, to Mary's announcement of her God-given pregnancy to Joseph:

She'd never seen him like this. He was furious. She thought at any moment he might strike her.
"Who was it?" he shouted.

Mary duly explains that "the angel says..." but Joseph's answer is to ridicule her in a falsetto voice:

"I'm six weeks overdue, God, and already half married to that simpleton carpenter down the road but if I can say you were the one who put me in the club he's bound to be impressed!"

Joseph reminds her that stoning is the usual punishment for such behaviour, before calming down and – sounding remarkably like a twentieth-century vicar still coming to terms with the death of his beloved wife, Ginny – reflects unhappily:

He had loved her so much. Life had seemed so perfect. Why had everything gone wrong?

Another extract from Simon's *Life of Christ* (by now entitled *Firebrand!*) portrays the reaction of Mary's parents to the news of her and her sixty-five-year-old cousin Elizabeth's pregnancies – "Don't talk so daft!" and "Oh, my lass, my poor demented lass, is it a fever you've caught?" – and with this simple, powerful technique we, the reader, are effectively required to review our own scepticism and as a consequence are led into the ensuing debate.

In his own writing Simon begins to see how to incorporate a short story he'd once written about "the apostles, after Jesus had sent them out on a journey to win converts and supporters and to spread the word" and although he has not yet reached the momentous conclusion that his own life should reflect this design, he does wonder all the same if this is not "the pattern in the carpet", a pattern of which he is being allowed "piecemeal glimpses". The book is scattered with references to Simon's overwhelming need to find a reason for his existence: "You couldn't face life feeling that it's got no point." The purpose he is seeking is slowly but clearly beginning to take shape.

So what exactly is the message delivered by the angel, the message from God? Simon sums it up very simply when answering a journalist's question as "Love thy neighbour" and getting "back to the great Christian truths...a byword for loving and caring and *doing*..."

But how to change "the world's priorities – prestige, power – when there are still millions living on the breadline?" Before Simon decides on a course of action, not only has the boys' father, Josh, made a substantial profit out of the angel, through a very calculated approach to giving interviews, but a local impresario has already started turning the car park behind Tiffany's into a tourist spot complete with souvenir badges and T-shirts, and we are forced to agree with the young, pre-vicar Simon's frustrated words that "the only thing this world cares about is money, money, money. I'm all right, Jack, I couldn't give a sod what happens to the rest of you."

The angel's message is urgent. We must all learn to love, to care about one another, if the world is to survive. Gabriel tells the boys that "people have to be made to realize, wake up, take action." It is Geraldine, the journalist who is in love with Simon, who puts into words the thoughts he scarcely dare acknowledge, namely that he will have to be the one to wake them up: "Simon, it seems to me that you should mobilize those followers, take the land by storm..." Simon is, of course, the rabble-rousing dangerous man of the title – the *firebrand!* – but she too has her role to play; as he says to her, "You are a very persuasive young lady. Possibly a dangerous one."

IV

And so is born the idea of the march from Scunthorpe to London – reminiscent of the Jarrow March of the Thirties – which will have gathered "millions...many, many millions" by the time the marchers finally storm Downing Street. (The fifty-odd gathered in Westminster for a 'last supper' of pasta and ice-cream before Simon leaves to deliver his message to Mrs Thatcher have mainly been coached in for the day.) We are never in any doubt as to the sincerity of Simon's motives for spreading the word of God but his religious beliefs do not, cannot, exist in a vacuum and despite his claim that "politics and religious principles never seem to mix" his final act of heroism/ fanaticism/ selflessness/ selfishness/ glory/ tragedy and *waste* would beg to differ. As a young man Simon contemplated a career in politics in order to "influence things for the better" and "make big improvements in people's lives." At the end of the book he chooses to make his statement in front of the Prime Minister, not before a religious leader; albeit a prime minister who – in the opinion of Simon's mother – "certainly *thinks* she's God." That politics and religion are completely mixed is, of course, integral to the novel and Simon's "urge to shake his fist at God and the government and everybody who supported it" reminds us that *Such Men Are Dangerous* was originally – and uniquely – published by Scunthorpe Borough Council, eliciting comments in the local newspaper about the appalling waste of local resources on works by "pot-smoking lefty hippies" or, as more elegantly phrased in the novel, conforming to "the airy-fairy notions of idealists everywhere who seek to change the world." The sort of comment that the Tiffany angel might well have predicted himself.

Equally, Simon does not live in an emotionless void and various phrases almost tossed away innocuously throughout the book return to haunt us in the light of his final choice. In fact, seemingly innocent clues litter this book and it is only on a second reading that one can see how clearly they are pointing the way. One cannot, for instance, help but remember that it is Ginny who always claimed (to Simon's horror) that he should be a vicar; help but remember her words at his "first married-life birthday" meal. If she were prematurely to die, she asks, what would he do? "Commit suicide," he answers. But apart from that? "Something wonderful," he says.

"All right. I'd haunt you every minute, to make sure you did. I'd clank my chains at you and demand some magnificent memorial, some golden piece of evidence..."

Well, of course, read like this, she sure gets it. So is the march and its tragic-glorious finale an entirely personal quest, a memorial to his dead wife? A culmination of the "feeling – bordering well-nigh on hatred" he harbours within him, the seeds of which were sown fourteen years ago at Ginny's death?

Or is it the ultimate sacrifice required to make a people in jeopardy wake up to the need to love thy neighbour, to respect the fundamental principles of Christianity? Is it an act of Christian redemption? Is Simon, a profoundly religious man, prepared to undergo the extreme suffering to save (the sins of) the world? He is after all, according to his mother, "bent on doing good – at times almost fanatically so."

But what, too, to make of Simon's charismatic character, the part of him that feels like 'an emperor' preaching to a huge congregation "with people standing four or five deep"; the Simon who is tempted by the idea of playing at "Henry V leading the English towards Agincourt"; the Simon mocked in the newspapers for wanting to play *Simon Says*; "the knight-errant in shining armour, riding into battle on a milk-white charger"...? Has history not taught us to be extremely wary of such leaders, to be frightened of the fanaticism of "a charlatan with charisma"?

It is ironic that Josh of all people, after his boys had seen the angel, should have thanked Simon for having made no "serious effort to convert" him, for Josh brings hope. Redeeming hope. He joins the march as a means of escape from his marriage, from a desperate lack of fulfilment, from the person he has become. When Dawn tells him that he "ought to be pleading for forgiveness, ought to be begging for salvation," his unvoiced

VI

response is, "No, I ought to be getting the hell out of here. I ought to be *doing* something with my life." Initially, he comes across as a fairly seedy, unpleasant character who has been fired from his job as a teacher for having had sex with a pupil and who would be prepared to leave Dawn for Geraldine on the strength of a couple of meetings. And yet by the end of the life-affirming march we are sure, although Benatar does not spell it out in depth, that not only have he and Dawn salvaged their marriage but that it is he who will return to Scunthorpe to continue Simon's work in his own way.

The title of Stephen Benatar's novel is beautifully apt. Such men are dangerous; such books are dangerous: they raise questions to which they do not always deliver answers, forcing us to think about our own lives, our own behaviour and attitudes. They make us look hard at our own priorities and question whether we would be prepared to stand up for our beliefs and follow a man like Simon (Geraldine is the only character in the book to throw in her job and join the march and she has an ulterior motive) and, indeed, even whether we would be right to do so. Like Simon, we have to ask whether the "coolly analytical frame of mind, expectant of little, mistrustful of much...circumspect and cynical," which could be said to apply to so many in our present age, is actually a prison that effectively shuts us out of a world where the norm is "to love thy neighbour".

Such men, such books, succeed in shaking us out of our apathy, out of the "lack of concern" condemned by the Tiffany angel. And such things can only be positive.

Prudence Hope,

May 2010.

VII

Part One

1

When the call came Simon had been changing a light bulb. For a modern house the landing was unusually high and his mother had insisted on holding the steps.

With one foot still pressing on the bottom rung, one hand still firmly in position, she reached out and fumbled for the switch.

"Let there be light," she proclaimed.

"I always knew you wanted to play God," he said.

"Then that makes two of us. But yes. Let there be light. Let there be peace. Let there be tomatoes with a bit of flavour. Let there be repairmen who actually turn up on the day they say they will."

She went on – as the telephone rang in the study – "And let *that* be something unutterably lovely. Like, for instance, a pools win or a wrong number."

Her son jumped down from the ladder, well-built, good-looking, as darkly blond as she'd once been; she was now brunette. He took the stairs two at a time. "Anyway," she called out after him, "we could do with a female God for a change. I may think of standing at the next election. Fight you for it!"

He glanced up at her quizzically before hurrying on.

"On second thoughts," she added quietly as she followed him downstairs en route to strain spaghetti, "I'm not so sure. You'd fight too single-mindedly." Her tone contained an element of pride. "And in any case... Isn't it enough for the time being to have a female *prime minister*? One who thinks she's God."

He picked up the telephone. "St Matthew's Vicarage."

"Oh, Simon, I *am* glad you're home! I've something wonderful to tell you! Can I pop round?"

Dawn Heath spoke with even more than her customary zeal and because Simon often doodled on his blotter, reducing life to a clichéd absurdity, he no longer needed a pencil in his hand for silly captions to occur to him. *It was Devotional Dawn on the blower. Sinful Simon felt his heart sink.*

"Dawn, I've got to be at the youth club at six. And I've a meeting after that. Can't you tell me now?"

"If you're having your tea," she said, "that's perfectly all right. You mustn't think I'll mind you eating."

Yes, I just have to do it sometimes, he wanted to confirm. Sorry. Sometimes I even have to shit. He wondered how she might react.

"Somehow it wouldn't seem proper on the telephone," she said.

Simon raised his eyes to the ceiling; then let them, on their way down, dwell briefly on the crucifix above his desk. "Fine. See you shortly." He went into the kitchen.

"Friend or foe?" asked Mrs Madison. Her look suggested that anyone who rang at this hour could only be the latter.

"Dawn Heath. Coming round to talk."

"What? Now?"

"She says she'll watch us eat."

"That's extremely kind of her. I shall stay in here, however. *You* can take a tray into the sitting room."

"Thanks."

"But what in heaven's name can suddenly be so all-important – ?"

"Well, yes, *of course*!" he exclaimed. "Her husband's found a job! In that case she can peer at every forkful, count my chews and wipe my mouth. Let her spread the news in any way she wants."

"Oh, do you think that's it? Then how fantastic! No wonder she's excited!" His mother's words were heartfelt and she touched his hand. "But even so. I think I'll stick with my Ross Macdonald."

The doorbell rang after barely five minutes.

"Dawn, you must be in training for the Olympics!"

"No. But I was all ready to come, you see, when I phoned you from the neighbours'. And it doesn't take a jiffy on the bike."

He helped her off with her anorak and she removed her headscarf and shook out her brown curls. She wasn't yet forty but looked older; despite the cycling she was overweight. She never wore makeup and was often shiny-faced. The hair remained her best feature.

"I'm taking you at your word and going to eat my supper whilst we speak. Would you like some coffee?"

"No thanks. But thank you anyway."

He showed her into the sitting room. She sat down gingerly, waiting for him to do so first, but already he realized there was something new about her: an air of confidence more gentle than her normal determination to bear witness to the Lord. He smiled. He could understand it. In a steel town such as Scunthorpe, in the nineteen-eighties, a man's finding a job was very nearly proof of divine intervention. Comparable to the kind of career guidance Joseph got in Egypt.

Simon twirled a forkful of spaghetti.

"You do that like an Italian!" she remarked.

This, too, seemed untypically relaxed.

She went on: "You're never going to believe this."

"Good."

"You've met my boys, of course."

"Your *boys*? I know I've met your husband."

He tried to think back: to the early weeks of his incumbency, about three years previously, when he'd visited the home of every member of his congregation.

"Oh, yes," she said. "In the past they haven't been to church a lot but you'd certainly have seen them every Christmas and Easter." She laughed self-mockingly. "At those times they didn't have much choice!" Dawn herself attended twice a week. "From now on, though, it's going to be different!"

"Great," replied Simon. He was having to adjust his expectations.

3

"You don't remember them, do you?" A strange mixture of disappointment and mild accusation suffused by tolerance and joy.

"I'm afraid not."

"Well, William's nearly sixteen, Michael's a year younger. They're good boys, both of them, not too noisy, helpful round the house." (Flat, wasn't it? One of those awful high-rise buildings near the town centre?) "Oh, sometimes they squabble a bit; I'm not saying they're perfect. But they don't tell lies. No. They never have."

These last words came out sharply – oddly – cutting a swathe through her serenity.

"Has anybody said they do?"

"Not yet."

He looked at her more curiously.

"Usually, you see, they don't come home together."

He thought *you see*, if intended to convey a sense of logical progression, might be overoptimistic.

"You mean, after school?" he asked. "Well, I imagine that each has his own friends."

"But today it was different."

It occurred to him he would have liked a glass of wine with his *Bolognaise*. Yet he supposed he oughtn't to let it seem he began to drink at half-past-five.

"They always walk the same way," she said. "Along Doncaster Road. Past Tiffany's. You know? That disco place that used to be a cinema? Big car park behind?"

He'd have thought Tiffany's, with its strident shades of blue and yellow, was garish enough for anyone to notice. Anyone. Even a vicar.

Yes, I often go there looking for girls. Again he wondered what sort of response this might elicit.

"Well, then. Something made them go round the back."

"What do you mean, something?"

"That's just it. They said they didn't know they'd done it. Not until afterwards."

4

He felt his stomach tighten. She was staring at him with eyes which were wide and challenging and gave the faint impression of a squint. He knew he wasn't a patient man. Let him at least remain a courteous one. "Dawn, I'm sorry. What are you trying to tell me?"

"Well, you see, it's like this. At the back of Tiffany's my two boys saw an angel."

Her tone was almost matter-of-fact. There hadn't been any slight pause for effect. And yet those last three words in some way glittered.

"Saw an angel?" Simon said.

Count up to ten, he advised himself. Count slowly up to ten. He counted up to five.

Dawn Heath leant back in her chair; ceased playing with her wedding ring; now gazed at him with more than just her earlier assurance. Now gazed at him in wonder.

"And he spoke to them," she added.

Without haste, Simon put his tray on the floor, the food unfinished. He wiped his napkin across his mouth, scarcely aware of doing so. He sent off a silent prayer for assistance.

"So what did he say?"

"That we were heading for disaster." The expression in her eyes was more suggestive of delightfulness. "And how we'd have to mend our ways."

"Heading for disaster and needing to mend our ways?" Again Simon had resorted to unhurried repetition in the hope this might provide a moment for reflection. "Anything else?"

"Well, the boys will be able to tell you better than me. I mean, I made them repeat it several times but I couldn't take it in."

"And what did he look like?"

"Oh, like you'd expect. Wore a white robe. Was all bathed in light." And she opened her arms to indicate the spreading radiance she was sure there'd been.

Simon stood up.

"Listen, Dawn, it strikes me it isn't you I ought to hear this from. Supposing I come round tomorrow after the boys are home from school?"

5

"Tomorrow?"

"If your sons have truly had a vision," he pointed out gently, "it's not going to evaporate by then."

"But you don't really think they have, do you?" Now her tone came as something of a shock: the very flatness of it. "You don't believe they have."

"Dawn, at this stage how can I possibly say?"

"You think they might have made it up."

"There could be other explanations."

"How could there? They *both* saw it."

"There's a thing called shared fantasy," he said. "The mind can play strange tricks."

"Why should it? Why suddenly like that?"

He shrugged. "On the other hand, of course, there've been plenty of similar experiences in the history of the Church."

They stood regarding each other in silence. She half turned towards the door. Sullenness gave way to supplication.

"Please can't you come tonight? Otherwise they won't sleep."

"I don't suppose they'll sleep much anyway. Nor you either. But all right."

He paused.

"Expect me around ten."

2

His mother was reading *The Zebra-Striped Hearse*. "Help yourself to pudding," she said. "I've just come to a good bit. Has her husband got a job?"

For a stupid moment he imagined this the current point of interest in her book. "No."

"What did she want, then?" She again directed his attention to the fruit salad.

"To tell us that her sons have seen an angel."

"What!"

"That her sons have seen an angel."

"Holy Moses!"

"No," he said. "Holy Gabriel."

"She isn't serious?"

"Never more so."

"And since it's Dawn Heath we're speaking of, that certainly does mean serious. I forgive you now for having left your tray."

He stared down at the table; pursed his lips; shook his head.

"What are you going to do?" she asked.

"God knows." Finally he stirred himself. "For the moment, go to play Ping-Pong." He kissed her. "I shan't be back till late. See you at breakfast."

"Bless you, my love. All part of life's rich pageant. Win the tournament."

After he had gone, she finished clearing up then watched the end of an old Frank Capra comedy: *Mr Deeds Goes To Town.* She liked films in which you knew good was good, bad was bad and right would be triumphant. And for vaguely the same reason – although the issues here were less clear-cut – she enjoyed books by Chandler and Simenon and Macdonald. The fictional private eye, Simon considered, was part of the apostolic succession reaching down from Sir Galahad.

These days, indeed, *he* reminded her of someone like Lew Archer: bent on doing good, at times almost fanatically so, despite his occasionally appearing a shade too cynical, a shade too detached. And yet she herself knew (who better, still living?) of the capacity he'd once shown for deep emotional involvement and unashamedly romantic belief. He was thirty-three. She wished he would get married again – or at the very least find a really good friend.

After the film she put on a cardigan and walked briefly in the garden. It was mid-September and the twilit air smelled fragrant. She was proud of her dahlias and roses and chrysanthemums, proud now of the garden as a whole. When they had come, this new vicarage had only just been built, with the land around it mainly mud and hillocky grass – though blessedly there'd been a few good trees. It was a mile or so from the church, which Simon regarded as a disadvantage since it clearly made him less

7

accessible; but she herself felt grateful for the distance. Also, St Matthew's stood in the poorer – poorest – section of the town; and *there* they might have had little more than a back yard. The very thought could make her shudder.

Mrs Madison didn't like Scunthorpe. Granted, it wasn't nearly so bad as those who'd never been there had relentlessly implied. The town was far more open and green than she'd expected, with pleasant parks and in many places wide and tree-lined roads. But she had much preferred their time in Bournemouth where Simon had worked as a curate before opting to move north. She had preferred it not simply because the climate had been softer and she had liked the sea but because she had felt closer to the people who lived there; life had seemed more civilized with its nice little tearooms and bookshops – here, there were no bookshops, except for Smith's. Maybe all these factors were superficial. Simon had certainly reckoned them so. But...well, the truth was, she supposed, she had grown into a snob.

"Sally Madison, you're a snob!"

She said it aloud and gave a little laugh.

"An unmitigated, unregenerate snob!" And yet her laugh was only partly an acceptance. It was also an ironic reminder that she had once strongly blamed her own parents for the same thing. She had met Henry Madison in 1948 when he had first served her at Francis Edwards'.

"But, Sally, the book trade! How far will he ever go in that?"

She stooped and put her nose to one of the warm pink flowers of a *Wife of Bath*. "Though that – my sturdy, aromatic friend – wasn't really the heart of it. Oh, not at all. Henry was illegitimate! Adopted at the age of four! An errand boy when he was twelve! A factory hand soon after that! But a factory hand who went to night school and who even managed to go on learning as a soldier in the war. And if only...oh, if only...!" But now she wasn't talking any longer to the rose bush; she had straightened up and put her hands into her cardigan pockets and was walking abstractedly across the grass. "If only he were still here, how proud he'd be of Simon's progress: his knowledge and his position in life! Oh, my darling one," she smiled – and this to her husband, not her son – "you certainly did work for it!"

Oh dear.

She remembered the time when Simon had been promised a bicycle: on condition he received a first-rate end-of-term report. The poor boy had talked incessantly about this beautiful machine, literally dreaming of the day when it would be taken out of the shop window, an almost unimaginable possession, already christened *Argo*. The report had been excellent – in all but one subject: Scripture. *Simon needs to try a little harder.*

"But I did try! I did try! He's muddling me with someone else. He often gets confused, he's famous for it!"

Yet when that bicycle left the window it was for some other child. Simon had cried himself to sleep for three nights in succession and Sally, listening helplessly outside his door, had argued and cajoled on his behalf. But Henry, who was usually no tyrant, was fanatical about Simon's education. Dr Jekyll, she had sometimes mentioned to her son, had also been a Henry.

A year later, of course, the bicycle was still a welcome acquisition but it was no longer that passionately desired and dreamed-of trophy. "And next time," said his father, "make sure you do so well in everything there's just no possibility of *anybody* ever mixing you up with *anybody*! If you do that, we'll have a holiday in France!"

Heigh-ho!

Mrs Madison sighed.

Happy days.

As she went in she became aware again, just a little, of the demoralizing arthritis which she suffered in one knee (but she was sure it wasn't as bad as it had been before Simon had prayed over it) and also – more annoyingly – of the fact that the telephone was once more ringing. Ye gods, that made it the fifth time since Simon had gone out, or was it the sixth? She responded with defiance. "Sorry, zey theenk thees ees ze wrong nomber, very pardon." She replaced the receiver, took it off again and laid it on the blotter with the happy sensation of being an alumna of St Trinian's.

9

Much later, when she was in bed and practically asleep, trying not to think about the funeral she'd been present at that morning, she recalled the disconnected telephone; and after a great deal of effort forced herself to go downstairs to reconnect it. Oh, thank heaven she'd remembered! It was a foolish thing to be scared of incurring the displeasure of your own son – a son, moreover, who very seldom grew impatient with her and who had never addressed her with the least desire to hurt – but there it was: she would rather have provoked anyone's annoyance than Simon's; and that had nothing to do, so far as she could make out, with the fact that she loved him and didn't want to cause him grief.

Sometimes she even wondered whether it had more to do with the possibility she really did find him...on the very rare occasion...just a little frightening.

But why?

Was it because he was so single-minded, so driven, so...? Well, no, he was never as demanding of others as he was of himself – not nearly so – but, still, his standards were obsessively high. This could be daunting. Uncomfortable. You wondered if you'd ever have a hope of meeting them. And you remembered that his father had also been – even if purely in one sphere – a person you could call fanatical.

3

Simon was good at table tennis but to his chagrin – as well as relief – was beaten in the third game of the finals.

The chagrin came because at heart he was a bad loser and would never have played less well than he could; the relief, because it would have been despicable to deprive a lad, already sufficiently deprived, of a victory bound to develop self-respect.

"Christ, I beat the fucking vicar!" he heard Earl Davis bragging afterwards, in whispered awe.

Yet, whatever Simon's form of self-reproach, almost nothing but the game itself had mattered whilst in progress and his absorption in it had been both merciful and marvellous. At seven-fifty, when he went into the empty, darkened church and spent several minutes kneeling by the altar, his gratitude for the tournament was the one uncomplicated thing he felt travelling between himself and God.

The youth centre not only abutted on the church, it was an extension of it. St Matthew's itself dated from the twenties. Other additions included a new main entrance – made chiefly of glass – a vestibule and an office. Because the office was one of the easier parts of the building to warm, most of the church committees chose to meet in it. Simon left the altar rail shortly before eight.

Education and Mission had only five members on it, all of them women. They began light-heartedly: a few holiday reminiscences; hilarity at his and the youth leader's rashness in allowing wet sponges to be thrown at them during a recent fête. More aggression had been unleashed than had been bargained for – "Some of it mine!" laughed Simon, who had slightly lost his temper. "And all for just tuppence a throw!"

"But talking of aggression, have you seen our Reginald's latest in tonight's edition?" Alison was about forty, shortish, dark-haired, lively. "My husband thinks the pair of you must be doubling the paper's circulation."

"Well, Reg certainly isn't doing it with his syntax," answered Simon. "So it must be with his sarcasm."

"Let's hope it isn't with his prejudice!"

"What sweet new fascist principles is he flaunting for us now?"

Before Alison could reply, however, one of the others spoke. This was Paula, who was in charge of St Matthew's Sunday school – *Pious Paula*, closely related to *Devotional Dawn* in every way excepting that of actual family tie and the fact that she was single and evidently 'stuck' on him: his mother's terrible

11

expression when teasing him with her own macabre vision of what the future might be offering, unless he took strong action to avert it. *Pious* was roughly his own age and rather dumpy. She wore a pancake makeup over a coarse complexion but she had a pleasant smile and she always smelled nicely of Bluebell. (She had told him recently, with a violent blush, that that was what it was – "Do you really like it?")

"Oh, Simon, I just don't know how he can be so rude to you! He should respect you. Not only because you're a vicar and write much better letters than he does but also because you're the vice-chairman of the Community Relations Council and really ought to know what you're talking about. That's what *I* say, anyhow."

He took compassion on her flustered countenance. "Thank you, Paula. That's what I say, too. But now I honestly feel we'd better do some work."

Tonight there were four main topics they wanted to discuss: problems to do with house groups; the forthcoming visit to Nigeria of a missionary who was going to keep a link with St Matthew's during his time out there; the possibility of some Franciscans coming to work in Scunthorpe; and what improvements could be made to the parish magazine. Throughout all this Simon did his best to concentrate and it turned out to be a satisfactory meeting, with some practical decisions reached.

When his concentration did lapse, furthermore, the direct cause was less Dawn Heath than a newspaper which the church secretary, who came in every Wednesday, happened to have left behind. This was folded in four but still revealed a couple of typically disquieting headlines: more provocative comment from Reagan at the expense of Russia and the death of yet another soldier in Belfast. There was also something about the government making further drastic cuts in services to the old and the mentally ill. Simon bit his lip. *Well, he said that we were heading for disaster. And told us how we'd have to mend our ways.*

Hmm.

It reminded Simon of nothing so much as the sort of 'encouraging' message delivered with such vibrant intensity at séances. Yet you'd think an angel could come up with something a *bit* more convincing. Surely?

And why on earth should he choose to deliver it in Scunthorpe? *Scunthorpe* of all places! The very name was a music hall joke; the easy butt of every second-rate comedian. Over the past three years Simon had become genuinely fond of the town and was often vociferously indignant at the rotten press it received. But the fact remained that, by and large, Scunthorpe was not a spot that the British media, or indeed the British population in general, treated with much seriousness.

Could anything good, they would say, come out of Scunthorpe?

These reflections occupied a few minutes. During the remainder of the meeting only one other thing distracted him: the memory of a burial service he had conducted that same morning. It was a death which had bothered him all week.

A man whom Simon hadn't met had hanged himself in a local wood. He was twenty-three and had been out of work for five months. He left a widow of nineteen who was pregnant with their third baby – which even yet the doctors were struggling to save. The man's father hadn't attended the funeral either, "because, if you must know, I'm just too bloody well disgusted by that bloody boy!" Nor had the man's mother, a recovering alcoholic. There had been eleven mourners at the service; these had included Mrs Madison and seven other members of the congregation who also hadn't met Jerry Turner. The remaining three were a former workmate, a schoolfriend and a teenage Pakistani boy, the son of a neighbour. They stood around the graveside in warm sunshine under a cloudless sky, awkward, their dark clothes incongruous, and as they came away the schoolfriend said – there were tears on his pockmarked cheeks – "And he was always so sodding cheerful!" He had hung in the wood for nearly a week before he'd been discovered by two eight-year-olds playing at being savages.

Well, as a vicar, of course, you had to guard against becoming bitter. Either bitter or sentimental. Simon now chewed his lip again – a habit his mother kept trying to break him of – and suggested giving a party at the vicarage for this other unknown young man who would be stopping there for a weekend, *en route*, eventually, for Nigeria. "Better than having the kind of get-together here in the hall where you're half afraid no one will turn up!"

The meeting ended. As he locked the office he saw Paula waiting for him by the main door.

"I was wondering if you'd heard on tonight's news, Simon, about the vicar who's just resigned from his parish near Stoke-on-Trent?" She was forever storing such snippets for him and – as usual when they were alone – spoke more breathlessly than at other times. "He's caused a split in his congregation by setting up a rival church nearby!"

Simon shook his head. He guided her onto the pavement and locked the outer door.

"And can you guess why?" she hurried on. "Because his son went to Lourdes and was cured of his convulsions! Imagine something inspirational like that, Simon, creating so much controversy and so much bad feeling!"

"Strangely it often seems to."

"And after seventeen years! Feels drawn to Rome! It's wonderful about his son, of course, but I really can't see – "

"Perhaps he thinks the Church of England pays too little attention to miracles? Perhaps, what's more, he could be right. But excuse me, Paula, I'm on my way to an appointment."

"Of course," she said. "Please give my love to your mother," she called across the broad expanse of pavement.

14

4

Josh Heath had gone to the pub. Dawn hastened to excuse this by declaring that it was for the first time in months; and then, although Simon wasn't in the least offended, realized the excuse itself could need excusing.

This worried her for a bit – until she saw it didn't matter. Tonight, nothing mattered. Her sons had been picked out by God for a glorious revelation and whatever Mr Mad–, whatever Simon, might have said earlier about queer tricks of the mind, now he would recognize the truth of it, simply by listening. Soon the whole of Scunthorpe would recognize the truth of it; the whole of Humberside; the whole of England.

She had the tea and biscuits waiting.

Both her boys sat on the sofa: William wearing jeans and jumper, Michael in pyjamas and dressing gown. William had acne. Michael wore a brace across his teeth. Each appeared small for his age. Simon, who'd have sworn he had never seen either of them before, thought they looked intelligent.

There was about them an air of quiet excitement. Naturally.

"Stand up," whispered Dawn. "Stand up and shake hands with the vicar."

The sofa was part of a three-piece suite whose chairs also looked towards the television – Simon asked if he might pull one round. Needlessly, but likably, William stood up again and helped him. They drank their tea and Dawn chattered about St Bernadette: recently they'd seen the film and Dawn offered this fact itself as though it might be significant, a form of preparation. She asked him vaguely about Fatima. Simon answered her questions as best he could but wondered whether he ought to be interviewing the boys individually and without their mother. Yet he didn't want to seem like a policeman, and besides, if they were meaning to deceive him, they'd have got all the details worked out beforehand. He asked about school. They said they didn't see themselves as being in any way unusual. They found religious education boring, apart from the occasional debate.

15

(Yes, they'd both been confirmed; when Mr Apsbury was vicar.) In English they were thought to have strong imaginations. William was fairly interested in politics, Michael wasn't. Simon didn't know if he'd hoped to deduce anything of value from this line of questioning.

"What were you talking about as you came away from school?"

They listed a few things, none of them obviously relevant to heavenly visits.

Of the two or three minutes prior to their encounter they could remember nothing.

"All right. When you saw the angel what can you remember then?"

Simon had to prompt them further.

"Did you feel surprise? Astonishment? Fear?"

"No," said William. "It seemed...it sounds silly...just natural."

"How do you mean, natural?"

"Like meeting somebody you knew."

"And liked," added Michael.

"I see. Well, what happened then? How did he greet you?"

William shrugged.

"He said hi, asked how we were, didn't want to shake hands or anything. Knew our names. Called us Mick and Bill, the way most people do."

"Did he tell you his own name?"

"No."

"You automatically assumed he was an angel?"

"Not really. It was Mum who did that. To us he was only a person dressed in white."

"Because he didn't have any wings, you see," said Michael. "I thought at first it might be Jesus."

Dawn, who was being good about not interrupting, made a slight movement, indicative of worry.

Michael turned towards it, briefly. "But then I changed my mind," he said. "Because he didn't have a beard, either."

"So he could almost have been just an ordinary man, you're saying, dressed in – what – a robe? Sandals?"

16

"Except there was all this brightness which shone round him," agreed William. Simon had forgotten about the light.

"But you didn't need to screw your eyes up?"

"No, I don't think so. Did we, Mick?"

"*I* didn't. And he hadn't got sandals. I remember wondering about the soles of his feet: whether they'd be dirty or not. Or maybe I only thought about that afterwards."

"You see, it's hard to tell now what we noticed at the time and what we pieced together later, by comparing notes."

"Because it was really what he said that mattered."

Simon drew a deep breath. "All right, then." He looked slowly from one to the other. "Now what exactly *did* he say?"

"Who do you want to hear it from?" asked William.

"Whichever you like. Why not you?"

"Okay. We can both remember it off by heart." He paused. "Well, after he'd asked if we'd pass on a message for him, the first thing he said was that God's pretty cheesed off with the world, and now more than ever..."

Here Simon noticed that William's eyes were closed.

"'Don't you see? You have the know-how, you have the means. If you'd wanted, you could have put an end to such quantities of suffering. All it needed was the one ingredient which your so-called realist dismisses as naiveté but which we describe as love. That's all it still needs. But only look around you. What do you mostly find? Grab, grab, grab on the part of the big fry; helplessness, or an equal lack of concern, on the part of the small. This can't go on. You've got to learn, all of you, you've got to learn to let go. To have faith. To care about one another. It's really not so hard and it even feels good, too. But it *is* urgent. People have to be made to realize, wake up, take action. To move forward generously, insistently and without fear. In the name of the Lord. It *can* be done, you know.'"

William opened his eyes.

Michael had been gazing at his brother, Dawn had looked flushed and shiny-faced with pride. Simon's own eyes had been directed mainly at the carpet.

There was a lengthy pause.

17

"And then he...just disappeared?" asked Simon, finally.

"Yes. He ruffled our hair, said, 'Well, good luck, see you both again someday,' and was gone. It was over. We realized we were in the car park behind Tiffany's."

"Feeling what?"

"Tremendous."

"We haven't squabbled at all since then, not once," Michael said. The brothers looked at each other with affection.

"Uh-huh. Let's hope you can keep that up." Simon bit his lip. "Do you think one of you could write me out a copy?"

"We already have." Michael had taken a piece of lined paper out of his dressing-gown pocket. It was folded into four.

"Thanks."

Simon then spoke as much to the mother as her sons.

"Look. For the present I don't want to make any comment. I need to think this whole thing over, quietly and alone. But I'll be back before the weekend. In the meantime I'd suggest you try to keep it all very much to yourselves."

He paused.

"And, William, Michael, if anything else occurs to you...well, of course you'll let me know."

But driving home he wondered if it would have been better simply to come out with it: "I can't believe in this. How could you expect me to? A message so *incredibly* banal!"

Then, on impulse, he made a small detour. He stopped the car outside the church.

Yet the half hour which he again spent before the altar, on his knees and in the dark, supplied no sense of certainty or calm.

When he arrived back at the vicarage it was after twelve. He went into his study, poured himself a large whisky and telephoned the hospital.

"Can you tell me how Mrs Turner is tonight?"

"Oh, yes, Reverend Madison. She was allowed home after supper. Dr Patel thinks the baby's going to be fine. Naturally, she'll need to take things easy for a while."

"What, with a baby in the house and two young children to see to already? And a mother-in-law who – even when she's

18

around – has a problem with the drink? Still," he said. "Thank heaven for Dr Patel."

He wished the sister a peaceful night but didn't feel that he himself would have one. On his desk there stood a framed photograph. He picked it up and for a moment merely stared at it. Then he kissed the glass. There were tears in his eyes.

"Oh, Ginny," he said. "My Ginny..."

5

"Ginny," said her mother, "you know that table in the window, the one I thought of bagging for ourselves? Too late. But at least the newcomers look interesting."

"Appearances must be deceptive."

"Why?"

"Because we're the only interesting people who ever came to this place. Lightning doesn't strike twice in the same dump."

"They're certainly more decorative than Mr and Mrs Simpson."

"They could be a dozen times more decorative and still make Quasimodo seem like a sex symbol."

"Clearly you *are* feeling better. Excellent. So do you think you'll be getting up soon?"

"I suppose so."

"There's my good girl! But when Daddy phones this evening you won't speak of *Sea View* as a dump, now, will you? Which it isn't, anyway. And it would only worry him."

"Hmm. I'll see. Tell me about these people whom you find so fascinating."

"They're a mother and son."

"Yes, that does sound fascinating."

"He's blond and very handsome. And about twenty."

"Have you spoken to them?"

"No. I smiled across the dining room most pleasantly."

"Then how do you know he isn't her boyfriend?"

19

"Because when you're a woman of a certain age, to have a young man like that in tow you have to be very rich indeed. (I mean, I'm guessing; I haven't made inquiries.) And when you're very rich indeed you don't come to stay at a place like *Sea View*."

"Because it's a dump?"

"From the point of view of giving the most lyrical expression to a grand illicit passion...yes."

"Anyhow, I'm quite impressed with the reasoning. So let's see what you make of this. If they're indeed a mother and son and he's about my age why are they down here together? Eastbourne doesn't seem the most exciting place for any *truly* interesting young man who, remember, doesn't yet know I'm in it. Could it possibly be that he's still tied to the apron strings?"

"Darling, I've noticed recently that you're becoming very cynical. I hope it's just an act. I think I prefer the softer centre."

Ginny at once pushed back the bedclothes and kneeling on the rumpled sheet put her arms around her mother's neck. "Oh, of course it's just an act. I approve of people who like their mothers." She added: "Especially when they're very handsome."

Mrs Plummer returned a quarter of an hour later, when Ginny was dressed.

"Are you really feeling better?"

Ginny nodded. "And I don't intend to waste even one more minute of a sunny Saturday."

"You know, the further I consider it, the less happy I am with regard to Mr Heddingly. I honestly do believe we'll have to find another gynaecologist."

"Oh, hell. Oh, hell. Well, at least let's make it one who doesn't tell me, every time, to go and have a baby!"

"How I agree! Even your father's jokes are marginally less wearing. But, turning to more cheerful things, I came back because I've just spoken to Miss Bryanston in the office. Their name is Madison. They come from Basingstoke."

"Oh, do they now? But why should I feel this is really the right moment to remind you...?"

20

"*His* name, by the way, is Simon. Miss Bryanston says that he's delightful. Remind me of what, dear?"

"Of how when I was younger you were always trying to pair me off with someone else my age, saying, '*She* looks nice,' or, '*He* looks nice, you're bound to have a lot in common, now run off together and have a good time!' And we never had a good time; we never had more than a dozen words to say to one another! I've got no confidence that things have greatly changed."

"No, darling, you may be absolutely right. How glad I am, though, that you've chosen to put on that particular frock. We always agreed it was your prettiest."

"I didn't suggest I wasn't still part of the human race. All I do hope, however, is that there's no connection in your little brain between all this and what Mr Heddingly has *said* – and *said* – and *said* again – "

"Oh, Ginny, don't get me wrong! I'm talking about a fleeting holiday friendship, not a lifelong passion, nor (dear God forbid) a regrettably pregnant daughter when we go back to Gerrards Cross! Good heavens, quite apart from anything else, how should we ever explain it to Mr Gatling?"

Mr Gatling was the vicar, an exceedingly sweet man but definitely one of the old school. The thought of having to explain it to Mr Gatling gave them both hysterics; they had to hold each other up and wipe away their tears, as their delicate attempts to break the news to him grew ever more incomprehensible, even to themselves.

6

The following evening, providentially, had been earmarked for *Saints Alive*, a course whose object was to explore the workings of the Holy Spirit and one which Simon conducted every fortnight for the house group leaders. By eight o'clock the sitting room was full. His mother, invited from the outset to be a member of the group, had handed out the last mug of coffee and resumed her seat. There were no absentees tonight, a fact which, seeing what it was he had to say, made Simon feel especially glad. The various shifts at the steelworks rendered such a turnout rare.

"Early yesterday evening," he began, "Dawn Heath phoned."

There were one or two flippant rejoinders but after that he spoke for about ten minutes with scarcely an interruption. Finally he read from the sheet of paper Michael had given him.

The silence which followed that reading was like the one after William's own delivery.

"I think that first, before we start to discuss this, we ought to try to prepare ourselves, both individually and together."

So there ensued several minutes of contemplation, several more of spoken prayer.

"Right, then. Who would like to begin?"

After a moment his mother looked around with the breezy encouragement of a hostess. "No answer, came the stern reply!"

Simon was asked to re-read the message.

During the previous night he had discovered he could recite it wholly accurately and without effort but for the present he preferred to keep his eyes upon the paper.

"Well, it's true enough, isn't it?"

"What is, Jack?"

Like four of the other men in the room, and two of the women, Jack Owen worked for British Steel. He was a burly fellow, with hair that was prematurely white, whiter than his high-necked cable-stitch sweater. "Grab, grab, grab. That describes the world's leaders to a T. Wouldn't you say so, love?"

Dulcie, auburn-haired, a good foot shorter than her husband, agreed readily. "And helpless just about sums up the rest of us. Well, I know it does me." She gave a nervous laugh.

Everyone murmured that she wasn't on her own.

"Well, now, there are three possibilities," remarked Simon, after a pause. "A, they're having us on. B, they think their experience was genuine. And C..."

22

"And C, it was." Tony, the parish youth worker, two years older than Simon, could easily have been thought the younger, on account of his willowy form.

"Exactly."

"But why should they be having us on?" Ethel, the oldest member of the group, was in her middle eighties.

"Who knows?" Simon said. "Pure devilment? A practical joke, to test how gullible we are? A way of hitting back at their own mother if they think she's grown too pious?" He gave a shrug. "What they're after could be recompense for any number of joint frustrations."

"Darling," said Mrs Madison, "stop sounding like a professor."

"Sorry," he said, a little curtly and without a smile.

"What kind of frustrations?" asked Jack.

"The fact that their father's been unemployed for four years and that there's no money in the house. A feeling they're lacking in status."

"Oh, come off it! There must be hundreds of kids in Scunthorpe whose dads are unemployed."

"There are also hundreds," put in Tony, "who are having holidays abroad, get ridiculous amounts of pocket money, have home-computers, music-centres, TV in their bedrooms, and expect at least a fifty-pound reward for doing well in their exams. Or sometimes twice as much."

Ethel had been turning up her hearing-aid. "Do you know something dreadful I was told today? A man down our road was out of work for five months before finally telling his wife. Out every morning at the usual time, back every evening. Drawing and drawing on his savings. At last he just broke down. Well, can you wonder?"

"Actually that's not uncommon." Simon bit his lip, then waited for the return of comparative quiet. "But there's another reason the Heath boys might have wanted to make themselves noticed. You see, it could depend on whether or not they get teased at school. William suffers from a terrible case of acne; it's really very bad. And physically, too, they're both quite weedy."

23

There came a groan from Tony. "Oh, yes, you six-footer macho types are all the same! You think broad shoulders rock the world."

"I said weedy, not slender. Sadly, you streamlined calorie-consuming types are all the same! Secretly quite smug."

"Hear hear to that," said Alison.

"Anyhow, perhaps you think I'm scraping the bottom of the barrel, but what I'm trying to show is – there could be all *kinds* of possible motivation."

"But, darling, you saw them," said his mother. "Did you receive the impression they were trying to hit back at poor Dawn?"

"No. Not at all."

"Or that they might have had some other kind of chip on their shoulders?"

"They struck me throughout as completely sincere, likable and convincing."

Everybody looked at him in some surprise. He himself felt surprised. He really hadn't meant, or even wanted, to acknowledge quite so much...although he wasn't altogether sure why not. "Yet this, of course, applies to every con man since Creation."

"Vicars themselves being particularly prone to it," suggested Tony.

Simon gave a quick smile. "And in a way they may even have sounded a little too pat. As though at times they were almost feeding one another their lines."

"'Oh, Mr Gallagher,'" said Alison. "'Yes, Mr Shean?'"

"That's it. There was actually a point when they told me straight out they'd been careful to compare notes."

"Either *very* cunning," remarked Tony, "or very ingenuous."

"What the hell does ingenuous mean?" asked Jack. "Listen, Simon, this isn't meant to be disrespectful – "

"Be disrespectful as you like."

" – but it seems to me a lot of what you're saying sounds a bit too clever. All I know is, if two boys had the same vision, then something must have triggered it off. And I don't think God

24

would allow them to make fools of themselves while they were trusting in his name."

Simon decided neither to question the word 'vision' – after all, it was one that yesterday he'd used himself – nor the basic assumption which Jack was making, but he still said, "No, that's too simple. You're forgetting there are bad spirits in this world, as well as good. You're forgetting the devil could say, 'I'm sent by God,' every bit as easily as I could or you could or anyone."

"But, Simon, what would be the point?" This was Mr Burgess, one of the bank managers in the town: serious and balding yet with an air of being ten years younger than he was – he was now approaching forty – that confounded the stereotype. "All this message says, fundamentally, is 'Love thy neighbour.' What sort of satisfaction would the devil get from that?"

"Well, for one thing, George, he'd most certainly enjoy the idea of decency being mocked. Which is what would happen here. For every person who believed that a bona fide angel had given us a warning, there'd be a thousand others who would jeer not only at the angel but at the whole idea of Christianity – *and* at the airy-fairy notions of idealists everywhere who seek to change the world. Only they wouldn't say idealists, they'd say do-gooders. So, you see, it could all be a vast undermining ploy the devil has in mind. Satan, don't forget, is first and foremost a saboteur."

"Then it seems we don't stand any sort of chance?"

"If an angel has come to us from God we stand every sort of chance!"

"But how do we *know*?"

"We pray about it. Here, tonight, as a group. We test the spirit."

"You mean, we'll ask for a sign? Then what's to tell us that this, too, won't be coming from Satan?"

"Not asking for a *sign*. Asking for *direction*. And when one prays to God it can't ever be the devil who answers."

"Why not?"

"Because God wouldn't allow it. We talk about a father loving and caring. What sort of a father would it be who – ?"

Now it was Jack who pounced. "There you are, then! What did I say? About God not allowing two trusting lads to be made fools of in his name?"

"No, you're wrong!" Simon wasn't the type who either through weakness or good nature let an opponent mistakenly believe he might have scored a point. "As far as I can make out, just before this happened they weren't in any kind of contact with God. 'Beware of false prophets, which come to you in sheep's clothing, but inwardly they are ravening wolves.' God assuredly wouldn't send you a wolf in answer to prayer. But that doesn't mean there aren't plenty all ready to leap out if you strike them as someone worth sticking their fangs into."

"Okay, then." Jack gave a lengthy sigh and Dulcie patted his knee reassuringly. "In that case, what are we waiting for? Let's get him to help us sort out the sheep from the ruddy wolves without wasting any more of his time."

"May I ask you something?" Mr Guthrie, a short, sandy-haired and slightly timid young man who worked in the haberdashery department at Binn's, stared at Simon through thick-lensed spectacles. He and George Burgess were the only two in the room who wore suits.

"What is it, Alan?"

"Well, 'naiveté'. Do you know if it's spelt right?"

Simon grinned. "Yes, I think it is. Why?"

"It struck me as a little odd, that's all. I mean, if those two boys were pulling our legs or anything or if anybody were pulling *theirs*. I'm just not sure it's a word which...well, which fifteen- or sixteen-year-olds would ever use. And the whole style of that message – what I mean is, we haven't talked about it yet, have we? Not at all. Do you see what I'm trying to say?"

"Yes, I do. Thank you. That's a good point."

7

When, the following afternoon, Simon went back to see the Heaths it was the boys' father who opened the door. "Sorry you've been brought out *twice* on such a wild-goose chase," said Josh Heath, with a smile. "You'll note I didn't say fool's errand?"

He looked younger than his wife. Or at least his style was more youthful. T-shirt, jeans. sneakers. Also, he wasn't a tall man but he was lean and muscular. Simon, who wore a sweater under his denim jacket, knew the T-shirt was intended to make this clear.

"Fool's errand? Yes, I'm grateful for that. What a tan you've still got!"

They went into the sitting room. Dawn called the boys from their bedroom, explaining to Simon that even on Fridays they got straight down to their homework. She then offered to put the kettle on.

"We would ask you to stay for a meal...," she told him.

But Simon said he had an appointment to keep and that anyway he'd just been given a cup of tea. Instantly relaxing (not needing to go into the kitchen and miss possible disclosures) she sat on one of the arms of the sofa and this time it was Michael who, without being asked, pulled round a matching chair.

"Well, then?" Dawn inquired, in a voice that sounded strained. "Have you decided?"

"Yes. I believe these two have been quite amazingly blest."

"You mean...?" she said. "You mean...?"

Then after a second she clapped her palms together, stood up, sat down, leant over and kissed Michael on the cheek, squeezed William's hand. There were quick tears running down her face.

"Oh, how silly I am! I feel so happy!"

She stroked her husband on the arm.

The boys just grinned and seemed uncertain where to look. In the end they both gazed warm-cheeked at the floor.

Their father stared at Simon. "You – must – be – joking!"

"No. I promise you I'm not."

"Oh, you mustn't mind Josh," said Dawn, tolerant, laughing as she wiped her eyes. "Sometimes I can't think how we stay together!"

Simon remembered wondering, on that other occasion he had met her husband, how they had ever got together in the first place.

He still wondered it.

"But please tell us, what made you change your mind?" In her excitement she even touched *him* now, briefly, on the knee.

"I don't know, Dawn. It wasn't exactly that I changed my mind. Let's simply say – conviction didn't arrive at once."

The truth was, there'd been a moment during the previous evening when sudden euphoria had spread like wildfire round the group. (Comparable to what had taken place at Pentecost?) Smilingly, he had ascribed it to a form of mass hysteria but if so it was one to which he himself had finally succumbed. He had experienced a warm feeling of love for those eleven people; and, along with it, a sense of deep tranquility. Enjoyable, of course – though he had warned himself it couldn't last.

And had been proved wrong. Had been attempting all day to talk himself out of an attitude which he believed to be so very weakly based. It was a transference of responsibility from mind to heart and he was by no means sure he could respect it. But it had happened.

Dawn nodded, reverently.

"Yes," she breathed. "Part of the miracle."

"Part of the hogwash," said her husband, agreeably.

She frowned at him and shook her head.

"Oh, but very entertaining hogwash," he conceded. "In fact, I'm totally enthralled. So tell us, vicar. What's the next step?"

"The next *series* of steps? Why, working out how best to spread the message."

"But surely that's more straightforward than you make it sound? Here's what to do. You contact the *Sun*."

They held each other's gaze. "A nine days' wonder wasn't wholly what I had in mind."

28

"I follow. You want to prolong it a little, find yourself some laid-back guy who could start outside Binn's in the morning, with a megaphone and a soapbox and a sandwich board?"

"Well, certainly that would be *one* approach. Though of course when you read about the Old Testament prophets, what interesting fact always occurs to you?" (Josh looked instantly ready to reply but Simon didn't give him the opportunity.) "That they never spoke out in the market place. They went to the king and the courtiers."

"What a relief, then, we still have a monarchy?"

"Or an Archbishop of Canterbury."

"*Mit* courtiers?"

"Certainly *mit* courtiers. With two, indeed, right here at home: the Bishops of Lincoln and Grimsby. Naturally, I shall go to them first."

William said: "It's likely to be a slow business, then?"

"You see, he told us it was urgent." Michael sounded similarly disappointed.

"I realize that. But rest assured: this matter will receive priority. From all concerned. And just remind yourselves of something. God knows about bureaucracy. A message would be pointless, Bill, if we weren't going to have the time in which to spread it."

"But you're sure he doesn't mean us simply to go to the papers, like Dad suggested?"

"Yes. Quite sure."

"Why would it be a nine days' wonder?"

"Because it wouldn't have the authority of the Church behind it. And if people begin by holding it cheap, no amount of endorsement later on is going to compensate. You wouldn't even get endorsement later on. The Church would treat it no more seriously than anybody else."

"So *easily* influenced?" bemoaned Josh.

"But why can't you go to the Archbishop direct?"

"Because he, too, is only human. He, too, is going to need convincing. By the people closest to him, whose judgment he respects."

29

"God will convince him," said Dawn.

"Yes, but God may wish to do so through advisers," responded Simon, every bit as firmly.

"Why?"

"Who knows? But you could just as easily ask why the angel who came to your sons didn't go straight to the Archbishop."

"Or straight to you," suggested Michael.

Josh stretched himself, happily. "Of course, you can't be wholly sure, can you, that he didn't in fact pop in on His Grace? Remember, now: the time was about four. He might have thought he'd get a classier tea at Lambeth Palace than either here or even, with respect, at the vicarage. Or, again, couldn't London be in the jurisdiction of some different angel? Yes, that might be the answer: the beat, let's say, of the Islington Angel. Perhaps there's a plethora of angels. All sorts of exciting possibilities."

Simon laughed with genuine enjoyment; realized it would have been more tactful not to, when he glanced at Dawn. Probably only St Paul's strict injunctions on womanhood had prevented her from interrupting, or from rebuking her husband a moment ago when he had stretched.

Josh became more serious. It might well have been from kindness.

"And after you've been to see the home team, what then?"

"Well, next I'll approach those experts in the Church of England who have special knowledge of mystical experiences and/or of nuclear weapons." He smiled. "I'd chiefly want to interest those sceptical about the first and in favour of the second. To win some of *them* to our side would wonderfully strengthen our position."

"You talk as though it needed strengthening," said Dawn. Unfairly, Simon found the woman of faith more irritating than the man without it. He said:

"I know we're going to win through eventually. I just don't believe it will be easy."

"What happens," asked William, "if in the end the Archbishop still isn't convinced?"

"He will be," stated Dawn.

30

"Yes, your mother's right. It can't be God's will for him not to be." Simon paused. "Unless, of course, he has some other purpose in mind – God, that is – at which we can't begin to guess."

Josh was surveying his fingernails.

"Like, you mean, keeping himself indefinitely amused? And us, as well: we lucky ones who can appreciate the comedy. Do you know something, vicar? I begin for the first time to feel a spiritual lack in my life. This, surely, would be a God after my own heart."

"Excuse me." Dawn, whom even St Paul couldn't always hold in check, stood up and left the room.

"Oh dear. Might I have spoken out of turn?" Josh gave a chastened grin. "Poor old Dawnie; she could never take being ribbed."

"Then why do you think you can change her?"

"Why do *you* think I can change myself?"

"I'm not sure if I do. I don't feel that you want to."

"Yet supposing I did?"

"You implied just now you couldn't."

"But how defeatist! Especially when proceeding from a gentleman of the *cloth*!"

"Well, can a leopard change his spots?"

"Worse and worse! And with a friendly sort of smile, as well! You seem almost – what do you seem? – *glad*."

Simon ignored this. "If you were to call on outside help, of course, then it could be altogether different. But that goes without saying."

"Says he, having said it. What was it you had in mind? A psychiatrist?"

"No, not exactly."

"I know it wasn't. You were thinking of That Big Psychiatrist in the Sky."

"Well, certainly he is that, amongst other things. Because, although I talk of change, what I really mean is liberation." Or am I waffling, he thought.

Josh now stretched out his legs, lifting them off the ground a little; then crossed them at the ankles.

"Can you liberate people into a sense of humour?" he asked, lazily.

Simon stood up. "Yes, I believe so; if that's something truly basic to a full life."

"Oh, it is. Let me assure you. It is."

"You're the authority, are you?"

Josh laughed. "Now that was a very underhand remark." He applied to his sons, still sitting on the sofa. "Would you two call a jibe like that quite worthy of our vicar?"

Simon had forgotten the presence of the boys and felt a little awkward at having, however indirectly, discussed their mother in front of them. Now, as he took his leave, he promised that he'd keep them posted. "And before long you'll be able to bore everybody rigid with every detail of all this. But not yet, remember." In the tiny hallway he called goodbye to Dawn. She came to the kitchen door, with a polite smile and a word of thanks but in a rather subdued manner. "Cheer up," said Josh. "Your children are going to make history and I think you've found yourselves the perfect champion."

He stood with Simon for a minute on the stairs outside the flat.

"I meant that. A knight-errant in shining armour, riding into battle on a milk-white charger. 'A verray parfit gentil knight.'"

Simon pulled a face. "Heaven forbid!"

"Heaven forbid what? That people should regard you in that light?"

"That *I* should regard me in that light."

"Oh, but, surely...an occupational hazard? One of the perks of the profession?"

"No, I don't think so. Not if you know yourself even half as well as you ought to." In trying to escape one aspect of smugness, however, he had merely ended up with another.

"Anyway, at least you haven't made any serious effort to convert *me*, for which I'm duly grateful."

32

Simon was by now at the bottom of the flight of stairs immediately below the flat; the Heaths lived on the first floor. He raised a hand in casual valediction. "Not much of one, I agree. You see, I recognize my limitations."

As he turned the corner and went swiftly down the remainder of the stairs it occurred to him that this was hardly a characteristic for a vicar, or indeed for anyone, to boast about.

8

"Oh, hell," said Mrs Plummer. "What an anticlimax!" The table in the window was unoccupied. Except for condiments, the cloth was bare. "But why bother to leave your name, and where you come from, if you're only passing through?"

"Shall we puzzle it out later," suggested Ginny, "while we seek to drown our sorrows at the bar?"

Shortly afterwards the manageress moved amongst the diners with her usual bright inquiries.

"Oh, Miss Bryanston. If that table over there happens to be free again...?"

But it appeared that the Madisons had merely asked for an early dinner because they had needed to take care of something in the town and then wanted to see the summer variety show.

"Darling, shall we go to that ourselves?" Miss Bryanston had barely moved away before Mrs Plummer was energetically peering at her watch.

"Tonight? But why? *We* didn't have an early dinner, so we'll have missed the beginning. You'll also be missing Daddy's call."

"But I suddenly feel in the mood for a little entertainment."

"No, you don't. All you feel in the mood for is a manhunt. Well, count me out."

Yet on the other hand the prospect of spending the evening listening to the residents in the lounge, who switched on the television and then unfailingly chattered above it, wasn't enormously enticing, either. And it *had* been a long day of

33

dragging pains, resentment and frustration – they arrived at the theatre some half-hour after the curtain had gone up.

In the interval Mrs Plummer looked about her with animation.

"I think I'd like to stretch my legs."

"Okay. You won't mind if I stay put?"

"I'd rather have your company."

With some difficulty (again) they squeezed past the three old ladies who were the only people now left sitting in their row.

"Oh, look, darling."

It seemed that most of the audience was already congregated, shuffling, in the aisle but Ginny could easily see, over the heads of everybody else, the one Nordic head her mother was drawing her attention to. At that point it happened to be lit from above and she was struck by the gleaming arrowtip the thick hair formed upon the neck.

When Mrs Plummer finally tracked them down, the Madisons weren't at the bar but standing just outside the theatre, enjoying the night air. They had turned to face the sea and in the darkness the waves were rhythmically pulling themselves up the shingle, then slipping back with a slackening, gravelly sigh. The moon's path lay brilliant on the water.

"Oh, do excuse me, but didn't I see you at lunchtime in the dining room of *Sea View*?"

By then Ginny had caught up. Introductions were made; comments – mostly favourable – passed on the songs and sketches. "But what a relief to be able to get out into the fresh air!"

"I can't think," agreed Mrs Madison, "why everyone chooses to crowd about the bar on a stifling night like this."

"Poor lost souls. It must be the demon drink that drives them on."

"Oh, please, Simon, *smile* when you say a thing like that in front of people whom you've only just met."

"Well, if you ask me," said Mrs Plummer, "they're simply a lot of sheep."

"Poor lost sheep."

34

Simon and Ginny laughed delightedly. The two of them had said it in the same instant.

By the time they all returned inside, Mrs Plummer had arranged that she and Simon Madison should exchange seats. The second half began nearly as soon as he and Ginny had negotiated the knees, the walking sticks and handbags; but even so the tactic wasn't wasted. Ginny was impressed by the kindness of his apologies to the three old ladies and by the patience with which he hunted for the programme one of them had dropped. Also, throughout the rest of the performance, she was very conscious of his being beside her: of the white pullover sleeve sharing her armrest, of the occasional deep laugh, the almost continual half-smile, the infectious and unstinting quality of his applause. The clean-cut profile.

No.

The tactic was not wasted.

9

He went straight from the Heaths' to one of the shabbier of the small terraced houses in Dale Street. The narrow area between the gate and the front door – concreted; he couldn't think of it as a garden – was filled with rubbish that the wind had blown in or that people must have tossed over the low wall: sheets of newspaper, an empty beer can, a small polystyrene tray that had once held fish and chips and mushy peas (even the tiny wooden fork was still imprisoned in its remnants), a cloudy milk bottle, a claret-and-blue rosette. When he rapped on the frosted glass – there was no bell – he was a little surprised that the person who opened the door was Sharon Turner herself. "Hello," he said. "I hoped you'd be in bed."

She stared at him, with sullen incomprehension. He suddenly remembered that he wasn't wearing his dog collar. "I didn't recognize who you was," she told him, frankly. "What you said...it took me back."

35

"I'll bet it did. I should have realized." He bit his lip. "I thought your mother would be here."

"She was for a bit, earlier. You mean Jerry's mum, don't you?"

His irritation with himself deepened. He knew perfectly well that her own mother was dead. Her father had married again and moved to Ireland.

"And she doesn't know yet if she's coming or going and keeps crying all over the place; so she's not much good. But anyhow she means well. Do you want to come in?"

"I... Well, not if I'd be in the way."

She shrugged. "It's a real awful mess but at least the kids are settled. I hope to God they sleep through."

There was some western from the fifties showing on TV. Virginia Mayo, with her shiny Technicolored mouth, seemed a coyly mocking incongruity: best peaches and cream served in a grubby-looking bowl. Sharon neither switched the picture off, however, nor turned the volume down.

"It's partly about the children that I've come to see you. I meant to call round earlier."

She said: "I know I ought to have them done. We'd been talking about getting them done for months; honest we had. But I couldn't face it now, not for a bit, not without him..." She started to cry.

"I wasn't speaking about baptism," Simon told her. But at first he wasn't sure she could have heard him over Robert Stack. She was fumbling in the pockets of her dress. He offered her his Kleenex.

"What, then?" she asked, having wiped her eyes and blown her nose and palmed the crumpled tissue. She sat very much on the edge of an orange-painted kitchen chair, although the fireside chair in which he himself sat had its equally dilapidated counterpart.

"Well, my mother was wondering if she could take them off your hands a bit. Also, a couple of other women were asking only last night if they could be of any use – shopping, cooking, cleaning, all that kind of thing." He had told the group about the

36

Turner situation almost as an epilogue to the main business of the evening; perhaps it should have been the prologue. In any case it had certainly achieved the right results. Alison and Dulcie had practically offered to move in.

"No thanks," she said. "That's very kind, I'm sure. But I can manage. Even if right now it don't look like it."

"Grief, you only came out of hospital yesterday!"

"The day before."

"Not till the evening," he said.

"Besides, I've got good neighbours." Perhaps he looked doubtful. "The lady three doors down took in the kids while I was ill."

"But will she do so now you're back?"

"I'll be all right." She caught him glancing at her stomach. The bulge was not pronounced. "And so will he," she added. "It was very nice of you to come round, I'm sure."

Reluctantly, he stood up.

"What about your father, Sharon? I reckon we could take care of your fares, you know, if there were any chance that a change of scenery – "

"That pig?" she said. "I wouldn't go within a hundred miles of him. Nor the slaggy bitch he married." She sounded more bored, though, than aggressive.

"Well, it was just a thought. If there's ever anything that any of us can do... You won't mind if I keep in touch?"

"Please yourself."

"Have you had some supper?"

Unaccountably, her eyes began to fill again. She turned away abruptly, switched off the set. Those Technicolored lips had just been lifted for a kiss. The room seemed darker without them but Sharon immediately looked less scrawny, less pallid. Simon wondered, fleetingly, if they ever showed such pictures in the Third World.

"Do you like Chinese food?"

"Never had it."

"Like to try some now?"

"Up to you."

37

He chose Chinese because he believed it would be more nutritious; he also bought some wine. When he arrived back at the house, she had tidied up a bit, removing plastic toys and bricks, colouring books and crayons, clothes, a cast-off nappy. He thought she might have combed her hair too.

She ate the food totally without remark, except when he said, "Is this all right?" and she told him, "Fine." She finished everything he'd put on her plate but rather as though she didn't notice and would have eaten less or more with equal compliance and equal satisfaction. It was similar with the wine: she drank what he poured into her tumbler, yet he felt it could as easily have been water. He'd been the one to find the corkscrew in her kitchen drawer – and also the piles of things that needed washing up. She was obviously quite incapable of looking after herself, let alone two small children; and he could only suppose her condition had deteriorated since the hospital discharged her.

It was the box of chocolates which drew the first real comment.

"Jerry used to get me things like that."

In the paper shop next to the takeaway, Simon had wondered about the wisdom of buying it. "But there wasn't much else," he explained, "that would have done for a pudding."

"When we were courting," she went on.

He said nothing.

"And after we got married, too. He was never mean with money, not like some. Right up to when he lost his job."

He hesitated. "Did it get him down – that – from the very start?"

"Well, what do *you* think?" Her tone still wasn't aggressive, yet the mere phrasing of her retort made him conscious of what he so often tried to ignore: the possibly uncrossable gulf between himself and the bulk of his parishioners; the haves and the have-nots; the respected, the dismissed. "Oh, it wasn't too bad to begin with..." (He sensed a part-apology.) "He had a bit of redundancy pay, which we had to spend quick, else there wouldn't have been no dole. Well, he'd been trying to save up for a car ever since we got married. It was only secondhand;

Jerry 'n' Sharon, it said, right there on the windscreen. And then he bought me a decent coat, too, lovely red wool it was. He was just so sure he was going to get something quite quick, you see. Other people might be out of work. Not him."

"Because he was bouncy, you mean, had plenty of go?"

"On his good days he half thought he'd be Mayor by evening."

She was almost smiling when she said that; almost pretty. You remembered that she was nineteen, roughly half the age of Miss Mayo in that shiny western. Simultaneously, he felt the urge to comfort her *and* to shake his fist at God. At God and the government and everybody who supported it, oblivious to all the harm it was causing – the stress, the breakdown, the suicide – either oblivious to it or more or less self-absorbed and condoning. And all (of course) rationalized in the name of the omnipotent economy, this steady withdrawal of hope from millions of apparently expendable lives, each one as blessed well important as...well, as any other in this land, or world. He remained silent, however: rapidly apologizing for his moment of blasphemy and for that feeling – bordering well-nigh on hatred – which he had come reluctantly to recognize in himself with increasing frequency over the past five years. Its seeds had been there for the past fourteen.

"His neck was broken," she said suddenly. "Did you know that?"

"Yes." The inquest had been lengthily reported.

"He'd been hanging in that wood a week." She looked towards him now with eyes which seemed enlarged by bewilderment; but at a time when one might have expected tears they remained dry, and slightly out of focus. It appeared she had to justify herself. "He'd been depressed, you see. I thought he'd just gone off again without saying nothing. He'd done it before."

This he knew as well.

"Once he walked to London and back – well, anyhow, walked most of the way there, because people don't like giving lifts and by then he'd had to sell the car. But he didn't find no job."

39

To his consternation Simon found his own eyes growing moist.

"I used to talk to him quite spiteful," she said.

"You can't blame yourself for that, Sharon."

"How do you know?"

"Listen. When anybody dies, even in the most ordinary of circumstances, those closest to them *always* feel a lot of guilt. But people are people; very few of us are saints. You were both under great pressure."

"Well, even if that's true...," she said. (Surreptitiously, he wiped his nose on the back of his hand, thought of the box of tissues in his glove compartment.) "I could still have been a lot nicer."

"We could all have been a lot nicer."

"And I was mean about his pictures."

"Pictures?"

"He and the son of that neighbour I told you about. He was teaching Imran to draw: animals and things. Jerry had a knack for doing pictures. He often joked about someday being a famous artist. But they used to go off all the time, you see: into the parks and the warren and suchlike. I got jealous of them having fun..."

"Sharon, there's nothing you could have said that didn't arise out of your situation and out of the kind of people you both were. Honest."

"Meaning, I suppose, that everything, bloody well everything, is forgiven? Just like that? I think that's daft."

He tried to make her see the truth of it, as far as he was capable of seeing the truth of it himself. (Hitler forgiven? Stalin forgiven? Pol Pot?) After little more than three minutes, though, he cut his fumbling explanations short, aware that he'd said enough, probably too much, for the time being. But he was pleased to have seen evidence of anger. It offered up some hope.

He asked after an appropriate pause:

"Have you any of Jerry's pictures that I could look at?"

"I suppose so." She gave a shrug. "Sometime."

"Would you like me to go now?"

40

"I just want to get some sleep. I wish I never had to wake up, neither."

"Yes, I can believe that."

"Jerry's well out of it, if you ask me."

"But it *will* get better. It may be impossible to imagine, but it will."

"How do *you* know?" she asked again.

Because it has to, he thought, with some vehemence; if there's a God, it has to. And because I *do* know. I've been through it all myself.

Oh, yes, indeed. *Simon the Self-Pitier. Simon the Competitive.*

And sometimes, too, at moments such as these, he really had to wonder.

Simon the Hypocrite?

10

On his way home he called in on both Alison and Dulcie.

"You shouldn't have left her," said Alison.

"What choice did I have? I could hardly have put her to bed. And she hasn't got a phone. Well, even if she had, I couldn't have used it in front of her." He was edgy.

"She'll be okay until morning," said Alison's husband, who was short and fat and smoking a cigar, his slippered feet at ease upon a pouffe. "That is, unless those kids wake up in the small hours and start to bawl."

"You're not either of you a lot of comfort. Should I get in touch with the hospital or something?"

"No," said Alison, reassuringly decisive. "Robert's right. Tonight what can one do? In the morning I'll get round there good and early."

"Not too early," warned her husband, dropping cigar ash. Simon jaundicedly assumed that he was thinking of a lie-in. "Or, anyhow, you'd better wait outside until you hear the first whimper."

"I suppose," said Alison, "that the social services *have* been alerted about all of this?"

Simon groaned. "Oh, it didn't occur to me! How stupid can I get? And surely Sharon would have told me if she were expecting a home help."

But all the same he was feeling a little more optimistic by the time he got to Jack and Dulcie's.

"Did you look at the kids?" she asked a few minutes later.

"No. Why should I?"

"I hope they were all right," she said, lugubriously.

Despite Jack's solid reassurance, and even Dulcie's own smiling acknowledgment that when her Harry was a baby she'd looked in on him six times an evening to make sure he wasn't being gassed by fumes emanating from the radiator, or the steelworks, or the oil rigs in the North Sea, Simon felt so stricken by what he thought of as an oversight that, on leaving, he seriously wondered if he ought to see the police. It wasn't that he visualized the children with their throats cut; he imagined them, rather, as having slipped into a coma, weak from lack of nourishment and incessant yet unnoticed crying.

He was tired; he knew that he was tired.

Notwithstanding the usually sympathetic presence of his mother, he didn't for the moment wish to go home. Instead of the police station he pulled up outside a pub and as soon as he had walked into its noisy, welcoming and warmly lit interior he was sure he had done the right thing. Better tonight a double Scotch in company, soothed by the hum of Friday night vitality, than an even larger one in the seclusion of his study.

He revived. Things returned into perspective.

Then he realized that, oddly, neither Alison nor Robert had once mentioned the angel. Nor Jack. Nor Dulcie.

But, come to that, neither had he. So why should it seem odd?

"Good evening, vicar!"

No collar; no clerical black; and this was a pub he'd never been into. He looked in perplexity at the thinly fair-haired man standing with a pint of lager in his hand.

"Benson," the man said. "High Ridge. Religious Education."

"Oh, yes! Forgive me."

They shook hands. Simon, who'd spoken at Morning Assembly on two occasions and had, on the strength of this, played in the staff-versus-school football match last April, would still have supposed he was looking at a stranger.

What made it worse, the fellow then inquired, smilingly, "And how are you getting on with that book?" Evidently they'd shared a conversation. Simon seldom had time to read and couldn't think what book was being referred to.

"No," said Benson, "nothing that you'd been reading. The book you were thinking of writing."

And then he remembered. He had passed on a remark made by Paula, who, at round about Easter, had been looking for a Life of Jesus to enthral her dozen or so charges on a Sunday. "Simon, everything I come across is either utterly turgid or hopelessly sentimental; there seems to be nothing in between. And yet our Saviour's life should be the most dramatic and exciting on record, wouldn't you agree?" Yes, he had certainly agreed, although he hadn't passed on the remainder of her comment. "Simon, *you* could do it! *You'd* have the proper magic touch! I know you would! And only think of all those little ones you would be leading closer to the Lord!"

Oddly, Benson had made the same suggestion. "If there's a gap in the market, why don't you try to fill it?"

"Well...who knows?" He'd been intrigued by the idea but had rapidly pushed it aside (along with, apparently, the whole encounter). Now he felt embarrassed and experienced no wish to reopen the topic. Such a project might have proved satisfying but it would surely have entailed too great a sacrifice. He couldn't consider it.

"I wonder," he said now, to minimize the danger of his companion pursuing it afresh, "do you happen to know either of the Heath boys?"

He asked this both for the sake of something to say and possibly because his failure to remember *any* of their faces had somehow linked the three of them as positively as their shared scholastic background. He habitually tried to remind himself that

43

everyone he came across was special; therefore it was worrying, this new awareness of not recognizing people whom he had most likely seen on at least a couple of occasions. He swirled the whisky at the bottom of his glass and endeavoured to give his companion the whole of his attention.

"Yes, I know them quite well," Benson replied. "Taught their sister, too."

"I wasn't aware they had one."

"I think she's now a trainee nurse. Outstandingly...well-favoured girl; high-spirited; you'd never take them for the same family."

"The boys certainly seem..." Simon hesitated over his choice of an adjective.

"Earnest?"

"No, I wasn't going to say that. You must be thinking of their mother. Beside her, I can assure you, they seem positively frivolous."

"Well, in school, let me assure *you*, they are not frivolous. Thank God! For instance, only a few days ago I let their joined classes hold a debate on nuclear disarmament and some of the facts and figures I gave out seriously alarmed them, while most of the other kids just shook them off like water."

Simon asked tonelessly:

"When was this?"

"When?" Mr Benson looked puzzled. "Well, like I say – "

"I mean, was it before Wednesday? No, don't worry. Forget it." Simon left his drink unfinished on the counter.

"As a matter of fact, now you mention it, it *was* last Wednesday."

"Yes. Well. Monday, Tuesday, Wednesday, it really makes no odds. Good to have spoken to you."

Glancing back from the doorway, he saw the man watching his exit, curiously. He knew he'd behaved badly but didn't much care. Or, rather, he did – yet what was one more care among so many others?

44

Disgustedly, he found that his predominant feeling was one of self-pity. *Still*. Even more disgustedly, he found the mere fact of having recognized this did nothing to dislodge it.

Why did God play these little games?

Or even... This was hardly a thought new to him of course (and, indeed, hadn't it fleetingly crossed his mind within the past hour?) but nowadays he found it difficult to give it entry, let alone respect. Couldn't people simply be fooling themselves when they said that God existed?

It was a terrifying notion. Too terrifying. Apart from all else...the sheer *waste*! Of time, money, effort, passion, dedication. The sheer waste of every life sacrificed; of every life lost through a billion acts of cruelty.

But thankfully it was a notion which for years he had known he would never be able to accept – and he pitied those for whom it had become a truth. In what small things did they find meaning? Comfort?

When he reached home his mother was in the kitchen filling her hot-water bottle. "My poor love, you do look done in! I thought Fridays were supposed to be your day off?"

He answered apathetically: "We can forget all about that angel business. It was just some sort of...well, freak hallucination."

"Oh, no! No, it can't have been! And after all that hard work you put in! Darling, I *am* sorry. What a shame! Still, I don't suppose they meant it."

"It seems they'd been very much affected by some debate in school. Nuclear disarmament. But if only they had said so."

"They probably thought it would lessen the impact."

"That in itself then was a form of deception."

She was now hugging the hot-water bottle to her chest. "Tonight, shall *I* build up the fire?"

"Why? What's so different about tonight?" He didn't say it with a good grace.

"Well, if you're quite sure? But please don't be downhearted. Shall I bring you some cocoa in bed?"

"No, I don't want cocoa. I'm off into the study." He kissed her, very perfunctorily, on the cheek.

"Just don't stay there for hours; you need your sleep. Oh, by the way... How was the Turner girl?"

"None too good. She wants looking after."

"Oh, my darling, don't we all?" The cry was humorous, not unfeeling.

The phone rang.

Oh God, he thought, who's dying now? That's all I need. For the instant before he lifted the receiver he looked up at the crucifix. Help me, Lord – give me strength. He changed the pronoun, made it plural.

"St Matthew's Vicarage."

He listened drearily to the pips; it was either a faulty coin box or some idiot trying to work it. Occasionally the telephone rang as many as six times before there was finally a voice at the other end.

"Oh, Simon. It's Dawn here. Dawn Heath."

He had an eerie sense of *déjà vu*. He remembered a film where someone had been relieved to wake from a bad dream, only to find the circumstances of the dream beginning to repeat themselves in real life. In a moment she was going to say she had something wonderful to tell him. Could she pop round?

"I'm sorry if it's late. But... Well, we thought you ought to know."

"I've got to be at the youth club at six."

He realized with a shock what he'd just said.

"Know what?" he asked quickly. He saw his mother standing in the doorway.

Dawn obviously hadn't been listening. "Two things. One of them's incredible." Yes. The scenario was clearly by the same scriptwriter. "You see, they suddenly remembered, both of them, wholly out of the blue, a scripture lesson they'd had last Wednesday. One of the teachers was away; their classes had to double up. Well, it doesn't really alter anything, I told them that but they were worried that it did. 'It's still a miracle,' I said. 'Mr Madison knows far more than we do and even he thinks it's a

46

miracle.' William said, 'But when we tell him what we've remembered he won't go on thinking it. Nothing will make him believe it any more. And then we'll just be on our own.' And after that he started to cry."

Dawn paused, perhaps for breath. Simon said: "Poor lad. It isn't anyone's fault. These things...happen. If he's with you could I speak to him?"

It seemed that Dawn was trying to take this in; her pause extended itself.

"But you don't understand," she said, at last. "You see, I haven't told you yet about the second thing. And, Simon, it really is a miracle. Because we've had a sign. God's given us the proof."

"Oh, yes?" said Simon. He decided this was hardly the moment to point out God wasn't in the business of providing tidy bits of proof. *Quod erat demonstrandum* was not, noticeably, in God's vocabulary.

"You see, it was when William started to cry because he thought it *wasn't* a miracle. Suddenly he clapped his hands to his face as though his tears were scalding him. At first that didn't occur to me. I just supposed he didn't want us to see. Afterwards he said it was like a great tingling sensation, like little currents of electricity shooting here and there beneath the skin. Not in the least bit painful."

"And?" Simon was scarcely paying attention.

"Well, it was when he took his hands away. He wasn't crying any more. That only lasted for a few seconds, maybe six or so. But his tears had washed him clean."

He imagined she was using blood-of-the-Lamb type language. He somewhat listlessly repeated her last three words.

"Well, don't say you didn't notice!" she laughed. "Up until this happened, there was nothing we could ever do about it, no matter what the doctor gave. Well, now it's all gone, every last trace."

"What has?"

"His *acne*. He's got the best complexion in Humberside. Even Josh can't come up with anything to explain it away." She

47

giggled. Dawn – Dawn Heath! She was giggling like some giddy and triumphant ten-year-old. "And, truly, you mustn't think he hasn't tried!"

11

Oh, yes. He had certainly tried. Even at half-past-two in the morning he was still trying. It was about then that Dawn mumbled:

"You all right, Josh?"

"Yes."

"Wondered if...some pain or something?"

"Go back to sleep."

He listened to her turn over and before long resume her regular breathing; listened with relief, listened with resentment. He confessed himself unreasonable. In some ways it was this very placidity of hers which made her a good wife, and often he felt grateful to her. But his gratitude was more of the mind than of the heart and in his heart she irritated him.

Even on Gabriel-night she had soon achieved soft snores.

He had a favourite fantasy: his moon-and-sixpence trip. But tonight he felt nothing could have soothed him into sleep.

What's more, it didn't have to be Tahiti. London would do. Anywhere that gave you the feeling of life being lived, of possibilities being possible. Forty-six wasn't old.

In any case, if he were starting out anew, he believed he could get away with forty. Even thirty-eight.

The obstacle, of course, was money. He did the pools. He was trying to write an English textbook. Textbooks could be lucrative but... Well, he only wished he had the nerve to rob a post office. Something like that.

Dawn wouldn't miss him. Nor would the boys. He couldn't fool himself he'd been much of a father – not since they'd moved out of childhood, become teenagers, learned to rely more

48

on friends than fathers. Not since they'd no doubt grown ashamed of him.

And none of them, financially, would be any the worse off. The opposite. If he ever got the money to escape he'd make sure he had enough to send some home each payday.

Sometimes he saw it as a real possibility. Even when he didn't, hope hadn't fully died. Every time he went walking through the town he was vaguely on the lookout for a new relationship: something with depth and durability. At bottom it wasn't just a carnal thing he was after, although Dawn no longer attracted him and seldom wanted sex. In truth it was more a friend he hankered for. Somebody to hug, yes – a ready hand to hold – yet still, in essence, more a two-way flowing of concern, support and understanding. Only when depressed did he tell himself this wasn't realistic.

Even one-night-stands eluded him. From all he read he would have supposed that to pick up a girl in 1984 was an easily achievable aim for any man who was at least averagely attractive; and he knew that he was probably more than that. He hadn't got those film-starry looks which, for instance, the vicar from St Matthew's had. Nor did he have his height. Yet on a one-to-ten scale he would surely be amongst the sixes or the sevens.

He had envied him this afternoon, that vicar. Envied him his stature, envied him his certainty and singleness of purpose.

Envied him his singleness.

But since then, somehow, his other feelings had completely changed. In fact, it now made him cringe, the memory of how he had buttered him up on the stairs. The man was nothing but a prig. Josh could neither understand his own attitude at the time – he wasn't normally a person who *fawned* – nor, to be honest, what had afterwards enabled him to get things back into perspective. He was only thankful that something had.

"Josh, what *is* the matter with you?" Dawn yawned lengthily. "Do you want me to get up and make some tea?"

"No. Go back to sleep."

49

"You keep on saying that. But how can I? With you so restless?"

"Sorry. I'll stay still."

"You're not worried about money, are you? I tell you and tell you, Josh. God will take care of all of that."

"Yes. You tell me and tell me."

"'Consider the lilies of the field, how they grow; they toil not, neither do they spin.'"

At least once every week Josh was urged to consider the lilies of the field. He had never before been urged to consider them at two-fifty-five in the morning. He felt seriously tempted to suggest that the lilies of the field go screw themselves. After all, what else had they to do in all that stupendously undeserved free time? But he found that he couldn't bring himself to say it. Not to Dawn.

My God, she tried though. In a way, you had to admire her for it; feel sad to see such effort misdirected.

"'And yet I say unto you, that even Solomon in all his glory was not arrayed like one of these.'"

"Sod Solomon."

"What?"

Four years ago she wouldn't have been able to recite that. Probably the extent of her biblical quotation then would have been *Adam and Eve and Pinch-Me went down to the river to bathe*. Now she had whole passages by heart. The fact that many were in rather pleasant English did little or nothing to compensate.

"Sod Solomon in all his glory." Yes. Why not? Even to Dawn.

"Please don't blaspheme. It's childish. Just because you're cross at being proved wrong! Yes, that's why you can't sleep, suddenly I know it is. Well, Josh, you ought to be ashamed. You ought to be down on your knees and thanking God for all his goodness. You ought to be pleading for forgiveness, you ought to be begging for salvation."

50

"Is that right?" he said. No. I ought to be getting the hell out of here. I ought to be doing something with my life. I ought to be getting the very most out of every fleeting minute, hour and day.

He turned his bedside lamp on and thought about, as a first step, going to make them both that cup of tea.

Dawn lay her head back on the pillow and looked towards the ceiling. "The wondrous thing is," she said – and the note of reproach had entirely disappeared – "that *I* could sleep. I mean, after I'd just witnessed..."

Perhaps, then, it wasn't mere placidity. "It must be the sleep of the innocent," he told her, gently.

She turned her face towards him.

"Oh, Josh, I don't see how you can fly in the teeth of all the evidence like you do. I really don't. It's like when we watched that programme on the Turin Shroud. Only more so. Are you going to spend the whole of your life just running?"

"Probably."

He got out of bed and started pulling his clothes on.

"Right now," he said, "I'm going to spend it, at any rate, just walking. Building up to it, you see, in easy stages. Whatever you may think about my present showing I've not yet reached the top of my bent."

"Oh, but that's silly. Where can you go at this time?"

Nowhere. He would have liked to walk to London, before his energy wore off. He got as far as Ashby – two miles? Here he finally acknowledged the uselessness of it all; turned round; feet dragging. He encountered scarcely anyone: a cyclist; an old man in too large an overcoat shuffling along in gym shoes; a very occasional car. The wind had acquired an extra edge. As a last gesture of hopelessness coupled with defiance, he deviated from the road home, trudged recklessly across hilly, hillocky, pitch black common land – "I couldn't give a fuck, not a fuck, whether I stand or fall!" – found himself, ironically, outside St Matthew's Vicarage and shuddered violently several times, while continuing to cry out loud at intervals, "I couldn't give a fuck, not a single fuck!" (He wished that precious, posing, pontificating hypocrite might have heard – and, indeed, if the

51

study hadn't been at the back of the house, Josh would have seen its light shining through the thin curtains.) On the last stages of his journey home he began to see some daylight. Incredibly, he was relieved to get back into the snugness of his bed. "You stubborn man," murmured Dawn. "I'm glad you're back..." Her hand reached out for him. This didn't often happen. Almost against his will he responded.

12

Simon had also got up before three. Unable to sleep, he hadn't been able to pray either, or not as he'd have liked. Although he'd often told his parishioners their prayers would sometimes sound laboured and dull (but that they shouldn't feel discouraged, for God would still be pleased and listening and receptive) tonight he couldn't draw much comfort from his own advice. The words that left his lips – or, rather, his heart, since he wasn't speaking them aloud – struck him as wholly worthless, insincere. They were certainly a little wooden, when what he'd asked for at the start was spontaneity and joy. And wisdom. In the end he left the sofa and sat at his desk, beneath the crucifix, drew several sheets of paper towards him, picked up a Biro...and eventually began to write. Resolutely, wildly, hoping that this, too, could represent a form of prayer.

*

He wrote: She had known him as long as she could remember, yet she had never seen him like this. He was furious. She thought that at any moment he might strike her.

"Who was it?" he shouted. He held a hammer; she wished he'd put it down.

"I've told you. The angel said – "

"The angel said! The angel said! Another bloody word about this angel of yours – " Then suddenly he sagged. He sank down

52

on the stool behind him, his face covered by both hands. "Angels may have come to the prophets in ancient times," he said, brokenly. "They don't appear to unknown girls in Nazareth today."

"But this one did," she persisted. "And he told me that my pregnancy came from God. He asked if I would bear it."

"And you, of course, said 'yes'." The moist eyes and the falsetto voice and the rugged frame were all oddly at variance. "'I'm six weeks overdue, God, and already half married to that simpleton carpenter down the road but if I can say you were the one who put me in the club he's bound to be impressed!'" The man's voice became his own again; the hammer dropped out of his limp fingers; he watched it strike the sawdust. "Oh, what the hell does it matter whose child it is? Don't you know what the punishment can be for a girl who's betrothed to one man and gets herself pregnant by another?"

When she didn't answer, the savagery came back. "Well, don't you?"

She nodded. For the first time a tremor appeared in her voice, a reminder to him that, after all, this was only a sixteen-year-old girl and he was a man of more than twice her age. A man almost old enough to be her father.

"Stoning?" she wavered.

He looked away. "Yes, well," he mumbled, "there's no need for it to come to that. There'll be shame for you, shame for both of us, that's unavoidable, but we can hush the thing up as far as possible. Do your people know?"

"No. You were the first one I wanted to tell. Oh, Joe, I felt so proud."

She clenched her fist to her mouth to keep back the sobbing that suddenly welled up. Then she ran from the shop and the carpenter watched her go.

He had loved her so much. Life had seemed so perfect. Why had everything had to go wrong?

*

53

Now the time was half-past-six. Simon put down his Biro, went and drew back the curtains, stood at the window, yawning, stretching. He looked out at the garden; realized with some surprise that he was still in his pyjamas but nonetheless opened the French window and strolled out on the grass, enjoying the damp softness beneath bare feet, enjoying the bright freshness of a new day. He felt pleased with what he'd written, although he knew he had no right to, "For thine is the kingdom, the power and the glory," and knew, also, that on a later reading he might well feel disappointed. That often happened with his sermons. Despite the countless crossings-out and substitutions and battles against cliché (for instance, he still wasn't happy with 'almost old enough to be her father', and things like 'she clenched her fist to her mouth', when naturally a fist would already have been clenched) and *despite* the passage being so relatively short, perhaps not even long enough to be regarded as a first chapter, he knew that it would still require a second draft. Possibly a third and a fourth.

But yes, he thought, as he peed behind a rosebush (his mother would have given him hell if she had happened to be looking out!), he was actually quite pleased with it, and excited – and despite the initial sense of aggression with which he had started, *virtual* aggression, he was already aware that constantly throughout the day he'd be thinking about it and wanting to get back to it, and the true self-discipline which any writer was supposed to have would lie in his *not* allowing that writing to get in the way of everything else he ought to be getting on with.

He said to himself the Lord's Prayer and then went on to pray about the Heath family and the conundrum with which they were presenting him; and this time found that his words flowed and seemed far more acceptable.

Which made him laugh. "Acceptable to whom? Who the *heck* do you think you are!"

He went in then to have his bath, and was already looking forward to breakfast. It struck him that he didn't even feel tired. On his way through the study he said his usual good morning to Ginny.

"And, darling, sorry I was so peevish and shirty last night! Such a pain in the arse! Forgive me."

13

"Joshua, Joshua,
   Sweeter than lemon squash you are...
   Yes, by gosh you are,
   Joshu-oshu-ah!"

"Oh, do have a *heart*," begged Simon.

"I'm sorry. I can't help it. Blame my mother. *She* was singing it before breakfast."

"Oh God!"

"My own feeling precisely."

They were stretched out on their backs near the top of Beachy Head, the remnants of their picnic lunch now tidily returned to Simon's knapsack. Below them the sea sparkled and the gulls soared.

"Added to which," said Ginny, "I don't even think that lemon squash *is* sweet, particularly. I hope that doesn't sound too crushing."

"It sounds moronic. Of course lemon squash is sweet."

"No, I find it sharp."

"Refreshing. Tangy."

"Sharp."

"I grant you, it isn't cloying. But how can you say it isn't sweet? Even if at your first swallow, perhaps – "

"I do wish you had some small talk. Why will you only speak of the big imponderables?"

"Life's too short for trivialities."

She smiled but didn't answer. She continued chewing on her blade of grass.

"As a matter of fact," he said, "my own mother also liked that memories-of-the-music-hall bit; she thought it was the best thing

55

in the show. But I can't help feeling that 'By the Light of the Silvery Moon' didn't *exactly* hit the right note when offered as a humble tribute to Messrs Armstrong and Aldrin; not even when backed up by 'Moon River' and 'Shine on, Harvest Moon'."

"Our humble and very *sincere* tribute. Don't forget that."

"I'm sorry," he said.

"The trouble is, you're a perfectionist. You cavil. At least it was topical."

"But think how you'd have cringed if they'd actually been with us: Armstrong and Aldrin."

"I wish I could have been with *them*. Last week. Up there."

He expressed surprise.

"Don't *you*, then?" She rolled over and looked at him, her head propped on her hand, the blade of grass now held between her thumb and forefinger.

"I'd have been petrified."

"Yes, of course, everybody would. But I mean, apart from that? The sheer enormity of the thing! Something to leave you awestruck and gasping for ever!"

"Well, I agree with that, naturally. It'd be interesting to know the long-term effects it'll have on those two fellows. But I still wouldn't have chosen to be up there with them. I'm not a brave man."

She looked disappointed although she totally ignored that last, short sentence. "I suppose you'll tell me next you don't even think it was a good idea?"

"It's progress," he said. "It's a tribute to the ingenuity of the human race. It's even a very *sincere* tribute." He paused. "And it's partly that selfsame ingenuity which makes me so certain there's a God. The potential for such brilliance could never have been purely accidental."

"But?" she prompted, after a moment, again ignoring the latter part of what he'd said.

"But the world's priorities are wrong. Prestige. Power. That's what it's all about, not simply the advancement of science. Yet even in the States there are thousands – millions – still living on the breadline."

She surprised him again: by the readiness with which she acquiesced. He felt pleased by it, as well; not because he had persuaded her of anything but because in fact he hadn't. It indicated, he thought, that fundamentally they would agree on most things.

It was as if she knew what he was thinking. "I hope you realize that I'm not just a yes-girl. I take a hard line on lemon squash."

"Oh, I do realize. But what became of your eternal gasps?"

"For the time being...yes, I concede they're a luxury."

"Then I must ask you again in another, say, twenty years."

She rolled over once more and squinted up at the sun; it shimmered between her eyelids. Of course, it was silly to take an unconsidered remark of that sort seriously, but even so it instantly reinforced the feeling of wellbeing she'd had since the previous night, inside the theatre.

"Anyway, I think we've established by now that you don't want to be an astronaut. So what does that leave?"

"I don't know. I feel that the right thing's going to present itself quite soon." Not books, he said, for although they still lived above his father's bookshop, the business itself had now been sold. Not teaching; he didn't think he had any vocation for that. He listed a number of careers that he felt the right thing definitely wasn't. "Does it strike you," he said, "I must be rather negative?"

The question had been meant rhetorically but Ginny answered it. "No. I can truthfully say it doesn't strike me at all in that way."

He himself moved onto his side and reached over and brushed his knuckles against the back of her hand. She turned the hand round and took hold of his fingers, stroking them. They smiled at one another but neither referred to the contact. Ginny merely said, easily, "Has there never been *anything* that's really appealed to you?"

"Well, let me think. I shouldn't have minded being a doctor. Except that I'm squeamish. I shouldn't have minded being a dentist. Except that I don't fancy spending the bulk of my life

57

potholing in people's mouths. And besides, could I ever bring myself to give them an injection? Only on the understanding I could always look the other way."

"No, be serious, though."

"I think I am being, more or less. I sometimes wonder about politics. The idea of being able to influence things for the better, maybe even make big improvements in people's lives...I find that quite exciting, I really do." He smiled. "Clearly I'm an egotist."

"You know what I can see you as?"

"Mm?"

"A vicar."

He pulled his hand away. The dreamy quality had gone.

"No, you can't! Of course you can't! What makes you say that?"

She sat up quickly.

"Simon, what's the matter? I don't *know* why I said it. It wasn't a very serious suggestion. You seem..."

"What?" He asked it sharply.

"Like a girl I once knew who went to a convent school. Somebody told her he thought she would end as a nun. I remember her face. It was frightened."

"And did she?" He, too, had sat up.

"End as a nun? Oh, I don't suppose she will for a moment."

There was a silence. They watched a linnet hopping on the grass nearby.

"I'm sorry," he said. "I don't know why I reacted like that. In a way, I believe, I actually *was* frightened. My father once told me that I ought to be a vicar. Perhaps I suddenly felt hounded."

"Oh, look! Isn't he pretty?"

But although the linnet had drawn even closer, he abruptly seemed to sense her interest and to find it threatening. He flew off.

"Now who would believe that? Stupid bird! You go on talking in a normal tone; I whisper half a dozen words. Is it symbolic? Was he also feeling hounded?" She laughed.

"Symbolic, nothing!" Unexpectedly, Simon jumped to his feet, took both her hands and pulled her onto hers. He put his arms about her and they stood together for at least a minute. Then he kissed her lightly and said, "Let's walk a little." He pulled his shirt on, slipped his arms through the straps of the knapsack. They started down the narrow path, laughing, running, swinging hands.

"Isn't it incredible?" he exclaimed. "Twenty-four hours ago I didn't even know you."

"Eighteen," she said. "Eighteen! What kind old fate directed you to *Sea View*?"

"The kind old fate that made my father a very distant cousin of the manageress. Well, anyway, sort of, by adoption. We came here once before; when I was a child. This year...you see, my mother badly needed a rest and...and suddenly she just wanted to return. Though I myself, if I'd lost someone whom I'd loved as much as that... *Your* father's still alive, isn't he?"

She nodded. "Oddly enough, we're both here, Mummy and I, because he too knows someone who's connected with this place. Daddy's an architect. He and Mummy had their real holiday earlier in the year, in Jamaica, and since he's all tied up at the moment – "

Simon interrupted her. "I think that's pathetic," he said, "your parents swanning off to Jamaica and you only getting a fortnight at *Sea View*."

"No, it was a client who'd invited them. It couldn't be at any other time. I was invited to go but the dates conflicted with my A levels."

"Well, now I think it's even more pathetic." Neither his mother nor father would ever have thought of leaving *him* if he'd had some major examination to sit. "Although I do have to admit that it's also..."

"What?"

"A bit of a miracle." It occurred to him, briefly, that somehow he meant it as more than just a figure of speech. "There was clearly a most magnificent reason for it."

"A point? A purpose?"

59

"Yes."

"Oh, don't get cross with me, I really can't help it. I *said* you ought to be a vicar!"

"You needn't think I've forgotten! So now you can go and – what? – "

"Take a running jump? Oh, please, no! Not off Beachy Head. Let me sing you something as a penance." She assumed permission. "'Joshua, Joshua, sharper than lemon squash you are; yes, by gosh you are...'"

"Whose penance?" he asked.

14

The first phone call of the day came before seven-thirty.

"I hope I haven't gone and got you out of bed, vicar, but I'd have been frantic if I'd missed you. I've been awake all night."

"Mrs Philby, isn't it?" (Oddly, he might be better with voices than with faces – a sort of compensation. *Thank you, Lord.*)

"It's about my mother," the woman added, in the same self-evident distress.

"I'll try to be with you in half an hour."

"Could you make it about nine? I've got to see to her breakfast first and get her washed and settled and not fall behindhand with the chores."

Mrs Philby lived in Crosby Avenue in a house with polished windows and a shiny doorstep and crisp net curtains. When he got there, shortly after nine, she'd been looking out for him. He didn't even need to ring.

She was a straight-backed, stringy woman in her early sixties, with a retroussé nose and grey hair stiffly set; she wore a nylon overall. At first she showed him into the lounge but then asked if he would mind coming into the kitchen, where she could get on with her work. Since she was already preparing vegetables for lunch, three potatoes and a quarter of a small cauliflower, and storing the segments in a pudding basin filled with water, Simon

60

couldn't feel that she was very much behindhand with her chores.

Mrs Philby had come home five years earlier, after her husband had died, back to the house where she'd been born and raised.

"She's got lung cancer," she blurted out, and her lips trembled. She took an eye out of the potato about a centimetre round; the potato could hardly spare it. "The doctor told me yesterday. I don't know what to do."

Simon looked down at the scrubbed deal table by which he sat. Ran his forefinger along one of the well-worn ridges.

"I'm sorry," he said. "I'm not surprised you couldn't sleep. Has...? Has your mother been told about it?"

"That's why I wanted your advice. Do you think she should be?"

"Yes," he said, slowly. "From what I know of Mrs Beecham..."

Yet then he began to wonder. Supposing he himself were told he had only months to live? Would he really want to know? Very easy to say, I'm a religious man, I'd wish to have time to prepare myself, get the utmost out of however long I've got left, not fritter all my energies – very easy to say, of course, while the question remained safely academic.

Granted, Mrs Beecham was nearly fifty years older than him. But at any age, surely, life was precious. (Unless it wasn't; he thought of Jerry Turner.) The fear of the unknown was just as great.

"The doctor said it might be better to leave her as she was. You see, she's usually quite chirpy – except on her off-days. He thought it would be a pity to risk spoiling things, without a proper reason."

Without a proper reason! "How would you feel, Mrs Philby, if it was *you*?"

"Oh, I'd just want someone to put me out with an injection, very quietly, not a word. 'You'll be right as rain in no time, dear.' That's how *I'd* like it. Oh, why do people have to die?" Her voice shook, as she asked that. He went over to where she

61

stood at the sink, with her gaunt back turned towards him, and put an arm around her shoulders.

"I can't tell her, vicar. I just can't do it."

"That's all right, Amy, you don't have to." Again, he thanked God that her Christian name should have come back to him just then. He noticed that she wore a hairnet; he wondered why she thought she needed it.

"I can't go through it all again."

"Your husband?" he asked.

"My husband. My sister. My father-in-law. I can't take any more of it. I can't!"

He held her while she cried. His lips moved rapidly and silently.

"It's going to be all right," he repeated soothingly, from time to time. "There'll be people who can help. Try not to worry, it's going to be all right."

Suddenly he heard that phrase, himself using it, nearly as if he had never heard it before. Try not to worry. *Try not to worry*! He was startled by the glibness of it, by the fact that, despite everything, he remained callow. If he'd been in this woman's position he thought he might have said: "What right has *he* to tell me that? What experience has *he* ever had of real suffering? Him with his mother and all his home comforts and people always inviting him for dinner. His posh southern accent. How much can *he* know about the true nature of things?"

But he was so very far from being in this woman's position, he realized with a further slight shock, that even at this moment, with another human being's unhappiness as rawly manifest before him as in ordinary circumstances it very well could be, he was still actually thinking of himself; absorbed neither in *her* grief nor in his own prayers.

God, he thought.

When her sobbing had grown calmer, Simon said:

"Amy, shall we put the whole thing in the hands of God? Just stand here for a moment and ask for his guidance and for the knowledge of his presence?"

She asked him to wait a second while she blew her nose and dried her eyes. She apologized for the spectacle which she'd gone and made of herself.

When he had finished praying, he gave her a final pat on the side of one shoulder and walked back to the table. She blew her nose again and put the kettle on.

"Thank you, vicar, that was nice. I feel better now. I want her to be told. I think she should. She's different to what I am."

"I'm sure that's right," he said. "And I'm not being presumptuous, am I, in thinking you'd prefer me to do it?"

"Oh, if you don't mind. If you would. I'd be happier." She was taking down cups from the dresser and she gave him a pinched smile of gratitude across her shoulder.

"How long does the doctor give her?"

"He thinks she'll still be with us for Christmas. She always liked Christmas; I never much cared for it myself. Funny thing, you'd think it would run in the family, one way or the other. I don't want her ending up in hospital," she added, fiercely.

He tried to tell her that towards the finish her mother might be better off in hospital, but she wouldn't accept that and, after all, he was no expert. "And especially not at Christmas," she said twice.

"What I mentioned earlier about there being lots of people to help, I very much meant it, you'd – "

"No," she said. "That's very kind. You don't want strangers at a time like that."

"Amy, they wouldn't be strangers. They... People you've seen at church," he ended rather lamely. But again he decided not to push. He asked about her family. A brother in New Zealand who wouldn't have the money nor the inclination to come over, it appeared. Her son perhaps somewhere in London; she hadn't heard from him in more than three years, he could be dead for all she knew. A few odd cousins scattered here and there, there wasn't one she could be sure she'd recognize if he walked into this room right here and now. They had some good neighbours but neighbours weren't family; and as for family – useless, worse than useless. Amy Philby and her mother were completely on their own.

"And that's the way I like it," she affirmed. "I won't go crawling after any of them! Let them find out afterwards and feel about it whichever way they choose."

She sat down whilst she drank her tea, sat with rawboned hands clamped round the cup, as though even that could soon be taken from her.

The ironic thing was that he himself felt basically so grateful and at peace. Ironic? Almost shameful. It was a desperate world, teeming with Sharon Turners and Amy Philbys (for in the mere half-mile dividing *them* how many others were there, each in his own proud ring of suffering, one in a chain of beaten lives that fell across the country?), and yet he knew now that hope remained. Real; abundant. God was there. God cared. He *cared*. Yes, naturally one had believed in that before but it was joyous suddenly to have the confirmation. A boy's face... Simon hadn't been to look at William. In fact he didn't need to. The miracle had conveyed itself along those telephone wires as surely as if a burning bush had sprung up in the centre of his study.

And yet he couldn't tell her of it, this woman who sat across the table, this woman who so very desperately needed it. He wondered how much it might have alleviated her suffering.

Enormously! Enormously! How could it not have?

When they had finished their tea she led the way upstairs. She opened the door to Mrs Beecham's bedroom while Simon waited on the landing. "Mum! I've got a visitor for you. You'll never guess."

The daughter went into the room to arrange the mother's shawl, smooth over the surface of the bed, close the window she had opened earlier. Simon heard her say: "It's the vicar, Mum. He's come to see you. Isn't that nice?" It sounded like the voice, the personality, of a different woman. He didn't catch the old lady's undoubtedly less buoyant response.

Amy Philby beckoned him in. "I'll just leave the two of you to have a little chat, then, shall I?" He was barely into the room

64

before she herself was out of it and with the door firmly shut between them.

"Good morning, vicar. What a surprise!"

The woman sitting up in bed had the same turned-up nose as her daughter but otherwise... Well, life had probably been kinder to her. Her hair was softer (white and gently waved and pretty), her cheeks were fuller, her body was, as well. She was unquestionably more pampered: she smelled of powder and perfume and her fingernails were polished.

There were flowers in the bedroom, and books and photographs. Her bed, plump-pillowed and inviting, was set by the window and from it she could look into the road; Simon was reminded of his boyhood dream of what a bedroom ought to be. Full of sunshine on occasion, snug, a wholly welcoming, picture-book retreat. Secure from all the outer harsh realities, a kind of cosy sealed-off kingdom from which to view the world.

"Good morning, Mrs Beecham. I like your room."

"Thank you. Yes, I do, too. Now, where are you going to sit? Here on the bed would be comfy and I could see you better. *And* hear you better." He sat down at the spot where she was patting the side of the eiderdown. "Maybe you're worried I could also eat you better?"

"Oh, I think I'll take my chances."

"I'm not sure if vicars should gamble!" She wheezed a little upon this.

"But I don't feel they should be scared of a calculated risk."

There was a short, companionable silence.

"Would you like a cup of tea?"

"No thank you, Mrs Beecham."

"Just had one, have you?"

"It isn't long since breakfast."

"Ah... I thought that perhaps Amy might have made you one before you came up?"

He hesitated, smiled.

"Yes, you're right. She did."

"And the two of you had a wee talk?" Then before he could answer she put up a hand to stop him. "It's all right, vicar. I

65

know why you're here. It's very good of you and I appreciate it but I *know*." And she lay her veined, arthritic hand on top of his for a moment and gave it a slight squeeze, as though she was the one whose job it was to offer comfort.

"How did you know, Mrs Beecham?"

"Well, now, you guess. I have a few simple tests at the surgery, then some others a shade more complicated at the hospital, x-rays and things – oh, just a routine check, they try to tell me, everyone over sixty has them now. Then yesterday the doctor comes to see me, spends a long time talking to my daughter at the front door. Through the evening Amy hugs me about six times, kisses me on the cheek, is ever so bright and breezy but tense and snappy with it, if you see what I mean. And as if all that wasn't enough, you yourself turn up around the crack of dawn, the second visit you've paid us in about three years, and without even ringing the doorbell, what's more! Well, vicar, let me tell you something. Up to now, for silly reasons of my own, I may have gone along with it but even so I was *not* born yesterday." She gave a cheerful laugh, until he saw her upper dentures start to slip. "I'll let you into another little secret if you like."

"Please."

"I don't mind. I don't mind dying."

He nodded, non-committally. It was now he who had his hand on hers.

"And shall I tell you why?"

He thought she was going to tell him she was tired; had too many aches, too little energy, too little mobility and independence; had outlived so many of her family and her friends.

World-weary. Life offers no more hope, no more surprises. One's dreams are only of the past. It's just a question now of getting through with what degree of dignity one can manage to cling onto.

He would have known exactly what she meant. Despite her pleasant room, despite her books.

66

Despite, even, a messenger encircled in light behind Tiffany's: a heavenly torchbearer handing on his torch?

Then he felt guilty. That his lack of sleep was catching up on him wasn't any mitigation. He quickly sought forgiveness.

"I don't mind dying," she said, "because...well, because there are great numbers of nice people who are dead."

He thought about this. "People you've known?"

"Yes. And a great many more I haven't."

He smiled.

"Of course," she added, "*you* may say, and naturally I'd agree, that there are great numbers of nice people who are living. But how many of them do you ever get to meet? In *this* world?"

He sighed.

She looked at him inquiringly.

"I foresee," he said, "a thoroughly exhausting eternity. I'd been hoping for a bit of peace."

"Now, stop it! It won't be an unending series of coffee mornings, which I can tell is how you picture it. Besides, attendance would only be optional."

"Mind you." He laughed. "What coffee mornings! Leonardo da Vinci, Shakespeare, Jane Austen, Abraham Lincoln. Don't quote me if I say this, but a mite more interesting than anything we usually get at St Matthew's."

They became more serious.

"How long have I got, vicar?"

He spoke about Christmas. He stroked her hand, entirely without knowing he did so.

"Listen, Mrs Beecham, let's get back to basics for an instant. Only think of what Jesus has said – and St Paul – to give us comfort and encouragement in any situation whatsoever."

They spent at least ten minutes in reminding themselves.

15

In that morning's post there'd been a letter from their daughter Janice.

"Oh!" said Dawn, reading it. "Oh! All the good things are coming at once."

"What is it?" In spite of his severely interrupted night, Josh had got up at more or less his normal time. He was currently mashing the tea.

"She'll be here for lunch tomorrow. She says she's sorry that it's such short notice."

The nursing school was in Sheffield. Usually she got home at least once a month, and for the whole weekend, not just for Sunday lunch. "Well, what's so wonderful about that?"

"It says – listen – it says, 'Do you mind if I bring Don? He's someone rather special.'"

"*Who*?"

"Yes, you're right, I'm sure it's not a name she's ever mentioned. The little monkey. Oh, she's an artful one."

"What else does she say?"

"Nothing. Except that he doesn't like peas much, or apples. What a weekend this is going to be! Heaven knows how we're ever going to cope but... Do you realize, Josh, that this is the first time our Janice has brought home a young man? And from the sound of it, I'd say, it might even be the last! He must be one of the doctors, wouldn't you think?"

She handed him the letter with a dreamy expression.

"Fancy a man who doesn't care for peas or apples!" he exclaimed.

Michael arrived for his breakfast; even at weekends (or, for that matter, during the school holidays or at any other time) slothfulness was not permitted; no greater concession made – or dispensation given, said Josh – than one short extra hour in bed. "Who doesn't care for peas or apples?"

"Some man your sister's bringing home."

"Blimey! Is she going to marry him?"

68

"What, at nineteen? She'd be a fool if she did."

"I was only nineteen," said Dawn.

"Attitudes have changed in the past twenty years." Josh brought their four mugs over to the table.

"I don't see how."

"Then you must be one of the few women in the whole country who doesn't."

"I wouldn't want her living with anyone."

She glanced anxiously at Michael as she said this.

Josh laughed. "Especially somebody who didn't like fruit and veg! It sounds positively unwholesome to me. Unclean." He got up from the table, to fetch a new jar of marmalade; and having done so ruffled Michael's hair. "Thank God *we* never had fastidious children. Ugh! I bet he's all covered in pimples!"

"Stop that, please!" said Dawn. "You really aren't being funny."

He and Michael exchanged a covert smile. Michael clearly thought he was.

A few minutes later William came in, who *wasn't* all covered in pimples. Josh, on his feet again, his breakfast done with, gave a small frown. For a moment he'd forgotten. Then he laid an affectionate arm round William's shoulders. "There, that's what you get as a reward for eating up your cabbage! And your carrots! My word, but you look handsome!"

"Oh, Dad...!"

William pulled away, embarrassed.

"Anyhow, I'm off for a workout. See you all later. And don't forget to tell Billy the good news!"

The Tannery was in Mary Street. Josh had become a member there four years before and had paid his first seventy-five pounds out of his savings. After that he had methodically held back three pounds every fortnight from his supplementary benefits. It had never occurred to Dawn to ask how he kept up his membership. To him this membership was more than just important; it was vital. In having developed his body he had done something constructive with his enforced leisure. It was the thing which had helped him most not only to hold onto his self-respect but even to enhance it.

He went three times a week: for a workout and a shower and a brief time on the sunbed. (He didn't want to be mahogany, just very lightly tanned.) He pretended to laugh at it, but was prepared to strive unflaggingly for things that he believed in.

Once, at the beginning, he had been sick after a particularly violent workout. Once, he had almost fainted. He wondered if he ought to see the doctor; on occasions he imagined pains in his chest, felt sick again – with fear. He questioned his priorities, resolved to give the whole thing up, then returned for an equally gruelling workout. It was at these times, surviving the session following the fear, that he felt unusually elated. He was continually testing himself. More than that. Continually pushing himself, continually forcing himself to surpass his own previous performance. When he was buoyant he didn't believe he would bring on any heart attack; when he was depressed he muttered that he didn't care; it was a possibility he even courted. He didn't want the pain, of course, but the solution – partial or entire, the rest or the oblivion – these sounded, at times, not undesirable: a welcome respite from his weariness, a final end to it. The strenuous exercise itself, however, especially if coupled with the beating of some record, almost invariably got rid of his depression.

This morning, for instance: for a while he totally forgot Janice and her 'somebody rather special'; he totally forgot that pustules on his son's face and neck had ever existed. And even during those moments when these things did come back to him they had grown more bearable: minor irritations around the periphery, rather than unthinkable threats full at the centre. On Saturday mornings the gym was at its most crowded; there were generally at least a dozen people. He didn't mind this. The place was small and it meant he might have to wait longer to use equipment but he enjoyed the atmosphere of clublike masculinity, the simple camaraderie made up of shared interests and a spirit of easygoing rivalry.

70

On a Saturday morning, though, he was often more aware of the absurdity of it all. Every aid to manly development appeared to be in constant use: the thigh machine and the lat machine and the curling machine and the rowing machine and the standing-press machine; the abdominal boards and the bench press and the power jog and the multi-purpose exerciser and the bike; the barbells and the dumbbells. Oh the pain of it, the grunting and the sweat, oh the heartfelt determination! Oh the concentration on the biceps or the triceps or the deltoid or the calf, the striving for perfection, for the godlike build, when in countries like South America people screamed out from the effects of torture, or in Beirut soldiers were having limbs blown off, when half the world was dying from starvation, when even in civilized England babies were mugged and little girls had their faces set on fire. Who ever knew what atrocities were being perpetrated in any part of the globe at any given instant, what accidents were taking place, what howls of agony were right *now*, somewhere, ripping at the air? Most of the men who came to the gym were younger than he was but one or two were older; did they all think (did he think) that they were going to turn themselves into objects of irresistible desire? Did they suppose (did he suppose) that, even if they did, it was going to make the world a better place for anybody, anywhere, other than (perhaps) themselves and the lucky women who might benefit from all their bulked-up charms? It was absurd all right.

But in a way he sometimes found it quite a comfort: the very fact that life *was* so inescapably absurd. It absolved. It cancelled out. It rendered unimportant.

It assisted you to laugh.

Supposing he were suddenly to say: "You know, my two lads met an angel behind Tiffany's the other night."

"Just hope she made a man of them!"

"Not that sort. The kind you read about in bibles."

"Christ! Is it glue-sniffing your lads are into, or drugs, or just old-fashioned alcohol?"

He tried it out, as he was drying from his shower. The other man was large and nearly every inch of him from the neck down,

71

with the exception of his hands, was covered in tattoos; you might, from the back, have thought him fully dressed.

"Terry? What do you think to miracles?"

"Dunno."

Josh found the word discomfiting. The ones which followed were even more stupid.

"The wife's sister went to one of them healing services. There was a man with one leg shorter than the other. Well, Rosie *swears* she saw that leg grow. She says she *saw* it. And when the bloke got up – they'd had the poor sod kneeling at the altar – he tripped and bloody nearly fell. Because the fucking leg which had the built-up shoe now made the *other* leg seem shorter!"

"I don't believe it," answered Josh.

The man just shrugged, amiably. "No reason why she should have lied."

"Perhaps she's got a good imagination?"

"What, Rosie? She couldn't imagine the yolk in a hard-boiled egg. Not without you helping out a bit: giving hints like 'small' and 'round' and 'yellow'. She might get it then, if you were lucky."

"Exactly. She's obviously open to the power of suggestion. Perhaps the lot of them were hypnotized."

"Yes. Well. All I'm saying is, you asked a question. Rosie believed it, my missus believed it, so did my mum-in-law."

For a minute they towelled themselves in silence.

"But if it were true, why didn't it get into the papers?"

Terry pulled on underpants; so jazzy in design that they became invisible. "People say that papers aren't interested in printing good news. They only want the horrors." Then something occurred to him. "Anyhow. Why you asking all this?"

"No reason. I was only thinking I could do with a fucking miracle or so in my own life."

When eventually he left he was hailed by a stocky man with a flattened nose who happened to follow him out. "Come for a drink?"

Josh hesitated.

"On me, mate."

Yes, why the hell not? Jimmy could afford the price of a pint and it would postpone, convivially, the moment when he had to go home. He knew that as soon as he opened the door of the flat – even before that, as soon as he set foot inside the block – last night's walk to Ashby would suddenly make itself felt. The French had an expression for it: *joie de la rue, douleur de la maison*: something like that.

They went to *The Parkinson Arms*. While Jimmy ordered their beer, Josh stood just behind him, in almost the identical spot where Simon had stood the night before. He looked about him at the guns, the hunting trophies, the dented suit of armour. They carried their glasses to an empty table.

"Cheers, mate!"

"Cheers!"

"You know something I've often wondered about you?" said Jimmy. "You're not a Scunthorpe man, are you? You talk too posh; I don't mean it nasty. But you're educated, like. Why do you live here, then?"

"Don't you get people in Scunthorpe who are educated?"

"You know what I mean. First time I heard you I thought you must be a vicar or something."

"God almighty!"

"Straight up! I said that to Dave and he said you must have been defrocked, because all he knew was you was out of work."

Josh smiled. "I wonder what he thinks I did!" Then, abruptly, the smile got frostbite. He said brusquely, "Well, there's no mystery. I was a teacher and we came here about a dozen years ago, because the property was cheap..."

16

It had been a mistake, of course, their coming here. Like so many other big decisions in his life. Hundreds.

For instance.

At sixteen he had wanted to study art in Paris. His parents, naturally, had been opposed. He had wanted to go to drama school. His parents, naturally, had been opposed. He had wanted to find work upon a farm: to build his muscles in the open air, to grow to manhood well-nourished on country food, and country lore, and noticing the seasons. His parents... And each time (because he loved them and was not unmindful of a sense of duty and felt a little scared, more than a little scared, of what he didn't know, no matter how it might attract him), each time he had allowed himself to be influenced by their combined advice. That was his first mistake.

His second came a decade later. He was twenty-six and still a virgin. Dawn was the daughter of a newsagent. He saw her regularly when he bought his cigarettes. They used to chat across the counter. She was pretty, trim, and sympathetic. She never said a lot but she had a nice smile, and the way she looked at him – somehow it made him feel almost tall, big, worldly-wise. She agreed with all his tentative opinions, which burgeoned swiftly underneath her gentle care. She agreed to his requests. He took her to the pictures and walking home across Wimbledon Common asked nervously if he might kiss her. The day had been a hot one. To their mutual excitement they were soon lying groping in the tall grass.

Dawn hadn't at all set out to trap him but she had often had sexual intercourse and she was used to its being the men who took precautions. It hadn't occurred to her that Josh was inexperienced. Even when she guided him into her she didn't notice the absence of a condom; it hadn't struck her that there'd been no fumbling pause. It was only when he ejaculated, almost immediately on entering, that her first suspicion came.

Even then she wasn't angry, merely reassuring. She covered well her disappointment. On subsequent occasions she made sure he wore a sheath, but by then, of course, the damage had been done. A few weeks later, just as he was beginning to feel bored by her lack of intellect and her insipidity, albeit admiring insipidity, she found out she might be pregnant. Janice was on the way.

Dawn wasn't a religious girl (to tell the truth, she said, she'd never really thought about it) yet from the first she held out stubbornly against abortion. He didn't need to marry her but she was determined to have that baby. She wanted that baby. She loved it already and nothing was going to stop her.

This wholly unexpected show of obstinacy, this evidence of incipient character, this clinging on in faith and devotion to that tiny life inside her, part of his own life, an embryo created by his own sperm – in some way all this moved him. Her charm became renewed. He wasn't in love but she was a goodhearted girl, she was endlessly compliant (except in that one instance), she looked up to him, she was thoroughly domesticated; and she enjoyed sex – was bringing on his own performance wonderfully. She would almost certainly become a good wife and a good mother. He didn't really care that he was marrying beneath him.

His parents did. They tried repeatedly to make him change his mind. They pooh-poohed his suggestion that there were certain codes of honour, codes which to some extent he genuinely believed in. For the first time in his life he opposed their opposition, intractably.

That was his third mistake.

The fourth one was again to do with his career. He'd increasingly disliked his ten years in insurance, and as soon as he left his parents' house and set up home in Camden Town he informed Dawn that he was going to look for something else; which she considered eminently sensible. Flushed with independence, and with only the occasional, easily suppressed shiver of apprehension, he handed in his notice at the Prudential. That wasn't the mistake. The mistake was this: that after several months of inquiry, indecision and delay, he ended up in teaching. Vaguely he had thought that he might enjoy going off to college and continuing with his education. (He did.) Vaguely he had thought that he would meet lots of interesting and cultured people in secondary-school staffrooms, to offset the dearth of any stimulating talk at home. (*Lots*? Well, no, he didn't.) Vaguely he had thought that teaching was a worthwhile job, full of long-term rewards and incidental satisfactions. (For some, no doubt, it was.) But well before the end of his first year Josh felt exhausted and demoralized: idealism all withered, like the second scattering of seed in the parable. By then, however, Janice was nearly four years old and Dawn was about to produce Billy. It was not a moment to consider training for some other job, even if he had known what other job to train for.

Four years after that, their rent went up, considerably. In any case, the flat was getting far too small; their third child was a lively toddler. Josh saw advertised a teaching job in Scunthorpe, one of the many in various parts of the country. Happened to mention it, without enthusiasm. Dawn, though, grew instantly excited. She had a married cousin living in that area and knew he thought most highly of it: lovely countryside, lovely people, lovely vegetables (the best he'd ever tasted), and not too far from Lincoln, not too far from York. (Her excitement seemed disproportionate, Josh told her; she herself couldn't fully understand her feeling of certainty.) Though the prospect of finding Dawn's relations all over the place held out small inducement to her spouse, something else enticed him more: the discovery that he could buy a house up there, comparing like with like, for roughly a sixth of the price being asked in Camden Town. Josh had a hankering to own his own house, become a man of property. Part of this hankering was due to a cherished dream of which he spoke to no one. He hoped to retire early. Very early. Perhaps at forty. (He was thirty-four now. Supposing he had to spend another thirty-one years teaching parts of speech, and composition, and comprehension – and *Oliver Twist* and *Treasure Island* – to a load of kids who were even more bored by the whole affair than he was; and most of whom, he guessed, referred to him as 'Weedy Heath' behind his back, judging from the few who brazenly whispered or even called it out in the playground and the classroom? Sixty-two more batches of end-of-term reports! Well, he couldn't face it; he would rather kill himself, quite literally!) And owning the few square yards on which you lived, your own demonstrable patch of territory, would clearly confer a sense of security. One day he hoped to write some novels. In the meantime, with only a small mortgage and the lower cost of living which almost certainly went with it, his six-year plan was practically a reality. No longer just a dream.

He found that suddenly, like Dawn, he had a very strong hunch about it.

And to begin with, the novelty of being in a new place and of having their own home to do up and improve certainly rendered life more enjoyable. But after a few years he had to admit he was missing London; and Dawn, uncharacteristically, began to complain about the difficulty of making ends meet; about the children not getting proper holidays or enough decent clothing and footwear. Unhappily, Josh hadn't risen far in his profession.

Yet he devised two ways of making the family budget stretch. He gave up smoking; and, unbeknownst to Dawn, he started betting.

Soon he was heavily in debt.

In 1976, finding it increasingly difficult to keep up repayments to the building society, not to mention repayments to the bookmaker, not to mention repayments on their many hire-purchase commitments, Josh put down their name on the council's housing list. He told his colleagues he didn't approve of people becoming slaves to their possessions.

In 1978 they moved to their present flat. For four nights running Dawn cried herself to sleep, because she'd had to leave her garden.

(Following this move, Josh took no further interest in any scheme of decoration; he left both choice and application to his wife and daughter. The flat in Camden Town and the house in Cliff Gardens had been full of bold effects, a daring use of colour

77

more eye-catching than cosy. Now it was Dawn's taste, modified only slightly by Janice's, which, after fourteen years, reasserted itself. Josh thought it supremely fitting, but knew he had no right to put this into words, to a council flat in Scunthorpe. Well, anyway – who cared?)

In 1979 he had a brief affair with one of the fifth-year girls at school. He didn't make her pregnant; for one thing, he had long since been sterilized. But she boasted among her friends about her latest conquest; and then boasted to her mother. Ten minutes afterwards her father was on the telephone to the headmaster's home. The following morning Josh was sent for after assembly. (He remembered, for some reason, that the hymn had been, 'Dear Lord and Father of mankind, forgive our foolish ways.') There were raised voices in the study. Josh left the school at five minutes to ten.

Strangely enough, he had never even fancied the girl – well, not greatly. She was a cocky bit of baggage, far inferior, both in looks and personality, to anyone like his own Janice. And even before he took her to the woods the first time he had known he wouldn't be able to rely on her discretion. He had hardly been unaware of the risk he was taking.

But at least, thank God, it never came to court.

Naturally he didn't tell Dawn the true reason for his 'resignation' – what mistake were we on by this time? But she discovered it, anyway. In the first place one of the local newspapers somehow got wind of the incident and in the second she received an anonymous phone call: a woman: "I just thought, Mrs Heath, that you ought to know..."

"Well, it was partly your own fault, in any case," he screamed at her at last. (The three children were huddled in the kitchen of the thin-walled flat.) "I thought you used to *enjoy* sex. It isn't me that's changed!"

Dawn had a minor breakdown. (Up to now, he had never looked after her so attentively; she had never shown less interest in his looking after her at all. But as if to compensate, the children, despite their knowledge, responded to him warmly and with a mutely sympathetic affection that was truly, as he realized even at the time, the one thing he'd been allowed to salvage from the wreck.) Yet it was less due to his own ministrations that she finally recovered, or to the doctor's, than to those of the vicar in Crosby. St Matthew's wasn't the nearest church to where the Heaths lived. None of them, indeed, would ever have had much reason to pass it: Frodingham Road was long and the far end of it frankly rather dreary. Added to which, St Matthew's was in a side street and anyone who didn't live nearby might have remained in ignorance of it for ever. Anyway, Dawn hadn't set foot inside a church since she was married, and even then it was her parents who'd insisted upon *that*. (Though heaven knew why – they certainly hadn't followed it through, regarding christenings for the children. Nor had Josh's parents. Well, *they* in fact had terminated all ties, together with any hope of an inheritance.) But in recent weeks Dawn had turned into an aimless wanderer and Mr Apsbury had found her sitting with her head down, sobbing, all alone in the nave on a Wednesday afternoon when "but for the grace of God, my child, the place should really have been locked." Mr Apsbury was silver-haired, rail-thin, close to retirement – and to death. He was gentle, encouraging, a good listener. Dawn explained why she had been sobbing, left almost nothing out; no other half-hour in her life had been so full of her own words. Throughout her recital Mr Apsbury saw much evidence of God at work. More to the point, he made Dawn see it, too. "We clearly found each other at the right time," he told her. When, over two hours later, after several cups of tea in the old and rambling vicarage across the road, she eventually went home she walked back to the Precinct without noticing traffic or traffic lights or even the two boys on roller skates who were infuriating the few others on the pavement – and she was smiling, beaming. Josh seriously thought, to begin with, that she was drunk. She kissed him, she hugged him, she kissed and hugged the children. She praised the tea he had cooked, told him he was both a good cook and a good husband. She apologized for her long, long period of apathy, declared herself to be as great a sinner as anybody caught in adultery but swore that a miracle had now occurred and that the five of them

79

were going to be the happiest, most united family in the world. Josh then wondered briefly, and almost as seriously, whether her mind had slipped across the border into madness. There at the supper table, over the baked fish and the mashed potato and before her three embarrassed children, she freely forgave him, forgave him everything, and humbly besought his own forgiveness and the forgiveness of them all.

That night she allowed, even encouraged, Josh to make love to her because she wanted to be generous in every way she could.

He didn't much enjoy it.

In most other areas her generosity survived the time when inevitably her exhilaration left her and was replaced by something steadier.

Furthermore, within a fortnight the children had all been baptized and she and they were being prepared for confirmation. Since the reverend gentleman would soon be leaving Scunthorpe – a fact which desolated her when first she heard it – and the four of them were the only candidates, the course was an abbreviated one. Josh once told her that her renewed withdrawal from sex was a way of getting back at him for not sharing in her belief and for not being so accommodating as their children. He privately allowed, however, that if this were so, it was probably unconscious. She took her religion with almost frightening gravity. "Thou shalt not be recalcitrant!" he informed Janice on one occasion in her mother's hearing after some minor misdemeanour. Dawn was exceedingly put out. She said that he'd been making a mockery of God and Moses *and* the Ten Commandments.

*

Naturally he told very little of this to Jimmy in the pub and what he did tell was in fact somewhat romanticized. Jimmy returned to the table with their second pints and said after a moment:

"I was thinking just now. It may seem daft but – all that – it's a bit of a success story."

80

Josh grinned self-deprecatingly.

"I suppose it could be on its way to becoming one. Yes! Why not?"

"What would you say, then, is the worst thing about being out of work? Apart from not having enough dough?"

Since, with alarming suddenness, a tremendous tiredness was now bearing down on him, complete with growing traces of nausea, he would have liked to say: "Not having enough hope either, not being able to break away, see even a signpost to an exit route." In any case, it was all part and parcel of the same thing. He would have liked to say: "Once you're in the system, mate, you're scared shitless that they've got you there for life. And then what is there?"

But instead, despite the exhaustion, he laughed and did his best to enjoy this fairly rare kind of moment, by pursuing the theme of his success story.

"Not being able to afford the vitamins to keep you young!" he said.

There was supposedly something on the market now – well, if you were gullible – that could take ten or even twenty years off your appearance. Something indeed which he'd scarcely bothered to take note of. Superoxide Dismutase.

"Vitamins?" his companion answered, pat on cue. "I wouldn't have thought that *you* were in need of any of those!"

17

On his way home – it wasn't really on his way home, merely another delaying tactic – he went to have a look at Tiffany's ('The Brightest Nitespot in Town!') or more particularly at the car park behind it. In the main this was just a stony, scruffy, potholed area, with patches of coarse grass, crushed coke cans, armchairs excreting their stuffing, a pink plastic bath jaggedly disfigured, a dead, limply-leaved candelabra of a tree branch. A notice on the back of the building read, "Mecca Ltd. Private

81

Property. All persons using or entering do so at their own risk."
(Angels included?) Another said, "Parking Fee 10p inc. VAT."
Who might collect the parking fee, however, remained a
mystery: was it the spectral figure of a once-splendid
commissionaire, from the days when this was a plushly-carpeted
cinema having its own orchestra? "Cars parked at owners' own
risk," Josh was further informed; there was certainly no shortage
of good literature. "No responsibility will be accepted by the
company."

Mecca Ltd. appeared remarkably anxious to dissociate
themselves from whatever went on in their car park. Wise
fellows clearly, he reflected, these modern lords of the dance.
Mecca, Birthplace of Mohammed, chief holy city of Islam,
economy dependent upon pilgrims. Josh wandered restlessly
across the holy ground, kicking aside an empty whisky bottle,
watching it roll, savouring almost savagely the senseless irony.

A car stopped on Parkinson Avenue. Simon got out.

"Good morning, vicar." That last word was clearly parodied.
"Tourists already converging on this hallowed spot? Let's call it
Angel Pavement. Or in the guidebooks will it soon acquire a
different name? Something more like – let me see now – well,
how about *Exploitation Corner*?"

"I think you had it right the first time." Simon was looking at
him, curiously. "Has something happened to you since
yesterday?"

But Josh ignored this. "Come to look for sacred relics?"

"Not really. Just to glance around."

"To work out the best location for the shrine? How about over
there, by the armchairs? If they're weary, people will be glad of
those."

"Josh, I'm not sure why you're doing it but stop trying to bait
me. I've come here to feel close to where a messenger of God is
known lately to have stood. I'd like to spend a little time in
prayer."

"Say one for me while you're about it."

"Willingly."

"I wasn't being that serious."

82

"In fact, I already do pray for you. For you and Dawn and the family. I mean, not only since last Wednesday."

"Oh, that's most terribly good of you, most terribly good. Not to mention most terribly, terribly patronizing. But I don't like to think of anyone wasting his time on my account. Not even somebody who gets paid to do it."

Simon bit his lip. "I'm sorry if I sounded patronizing. An irritating occupational hazard. I've got no call to be."

"Cant. I bet you believe you're better than I am. You'd never admit it but deep down – "

"I only believe I'm luckier than you are. More blest."

"There but for the grace of God and all that rubbish?"

"It's a grace available to everyone."

"Sweet Jesus Christ! And you don't call *that* patronizing?"

"Look," said Simon. "Let's go and have a drink."

"'Turning the Other Cheek...' Oh, I can see it in inverted commas. Paragraph four-hundred-and-fifty-nine. *How to be the Perfect Clergyman*. But no thank you. I only drink with my friends." He remembered Holden Caulfield, in *The Catcher in the Rye*, buying a trayful of his favourite food, then dumping it in a bin at the end of the cafeteria counter.

Simon gave no sign of finding the remark childish. Instead, he gave a wry smile.

"Please don't think I'm referring to you, Josh, but I can't help feeling it might have to come a lot earlier than paragraph four-hundred-and-fifty-nine. In case you should ever contemplate drawing up some sort of manual."

Josh didn't smile. Wryly or otherwise.

"In fact I'm glad to have this opportunity for a chat with you," Simon said. "Apart from all else, I wanted to add a little rider to something I told you on the staircase. (Where I actually believed we might be all set to become friends!) I implied I didn't want people thinking of me as a knight on a white charger. That's not exactly true."

"The perfect *introspective* clergyman."

"I feel one can overdo the introspection bit but I can't go round implying I don't wish people to think well of me. Or that I don't care much either way, so long as *I* know what I'm doing is right. One of my biggest faults, in fact, is that I do care."

"You're worried about the image of the Church? Oh, but that's not a fault, vicar. You haven't stained your precious little soul, I promise you. Look, here's another gold star."

Simon smiled again and persevered. "You see, I have too much ambition."

"Oh. You want to be Pope?"

"Not immediately. But I do want to succeed; I mean, in a worldly sense. I sometimes think I'm more concerned with making a name for myself than with the actual quality of my work. So I'm not such a perfect anything that I can afford to feel superior to anybody. I only wish I were."

"But you pray about it, of course?"

"Of course."

"Scunthorpe, it seems to me, remains a tidy step away from Rome. Or even Canterbury."

"'Step', however, is the right word. I've been here three years. In another three years I'll probably be wondering what the next 'step' ought to be."

"Oh, but don't make out you aren't already, *please*. It will demand a further little chat."

"Wondering seriously, I mean. Apart from daydreams."

"This sounds like True Confessions."

Yes, perhaps it did. Simon didn't normally indulge in breast-baring so why on earth should he be doing so now?

"Wouldn't you like to come and have that drink?"

"No," answered Josh. I can't be won over *that* easily, he thought. I'm afraid your charming ways won't work on *me*. Afterwards he almost wished he'd said it.

But drinks were certainly flowing in abundance today. He'd have to see if this were mentioned in his horoscope.

"Well, at any rate, how about our shaking hands to show there's no ill feeling?"

Josh, however, merely turned on his heel and said, "I thought you came here to pray, not just to hand out bullshit or go boozing." Then he walked off.

84

It was incredible to think that about an hour before, following his workout, he'd been feeling good. It was incredible to think that only the previous evening he'd said, "You've got yourselves the perfect champion," and 'perfect' had neither been ironic nor had it seemed exaggerated.

Now he thought, viciously, "By their fruits shall ye know them," meaning the effect that so-called righteous people had upon those chance unfortunates who happened to cross their path during their long bullshitting day. At the bottom of Parkinson Avenue he again remembered Holden Caulfield.

But Holden Caulfield had been a boy of sixteen, not a man of forty-six. The sudden recollection of this was startling and did nothing whatever to help.

Another thing that did nothing much to help, yet which, despite his mood, he discovered that he couldn't simply sneer at, was the spectacle of two men on a motorbike roaring along Frodingham Road. The one behind had his arms around the driver's waist – well, naturally – but while Josh was waiting to cross he saw this fellow lay his cheek against the back of the other's leather jacket. He straightened up again after several seconds but the quality of pure affection contained in that trusting and spontaneous gesture was unmistakable. Josh found himself gazing down the road long after the machine had gone.

Still he didn't go home. He strode past the turnoff to the flats and on towards the library. There he said to an assistant, "What have you got on miracles?" She walked him across to the religious section. "I mean," he amended, "on *alleged* miracles." He gave a twisted smile.

He spent over an hour there, but more because he was reluctant to heave himself out of the low chair than because anything he read proved so engrossing, or, after a while, even mildly interesting. His brain felt stale, sick, unable to absorb. If he could have pressed some button and thereby been wafted, painlessly, into an eternal sleep, he was nearly sure he would have done so.

Instead, he finally returned to the flat. Lunch was over, the boys were watching sport, Dawn had gone shopping. "Your

85

dinner's in the oven, Dad. Mum says she hopes it won't be dried up."

"Your mother's probably an optimist," he answered grimly, suddenly realizing how hungry he felt. "In fact, I know she is."

He paused in the sitting-room doorway.

"How can you just sit and gawp at wrestling, Billy, when on Wednesday you saw an angel and on Friday your spots fell off?"

William shrugged.

"Life has to go on, Dad."

"My God, how old are you? Already to have learned the whole tragedy of existence!"

The meal was sausages, mashed potato, carrots and broccoli, with onion sauce as well as gravy. It wasn't particularly dried up; it both looked okay and it smelt good. Careful to wear an oven glove on one hand but with the warmth of a kind of spontaneous premeditation swiftly spreading up his trunk he passed the plate into the other hand; made himself endure the pain; scraped the food into the pedal bin. Some of it spattered onto his sneakers, cleaned thoroughly the night before. An embossed brown ring was left around the edge of the white porcelain. He worked at it with the side of a fork. In the pedal bin the meal continued to steam. He made no attempt to cover it over, other than with the congealing but still fluid contents of his bowl of banana custard, for it mattered that Dawn should find it there.

A little later, however, he retrieved and ate one of the sausages, and then the other two. He did it further to punish himself, further to punish Dawn too, in the event of his becoming ill. But unexpectedly this made him feel better: sufficiently so to cause him to eat an apple and some cheese, and even wash the apple.

Before Dawn returned from her shopping he had emptied and cleaned the pedal bin.

He had also fetched his dog-eared manuscript pad and composed another exercise for his projected textbook.

Soon there were smears on it from the antiseptic cream he'd rubbed onto his thumb and index and middle fingers; under the cream, his skin had grown all red and blistered.

However, he'd unexpectedly managed a tight smile. Near the foot of his current page he wrote *How to be the Perfect Clergyman*, paragraph 459, and thickly ringed it round, then bordered it with crenellations. He went on to draw a figure on horseback. But for all his pretensions to artistic flair and frustrated hopes of a youthful course of study in Paris, no one would have recognized it, quite, for what it was meant to be. 'Behold a white horse,' he scribbled underneath.

18

On their last night at *Sea View* Simon asked her to marry him and she said yes. They had known each other for less than a week but neither felt nervous about having done something foolish.

Certainly nobody could have claimed they'd been carried away by a romantic setting: moonlight on the sea, the distant strains of a lilting waltz from the bandstand, a gently caressing breeze laden with the scent of summer roses. It was raining; not just a soft refreshing shower into which you could stride out laughingly with heads held back and Pakamac-ed arms securely linked – stopping occasionally to kiss the drops off one another's face. The rain was hurling itself down as if with an intent to penetrate and scar and shatter: rebounding off the pavements, forming fiercely bubbling rivulets along the sides of the promenade, turning the sea into a raging entity that would have been fascinating to watch; except that the sky had grown so dark that even from the windows across the road almost nothing of it could be seen.

In the lounge of *Sea View* there was of course no other topic; it looked as though everyone had congregated with the sole purpose of airing their views on such freak climactic conditions, those residents who normally retired to their bedrooms after dinner obviously needing further contact with their fellow beings: possibly worried that when the rowing boats arrived (or else the marshalling two-by-two began) they might not hear the summons from the upper floors.

"Oh, who remembers that dreadful Lynmouth flood, in 1953?"

Well, everybody did, apart from Simon and Ginny and a very bored brother and sister of about twelve; but there was much animated discussion as to whether the year was right – in the middle of which, Mrs Bates tried to steal unconcernedly across the room with a supposedly reassuring array of nods and smiles and a most urgently whispered warning to deliver.

"I don't wish to start a panic, dears, but should you two *really* be sitting in front of the window like that? Supposing that the glass were suddenly to cave in under all this stress?"

She turned fleetingly, for the benefit of everybody else, to give what she meant to be a jaunty little whistle but although her lips were nobly puckered her whistle proved less jaunty than inaudible.

"The glass cave in?" repeated Simon, also in a whisper, after he'd stood up. "Oh, I don't think that's very likely, Mrs Bates."

Their whispers were only whispers in a relative sense but even so he had to repeat what he had said; twice, and rather loudly.

"Well, I don't know, dear. I don't know."

"Then perhaps we *had* better move. Thank you for telling us about it."

When they were resettled and Mrs Bates had again nodded at them several times, wisely and approvingly, and they had nodded back with many smiles of gratitude, Ginny observed drily:

"For your own sake, Simon, it's probably for the best you're leaving here tomorrow. I think I detect a sympathetic softening of the brain."

"Well, what would you have had us do?"

"You're very good with old people, aren't you?"

"It's just that I like..." Suddenly he stopped. "I was about to make a very stupid comment. Some old people in fact, the same as children and people of every other age, are exceedingly difficult to like and only a halfwit could do it."

"Or a saint."

"No. A saint would love them but he, too, would be a halfwit if he liked them."

"Can't you have a saint, then, who's a halfwit?"

"I'm not sure. You might have to check with theologians. It could be just a natural state of innocence involving no effort."

"You mean, like a pussycat?"

"You took the words out of my mouth. *You're* like a pussycat!"

"Oh, good, if that lets me off the hook about trying to be a saint. Do you realize that no one's put the television on?"

"You feel you could be missing all the action?"

"No more than I do in this place when it's actually switched on and going at full blast."

"Maybe you'd like to pop into the next room and watch our respected mums play bridge? If you're looking for excitement."

"Believe it or not I'm honestly quite happy here with you."

"That's good. Because I'm honestly quite happy here with you."

"And all the old folk."

"There's a difference, I think. Subtle, indefinable, but *there*."

"Will you miss me a little tomorrow?" She was cross with herself for asking that. She tried to mitigate the offence. "Or have you plenty of nice almshouses back in Basingstoke?"

"Innumerable," he said. He took her hand, right there in front of Mrs Bates and Miss Retford and Major Blackburn *et al*. "I tried to count them once but I got helplessly distracted by all those dizzying geriatric charms waving to me from the windows. Oh, hell!" Bobby and Sandra had just thrown themselves lackadaisically onto the nearby couch where Ginny and he had recently been sitting. "We'd better lead them off and have another draughts session or snakes-and-ladders or ludo or something. What if the glass were suddenly to cave in?"

"Under all this stress?"

"Under all this stress," he affirmed, solemnly.

"Under all this stress you could turn just as batty as any of them," she prophesied.

89

"More than likely," he agreed. "But in the meantime, Ginny, I'd like to put to you a question. Would you ever consider, do you suppose...?"

"What?"

"Well. Would you marry me?" he asked.

19

That same evening her mother was making matzo. Her father was tending a sick sheep. Mary said suddenly:

"When we go to Jerusalem next week shall we see Elizabeth?"

"Don't we always?" Her mother didn't even look up.

"She's pregnant," said Mary.

A short silence. Then:

"Don't talk so daft!" Her father wasn't angry; he seemed to consider it some kind of joke. "Your cousin's sixty-five if she's a day."

"In the scriptures Sarah was over ninety."

But by now her mother had certainly looked up. *She* didn't treat the matter as a joke.

"Has the girl taken leave of her senses?" She addressed the house at large: husband, daughter, animals and all. "I never heard such disrespect!"

"But it's the truth, Mum. It's the truth."

"Oh, stop it! Not another word! And how do you mean, the truth? Something so downright ungodly. Yes, my girl, *ungodly*! Who ever put it in your head?"

"God did," she said.

She didn't want it to sound flippant. That was the last thing she'd have wanted. Yet she could see it had its comic side.

"God did," she repeated.

Her parents looked at one another in horrified dismay. Now her father no longer seemed amused.

90

"I think he felt the message would bring me comfort. He told me through an angel." But he must have *seen* what would happen, she reflected.

"An angel?" exclaimed her father. He might have been saying a *dragon*, or a *flying horse*.

"His name is Gabriel. He's the one who spoke to Daniel."

Her mother started to cry. She ran across to kneel at the stool where Mary sat, to cradle her determinedly, press her head against her bosom and rock her gently to and fro. "Oh, my lass, my lass, my poor demented lass, is it a fever you've caught? Have you had a fall? Quickly!" she urged her husband. "For Pete's sake run for the doctor!" Her husband appeared incapable of stirring, let alone running.

"No, Mum, I don't need a doctor." The words came out muffled yet intelligible.

"There, there, love, of course you don't! Now you just rest a little and don't you fret about a thing!" She gave a series of mute and frenzied jerks designed to move her husband faster through the door – and this time, indeed, he did take a step towards it. The abandoned sheep bleated forlornly.

Mary continued mentally to pray. "There's perhaps one other thing you ought to know."

"Hush, hush, my precious."

Her father was more curious.

"Well, lass?"

"I'm pregnant, too."

The sheep bleated again; as if in fellow feeling.

*

This time it came more easily. He had finished in an hour. He began to feel it was something he was being inspired to go on with; more than that, something he had a duty to go on with. It would have been too great a coincidence, he thought: the eruption of Gabriel into the lives of the two Heath boys – and indirectly, of course, into his own – and then, last night, Mr Benson reminding him of Paula's six-month-old suggestion: one which had assumed implicitly, as its starting point, the eruption of Gabriel into Mary's life.

Simon couldn't believe it was coincidence.

Also, he had once written a short story he now saw he could incorporate quite seamlessly. It had to do with the return of the apostles, after Jesus had sent them out on a journey to win converts and supporters and to spread the word.

That was only a small thing, obviously, but he asked himself whether it would be wrong to regard this, too, as a sign; and to wonder whether a mass of loose threads was now being pulled cohesively tighter.

To wonder if he were being allowed a few piecemeal glimpses.

Of the pattern in the carpet.

20

The next day's lunch didn't get scraped into the pedal bin but in its own way it proved more traumatic.

Janice, he thought, looked prettier than ever, with her bright blue eyes and silky honey-coloured hair; yet this time he could only partly ascribe it to the fact he hadn't seen her for several weeks. (Indeed, often it worked the other way: she was at first *less* pretty than he remembered her.) Usually vivacious, her vivacity today was so much more pronounced that it was almost a little...well, yucky? Her solicitude for everybody's comfort and enjoyment might be sincere but it was overdone. The flat seemed smaller on account of it, smaller and drabber.

The fact that the walls had drawn in, the ceiling had come down, was also due to the presence of this hulk she had brought with her. The incredible hulk. He wasn't a doctor. He was a swimming instructor. They had met at the Sheffield baths.

Don. He was six-foot-three, she had informed her family proudly; the two of them were scarcely through the door. "And a half," he had added, with a deep, self-disregarding laugh. He weighed fourteen stone and five pounds, she told them. "Stripped," he made it clear, with an extension of that rich, embarrassed chuckle; and even Dawn, Josh coldly saw, seemed to signify amazed approval. "And not one ounce of... But, Billy!" Janice said. "What ever's happened to your spots?"

"Oh, we've got so much to tell you!" exclaimed her mother. "But first we must hear all *your* news."

"We must?" said Josh. There was only the merest suggestion of a question mark but he shouldn't have introduced even that. He started things and then – with everyone looking at him – he had to do his utmost to pretend he hadn't. "That would be really nice," he said, grateful that at least he had resisted that other small piece of sabotage: the strong temptation to give a heartfelt sigh.

"Yes," said Dawn, and he sensed the air of a woman who wanted to leave the best till last; for which, in fact, he was not altogether unthankful, even if it did mean that they were then back with Janice's promotion of Don, and Don's promotion of himself. Don laughed about everything, expressing manliness, simplicity, good nature at each new boring detail Janice trotted out, details to do with their meeting, their initial thoughts on one another, the things they'd both said, Janice's frequent returns to the pool, their first date, everything they'd eaten upon it, even the piece of Turkish Delight served up with their coffee. ("What colour was it?" asked Josh.) But worse than that – far worse than that – as well as being the strong, silent, amiably indulgent male, Don was also sickeningly proprietorial, with an easy, familiar bossiness that extended from Janice even to her mother and brothers; and with a way of touching Janice, repeatedly touching her, on the shoulders, on the arms, on the back of her neck, of brushing his hairy knuckles up and down her cheeks, that increasingly pulled tighter, with each slow turn of the rollers, the already lacerating thread of tension in Josh's stomach, chest and genitals and finally brought him to the point of feeling that if it happened again – no, *when* it happened again – he would actually have to leave the room and relieve himself by doing violent exercise or causing violent damage or committing violent self-abuse.

It came as no surprise, of course, to learn they were engaged. Josh would have preferred to hear they were already living together; that at least the consummation had been got out of the way, beyond all doubt; and that one no longer had to think, therefore, that on such-and-such a date and at such-and-such a time...

The only surprise, in fact, was that Dawn should feel the way she did. (It couldn't be merely those two bottles of champagne they'd brought with them.) Dawn didn't approve of macho men. Josh didn't regard *himself* as macho but still these days she nagged at him because she said his T-shirts and jumpers and jeans were too tight; because, when his shirts were open-necked, he left too many of their buttons undone; because he wouldn't wear pyjamas. (He resisted her, categorically. She was never going to change *him* into her own brand of nonentity!) But now the thought of this smirky, sweaty-palmed Lothario, with dark hair fringing the base of his throat above the top of the crewneck sweater (he probably spent hours in training it to do that), the thought of him smugly soiling their daughter's cool and virginal young body with that clammy, tacky, suppurating contagion of his own: apparently this did nothing to disgust her, despite her saintly views. Yes, he himself wanted to be sick, whilst *she* talked of wedding plans and trousseaux and of meeting his family and of where they were going to live and seemed nothing but delighted to think that within six weeks, six *weeks*, they would all be standing on the pavement outside St Matthew's throwing handfuls of confetti over the happy pair.

"Oh, praise the Lord!" she said. "Praise the Lord! Another lovely thing to be able to tell Simon! And the church hall, too, will be the perfect place for the reception, that part of the hall named after Mr Apsbury, because we'll be able to think of him standing there in spirit, feeling so very pleased to see the young girl he prepared for confirmation returning four years later as a bride." She went on like this, thought Josh, for roughly a further four years herself.

94

The reception was going to be paid for by Don's parents. "So now you mustn't worry about that, either of you," declared their future son-in-law. "And I don't want to hear one single word of gratitude. We all know how it is, you see. And, as I told you, my father's doing all right and always likes to share with others far less fortunate." His father was one of the head buyers in a large department store.

Josh felt momentarily obliging. He didn't let Don hear one single word of gratitude.

Not so Dawn.

"Well, I don't mind saying," she didn't mind saying (at some length), "that that would be a great anxiety taken off our shoulders, even though we've found, time after time after time, that the Lord unfailingly provides."

"Though why must he always shop at Woolworth's?" wondered Josh, aloud. "Doesn't it give forebodings of a very cut-price kind of heaven? But talking of money, what sort of dazzling future does the career of a baths attendant in Sheffield offer these days?"

Don laughed his good rich laugh.

"Swimming instructor," he said.

"Forgive me."

"Naturally it's only a stopgap. I'm always on the lookout. But in this day and age I feel you're lucky to have anything at all that keeps you from spinelessly relying on the dole queue. Heck, sir, that wasn't meant to sound offensive. I wasn't meaning – "

"Of course you weren't," said Dawn. "And, good gracious, this isn't the kind of household where everybody has to mind their p's and q's" – she smiled at her husband – "well, is it, dear? Besides, Josh, I think you've forgotten what it's like to be young. When you're young and just getting married you live on love. It's the happiest diet in the world. The happiest and the healthiest."

"Yes," said Don. He nodded and grinned and stroked one of his massive forearms. "Haven't I mentioned? I intend to live entirely off my wife!"

95

Janice said, "Anyway, Mum, that's enough about us now!" Though she didn't look as if she actually believed that. "What's this good news you said *you've* got? You mustn't keep it from us a second longer!"

Dawn wet her lips. Her own eyes shone almost as much as her daughter's. "Well, you've got to promise not to tell anyone. Not for the time being, anyhow."

"Ooh, Mum! Cross my heart and hope to die."

"Me, too," appended Don, pushing back his chair and crossing his long, large and no doubt coarsely hairy legs in comfortable anticipation; a willing and absorbed conspirator.

"You see, it all started last Wednesday afternoon, when these two monsters were coming home from school..."

No, Josh didn't enjoy his lunch. He didn't enjoy the hour or so preceding it, nor the four or five hours that followed it. There had been only two mildly pleasurable parts of the day: the first, when he himself had been preparing the meal (for Dawn, of course, had gone to church, taking the boys with her) and the cooking had turned out well – though not so well, he thought, as if he'd had the courage to put apple in the pie instead of rhubarb; and the second, when after the visit was over and his daughter had driven away with her chosen ravisher he'd taken three-pounds-seventy-five out of his wife's housekeeping tin and had strode off to get as drunk as three-pounds-seventy-five would allow. Then, incredibly, somewhere between his third and fourth pint, the thickly encompassing fog of misery began to lift and through the rapidly disbanding eddies a sudden glimmer of light, both shocking and supportive, started tremulously to focus his attention – as, indeed, he told the little Indian fellow with the serious eyes and the sparse goatee who sat about a yard away from him along the plastic-covered bench.

"The thing is," he said, "I've got to get away within the next six weeks! Imperative, my friend, *imperative*! Within the next six days, if possible."

"Yes, sir."

"It could be possible."

The little Indian nodded – and glanced towards the door. But he quickly looked back again, and with the same expression of polite interest.

"I mean, consider it like this. Billy goes off to school tomorrow, as per usual. Well, people are bound to notice, aren't they? It *is* quite noticeable. And what does the boy say then? Are you going to encourage him to lie? Is that what his mother would want? Is that what the holy vicar would want? After all, a lie is a lie is a lie, wouldn't you agree, even if you use no words to speak it."

He paused and looked expectant. "Yes, sir," said the Indian, gravely.

"*You* wouldn't encourage him to lie?"

"No, sir."

"So the news is going to break, anyway. Surely you can see that? *With* me or without me. Even by tomorrow night the air could be thick with speculation; speculation leads to rumour – 'Rumour is a pipe blown by surmises, jealousies, conjectures' – one can't approve of that. It's dirty. It's debasing. It hasn't got the drama of a cleancut scoop. Nor the honesty. Nor the money. Pounds, shillings, pence, my friend. (I don't mean to confuse you.) My escape fund; that's what I'll call it. Escape to happiness. To a new life. To love. *Comprenez-vous*?"

"Excuse me, sir, I'm very sorry but – "

"Oh, by the way, *King Henry IV*, I believe. Yet maybe you knew that already? In which case I apologize, how patronizing, now he's got me doing it too! Just don't ask who says it, though, or quite where it comes in."

"Excuse me, sir, I'm very sorry but I have to go. My wife is, most happily, expecting our first baby."

"Of course. I understand. That's very good. But tell me just one thing." Josh held on for a moment to the fellow's dark and scrawny wrist, beneath the clean white cuff. "*The News of the World*, would you say? No. The name appeals but then we'd have to wait another week. *Daily Express*? *Daily Mail*? Which of these would you consider the most suitable? *The Mirror*, maybe?"

The man murmured something unintelligible. Josh asked him to repeat it. He did so, sorrowfully.

"Oh? *The Evening Telegraph*? Good God! No, no! Nothing local. Not if you mean to make a splash, my friend... Why, next you'll even be suggesting the parish magazine!"

He let the Indian go. His fingers had left small livid marks on the brown skin.

"My congratulations to you and your wife. Be happy with your first baby. I hope that it's a boy."

(But was that really any better? Boys grew up and brought home nubile and attractive girls and that was another thing which would be coming his way before too long. Twice over. Or...correction: would have been, if he'd been wimp enough merely to sit around and wait for it. But no, sir! That is *not* my baby! He would hear about these branchings-out and blossomings from afar; care of a rich and fully satisfying life of his own, thank you very much.)

He'd fulfilled his aim: he was at least a little drunk. He must go home now, he decided; home to his very boring wife, home to his very *pious* wife. (He giggled a bit. How many of them were there? It was a harem, a harem full of extremely *dull* women. But it was just a little sad, too, because once, twenty years ago, one of those wives had used to giggle a bit herself; enjoy a silly joke; even – whisper it, whisper it – one about *vicars*, or *God*, or the *Church*, or other crazy things like that. "It's the happiest diet in the world," she had said, "the happiest and the healthiest." Unbelievable, not that she'd once thought that, but that she should now remember having done so and, remembering, *admit* it!) Well, he must now go home, he decided, and try to sleep on it. In the morning, after he had signed on at the jolly old employment exchange, with all its books and pictures and dance music and TV and its warmhearted air of welcome that invariably made you feel like somebody, somebody who mattered...after he had stepped in for a cosy little chat and a cup of coffee and a selection of chocolate biscuits, he would then go along to that big post office on the corner and ring – eenie, meenie, minie, mo – he didn't yet know whom. But somebody somewhere would be made happy. He would reverse the charges.

Part Two

21

"Newsdesk."

Afterwards, the thought that it could so easily have been someone else who answered...even on the warmest of nights that thought could still induce a shiver. (Paradoxically, there were times when her anguish made her cry out through her tears. "Why did it have to be *me*? Why *me*?")

"I have a call from Scunthorpe, in South Humberside, Miss Coe. It's reversed charges." The new girl on the switchboard was endearingly punctilious about such things. Geraldine believed it worried her that the *Chronicle* should have to incur these costs, that people might be cynically exploiting its trusting good nature.

"All right. Thank you, Iris."

"I'm putting you through."

"Newsdesk. May I help you?"

"Well, I hope we can help each other." A man's voice. Youngish (though you could so often be mistaken about that), middle-class, none of the northern accent which she'd half expected. "I'm offering you a big exclusive scoop."

Despite the boldness of the words, no doubt carefully rehearsed, the trace of nervousness she had detected in his first sentence was still apparent in his second. Because of it she held back the kind of retort she would otherwise have liked to make. She respected people's nervousness.

"That sounds interesting."

"But before I tell you, I want to know something."

"Go on."

"How much you'd be paying me for the information."

103

Her respect began to diminish at the same time her instinct for a story suddenly began to stir.

"Well, that would depend. If it's really as big as you say it is..."

"Thousands?" he asked, a little hoarsely.

"All I can tell you, Mr..." She wrote down his name. "All I can tell you, Mr Heath, is that it is...always...in theory...a possibility." She pulled a face at Bob Clarke, who sat at right angles to her and who – alerted perhaps by something in her tone – had paused in his typing to wink at her. "If you could give me some idea of what the story is, obviously I'd be in a better position to judge."

"Sorry," he said. "Didn't mean to put your back up." He was quick, she thought, and he had charm. "But I know absolutely nothing about the way you people work, and I have to protect my interests!" He laughed, apologetically. The nervousness had gone.

"Of course," she said.

"Impasse," he murmured. "How do we get round it?"

There was a pause.

"You know, Mr Heath, sooner or later you'll really have to trust us."

He continued to speak lightly. "But how do I know I *can*?"

"Because you picked up the telephone and dialled our number."

"Wrong," he said.

At the same moment she remembered. "Because you asked the operator to do it for you." And might, she added, but only to herself, come to the point a little quicker if you hadn't. "And because you know we have responsibilities we need to live up to, a reputation we have to maintain." She laughed. "And because we don't like anyone to take us into court."

"What's your name?" he asked.

She gave it to him. After all this his story had better be good and not just a storm in a local teacup – a teacup currently being slopped along the counter by some avaricious weirdo. She noticed that Bob had come to the end of his typing and now sat watching her with open interest, elbow on table and chin in hand.

"Do you believe in God, Ms Coe?"

Even as she experienced it she realized her disappointment was disproportionate. All right, then, so he *was* a weirdo. Phone calls from fanatics of every type were nothing new in the newspaper world. *Religious* fanatics were possibly the worst, since their long-windedness was usually a consequence of their concern and it was therefore harder, if you had any sensitivity left in you at all, simply to cut them short or cut them off. Only the previous week, for instance, she'd had an old lady wanting to give her a list of aeroplanes that would be crashing in the following fortnight – no flight numbers, just routes, dates and approximate timings – and the old lady had actually been weeping as she spoke because she'd thought that no one would believe her and she so wished her dear Lord could have picked on somebody a little younger to pass on these dreadful revelations.

But Miss Hester Johnson certainly hadn't asked for any thousands of pounds, nor had she reversed the charges. Geraldine didn't feel she would need to be quite so tactful in dealing with this present call.

She gave a small sigh.

"I don't see why it's relevant, Mr Heath, but to tell you the truth I've never finally made up my mind. Now I ought to mention that I'm extremely busy at the moment and so if – "

"It was relevant in that we know where we stand with one another. You're an agnostic; I'm an atheist. Now the position is this. Last Wednesday my two sons, aged fourteen and fifteen, had a vision in Scunthorpe. They saw an angel. He spoke to them and gave them a message for the world. Naturally, I myself didn't, and don't, believe a single word of it, although it's very clear that both my children are convinced they're telling the truth. What's more, our parish vicar, who's somewhere in his thirties, intelligent, analytical, by no means the kind to countenance anything dodgy (unless it happens to be in the Bible) and who at first was wholly sceptical, has now changed his mind. He believes that an angel did appear in Scunthorpe last Wednesday. At this very moment he's probably arguing the question with some small-fry bishop or other, *en route* to make a fat impression on the really big fish: he who rings the bell at Canterbury. And there's a silly little thing, too, which happened last Friday, which some people might call a sign, or a miracle, and which even I can't put down to coincidence. Tell me: are you interested?"

"Yes," she said. "Very." She had been making quick shorthand jottings. "May I have the name of the vicar? And what was the nature of this sign you mention?"

"And what did the angel say, and what are my children's names, and how does my wife feel about all this? No way, Ms Coe. (And is that Miss or is it Mrs?) No, if you really want to hear the answers to these questions – and, obviously, to a great number of others – I'm afraid you'll need to travel up to Scunthorpe, pronto. Cheque in hand, naturally."

"What's your address, Mr Heath? And phone number?" It was hard to keep her tone from sounding cool.

"No phone, and I'll meet you at the station. Then I can take you on a little tour of the sites. Or will you come by car?"

"I'm not sure it will be me who'll come at all."

But it was largely her resistance to him making her say that. She wanted this story; she thought it could be big; and she felt confident that Geoff would let her handle it.

She added, "We do have correspondents already in the north."

"Well, you can keep your correspondents already in the north. It's you I mean to deal with. You or no one. And you can damn well tell that to your editor, or subeditor, or whatever."

She wanted to say: "He who pays the piper calls the tune." But plainly it would be foolish to antagonize him to no purpose. (And he could very reasonably answer, anyway, "He who knows the steps will lead the dance.") She inquired instead whether he knew how long the journey would take by road, and they arranged to meet – still at the railway station; he thought it best – at about three.

"See you then, Miss Coe"...having decided upon her status without any direct assistance from herself. (The fact his decision was correct annoyed her further.) "I shall look forward to it. Oh, and by the way, you don't need to wear a carnation in your buttonhole or even have a sticker saying 'Press'. I'd rather recognize you by that chequebook you'll be waving."

"By now I can well believe it. But I trust to find you less repetitive, Mr Heath, a lot less repetitive, when it comes to telling me your story."

She heard him laugh. "A hit, Miss Coe. A palpable hit. I know I'm going to like you." And he put down the receiver before she could reply.

"From the sweet expression on your face," observed Bob Clarke, sympathetically, "my intuition tells me this could be the start of something big. And of something *very* beautiful."

She swore.

22

It hadn't been easy telling her mother. At first Mrs Plummer had said that she refused to believe it. "It will be *years* before he's in any position to marry you. It was extremely wrong of him to ask." She was still seated at her dressing table but at least she had accepted back the hairbrush she had dropped. "Years!" she repeated, as though deriving comfort from the very word or maybe hoping she had found herself a mantra. "Years and years and *years!*"

"We thought next month."

"Ginny, you're behaving like a child. Stop it! Even if you *are* besotted with this egocentric young man you must surely see – "

"He's decided he won't take up his place in college – and naturally I shan't take up mine either – "

"Just wait until your father hears about this!"

" – and then we'll both get fixed up in something very temporary, me in a shop or office, him on a building site. All we'll need is a cheap bedsit. In London that can't be difficult."

"And in nine months' time a baby comes along. Oh, that *will* be nice!"

"Well, at least Mr Heddingly should be pleased."

"Oh, for heaven's sake, grow up! I suppose he thinks it'll be pleasant just to drift from one thoroughly demeaning job into another. As I say, your father is simply going to love this!"

"No, we're hoping the only temporary jobs will be right at the beginning. Merely to tide us over. Afterwards, if we can, we'd like to find work together in a home for old people – and eventually to open one ourselves."

"What!"

"Simon feels he's never done anything to try to benefit the world. I tell him that's nonsense."

Mrs Plummer would have told him the same thing.

"Then love really is blind. As though any further evidence were needed! I've never known you express even the least bit of interest in old people."

"I'm very fond of Granny."

"That's different."

"And, in any case, I can learn. If that's what *he* wants it's also what *I* want. More than anything – apart from him."

"I thought you had a less dependent turn of mind."

"I thought so, too. But it's not something I appear to value any longer."

"That's simply because you're eighteen and think you're in love. But the sex thing wears off after a year or two; you can take that from me, my girl. Four legs in a bed may sound wonderful to you at this moment but there'll come a time when you're inventing headaches just like any other woman."

No, Ginny thought. No. Never. You're telling me about yourself and I'm sorry if that's the way things are, I truly am, I wish I could change them for you. But I'm not you and Simon isn't Daddy. It won't ever be like that for us. It couldn't be. I know it.

108

"*Romance* is not so easy to sustain in the face of dirty socks and dirty underwear and all the usual bathroom smells."

Ginny shrugged. "Who's talking of romance? I think dirty socks are perhaps a bit of a cliché but I love him for his dirty socks and for his dirty underwear and for all the usual bathroom smells. Why not? They're a part of him just as much as they're a part of me and I wouldn't want him any different. I embrace it all – eagerly."

Suddenly she laughed and put her arms around her mother's shoulders and her cheek against her mother's cheek.

"So help me God!" she said.

Their eyes met for a moment in the mirror and then Mrs Plummer abruptly pulled away.

"So help you God, indeed! You'll want all the support that you can get. For let me tell you one more thing, Virginia. Believe me, all old people are not like Granny and the aunts. They dribble, they become senile, they wet their beds. And worse – *far* worse! Emptying the chamber pots will be the very least of your worries!" It occurred even to herself that she was being a little lavatorial and maybe wholly unjustified. Certainly not like the mother she had always done her best to be. But she had never meant to encourage Ginny to do any more than lightly flirt with a good-looking boy, as she herself in some of her most secret dreams, a carefree hopeful girl again, sometimes lightly flirted. "What does *his* mother say about all this?"

"Simon thinks she'll be pleased."

"Obviously ripe for incarceration in this old people's home you talk about. Perhaps you were surprised to find that your own was made of slightly sterner stuff?"

"No, not a bit!" snapped Ginny. "If that's of any comfort to you."

23

It was only two-forty-five when Geraldine Coe and Graeme Peters drove into the station forecourt but Josh Heath was already there and she knew him instantly despite his appearance being unlike what she had pictured. His face was even fairly pleasant and although he assuredly gave her the once-over she didn't find this altogether offensive. He managed to convey that he'd been expecting her to be attractive and that he wasn't disappointed.

"Graeme takes the photographs," she said.

"Haven't had a good picture of an angel in months," drawled this smiling Australian. He was large and loose-limbed and thirtyish but he gave an exaggerated wince at the power of Josh's handshake. "Hell, what do they feed you on round here? If it isn't prime steak, at least the manna must be packed with protein."

"Look," said Geraldine, "before we start, all of us, let's make a pact. No bible jokes, please. Where's a good place for coffee?"

Josh always liked *The Buccaneer*; he considered it relatively sophisticated. Both the travellers had a sandwich, Josh a glass of fruit juice. Geraldine said, "I don't know about diet but you look as though you've been on holiday. Somewhere in the sun."

He smiled, a little ruefully; told them he was unemployed. In that case, Geraldine replied, his complexion said a lot for the gardens, parks and general climate of Scunthorpe. "As a matter of fact it isn't what I expected." She meant the town. "And it *has* been a pretty good summer. How long have you been out of work?"

"Four-and-a-half years."

"Hell's bells!" said Graeme Peters.

"Mr Heath, I have a small confession to make. On the phone I thought you sounded mercenary. Forgive me."

110

"But I am mercenary. There's nothing to forgive."

"What I mean is, anyone who's been out of work that long and has a family to support has a right to be." She took a notepad from her shoulder bag and pushed aside her plate. "Four-and-a-half years," she said. "What a mess it all is! What *was* your job, Mr Heath?"

"I was a teacher. I wish you'd call me Josh."

"Joshua?" exclaimed Graeme Peters, with considerably more surprise than Josh felt the name warranted and with an expression that dissolved into a grin.

Geraldine put up her hand warningly.

"Graeme, don't say it! Don't you dare say it!"

"Why, lady, can't think what's got your dander up! No notion what you mean."

And he glanced about him casually and began to whistle.

Josh knew the words that accompanied the tune.

Geraldine laughed.

"Oh, you bastard! I might as well tell you, Mr Heath, and get it over with: my poor dead parents either had a lousy sense of humour or were just so dumb they didn't notice. Perhaps they were drunk. Geraldine, of course, shortens to Gerry. You can guess, therefore, what they call me on the paper: the same very witty thing I've been saddled with since kindergarten."

"But you enjoy it, Jericho! Don't pretend you don't enjoy it!"

"Again forgive me, Mr Heath: for the playground mentality of those I have to work with."

"Josh."

"Yes, of course. I'm sorry. Were you teaching for long, Josh? What made you leave?"

He spread his hands. They were strong and well looked after. "I heard there were brighter opportunities in Germany. Better pay. I decided I had to take a gamble but unfortunately..."

"You're obviously a brave fellow."

"I suspect, though," Geraldine told Graeme, "that only when a gamble pays off do people call you brave. When it doesn't, the word is more likely irresponsible."

111

Josh nodded. "And actually, while we're on the subject, I've got to ask that neither of you will mention it before my wife. It's still a bit of a sore point."

"Then you did it off your own bat?"

"Well, I'm not the type who – once he has an idea – likes to waste time. I believe you really have to make a grab for what you want in life."

Geraldine wondered how much notice teachers had to give; she would have thought it was a term. But all she said was, "Mm. I think I might faintly have gathered that impression even before we met!"

"*Touché*, Miss Coe."

"Jericho," said Graeme.

"That may have sounded drier than I meant it to. I'm very much in sympathy. Both with you and your wife."

"Yes, it's been hard on Dawn, of course, and the kids. But in a strange way they've got something out of it. My wife has found religion. And the boys...well, they too after a fashion. And all of them, they've got their angel."

"And would you say," asked Graeme, "that *you'd* got anything out of it?"

"Oh, myself – yes, in all honesty, I think I have." His expression was wryly self-mocking. "You see, Dickens here has embarked upon the Great British Novel. The *definitive* Great British Novel."

"Has he indeed?" said Geraldine. "That's wonderful! What's it about?"

"The effects of unemployment. People who've not been out of work...they may be sensitive, imaginative, as well-intentioned as all getout but they really have no idea, no idea at all." He smiled. "Yes, I know! It all sounds very dreary! But I trust it won't be, any more than *Hard Times* or *Bleak House*."

"Have you a title yet?" asked Geraldine. "May I read some of it?"

"*Behold a White Horse*. But, no, I wouldn't want anyone to look at the book, not even you, until at least the first draft is finished."

112

"I can understand that. How long will it take?"

"A further six months?"

"You won't mind my mentioning it, though?"

"Advance promotion? Not at all." Josh told himself he'd better get to work on it – and fast! He could think of no better incentive. He watched her write in shorthand what he took to be the title.

"Then I certainly wish you luck with it. Now, what about this second thing you spoke of on the telephone? A sort of sign, you said, which even you couldn't put down to coincidence."

"No, I think I'll let Dawn tell you about that."

"*Her* miracle, is it?"

"She'll do it more justice. Besides, you're right, she's the person who actually saw it. Well, she and Mickey, I should say."

"In that case, what about this tour you promised, while the light's still good?"

It was not an extensive tour. Graeme took pictures of both St Matthew's and the vicarage. Geraldine had hoped to meet the vicar in the process but Simon was spending the afternoon in Lincoln and since Mrs Madison had earlier informed Dawn (whose husband had suggested Simon might feel flattered to hear of Janice's engagement) that she always grabbed the chance to accompany him and thereby shop at Sainsbury's, there was no one to photograph outside the vicarage...other than Josh, who had already been photographed outside the church. At four o'clock they went to High Ridge and met the two boys. There Graeme posed them together in front of the building and then shot them surrounded by several of their classmates. Geraldine afterwards spoke to a few of these. She was impressed, yet vaguely worried, by the fact that nobody appeared to know anything about what had happened to the Heaths last Wednesday. One of the younger girls asked shyly if they were making a commercial for some wonder spot-remover and there was a good deal of giggling and speculation until the headmaster himself came out, attracted by the growing crowd. But even Mr Dane told Geraldine he had no idea of anything newsworthy, nationally newsworthy, having befallen any of his pupils.

"Bar the spots?"

"Yes, that was strange, very strange indeed, but hardly worth the notice of Fleet Street I'd have thought."

He looked at her expectantly and was clearly disappointed by her reticence, no matter how politely she made conversation.

"But if you'd be so kind as to let me talk to you tomorrow, Mr Dane, after you've had time to read the *Chronicle*; and if perhaps I could meet some members of your staff...?"

Then seeing that Graeme had by this time got everything he needed, she excused herself tactfully and joined him and the three others for the brief ride back to Tiffany's, where Graeme wanted shots of the boys taken at the scene of their encounter.

After she'd looked around for salient details, she moved back a short way, to stand next to Josh. "Was that the school where you used to teach?" she inquired.

"No." He seemed to hesitate before telling her which that had been.

She asked him why he hadn't spoken to Mr Dane.

He shrugged. "Some deep, subconscious resistance to authority, maybe?"

It hadn't looked all that subconscious, though. "Must make it hard on open evenings."

"Oh, when your children are as bright as mine you don't need to attend those things." He didn't add that Dawn went to them unfailingly.

"I'll tell you what amazes me: that they could have kept all this so utterly secret for the past five days! They must be quite remarkable."

"They are. And if they hadn't been, why do you think this angel would have chosen them?"

"My goodness," she said.

"What?"

"Could the confirmed atheist be undergoing a change of heart?"

"Good God, no." He gave his swift, attractive grin. "I'm afraid my mind was on something else."

"Ah."

114

When the two of them were sitting in the car again, a little ahead of the others, who were choosing ice creams for themselves, he asked, "How long will you be staying? Or don't you know yet?"

"Well, at least until tomorrow. Graeme goes back this evening."

"The Royal's a good place. It's just on that corner, if you look through the rear window. Beyond the petrol station."

As she screwed round, instead of moving his body away to give her room, he appeared to bring it slightly towards her. The contact wasn't much, yet she was suddenly aware of a tension between them that was sensual and electric. She quickly drew back. And when she spoke again she was relieved to hear her voice sound normal.

"Tell me, Josh. Why did the boys look so surprised to see us just now and what did Billy mean when he told you he thought Mr Madison had asked for a few days of...something or other...and you cut him off and said there'd been a change of policy?"

"Simon Madison's the vicar."

"I know that."

"Did I say a change of policy?"

She smiled. "I got the impression you might be trying to keep something from me."

"It can't have been important. If I remember I'll let you know."

She nodded, reflectively: now formulating a suspicion she hadn't consciously admitted until then.

Could she trust him?

*

The boys returned soon after. This time Michael sat at the front while William squeezed in next to his father at the back. Graeme had gone into the *Scunthorpe Evening Telegraph*, whose office was hardly twenty yards from the parked car, and asked for any

115

photographs they might have of the vicar of St Mathew's. He came back carrying a Manila envelope.

Then they drove down West Street, to the block of flats where the Heaths lived.

There, Josh ran upstairs to prepare his wife for the arrival of the press. She flustered easily, he said; he'd thought it better not to give her any warning. And when the others followed him up after the agreed five minutes she was clearly far from happy. Yet, equally clearly, she responded well to Graeme, a fact Geraldine found less surprising then than later, and by the time he'd taken a dozen photos and said he must depart she was pressing him to stay for at least a cup of tea. Though he declined with lazy Aussie charm, and a promise he'd take her up on it the next time he hit Scunthorpe, Geraldine of course accepted.

"Not," she murmured sweetly, stooping at the nearside window, "that *I* rate even as a consolation prize, you great smooth layabout from Bondi Beach!"

"Jericho, stop griping, will you? Can't you see you're well in with the trumpet player?"

"Trumpet player?"

"And the walls came tumbling down!"

"Now *there*, as a matter of fact, you do find an example of a man with sex appeal."

"Well, you know the place they say you'll often get the best story?"

Back upstairs, she joined a mildly relapsed Dawn in the kitchen, where, while tea was being prepared, the talk was fleetingly of Graeme, then of the angel, finally of Mr Apsbury. Elderly vicars, it seemed, could make Dawn forget both about secret troubles and large young Australians and even perhaps about messengers from heaven; and to begin with Geraldine viewed such a fast-returning interest in church life as nothing more than sublimation – until she realized she was doing this and rebuked herself for indulging in not merely an anti-feminist but, maybe worse, a stereotypical way of thinking.

She fought, too, against forming glib judgments on the angel story: it was very plain the boys believed in what they'd told her.

116

And the business of the almost disfiguring acne...what was one to make of that? She'd been shown a snapshot, obviously a recent one. (Had borrowed it, as well.) She thought that Geoff would have to come up with some pretty solid medical opinion in the face of such evidence (ha, ha!) as indeed, knowing him, she supposed there was little doubt he would.

But, *from one moment to the next...* She would stake her career on it Dawn was neither lying nor even consciously exaggerating. So what was the answer? Josh Heath, out for fame and fortune, taking a crash course in hypnotism? The notion made her smile. Yet leaving aside such tempting possibilities, what were you left with? A miracle? Two miracles? A message?

Thank God though, she reflected, she had only to report, not interpret.

And, as to that, she did her reporting from outside the general post office. It took her fifteen minutes to dictate the story. Luckily it was a good line and so for once she didn't have to enunciate like Sybil Thorndike. But, all the same, this evening she tried extra hard to eliminate all chance of ambiguity. For, if the copy-taker's reaction was any real guide, people were going to be sufficiently incredulous anyhow.

24

Dawn Heath had insisted on her having tea with them: an omelette and chips, with bread and jam and homemade cake. They were a nice family, Geraldine thought. Although the boys didn't say much, they were attentive and polite, and if an angel were going to appear to any teenage lads, why not to them? They joined in their mother's speculations on the nature of the publicity to come and what the reactions of the world were most likely to be. What they *ought* to be, at any rate: Dawn furnished lengthy quotations complete with chapter and verse and rather warm, velvety cheeks. The quote which seemed to give her the most comfort, however, since she came back to it three times,

117

was not in fact from the Bible. *God moves in a mysterious way his wonders to perform.* Her second favourite was more orthodox: *All things work together for good to them that love God.* Geraldine noticed that on the five or six occasions Dawn looked at her husband and then appeared to falter again, one or other of these statements almost visibly restored her confidence. Only Josh himself remained apart from all of this: not silent but not serious. Geraldine became impatient of his comments. Once he even winked at her over the top of William's head. She felt prissily shocked and pretended she hadn't seen.

But then he also seemed apart from the other main topic of conversation: the engagement of their daughter to a young man from Sheffield who was 'really nice' according to Dawn, 'ace' according to Michael and 'okay' according to his brother. "She's a very lucky girl and so are we, Josh, aren't we, we're extremely blest! (Of course, Donald is, too, Miss Coe; I think I can say that, even if I do happen to be her mum!) Yes, praise the Lord, if we do half as well with the sweethearts these two eventually bring home (and indeed I know we will: every *bit* as well) then at least we'll never have much to complain about in *that* direction. Not that I'm inferring we should complain at all, ever, about anything... Oh, pay no attention to him, Miss Coe: those faces he's always pulling: you can never get him to show that he's in tune with the rest of us, it's really easier not to try." Geraldine made no answer but she could see that over four years' unemployment might have affected him far less positively than he'd acknowledged; and she felt she knew him no better now than after his telephone call eight hours ago.

After tea, though, she was given a further opportunity to put this right.

"Miss Coe's going to be stopping at the Royal," he announced. "I'll walk her up there."

"Oh, no," she said, "you mustn't bother."

"Can I come, too?" asked Michael.

"*May*," said his father, adding firmly, "No – you've got your homework."

118

"I noticed a mistake that Mum made earlier." The boy smiled ingratiatingly.

"Nothing to the mistake she made about fifteen years ago."

"You mean, when marrying you?"

"Then that would really turn you into one, wouldn't it?"

"No." He shook his head happily. "Only Janice and Billy. Not me."

"All right: that round to you. But if you're going to turn into a self-satisfied little stoolie you needn't reckon you don't also qualify. Besides..."

"What?"

"Angels don't have dealings with informers. At least, *I* certainly wouldn't trust one that did."

Geraldine couldn't be sure how much of this was staged for her benefit. The good parent syndrome: here you see more of a friend than a father! Then again she felt irritated with herself. In all probability it *had* contained an element of showmanship but if she hadn't been there she thought that it could still have taken place.

They walked through a shopping precinct towards the High Street, Josh carrying her small suitcase, and at the first crossroad he took her arm although there wasn't any traffic. She became increasingly certain that within the next half-hour he was going to make a pass at her. What was less certain was whether she would mind.

"I noticed that, back there, we Heaths all talked exclusively about ourselves. Nobody seemed much interested in hearing about the life and times of Miss Geraldine Coe, girl correspondent."

"Not true," she answered. "Your wife asked me a number of things while we were doing the washing up. Your sons were with us, too, and seemingly interested." She suspected that Josh might have been getting rid of his (not very heavy) six o'clock shadow at the time and splashing on, a little too liberally, more of that cheap aftershave.

"All the same," he said, "it's now my turn. Tell me, Miss Coe, are you happy in your work?"

119

"Yes, thank you. Mostly."

"Career woman?"

"Certainly. Any reason why not?"

"You wouldn't give it up, then, if the right man came along?"

"The right man wouldn't expect me to."

"Then the right man wouldn't want children?"

"Perhaps I'm unnatural. At the moment, to me, children don't seem all that necessary."

"Good."

"Why do you say that?"

"Oh, I don't know. A lot of women are pressured into feeling they ought to have children. It's nice to see you're different."

"Well, I think I shan't really know how different I am until the situation arises, if it ever does."

"Oh, come off it. You know that you're attractive."

"That isn't quite the compliment you think."

They arrived at the hotel. The receptionist had difficulty in finding her a room. Geraldine signed the register. Josh suggested they should have a drink at the bar. "I can't stay here too long," he added, on seeing her hesitate.

This struck Geraldine as pathetic. "All right. On the *Chronicle*."

"Very much on the *Chronicle*. By the way, when do I get my cheque?"

"I was going to give it to you in the morning or at any rate before I left. I can make it out now if you like."

"No, when you go. A nice little parting gift. Something to remember you by." He didn't ask about the sum involved.

He ordered a gin-and-It for her, a whisky for himself. Doubles.

They sat in comfortable armchairs in comfortable surroundings. The place was fairly empty.

"Why aren't you married, then, by the age of...thirty? Thirty-one?"

"As though marriage were definitely the be-all and end-all?"

"Isn't it?"

"Well, you tell me, then. Is it?"

120

"A good one."

But she didn't wish to hear about his marriage problems. "*And*, damn you, you're an unflatteringly good judge of age."

"You don't need to damn me. I'm sure I'm damned already."

"That isn't what you were saying in the coffee bar."

"Damn what I was saying in the coffee bar." They laughed.

"But in that case hadn't you better do something about it? You can't go round feeling you're damned...whatever that expression may mean to an unbeliever."

"Two lost souls on the highway of life," he said grandiloquently. He thought he might have heard it in a song.

"Why two?"

"Because I wouldn't even mind being damned if I were in the right company."

He smiled.

"Come to that, I wouldn't even mind being saved if I were in the right company."

"There's one thing. Nobody could call you a fussy man."

"But..."

"But...?"

"I do like a little bit of butter to my bread!"

"Of course! How *could* I forget?"

"I think you're meant to say, 'There, there!'"

"No. That's the wife's job. It was the Queen who said, 'There, there!'"

"It was also the dairymaid."

"I suppose I should be thankful it wasn't the cow."

They both remembered at the same moment. The cow *had* said it. It was a good moment.

His whisky was finished quickly. He went to fetch another. "Charge it to me," Geraldine called across.

"I have!"

He returned to his chair.

"You know, when you picked me up on the be-all and end-all, I wasn't thinking of it *only* from the woman's point of view."

"In that case, perhaps you're not as lost as you believe you are. Or, actually, as I believed you were when you said it."

121

"Friends?"

She nodded. "Friends." They raised their glasses to the concept.

"No, I'm not lost at all." He was very much a creature of moods, or contradictions. "*I* know where I'm going."

"In search of butter."

"It's just that...well, the dear knows who's going with me."

"I know who's going with me," she said. "Or, anyway, I hope I do. You see, there is in fact somebody I'd like to marry. But there's a snag."

"He has a wife already."

"End of sad and very ordinary story."

"It must be me."

"Except, as I say, I hope it's not the end."

"Again you missed your cue."

"Oh?"

"Is he happy with his wife, this man of yours?"

"Do you really suppose that if he were – ?"

"No, of course not. Sorry. Wasn't thinking."

"They live in the same house," she said, "but apparently don't talk. Or hardly ever. Only when it's unavoidable."

"My God! Then why don't they divorce?"

"He says they will...when the children have left school. The younger one is fifteen."

"Another three years?"

"Yes," she said. "Another three years."

"And in the meantime how often do you see him?"

"Two or three evenings a week. He stays quite late."

"And don't you worry he may be taking you for a ride? A wife at home who cooks his food and washes his clothes and knows his funny little ways. Respectability. And a sophisticated and intelligent girlfriend who looks the way you do and possesses her own flat..."

"Of course I worry. You call me intelligent and sophisticated, yet speak to me as though I were stupid and naive. How like a man! How like a certain type of man!"

"I'm sorry. You're offended?"

122

"Well, if so, there's only myself to blame, very clearly. But there's usually supposed to be a certain measure of relief, isn't there, in talking out your problems with a stranger?"

"A stranger? Is that the way you think of me?"

She returned surprised look for surprised look. "Well, isn't that the way you think of *me*? We met for the first time less than five hours ago."

"Two lost souls on the highway of life? Friends?"

She smiled – a little crossly – but didn't answer.

"Shall I tell you something? I don't know about this procrastinating boyfriend of yours. I would start divorce proceedings first thing in the morning if I thought there was a chance of having someone like you. I said there's nothing better than a good marriage. There's also nothing worse than a bad one. Take it from me. *I* know. Even if your boyfriend doesn't."

She hesitated. She attempted another smile. She said, "I'm not sure whether to be flattered or appalled."

"Does honesty appal you?"

"Yes. In certain situations. Most definitely, a man who wouldn't pause to consider the plight of two very pleasant teenage children might...worry me a little."

"And how do you know, then, that I haven't paused to consider it? And paused and paused and paused again? Let me explain. I've dreamed of nothing else for *years* but of being able someday to break free."

She stared at him.

"And, in any case, if you think that *I'm* being hard," he went on, bathetically, "I very well remember the way you talked about your parents...about your dead parents."

She said rather quietly, after a few seconds: "You noticed that, did you?"

"*Dumb or drunk*! It wasn't very nice."

"Yes. As soon as I'd said it I felt ashamed." She paused. "But sometimes when you're trying to amuse or impress or simply to avoid the sentimental, you come out with things which...oh, I don't know...which..." She shrugged and looked at him appealingly; and if at that moment he had responded with the

123

sympathy which actually he was well capable of, and which, too, she strongly sensed he had within him, she would have been very open to receiving comfort.

There were several strands he could have picked on.

"Are you saying, then," he asked, slowly, "that you were trying to impress *me*? *Me*?"

At any other time she might have been touched by this essential lack of confidence, in contrast to his habitual mockery, his attempts at the bold front, the peacock strut. She was reminded of his nervousness on the phone.

"Yes," she said, dully, "I suppose I was." It was true. She couldn't take it from him.

He grinned. "That means you find me attractive?" It was a bad time for the grin. It was a worse time for the question.

"Found," she said. "That was before I discovered you were someone who believes in spelling things out, someone who's merely waiting for the first bandwagon to roll into town on which to make his getaway. It was before I discovered other things as well: amongst them, the truthfulness of first impressions. "

"You think I regard you as a bandwagon?"

She said: "After only five hours I don't know what else you could regard me as."

"You clearly don't believe, then, in love at first sight?"

"Not since adolescence. Only in lust at first sight. Or opportunity."

"But don't you see? I could really give you such a lot. What with my book – and all this money from the *Chronicle* – and all the publicity. And *now*, not in any mythical three years! I'm a fellow who's going places. Don't you see?"

"If it's of any possible consequence...yes, I think I do see."

"Also," he said, trying to sound matter-of-fact but acquiring only a faintly pleading quality, "I can honestly tell you this. That I'm very good in bed."

"Oh, terrific!" she answered. "Should I offer my congratulations to you, then, or to Dawn? I'm sure she must really appreciate her luck!"

124

She thought that before he looked away she saw the beginning of tears – and only just stopped herself in time.

She'd been about to say:

"There, there!"

25

The first time after marriage that she had period pain and had to return to bed with it, Simon said, "Darling, we can't have this! Where does it hurt, exactly?"

"How do you mean: where does it hurt exactly? It hurts all over! Here, and here, and *here*! Just go away and let me die in peace. Mummy was right. Men never understand these things." But by the time she had got to the last two sentences, she was smiling a little, despite everything. She took his hand. "I'm sorry, Sim. This always makes me feel so very rotten. When you said *we can't have this* it sounded as if I might be throwing a tantrum to win attention and all I needed was a little self-control."

"But where did you say it hurt, again?"

"Oh, Simon, it isn't the sort of thing you can pin down. I told you. All over." She released his hand.

"Around here, would you say, mainly?"

"What are you doing? Massage won't help." Her testiness intensified. "Nor, funnily enough, will tickling."

"Be quiet a moment. I'm neither massaging nor tickling."

"What is it, then: Teach Yourself Obstetrics?"

"Gynaecology. Not quite. But I suddenly remembered something. When I was a child I used to have warts on my fingers. I had them for a long time. Then at bedtime one evening, while I was saying my prayers, my mother suggested I should ask God to heal them for me. And after a week or two they'd gone."

"How *sweet*!"

"And once – only a short time later – I was staying with an aunt who developed a migraine. 'Poor Aunty Madge,' I said and

125

put my hand on her forehead. 'Jesus will take it from you.' And not only did that one clear up remarkably fast but ever since, apparently, her headaches have just been ordinary headaches. No migraines."

"You must really have been rather a sweet child," she said, distracted. But it wasn't long before the irony came back. "What's the success rate nowadays, doctor?"

"Not very high, I'm afraid. I found it didn't work too noticeably on colds or toothache or – or on coronaries, either." He bit his lip and took his hand from under the coverings. "Oh, I don't know why I bother. You're right. It's just a farce."

"Oh, Simmy, *don't*! I honestly think it helped a bit, having your hand there. It felt comforting."

"Well, at least that's something."

"Who knows? You might truly have a gift."

"You go to sleep."

"Enjoy your walk across the Heath, my Simeon. *Next* Sunday I'll come with you."

But she didn't go to sleep, prescribed tablets being patently as ineffectual as faith healing. She turned from side to side, clammy and nauseous; with Simon gone, she groaned. At length she opened her eyes and lay on her back and listened to the bells. She wished that she could find it hypnotic: the counterpoint of church bells. But it was only soothing from a distance and in her present state she was soon impatient for its end; her stomach grew more jangled every minute, until she actually cried out in her frustration, hysterically demanding obedience. (She hadn't known she was going to do that; as well as being surprised she felt immensely foolish. She wondered what Mr Kurosawa might have made of it, or Mrs Gupta, had either of them been passing on the stairs; and the speculation made her smile, however bleakly.) She turned on her side again and gazed wearily around their home; Simon had left the curtains drawn but they were thin and offered only dimness, not obscurity. They had pinned up travel posters; put roses in a jar; been given gaily-coloured ornaments (what fun that day had been, eating bagels and ice creams as they went from stall to stall, returning with their garish

126

gifts and useful bargains – this time a week ago they had been there!); but what was really needed was overall replastering and fresh paint and wallpaper, and to such extremities they were not prepared to go. Even if they had been, the divan on which she now lay would have dominated and destroyed; like the tatty armchairs and the chest whose bottom drawer stuck and the wardrobe whose door you had to wedge – to say *nothing* of the shiny blue lino, cracked and cigarette-ringed, the furry matted rug, the gas fire with its broken mantle and black meter, the obtrusive ugly sink, the grease-encrusted cooker. She glanced from one pitiful object to the next, wondering with what affection she would look back upon them in the future...and then a solacing reflection came to her. She thought that despite the way she felt now, despite the bells, despite what her parents would have said about this room and about this house, with its unwashed walls, its unswept floors, its babel of strange voices, its spicy cooking smells and unappealing lavatory and bathroom – what they would have said, too, about their registry office wedding, streamlined, utilitarian, sparse not only in ceremony and frills but in family attendance (only Simon's aunt and mother there, who, bless her, had taken both them and their handful of guests straight on to a Lyons Corner House celebration); she thought that, despite all this, despite her temper and his temper and their tiffs and their frequently boring jobs (him at John Barnes, herself at Woolworth's), she was, against all the odds, indescribably happy. Radiantly happy, gloriously happy, spectacularly happy; enjoying her new life, when it *was* enjoyable, with an intensity, a clarity of sensation, an almost frenetic awareness which she had seldom experienced, certainly not in any reasonably sustained manner over a period of three weeks. She had never laughed so much, never found so many small things to take pleasure in, never been so interested, so uninhibited, so confident, so loving. Loving towards everyone, not simply towards him. *Doting* towards him. Yes, she doted on him, on every word he said (apart from the times when she didn't dote on him nor on any word he said), on every smile, on every frown, on every movement, on every line and muscle of his

127

body, whether it was clothed or unclothed. Indeed, it wasn't healthy, the way she doted on him, not for either of them, but since this doting phase was bound to pass – so books and plays and life informed her, not to mention, of course, mothers – why not simply give in to it, make the delicious and ecstatic most of it while she was lucky enough to have it, this new and ephemeral experience? Therefore she doted. Shamelessly. "See Naples and die," she told herself.

She shifted, realized something, frowned. A little strange, wasn't it? The power of mind over matter? The distraction of thought?

She moved back the bedclothes, put her feet to the floor, testingly. Stood up, walked over to the fireplace, walked over to the cooker. Filled the kettle, lit the gas, bent down, got out the coffee jar. Returned and kneeled upon the bed, drew back the curtains, pushed up the window. Leant there with elbows on the sill; listening to the continuing and infinitely more musical peal of the bells; conscious of a motorcyclist revving up and of the cries of children who were on the Heath.

She got down off the bed. She raised both arms in line with her shoulders and twisted her trunk as far as it would go, both ways, a fine waist-trimming exercise. She touched her toes six times.

Steam was issuing from the kettle but suddenly she decided she didn't want any coffee nor breakfast. Well, anyway not here. If she got dressed very quickly, if she hardly bothered about washing or makeup or brushing her hair, then she wondered if she could guess the path he would have taken: Siamese twin calling out to Siamese twin, Heloise calling out to Abelard: and so, by running, soon catch him up. She was almost certain she could track him just by love.

"Simeon," she would say. "Most lovely man that ever was. Why didn't you wait for me?"

26

Somehow Jericho, having fought the battle of Joshua, managed to get rid of him. She felt shaken by the episode. She had written out his cheque. It was for three thousand pounds and Josh's face, albeit briefly, had leapt back into liveliness at the sight of it. But then, again pathetically, he'd asked whether it might have been for more if he hadn't made a nuisance of himself, got on the wrong side of her, miscalculated the gamble.

She tried to reassure him, shook his hand, said she would see him before she left. She went with him to the entrance and watched him start on his walk home, the earlier spring now missing from his step, the legend on the back of his sweatshirt a pointedly cruel joke: *Keep your pecker up*.

On the front it said: *Think big*.

It was then nearly half-past-eight. Because she felt unsettled and not in the right mood to be alone, she didn't want merely to go to her room with the intention of staying there. She hadn't meant to return to the vicarage tonight, yet now it seemed the most sensible thing to do. She decided not even to telephone first. If the vicar wasn't there, or if he was there but engaged with something lengthy, she would at least have had the walk.

She thought she remembered the way but in fact got lost and on the first occasion she asked for help was wholly misdirected. The roads were very quiet. Not nervous about such things generally she now began to wonder whether she were being foolhardy. Several times, on hearing footsteps coming up behind her, she held on tightly to her shoulder bag. At one point, five or six youths who were going in the opposite direction – *and*, thankfully, on the other side of the road – plied her with laughter and ribaldry and several shouted invitations; she estimated the distance to the nearest house showing a sliver of light. Yet, anyway, the danger passed. Nevertheless she hurried; rued the impracticability of high heels, the price of vanity. She glanced back over her shoulder, was startled by the soft approach of a

129

beer-bellied fellow in a checked shirt and a Stetson who seemed to be regarding her with furtive interest. She knew she was overreacting but actually started to run...with even the wretched tap-tap of her shoes appearing to call attention to her, *here I am, absurd and alarmed, a natural victim, come and get me*! She passed a cemetery – ideal, she thought, ideal, what more is lacking? – but then saw cars going by at right angles and realized she had almost reached a busier road. On the further side of it, outside park gates, there was a man pacing backwards and forwards. Illogically, she supposed – yet only afterwards did it strike her as being that – she hastened towards him as if towards her saviour. "Excuse me but do you know St Matthew's Vicarage? I hope to God you do."

"I ought to," he smiled. "I live there."

This took her back so completely it was a second or two before she could adjust.

"Have you been having trouble?" he asked.

"I'm afraid it was my own fault. I was so sure I knew the way. You're Mr Madison?" She had meant but forgotten to glance at the photographs which Graeme had obtained.

He nodded. She would plainly have to discard at least some of her preconceived notions concerning vicars – and automatically wondered about her own appearance. She knew it had been all right prior to leaving the hotel but had her apprehensions made her shiny-nosed, dishevelled? A minute or two before, she had worried about being raped; now she worried about the condition of her makeup.

"Geraldine Coe," she said. They shook hands.

"We're only a few yards from the vicarage, Miss Coe. Or is it Mrs?"

As they began to walk in the direction he'd indicated, he moved round behind her, to be on the outside.

"But weren't you waiting for someone?"

"No," he said, "I had a headache. I was hoping a breath of fresh air might clear it."

"I always carry aspirin in my bag."

"I've already taken some. But thanks." (Even as she'd made it, she had known the gesture was without point.) "Are you a local woman, Miss Coe?"

"No, I'm staying at the Royal. Shall probably be returning to London tomorrow. I'm from the *Chronicle*."

"The *Chronicle*!"

"I hoped for a short interview."

"Good heavens. With me? Are you doing a feature on the town?"

"It isn't that." Something in his manner made her hesitate.

"What could I have done, then?" But she heard the anxiety that underlay his laugh.

"It's about the two Heath boys. Their claim to have seen an angel."

They had reached the driveway to the vicarage. He stopped abruptly and stared down at her in anger – she could have sworn that it was anger. "Who in God's name told you that?"

"The boys' father. He phoned our Fleet Street office."

"When?"

"This morning. Why are you so...so surprised?"

He didn't answer but started striding up the gravel drive, apparently unbothered whether or not she could keep up.

Yet at the front door he waited for her. In the hallway a woman of about fifty-five gave her an inquiring look.

"I was just coming out to get you," she said to her son – the resemblance was unmistakable.

"Why?"

"I didn't want you catching cold. Besides, I'm making you a milky drink. It ought to help your head."

"Mother, this is Miss Coe. A reporter from the *Chronicle*. She wants to talk to us about the Heaths, et cetera."

"How nice."

"No, it is *not* nice in the slightest. With all due respect to Miss Coe I could kick the bloody *Chronicle* from here to perdition and the bloody Mr Josh Heath along with it."

"Simon! Simon, *dear*."

131

"Why on earth did he do it? They all knew it was absolutely essential to stay quiet."

"Miss Coe, would you like a cup of Horlicks?"

"Miss Coe would probably like a glass of whisky. I know I damned well would."

"Darling, what *has* happened to your vocabulary? I haven't heard you swear so much since – "

"I feel I have a reasonable excuse. Here, let me take your coat."

"Thank you. If you don't mind, Mrs Madison, I think I'd much prefer that cup of Horlicks."

"Then you may have mine, with pleasure. And, Mother, so long as you don't harp on about my vocabulary, you'd be quite welcome to join us."

While he hung up her coat Geraldine had the opportunity to glance into a wall mirror. He held open the door to what was obviously his study.

Mrs Madison had gone to fetch the Horlicks. Geraldine was waved to a large and comfortable armchair. The room was a pleasing mix of ancient and modern – the armchair modern. Simon stood for a moment with his back towards her, looking up at the crucifix over his desk. While he did so, she noted the framed black-and-white photograph of an attractive young woman with dark hair. She noticed, too, the yellow plastic dog that sat by it, soppy-looking, quite sweet, yet curiously out of keeping with what other ornaments were in the room. But then he turned and took a bottle and a glass from a cupboard near the bookcase. "That's better," he said. "Do you find it warm enough in here?"

"Yes, fine."

"I apologize for my vocabulary."

"I've heard worse."

"Perhaps you were lucky not to do so this evening."

"I have to admit it wasn't the reaction I'd expected. Frankly, I still can't see the reason for it."

"Because as soon as this story breaks, tomorrow I imagine – "

"It may not be tomorrow. They were certainly holding space for it but it's possible they'll decide to wait until Wednesday, then launch it with a big splash: headlines, photographs, the works. "

"Tomorrow or Wednesday," he said, "it really makes no difference. Unless..." In the midst of pouring his whisky he stopped and looked at her more hopefully. "Unless that means you can get them to hold it indefinitely. Well, for a period, say, of three to four weeks. *Then* you can publish with my blessing, splash it about in luminous vermilion, in fiery letters six feet high." He must have seen her expression, Geraldine thought, because suddenly he gave a shrug and his optimism went. He turned, continued pouring the whisky, then replaced the cap. Mrs Madison came in with the Horlicks and a plate of biscuits but she didn't stay. "You can tell me all about it later." Geraldine noticed the habitual slight severity of her expression softened as she looked at him. "I'll see you later, Miss Coe. Or, if I don't, then I'll hope to meet you on some future occasion."

"Because as soon as this story breaks...?" prompted Geraldine, after Mrs Madison had left.

"Then it turns into nothing but a three-ring circus. The *Sun* gets hold of it, the *Mirror*, the *Mail*. We'll have 'The Disco Angel with the Song of Love' and the standard girlie photos all winking their encouragement. Sensationalism, ridicule! It wasn't what I wanted, it wasn't what I thought to get. I've already seen the Bishops of Grimsby and Lincoln. I've set up appointments to meet four more bishops during the week, plus a number of others in the C of E who hold a position of influence. I've made an application to the Church's Council for Health and Healing. I've done everything within my power to set the ball rolling...I mean in a controlled and dignified manner. And all for what, Miss Coe?" He clenched his free hand into a fist and pounded the arm of his chair with it, three times. "And *all – for – what*?"

She felt incensed, as though he were using his fist as a weapon of intimidation. It wasn't part of her job to put forward her own opinions at a time like this and on dozens of apparently more provocative occasions she had managed not to; but tonight (perhaps she was unduly tired) some demon of perversity appeared to take possession of her.

"Is dignity so all-important?"

"I should have said so, yes. Don't you think that a heavenly revelation, or what I for one accept wholeheartedly as such, deserves to be treated with awe, not with hysteria? It asks for action, not exploitation. For alarm, even. What it doesn't ask for is a retreat into jokiness and facetiousness. Just make a noise, pretend it isn't there."

"But awe – action – alarm." She slowly numbered these responses on her fingers. "Yet no mention of joy?" She felt that for better or worse she was committed now. "And there are a couple of other things which strike me as a little odd."

For a moment he massaged his forehead lightly with one hand, covering his eyes.

"Yes, Miss Coe, you're right. Of course one shouldn't leave out joy. What's happened here is obviously a proof of God's existence and of his wish to be merciful. Great! And joy is one of the fruits of the Spirit, should be totally – yes, *totally* – integral. But at the same time I can't help thinking that if a messenger arrives to announce what an awful cock-up the world has made of things and to warn it of imminent catastrophe, then your natural urge to shout whoopee may seem a little out of place. Particularly if you've always taken God's existence and the question of his concern pretty much for granted anyway. But clearly you see the matter differently?"

She gave a small, ironic laugh.

"Oh, no. I wouldn't dare!"

"Now you make it sound as if I'm trying to browbeat you." Naturally by this time he had taken his hand away from his eyes but he still looked extremely weary. "What were the other points you mentioned?"

"Well..." She slightly shifted her position in the armchair, straightened her back a little. "The first is, I get the feeling that in general you don't have a very high opinion of people. They're not really to be trusted."

He shrugged then gave a very faint smile.

"I wonder if that could largely be because...in general...I haven't?"

There was a mildly disconcerting silence.

"What about you?" he asked.

"But aren't you going to add anything to that?"

"If you like. I think that people are capable of great things on occasion, great moments of heroism and tenderness and sacrifice, especially when they forget to rely on themselves and when they place their full dependence where it ought to be. But otherwise..."

"Yes? Otherwise?"

"I think that on the whole they're more than merely weak and self-centred, more than merely ineffectual and misguided. I think that even if we omit altogether the problem of real hardcore evil they're still, by and large, petty-minded, hypocritical, uncharitable, jealous, greedy. Do I need to go on?"

"I didn't realize," she answered, equably, "that the Christian viewpoint was only another term for misanthropy."

He smiled again, and less faintly than before. "A Christian, surely, doesn't have to be blind to people's faults, shouldn't try to pretend they simply don't exist? Why are we here at all, if not for the sake of self-improvement? No, *surely*, while seeing how very far from perfect everyone still is, the Christian nevertheless attempts to love him, in the same way that he loves himself?"

"All the time you've spoken of 'them', the sinful wicked people, not of 'us'."

"I'm sorry. That wasn't deliberate."

She said: "Some people, perhaps, are more adept at loving themselves than they are others? Which, as it happens, is the second thing that rather struck me." She turned to the previous page in her notepad. "Do you mind if I read back some of your own words?"

"Obviously in a minute I'm very much going to. But, anyhow, fire away."

Now that she had come this far, however, she began to experience doubt. It was an unfortunate moment in which to

135

waver. "That is, if I can ever untangle this abominable shorthand of mine..."

"Miss Coe," Simon told her, "please feel free to be as blunt as you like. It really doesn't matter. My back is broad."

So he brought it on himself.

"Then listen to this," she said. "All taken from a single speech. 'It wasn't what I wanted, it wasn't what I thought to get...I've already seen the Bishops of Grimsby and Lincoln...I've set up appointments...I've made an application...I've done everything within my power...'" She looked up from the notepad and willed herself to meet his gaze. "'I've done everything within my power.'"

"I didn't say that twice."

"What sound do you hear the loudest behind those words?"

"Supposing you tell me?"

"Self-assertion, would you say? Self-concern? Self-pity? In any case, self of some kind."

"Why are you so bitter, Miss Coe?"

"I really don't believe I am. It's just that I resent complacency. '*I* know what's going to be best!'"

"And you're perfectly right to resent it. Thank you for pointing mine out to me."

"Oh, please don't turn the other cheek. I couldn't stand it."

"The perfect clergyman," he said. He grimaced. But his face still appeared flushed.

"Self-parody," she added. She looked into her lap. "Now I do begin to feel deflated."

"Is this the way, though," he asked, "that you generally conduct your interviews? The *local* press seems to go about it differently."

She shook her head. "Honestly I'm not too sure what got into me."

"Certainly not your Horlicks."

"No, I'd forgotten that. In fact, it's still drinkable. May I pass you a biscuit?"

A temporary cessation, or a permanent ceasefire?

"Have you heard *anything* of what you need to know?"

136

"Yes, certainly I have. I'd like to hear, however, why you changed your mind about the validity of the boys' story."

He told her, simply and concisely. Geraldine admired his fluency. Then he stood up; it was clear the time allotted to her had elapsed. "I suppose it's no good my asking you, is it, if you *could* possibly use your influence to try to postpone things? That would help, immeasurably."

She said: "You don't understand. Only the bosses can ever wield influence of that sort. I am sorry."

"Well, in that case there's no more to be done. It'll have to be left in God's hand...where, of course, it should have been from the beginning. I'd better drive you home."

They didn't speak much in the car. She had got into a muddle with her seat belt and he had patiently sorted it out. Again, he had to unclasp it for her at the other end; she was sure there must be something defective in the miserable device. He probably kept it that way on purpose: to demonstrate his superiority over anybody sitting on his left-hand. (Or was it the *right*-hand the privileged were said to sit upon?)

She had asked him if the girl in the photograph was his fiancée. He had answered only, "No." She had too much pride to pursue the matter – in any journalist, of course, another highly prized characteristic.

Standing now on the pavement outside the hotel she said to him through his drawn-down window:

"I hope your headache has cleared."

"Yes, thank you."

"I'm sorry we don't appear to have hit it off. Clashes of personality...I suppose they're sometimes inevitable? But please believe me: I'll be as fair as possible in whatever I write about all this." She added: "Thank you for the lift."

He didn't say anything, only held up a hand in acknowledgment. Then he drove away without another glance, as if already she were slipping from his mind. Well, sod that, she thought. At least he, too, could have made *some* attempt at an apology; could have got out of the car perhaps and shaken

137

hands? She'd always believed it took more than one to have a clash.

27

But did it really? She awoke next morning after a sound night's sleep and started to remember. It wasn't Josh Heath that she thought about principally, nor any of his family, nor indeed his contentious revelation; it was that whole strange episode at the vicarage. Oh God, oh God, oh God. And as she thought about it her entire body seemed to contract with embarrassment and shame.

Not to mention her soul.

Why *had* she been so resistant? Was it his sheer physical attractiveness she had reacted to? (Hey! Look at me, everyone! *I'm* not susceptible!) Was it that air he had of always having his own way? (A mother who ran out to make sure he wasn't getting chilled then scurried off to make him hot drinks – which, anyway, as like as not he spurned – had he even said thank you? Probably since childhood everyone had spoilt him, shielded him, made sure he'd never suffer.) Was it his smugness? *Especially if anyway you've always taken God's existence and the question of his concern pretty much for granted.* Or was it the irritatingly exaggerated respect a vicar still enjoyed amongst his parishioners? (Even in London – so what on earth must it be like up here?) Or was it, perhaps, none of the above? Was it the old woman with sour breath and a growth of beard and a collecting box who had waylaid her the other day on Ludgate Hill, wanting to know if she were saved and thrusting a pamphlet into her contemptibly docile hand? (Four printed sides of rubbish that had cost her 50p.) *Why* had she behaved as she had?

She reviewed their entire conversation; tried to sort out where things had started to go wrong. He had been angry but not with her personally. (Indeed, she agreed with his assessment of the gutter press and couldn't in any way have taken it as an indictment of all Fleet Street. She agreed, too, with his probable assessment of Josh Heath. The louse had played a deeply rotten trick on him – not only on him but on his own wife and children. Possibly on the world?) And then he had given her the full reason for his anger; well, there was nothing wrong with that and she had asked him for it in any case. Self-pity? Self-concern? (Had she *really* said those things? What single shred of justification had she had? He was only a man who'd been doing his job, to the utmost of his ability. And to be absolutely fair, he didn't even have an air of always getting his own way – that aura of smugness was likewise, she knew, purely something she'd been doing her best to foist on him: he simply stated his beliefs quite straightforwardly, without dogmatism but without apology.) And he was surely right about the ridicule which people tended to heap on things which, for whatever reason, they felt unwilling to accept; you *couldn't* trust them to be responsible, neither in their actions nor their attitudes. But time and again what she returned to was that dreadful allegation of hers; and, despite the repetition, her embarrassment lost nothing of its edge. Even as she'd read back to him what she had written, the evidence for such a charge had suddenly seemed thin, woefully thin. So, if even at the time... And, after all, the man was only human – besides being angry, disappointed, tired – and with a head that ached. Why in heaven's name, merely because he was articulate, should she expect him to express himself without flaw? Why in heaven's name should she expect him actually to *be* without flaw? Okay, then, a strand or two of egotism? Would that be so unnatural, so wholly unforgivable? Was she herself without it? Perhaps to be breathtakingly holier-than-thou, it wasn't necessary to be a Christian.

No.

Even if it should turn out to be the most humiliating task she had ever been called upon to undertake, she had to make amends for what had happened yesterday.

As far as it were possible.

She reached the vicarage at the very moment he was about to leave it. Had she stopped for breakfast she would have missed him altogether. She offered up a pointless little word of gratitude.

"May I ask for ten more minutes of your time?"

He closed the car door with a slam and led her back into his study.

"First and foremost," she said, "I want to apologize."

He answered slowly. "But you did that last night – and I'm not even convinced you have anything to apologize for." He motioned her to sit down.

"That's kind," she said, "but untrue. And that sad little spiel about a personality clash was not only tepid, it was insincere. I now want to apologize unreservedly and to own myself entirely in the wrong, with no excuse whatever for such terrible manners. *Those* I could have done something about, even if my sheer stupidity was maybe less controllable. I was snide and detestable throughout, as well as being just plain wrong. No, please don't say otherwise; I really have this need to grovel."

"Don't you think, though, you may now have grovelled enough?"

"No, honestly, I don't. But perhaps I'll let you off the rest if you'll shake my hand and tell me that I'm fully, however undeservingly, forgiven."

He did as she requested. They hadn't yet sat down. Now they did so.

Overhead, she heard the sound of furniture being moved about. Sporadic snatches of song. Short bursts of hoovering.

"And can you look me in the eye and say there's not a scrap of ill feeling left between us?"

"Not a scrap."

"Thank you." She drew her hand away and smiled. "I feel all cleansed and as if I'd been allowed to make a new start. I wish you had a church roof which was falling down, or something of that nature."

"That's a very kind thought," he said. "And as a matter of fact we have – what church hasn't? Yet why?"

140

"Then may I contribute something small towards it? I don't mean on behalf of the *Chronicle* but on behalf of me, as a sign that I wish to do something practical with my penitence."

"It isn't necessary."

"Couldn't you see it as my procuring an indulgence?"

He laughed, and accepted the twenty pounds she held out to him. "Well, I don't know I can see it quite as that but, if you're sure, the church roof will certainly be grateful. This is extremely generous. You wouldn't prefer more time to think about it?"

"I should only feel I hadn't paid enough."

"In that case, thank you."

"What I really wish my penitence could achieve is put off publication of the story."

He nodded.

"By the way," she said, "there isn't any word of it this morning."

"Yes, I know."

"I'd very much like you to believe me. If I *could* have suppressed it..."

"As recompense, do you think you could suppress Josh Heath?"

"That *might* – I'm not too sure – be marginally easier." She added: "Do you know what occurred to me earlier? Joshua's the Hebrew name for Jesus, isn't it?"

"Yes."

"Mildly paradoxical?"

Simon shrugged.

"Maybe," she said, "that's why Dawn doesn't appear to call him Joshua."

"No. It's more likely that if she tried – and I'll bet you a pound or two she has – he simply wouldn't answer."

"You say that almost with affection."

"Do I? Well, at the moment, let me assure you, I feel so little affection I could wish him as far from Scunthorpe as a person could possibly get."

He rubbed his eyes.

"Your headache hasn't come back?"

141

"What? Oh, no. I suppose, however, I shouldn't be uncharitable. Undoubtedly he has his problems. 'Father, forgive them; for they know not what they do.'"

"Is the situation really so grave as you implied?"

"That once the tabloids get hold of this miracle is it finished as a subject for serious discussion? Yes, I think it is."

She said suddenly: "Supposing I phoned my editor? Told him the Heath boys had withdrawn their statement? Had confessed the whole thing was a lie? Its news value would diminish into dust."

He smiled a little.

"What are you looking for?" she asked.

"The dust which that reporter with her scoop also diminished into."

"The very *penitent* reporter. So may I use your phone?" Already she was reaching towards it.

"No, hold on. Only if you'd like to explain the true situation to your editor or else let *me* speak to him."

"But that wouldn't do any good at all. He's by no means an unfair man, yet he's not going to listen just to pleas: mine *or* yours."

"Is he religious?"

"No."

"You're sure of that? No belief whatever?"

"None."

"Still, I'm convinced that a man in his position would have respect for the belief of others. And it's only a postponement we're asking for, not suppression. It's worth a try."

"I don't believe it is."

"Are *you* religious?"

"I'd like to be." When she removed her hand from the receiver it was only with clear reluctance. "Why won't you let me tell that lie?"

"Oh, come on now, you don't really need to ask."

"Yet if you genuinely believe the whole world will benefit...?"

142

"It's not the way God's business should be done – and I'm sorry if that sounds priggish. But, speaking more practically, what credence do you think those boys would have when the time came for retracting their retraction?"

"But the public wouldn't know. It would only be... And, after all, there *are* other papers." Yet she knew he was right and her voice held no conviction. "Or, when that time came, couldn't you simply give the reasons why you had felt it necessary?"

He shook his head. "No. Now we'd be asking Dawn and William and Michael to lie. Josh, also, of course." He paused. "However, after you've gone," he said, "I *shall* make that phone call. Possibly miracles can still turn up in threes? Or sixes? Or dozens? And to be honest I'd been going to do so anyway. When you came I was about to drive to St Matthew's to prepare for it with prayer."

"Well, if you're fully determined – which I can see you are – won't you phone Geoff while I'm here?"

Again he shook his head. "No, I really do need to pray about it first. But now I think I'll do that here, despite my mother's happy spring-clean from above. So I may not phone him for another hour."

She glanced at her watch. "Then don't leave it any later. Already they'll be working out what goes in and what..." She broke off, aware of how contagious was his faith in the impossible. And how forlorn.

But even knowing of the urgency she couldn't just get up and go.

"May I say how much I like your painting? I would have mentioned it last night."

"Strangely I'd only hung it in the afternoon. Before I went to Lincoln."

"Really? Who is the painter?"

While they stood in front of it he told her, briefly, about Jerry Turner. He'd given Sharon fifty pounds for the picture.

"I don't want any charity," she'd said, trying to push the money from her.

"Sharon, I promise you it's not charity. The only thing that worries me...it could be theft."

It was ironic he had used that phrase: the one thing that had really worried him was the thought of the kind of future Jerry Turner might have had in front of him. And Sharon and the children, too.

"Knowing our vicar," had called Alison through the open doorway (she'd been kneeling on the lino in the kitchen, cleaning the cooker), "it's almost bound to be theft."

Sharon said: "He did that picture the time we went on holiday. We went to Cornwall, had a whole week." She'd seemed more rested than before. More forthcoming, as well.

"Then, Sharon, I obviously can't take it from you."

"Oh, it's all right. He did a lot of others, mostly of the same thing. We had a really lovely time. He'd get on with his painting, I'd be on the grass nearby, reading my magazines."

"*A Beacon in the Mist*," he'd said. "I like its title." Which wasn't wholly true: he'd have preferred it didn't have one.

"There were half a dozen flaming beacons in the mist." He'd received the impression it might have been a little joke between them, her and Jerry, that adjective in this context. It was a small sign but definitely encouraging. He'd silently thanked God for it.

Geraldine found it hard to assimilate, emotionally, that the fingers which had swung the rope over the branch, tightened the knot, had earlier worked so lovingly upon this strong yet tranquil picture. The frightening transience of life, its total lack of certainty: these sounded so banal while you struggled for the words in which to communicate them afresh. After a further moment she turned from the painting and sought relief in bathos.

"I also like your dog. He looks all bright and happy."

"Petticoat."

"I beg her pardon. *She*. A slightly unusual name?"

"Given to us one Sunday in Petticoat Lane, along with...well, several other things." But he didn't dwell on that. "Anyway, in all of this, there could be something else we ought to be considering. That whatever your editor is going to decide in response to my phone call – it possibly doesn't matter."

144

"No?"

"Well, isn't this conceivable? That at much the same time our two were having their revelation here in Scunthorpe, others were having a similar experience in some other part of the world? Or *parts* of it. Not necessarily boys, or even children. And probably not white-skinned either, nor Christian. But why assume God would put all his eggs in one basket? Indeed – knowing us as he does – it becomes hard to believe he would."

"And, presumably," she said, "knowing in advance just what's going to happen to each egg?"

"Oh, well, *there*," said Simon, "we could be wading out into deep waters." But now it was he who glanced at his watch. "And this isn't quite the time to try to plumb them. Though I'm sorry if it looks like I'm wanting to hasten your departure."

"Which you are," she laughed. "*Again*! And rightly so. Truly, I'd only meant to stay a few minutes."

"I'll run you back to the Royal."

"No, you've enough to be getting on with. Besides, I shall enjoy the walk. It'll give me an opportunity to think." She felt conscious she was making a sacrifice: she would have liked more time in his company. "Incidentally... What was the connection of ideas between Jerry Turner's painting and God not putting all his eggs in one basket?"

"His wife said he painted the same thing time and again – to give it every chance of growing as perfect as possible."

"Right."

"When do you go back to town?"

"This afternoon."

"Shall we be seeing you here again?"

"Oh, yes." As he walked with her to the road, she added, "And say hello to your mother for me. Thank her for the Horlicks."

"I will."

"By the way, something else I meant to ask. The Bishops of Grimsby and Lincoln. How did *they* react?"

"One very encouragingly, with wonder and hope and excitement. The other – well, he's a chap who tends to try to

145

explain things away. Not only is that his natural disposition, he happens to be married to a psychotherapist."

"Josh Heath implied it might have been *your* natural disposition, as well."

"And he did so with complete justice." He laughed. "All the more reason, then – wouldn't you say – to be impressed by my present attitude? But it follows that Josh Heath doesn't *always* get things wrong! In fact I feel this strongly: that if he were only fighting for the world's true causes he'd be very much a force to be reckoned with...more so, maybe, than most of us. And now, quite definitely, Miss Coe, I *am* speaking of myself!"

At the moment he told her this she didn't entirely take in what he was saying, because they had now reached the highway and while he was talking he had stooped to pick a snail off the pavement, a large snail that had not simply left the shelter of a grass verge but seemed intent on crossing the very busy road. He cupped it gently and restored it to the safety of the garden wall, lightly wiping off his palms on the sides of his trousers.

"Goodbye," he said. "I still appreciate that offer."

"Good luck," she answered. They shook hands. "And if anyone can manage it I'm sure it must be you."

"Oh, something else," he called out after her. "That girl you were wondering about last night... Ginny. She was my wife. She died. She died in childbirth. Goodbye," he repeated, and gave a quick wave.

She started walking away again and looked back and saw that he was closing the front door. And she felt desolate.

28

That evening, when he got home, there was wine on the table.

"That's my girl," he exclaimed, kissing her zestfully. "Let's go to bed!"

"And I suppose you'd never guess that there's a chicken in the oven? 'Great heavens, now that's what I *do* call an appetizing

146

smell! *Cordon Bleu*, even in these cramped, impossible conditions! How on earth do you do it?'"

Momentarily, he put his hand to his head.

"Ginny, what were you saying? Sorry – I didn't hear – I was suddenly knocked speechless by this incredible smell that came wafting towards me... What I can never understand is – I think you must be a sorceress – how on *earth* do you ever do it?"

"Funny you should ask me that."

"What a truly extraordinary woman!"

"That's better."

"Let's go to bed."

"That isn't. Don't you know that the way to a man's heart is supposed to be through his stomach?"

"I was under the impression it was through his underpants."

"How crude. Tonight I have no wish for crudeness. Tonight I wish for glamour and romance. Me in a filmy evening dress, you in a dinner jacket. Candlelight and crystal goblets. Rose petals strewn across the floor."

"Rose petals? We could conjure up some wilted chrysanthemum leaves."

But this time his kiss was more determinedly persuasive. She let him keep his hand beneath her blouse. "Well, maybe I could spare you just a very few minutes," she conceded. "But after *that* we shall be civilized. I mean to hold a celebration."

"And what finer way to celebrate?"

"Since you've hardly tried any other, aren't you speaking from a position of almost total ignorance?"

They undressed in front of the sputtering gas fire and knelt to embrace on the new fluffy rug (machine-washable) which Simon had bought at least partly for this purpose. It was early December. With the curtains drawn and by the light of a rather pricey table lamp (another recent acquisition, thanks to the staff discount at John Barnes) the room had grown quite cosy.

She put his hand to her stomach; held it there a moment.

"Are you trying to tell me something?"

The eagerness of the question matched the eagerness of the answer. "Yes!"

"My God!" he said. "My *God*!" She gathered from the look on his face that these were cries of praise rather than profanity. "But why didn't you *say*? How many...?"

"Three-and-a-half months. And what do you think I'm doing now, you numbskull? But I wanted to be sure. It was only at lunchtime I became so."

"You should have phoned me."

"Why? This is much better."

"But all the time that you must have suspected..."

"Well, don't you feel that it teaches you right, a little? For simply not having noticed. For just taking those healing powers of yours so very much for granted. Besides, I somehow wanted to keep it all to myself, miser-like, until I really *knew*."

"Selfish beast."

"Pots and kettles."

He put his arms around her and held her to him, very close.

"Next summer, then?"

"Start of June."

They stayed for a while in silence, and in stillness, cheeks together.

"You know, you've got such lovely skin. Ginny by gaslight. Do you think our baby will have skin as soft as yours?" He was now holding her away from him. "A family... That's what I can't get over. I always wished I'd been one of a large and very *noisy* family. Constant comings and goings. Open house. More like a commune."

"Me, too."

"Terrific at Christmas!"

"Drive the old folks scatty!"

Eventually, after they'd made love, they had some wine as an aperitif, still sitting on the rug and making lazy conversation.

"'Your young men shall dream dreams,'" he said. "I wonder if this was what Isaiah or whoever it was had in mind when he wrote that: back to back in front of the fire. I'd like to think so."

"I thought it was your old men who were going to dream dreams. Weren't your young men going to see visions?"

"Well, okay. He must have had you in mind."

148

She nuzzled her head, appreciatively, against his shoulder. "If he was thinking of this precise moment, as you claim, then I hope he supplied you with eyes in your elbows." She laughed, and shivered. "Oh, how off-putting! Salvador Dali might enjoy it but otherwise *not* what the well-undressed young man is wearing this year!"

She sipped her wine, a little thoughtfully.

"And actually too, my whiz-kid hero, I don't believe it was Isaiah."

Simon rose lightly to his feet and took down Ginny's concordance from the mantelshelf. "Joel, would you believe? Who ever heard of Joel?" He closed the book in some disgust.

"I did." With her arms encircling her legs and her chin resting on her knees, she said suddenly, "Darling, if it's a boy, let's call him Joel, shall we?"

He considered. "Okay, that's nice. If by June, that is, you haven't thought of a dozen different things you'd like to call him."

"No. If it's a boy that's the name I know I'll want. Joel. To remind me of tonight. And of you. And of – "

"I've got no plans to go away."

"I mean, idiot, of you as you are this minute, simple and funny and kind and strong. Full of warmth. Don't change too much. Don't stop being the loveliest man that ever was. *Please*. I couldn't bear it. Oh, hold me, Simeon; I suddenly feel cold."

After their meal, although they took a fair time over it to do justice to the fact of its being civilized and *Cordon Bleu*, it was still early enough (if they left the washing up to the scullery maid) to think of going out. So they caught a tube down west to look at the Christmas lights. Yet because it was a fine night, cold but dry, Regent Street was more crowded than Simon had expected. "Try not to let anybody bump into you." He walked with an arm protectively around her and a ready glare for anyone who actually happened to be looking up at the illuminations. When they had a cup of coffee in a snack bar off the main route, however, he received a salutary lesson. Rather a pretty woman sat at the next table, evidently in the final weeks (days) (*minutes*?) of pregnancy. Yet with perfectly good-humoured unconcern she had a toddler repeatedly pulling himself up into what was left of her lap; and she was playing a game with him whenever he did get settled for a minute or two – walky-round-the-garden-like-a-teddy-bear – that made his arms and legs flail rapturously in the anticipation of anguish.

Simon grinned at Ginny. "Us in a few years' time?" He suddenly leaned towards the woman and said: "My wife's expecting, too!"

"*Is* she? That's nice. I bet you're pleased."

"If only because, as yet, they don't know better!" put in the husband. His voice was surprisingly educated and he had strikingly white teeth. "I take it, of course, this *is* your first?"

Ginny laughed. "And you're the first to hear of it, as well."

"Now don't you listen to him." The woman patted Ginny's arm. "He always makes these silly jokes but what matters is he's a really good dad, same as *your* hubbie's going to be. Sorry," she said quickly, colouring a little and glancing sideways as she did so, "I mean husband. For instance...he didn't think we ought to come out tonight but I'd have been really sad to miss them angels – those angels; just felt I had to see them. So he brought us, even though he didn't want to."

"Are *you* enjoying seeing the lights?" Ginny asked the very appealing child of five or six who sat at the table demurely sucking at her fizzy drink.

The little girl nodded, shyly. "It's a long way past my bedtime," she said.

"I'm not surprised. It's a long way past mine."

"It isn't!"

"It is!"

"I think you're telling me a fib." But there was the shadow of a question mark.

The mother beamed. The boy sat looking at Ginny interestedly, his thumb in his mouth, swinging a shoe rhythmically against his mother's leg. The father's reaction was the least expected. He was staring at his daughter with frank indulgent pride.

150

The woman noticed Simon's look.

"There, you see. What did I say? He's just as soft as all the rest of you. You tell this nice lady and gent, Janice, you tell them what a real good man your daddy is – inside. You tell them, too, Billy."

29

The *Chronicle* carried the story next day. Front page. Headlines. *Gabriel over Scunthorpe*? Above this, in smaller type, *Brothers allege meeting with angel – Message for the world – Charge of apathy and needless suffering*. Below, using a typeface somewhere between the two in heaviness and size, *Heaven on the side of nuclear disarmament – and love*.

The by-line was simply *By Geraldine Coe*.

There were two related photographs on the front page: William and Michael Heath standing in the car park and a much smaller one – just head and shoulders – of the boys' father; while on the back page, where the story continued, there was a picture of the vicar of St Matthew's processing with a donkey and a long line of out-of-focus parishioners in the previous spring's Palm Sunday act of witness.

By mid-morning the phone at the vicarage was ringing incessantly. Simon wasn't there but his mother had settled herself at his desk with a pot of coffee and a notepad and some knitting; and was being brisk and affable and joyous. "Yes, isn't it *marvellous*!" she kept saying. "There's hope for us all." Sometimes, depending on whom she was talking to, and very conscious of her role as Mother of the Vicar, she added "Hallelujah!" and even "Praise the Lord!" The woman from Yorkshire Television received both of these, the man from Radio Humberside neither. But as a form of rating it was variable. At first it was given only to those who were clearly sympathetic but later only to those who were clearly sceptical (partly on the grounds that they required it more, partly because she wanted to

151

annoy them). Paula Marshall, on the other hand, who was just too churchy by half but who'd have sacrificed the Holy Grail, given it to Oxfam, for the sake of one day becoming her daughter-in-law, hallelujah-ed *her*, and praise-the-Lord-ed *her* (*and* amen-ed her into the bargain!). *She* received a very crisp, "Well, thank you for telephoning, Paula, I've noted your offers of help and your suggestion of a round-the-clock vigil," without a single laudatory response. Mrs Madison wrote down the names of all the newspapers that called, both national and provincial, with a system of asterisks indicating the degree of her approval – except in the case of one of them, where an asterisk's range of expression appeared frustratingly restricted. "Give *them* the Turin Shroud," she scribbled furiously, "and they'd use it for net curtains!!!" (That was the call which, in retrospect, she regarded with the greatest satisfaction.) The rings at the doorbell, insistent or not, she totally ignored, since she wasn't anticipating any deliveries today and felt very thankful for their own net curtains, inferior though she reckoned them to be. At two o'clock, during a sudden lull, she removed the receiver from its rest (feeling on this occasion righteously justified), made herself a sandwich and lay down on her bed. She felt quite happy with her morning's work but she knew when it was time to halt. She experienced an invigorating sense of power.

By mid-morning, too, the telephone at High Ridge was very busy. The school secretary found herself being asked continually to fetch the Heath boys out of class. Twice she was offered a bribe. Usually, when everything else had failed, she was asked to put the caller through to the headmaster or his deputy. (She didn't.) Repeatedly she was invited to pronounce on the veracity of the two boys and on the prevailing mood in Scunthorpe and once she was actually implored to dispatch some child to the flat where the Heath family lived, with an urgent message for one of the parents to telephone: *that* optimistic gentleman hoped in this way not only to get in ahead of his own paper's telemessage but of everybody else's. Eventually, however, Mrs Nash received permission from the headmaster to do what Mrs Madison would do an hour or so later: simply take the phone off its hook.

152

By then the headmaster had already interviewed the boys, held an impromptu staff meeting, been harassed by the chairman of the governors and hastily convened a special full assembly at which he stressed the need for good behaviour, since the school would now be coming under widespread scrutiny, and for an open mind, since the possibility of God's having chosen Scunthorpe (like Nazareth or Lourdes or the road leading to Damascus) as a setting for one of his major miracles could neither be ignored nor taken lightly. Mr Dane, more by his own example than by anything he said, managed to create a good atmosphere, fairly matter-of-fact but one which could readily absorb a miracle if called upon to do so; which in itself was something of a miracle; for inside their school at least, William and Michael were regarded, on the whole, with respect not with ridicule. In view of the tremendous pressure they were soon to be exposed to on the outside this was a doubly fortunate blessing.

Meanwhile, their parents had also come to be a centre of attention. Although the *Chronicle* was not one of the more popular papers in the town, the news of what it contained had travelled very fast, not merely through the agency of paper shops and delivery boys (as well as that of a few actual customers) but on account of *Breakfast Time*, *Good Morning Britain* and, for those who might still prefer listening to watching at such an hour, the radio too. Long before the boys had left for school, friends, neighbours, acquaintances and even a total stranger had come knocking on the door – the stranger to denounce. When Simon had called round the previous evening Dawn just couldn't believe the warning he had given them but now she realized she had been naive. ("What else did he want?" Josh had inquired, coming out of the lavatory after the front door closed. "Only that," Dawn had told him, "and no, he didn't ask where you were and I certainly had no wish to advertise it, thank you very much!" Josh, who she knew would have had no inhibitions about keeping even royalty informed of where he was at such embarrassing moments, had stared at her sulkily and looked both studiedly indifferent and secretly put out.) Also, some of the nation's more enterprising reporters had managed to coax from

153

Directory Inquiries the telephone numbers of several nearby subscribers. Therefore Josh was constantly being called out to adjacent flats and on the one occasion when she herself had gone he'd seemed annoyed she hadn't had the caller wait for him...which she would have done most willingly, since the man had been a bit unpleasant and Dawn – who didn't enjoy talking on the telephone at any time, especially not in front of neighbours – had needed to remind herself she was a Christian and that others, even if she hadn't already told them, ought to be able to divine it simply from her forbearance and her exemplary demeanour. (Josh, on the other hand, was very good at coping with these importunities. You had to admire him for it, the manner in which he hastened to deal with them, almost like one of the very first disciples – for although he would impatiently deny it she felt sure there *was* something of that inside him – ready to run forward into battle, "singing songs of expectation, marching to the Promised Land," and she was proud of him, the way he handled this responsibility.)

The journalists, however, didn't remain just voices on a phone. By lunchtime they or their colleagues, or competitors from other branches of the media, were actually interviewing people in the streets: soliciting the Scunthorpe point of view: although already they found they were sometimes holding up the mike to tourists, for not only had some of the overseas visitors who'd planned to spend the day in York decided on a sudden change of itinerary, a few even believing vaguely they'd find on show a kind of upper crust ET, but dozens of the curious from Hull and Doncaster and smaller nearby places were coming in off every bus and train – a mere foretaste of what the weekend and possibly brighter weather (according to the Met Office) might now be expected to bring. One Scunthorpe man, when questioned by the BBC, gave it as his opinion the whole shemozzle had been dreamt up by some chinless wonder on the town council. "Bonanza time for trade!" he suggested bitterly.

"Still, perhaps it does take your mind off things a bit," he then added with a shrug. "A peepshow for the unemployed."

154

30

Simon, having spent a highly unsatisfactory day in and around York, parked his car outside the school at a few minutes to four in order to collect the boys. He had told Dawn he would do this – for whether they were going to be reviled, lionized, or only mildly pestered, it wouldn't be pleasant for them to have to walk home in the usual way and he'd been worried about it long before Geraldine Coe had phoned him, on his return from the Heaths, casually to offer payment for a taxi morning and afternoon. This evening he meant to organize a rota of willing car-drivers from amongst his congregation but he had never felt so keenly the absence of a curate. (Several times he had requested one; though always, he supposed, in far too relaxed a fashion.) Tony, of course, gave invaluable assistance, yet a youth leader had neither the time nor the training to take care of all the parish work at present being neglected. Over the weekend Simon had called on his brother ministers in the area, discussed with them what was happening, listened to their advice and asked them for their help; but apart from such things as burial services – which ideally had to be conducted by someone who'd been on friendly terms with the deceased – and visits to the bereaved which also couldn't be left to total strangers, there was still a number of people (like Sharon Turner, Mrs Beecham, Dick Evans, Molly Simpson, the list had at least a dozen names on it) whom he knew he couldn't just abandon, no matter how much aid he had at his disposal. Yet to every problem, he told himself now, there had to be a solution. He bit his lip, then tried to concentrate upon the job in hand.

The phalanx of pressmen and television reporters assembled both at the front door of the school and near another entrance – one which the children used – was sizeable but not as great as Simon in his heightened state of expectancy had feared it might be. He got out of his car intending to go straight to the

155

headmaster's office, outside whose door he had arranged to meet the boys, but he had overlooked the fact he himself might be recognized.

"It's the Reverend Simon Madison, isn't it, vicar of St Matthew's?"

Immediately, cameras were being trained on him, a microphone being held up. Later he'd be surprised at how little thrusting there had been, at the unity of their restraint and the logical sequence of their questioning: half a dozen voices co-operating singly or in concert to produce the next, most obvious point.

"Vicar, what do you feel about the alleged appearance of an angel in Scunthorpe?"

"I feel sure it took place."

"*Sure*? Isn't that a strong word in the circumstances?"

"No."

"But how *can* you be sure?"

"My sense of conviction, arrived at after prayer."

"Yet mightn't that have been wishful thinking?"

"No. It isn't what I wished for."

"But as a vicar of the Church of England it's certainly what you'd want?"

"If my own conviction could guarantee that of everyone else then naturally it would be different. But as it is..."

"Yes?"

Simon considered, shrugged. "Well, if we hear the specialist confirming cancer is it really wishful thinking that gives us our belief? And I can't feel confident even in the face of this (God prove me wrong) that anyone in authority will be induced to prescribe the right medicine."

"Which is?"

"Well, *love thy neighbour* in all its many forms and applications."

"Why can't you feel confident?"

"Because I'm afraid politics and religious principles seldom seem to mix. There's no acceptable reason why they shouldn't, of course." He smiled.

156

"Surely you're now arguing against your own case? Against the effectiveness of God?"

"God can only be effective – no, let me change that – God only chooses to be effective if people will allow him to be so."

"Would yours be the view of the Church as a whole? Concerning this matter?"

"Concerning this miracle? I don't feel qualified to comment on the view of the Church as a whole."

"Then would you feel qualified to comment, unofficially, upon the content of the message?"

"I endorse it, clearly."

"What about the style of it?"

"The style?"

"Doesn't it strike you as undignified?"

"No. It says what it wants to and in a manner we can understand. I don't imagine it was God's aim to produce a piece of literature. He could easily have sent a poem."

"Then what do you think the country should do now in the light of such a message?"

"What it should have done a very long time ago – and every other country with it. Get back to the great Christian truths as Jesus preached them. Remember that weakness can be strength. Show that at whatever the risk to itself it doesn't mean to be a party to the destruction of mankind but a byword for loving and caring and *doing*, both at home and abroad. Release the billions being consumed by our defence programme to help get rid of deprivation wherever it occurs. Well, I think that ought to do you, as a start."

"But what hope do you see for this message being effective in Britain if the nation's leaders should prove unsympathetic?"

"Then my only hope would lie in the power of democracy. After all, in this country we *are* still a democracy. Aren't we?"

As Simon moved away, to the nods and muttered thanks of several who had been busy with their notepads, one woman even made a smiling gesture of applause. He himself was pleased with his performance. Normally he believed that God sought to inspire him and – not simply that – actually to speak through him

157

so long as he felt himself to be in a state of grace with his channels of communication unimpeded. (Well, any dedicated clergyman must surely feel the same.) But so often things got in the way, human things, and he was enormously thankful that today, just now, so far as he was honestly aware, they hadn't seemed to do so.

Inside the building the bell had now rung and Michael was waiting at the appointed place. "They've got television out there," he said. "I won't know what to say."

"Just tell them the truth, whatever it is they ask you."

"I feel nervous."

"Of course you do. But they'll be very nice and as soon as it starts you'll feel okay. And, obviously, God will be looking after you. When William comes the three of us will say a prayer together."

Michael looked round furtively. There were now plenty of others walking down the corridor, with their satchels or their bags. "As long as no one sees us."

Simon laughed. "Anyone who does, we'll rope them in."

"All right. Though actually I already feel a bit better."

"Good. But that isn't going to let you off a thing. What sort of day have you been having?"

The brothers acquitted themselves well. They jointly gave a straightforward account, neither embellishing their experience nor detracting from it. Simon saw very much why God had chosen them, or thought he did, and felt (more optimistically than he had yet felt about anything that day) that the many millions who would later on be watching could hardly help being impressed. He began to think that whatever the cynics and the intellectuals might have to say about it the bulk of the nation would be very much moved by such a patent display of sincerity and in its heart would not only want to believe but actually might start to do so. When William recited yet again the angel's words (with just one brief omission – which was afterwards supplied by Michael – but with neither the flat delivery so often associated with recitation nor the injection of artificial stress) Simon could imagine that all over the country people would be nodding their

158

heads, at least in spirit, and saying to themselves and one another, "That's right, there's a lot of truth in that, it's the sort of thing I've always thought myself." If only, he reflected, if only there was some way in which to channel all that sympathy before the whole episode became played out, its novelty and impact compromised. A tidal wave of simple human feeling, harnessed and irresistible, that was what was needed, and very quickly too: a tidal wave flooding along the very backbone of the land, washing through it and down it and beyond it, from John O'Groats to the Houses of Parliament, from Land's End to everywhere.

31

As it turned out, though, it was neither the boys nor Simon who got the most television coverage that night. Josh Heath was seen not only on every news broadcast that went out, from *John Craven's Newsround* to *Newsnight* some six hours later, he was also interviewed on *Sixty Minutes* – a programme which claimed to 'present the issues of the hour, and some stories with a smile' and was a special, scoop, last-minute guest on the Russell Harty Show. Here he gave a graphic and fairly accurate account of recession-hit Scunthorpe, with some of its steelwork chimneys now smokeless and much of its machinery now silent, shops closed, dole queues longer, feelings of hopelessness growing. The account he gave, however, of the life of one particular family in the town was slightly less accurate: a cheerful, churchgoing unit, challenged, strengthened and united by its experience of unemployment over the past four-and-a-half years. When asked if its life style was likely to be greatly affected by the publicity, he said he hoped that neither he nor his wife nor children would ever exploit the fact of their having been singled out by God (at this point he needed to explain, with highly amused forgiveness, the misconception in that morning's *Chronicle* about his not being a Christian: "part of the endearing

159

charm of Fleet Street") but that being only human, he couldn't deny the emoluments for such little shows as this (much laughter: from the audience, the other guests, from Russell and himself) would certainly be highly welcome and come in rather handily for buying all those little things like pillowslips and tea towels and facecloths and shoes and clothing which the government clearly didn't imagine the unemployed should ever need to have replaced. Beyond such parochialism, he said, he hoped that the life style of every family in the universe was likely to be greatly affected by the publicity. He was in his element, had all the makings of a television star, and Russell, covering his eyes as if to hide the tears, expressed a good deal of concern for the safety of his own job – would Josh, perhaps, give *him* a spot on the show after *he'd* been out of work for four-and-a-half years? Josh promised that he would, he'd remember all his old friends. The audience showed how warmly it had taken him to its heart by the length and energy of its applause and the credits went up with each man having his arm around the other's shoulder and with the remaining guests capering self-consciously in attendance. The whole thing was a merry hoot and about thirty seconds of it was inserted by the BBC into its main news slot of the evening and was consequently the only part seen by Simon. He'd been celebrating a house communion with one of the discussion groups and his hostess had turned on the TV so that they could all watch 'Scunthorpe's red-letter day, its hour of fame and glory'. "Well, one hopes it's going to be something a little more than that," demurred Simon, drily, but he didn't press the point. The clip was taken from Josh's description of conditions in the town and Simon was very favourably surprised; he handed over to God, in a private word of thanksgiving, his still woeful lack of trust. "Lord, I believe; help thou mine unbelief."

He was rather less impressed, however, by the review of the Harty show which he read the following morning but by then he'd had further harsh reminders of the perfidy of the press and couldn't discount the possibility of prejudiced reportage. He had read, 'Vicar claims he could set the world to rights!' (*Daily*

160

Express), 'Car park angel urges Brake fast at Tiffany's!' (*Sun*), and an editorial in one of the so-called quality papers which spoke of 'the clergyman in the case who couldn't drive a base suspicion from the mind of at least one viewer that he hoped everyone would soon be playing a well-known game called *Simon says*.' That same editorial concluded with a sentence even more disquieting. 'Such men,' it summed up, economically, 'are dangerous.'

The *Chronicle* had followed up its 'exclusive' with a wholly neutral and therefore very welcome report on what Simon had said outside the school – and on the sentiments of the Scunthorpe community at large, with special emphasis on the people among it who actually knew the Heaths – as well as on the reactions of other local, and national, figures in the Church. All the dignitaries spoken to had been predictably guarded; Dr Runcie cheerful but entirely non-committal. There was only one clergyman, reportedly, who had cried "Hallelujah!" to the press and even *his* comment was merely to the effect that he was prepared to believe the thing was true rather than that he actually did...which, of course, was fair enough, thought Simon. As for the politicians – Mrs Thatcher had remarked with good-humoured tolerance that the way to hell was paved with good intentions, while the other party leaders had been less indulgent but equally dismissive. (Referring to the PM's remark David Steel, leader of the Liberal Democrats, had said she wasn't just coining a phrase, she really *did* know, although he admitted doubt as to the accuracy of her adjective.)

Simon didn't notice that the byline wasn't *By Geraldine Coe* until she rang him later in the day. He'd been working on his sermon for next Sunday – it felt almost strange that the ordinary things could still be going on – while his mother and the church secretary had been sharing the job of filtering his calls. Elsie collected Simon from the sitting room and the two women went to make their first pot of coffee of the afternoon.

"How are you?" asked Geraldine.

"Strictly no comment. I think that can be regarded as the standard answer of the moment from henchmen of the Church."

161

"But then you're not the standard model. You're allowed to branch out."

"In that case, I suppose I'm very well, thank you. Albeit a bit tired. How are you?"

"Did you see I've been demoted?"

"In what way?"

"I'm no longer covering the Madison assignment."

"The Heath assignment. But why not?"

"My editors weren't much pleased by that interview I had with you. That non-interview. I can't for one moment think why, can you?"

"I'm really sorry," he said.

"Don't be." She laughed. "I still don't know what happened, though."

"I do. *I* was feeling angry. And *you* countered."

"But I could understand your anger. And, anyway, you got over it. In fact I saw the way you stood before the crucifix and how it steadied you. I think I mentioned that I've always been agnostic? While watching you, however, I suddenly felt something stir." She laughed again. "My friends say it was sex, I claim it was religion. Or, if you like, religion plus sex."

Simon hesitated. She added quickly: "I hope that hasn't shocked you."

"No. No, of course it hasn't."

"As I get older I seem to grow more forthright. Anyway, to return to the other evening, that's when I began to behave badly: just at the point I was thinking, well, if someone like you could so clearly draw such strength from your belief..."

"In a way," he said, "it's reassuring: the very fact that you did begin to behave badly."

"Reassuring? How so?"

"Well, they say that when the Holy Spirit starts to move in somebody, that's when the devil goes to work as well, shaking up all the rotten things inside and sending them straight to the surface."

"It's strange you should say that. I kept telling myself it must have been some demon who had got into me – although I then thought it was purely a figure of speech, nothing more."

"Not a bit strange." There was a pause. "Anyhow, even if nothing else comes out of all this, we may still be able to feel it was worthwhile."

"All this, for one believer?"

"For one finally staunch believer? Every time."

"I think that you must be...pretty close to being a saint."

"That's nice. And how would you define a saint?"

She thought a moment and then said slowly: "As someone who can give other people a vivid glimpse of the kingdom of God."

He was surprised. He had expected her to say, "As a person who leads a very good life," or something of that sort. Recently he had heard one definition given by a Franciscan friar: as someone who, when lying sick in hospital, cares *more* about the recovery of the patient in the next bed than about his own. He told her this and then mentioned that on such a rating he was light-years away from being a saint, especially if there was any question of acute physical suffering involved. "You see, I'm such a baby, I would possibly make the most complaining patient in world history! This modern age may not be perfect but thank God they've at least done away with such things as the stake and the rack and the thumbscrew!"

"You mean, in hospital?"

He laughed but then swiftly changed the subject. "Are you phoning from the office?"

"Yes."

"Then you haven't had the sack?"

"Not yet. No, I rang simply because I wanted to let you know I think I believe in your angel – I know I believe in his message – and I know I believe in you. What's more," she added, "I thought you might find it encouraging to hear that six of the women in this office say they believe implicitly in everything that's happened."

"I do," he said. "Thanks."

163

"And they're merely the ones who'll admit it. Now if in just one office – I agree, of course, it's certainly a large office but to counteract this it's a *Fleet Street* office and where could you find a place reputedly more sceptical than that? – if in just one office there are six people who freely declare that they're with you, not to mention many of their children, mothers and spouses, then only think about the kind of following you've got throughout the country. Simon, it seems to me that you should mobilize those followers, take the nation by storm, not allow a single one of them the time to draw breath..."

He laughed. "Then all I'm left with is a lot of dead followers."

"Oh, please don't make a joke of it. Doesn't that excite you?"

"That's why I make a joke of it. I must confess it's an idea which isn't wholly new to me."

"And you could do it! I *know* you could do it! You'd be like Henry V leading the English towards Agincourt!"

"That strikes the right non-jingoistic note."

"I warn you: I shall start to believe that you and Josh Heath are interchangeable!"

"But you forget, there are still the more orthodox lines of approach, even if they *have* had the ground cut out from under them."

"That sounds defeatist. And slow. It doesn't fit in with my image of you."

"I grant it would be slow. But if we believe that God has everything in hand, will do all he can, other than interfere with free will, to help us propagate his message, then we know he'll take very good care of the timing."

"Yet how do we know he isn't doing precisely that right now, in urging you to throw all caution to the winds?"

"I suppose we don't." His tone sounded grudging. She was not deceived.

"Isn't Christianity a creed for heroes? Not for those timid souls who work only by the book?"

"It depends on the book," he answered, more briskly. "You're a very persuasive young woman. Possibly a dangerous one. You must give me time to think."

"Of course. Though I should add that at the moment I don't object to being considered dangerous. It throws me into rather good company."

"Dangerous company. It sounds like you've read that editorial?"

"Indeed I have. It made me very angry."

"*Simon says...*"

"Pure jealousy."

"I don't know about that. There could be truth in it."

"Well, my next remark isn't going to help. And who cares, in any case?"

"What is your next remark?"

"You've spoken about God having chosen those two Heath boys and what an appropriate choice he made."

"Did *I* say that? How patronizing! Forgive me, Lord."

"But do you know what occurred to me? It might have been *you*, not them, whom God was choosing."

"No. Don't say that!"

"Too late. Already have. Yet if it makes it any easier to listen to I can modify it slightly. You *as well as* them."

"Geraldine, stop! You're appealing to my basest instincts."

"As I've already suggested, that's irrelevant. And, anyway, base instincts were made to overcome. Lucky you! It seems to me you have an interesting array of challenges to rise to." Her tone remained light. "But to revert to more prosaic things. Would you mind if I returned to Scunthorpe for the weekend?"

"No, of course not. Why on earth should I?"

"Because by now it must be fairly obvious I'm throwing myself at your head and I wanted to discover your attitude towards women who do that."

He considered. "Well, in the normal way, I reach for my running shoes. In this case, however, I don't feel any particular urge to do so. Not yet. Is that a satisfactory answer?"

165

"Yes, thank you. Perhaps a *trifle* unenthusiastic but satisfactory. May I just ask: is there anyone else at the moment?"

"No. No one since my wife."

"When did she...?" Geraldine faltered. "How long ago was it she...?"

"More than fourteen years."

"Good God," she said.

"Yes."

32

They'd been sitting over breakfast when the letter came. "But surely we're not just going to give up?" said Ginny.

"What else can we do?"

"Find another house."

"We've looked at over a dozen already. This one was perfect. You know it was."

"I thought you had more fight in you than that. For something which you really believed in."

"Fight? It's Sharma that I'd like to fight! Do you realize it's for *months* he's been stringing us along? First one evasion, then another. And all the time he was waiting to see if he could get a licence to...to bloody well compete with the casino at Brighton or at bloody Monte Carlo." He again threw down the letter, in inexpressible disgust. "Oh, *hell*! The only thing this world cares about is money, money, money. 'I'm all right, Jack. I couldn't give a toss about what happens to the rest of you.'"

Yes, it had seemed the perfect house *and* at a rent that was viable. The others they'd explored had all been in North London but this one was to the south, at Lee Green. Most recently it had been a guest house: with roughly twenty good-sized rooms on three floors, quite pleasant furnishings, unfussy wallpapers: the whole place giving an impression of cleanliness, airiness and light. There had been two staircases, an excellent kitchen, washbasins in every bedroom, enough bathrooms and lavatories,

166

central heating, oatmeal fitted carpet. There had also been a splendid garden with fruit trees, flowerbeds, plenty of lawn and a large vegetable plot. Miss Calthrop from the Old People's Welfare Association had come to invesigate, spent a whole afternoon discussing possibilities, had declared herself delighted. Their bank manager, too, was sufficiently impressed – by them, their workings-out, the property itself – to promise them the figure they had mutually decided on. An officer of the fire brigade had stipulated fire doors and made several recommendations, not all obligatory, he'd stressed, but highly desirable. Although he'd spoken with the air of one who realized cost would inevitably outweigh good intentions he'd soon been told he was mistaken – Simon had a phobia regarding fires, nearly all his nightmares were inspired by it. Accordingly Mr Butcher had agreed to increase the loan and Simon had written a confirmational note to the fellow from the fire brigade.

And it was *not*, they said, going to be just another old people's home, charging iniquitous prices and run with clinical efficiency, like so many they had gone to inspect on the pretext of having an aged relative to settle. This one was going to be a *home*; with lots of interesting and self-expressive things going on in it and plenty of younger people being roped in – for between them they had many friends – to entertain and stimulate and listen. Mrs Madison had offered to help with the housekeeping and the cooking, and an older sister of Ginny's best friend, who even had several years' nursing experience to contribute, was also going to move in. The 'staff' would all live on the top floor, leaving the two lower ones for those who found the stairs more difficult, and it was all going to be great fun, both for themselves and the residents. They wouldn't even think of it as an old people's home. More as a kind of commune.

And now – this.

"Well, we can't pretend we didn't see it coming," said Ginny. "You kept asking why there should be such holdups with the contract."

"I still can't believe it."

"Because you close your eyes to things."

167

"Nonsense."

"You expect everyone to be as straightforward as you. You feel all hurt and bewildered when they don't do what they've said they will. You see something as being self-evidently good and can't understand why anybody should ever choose to get in your way."

"You know, I'm really not in the mood for character analysis. Or are you just getting something off your chest with your usual impeccable timing?"

"Like what, for instance?"

"Perhaps you're trying to say I'm bossy? Demanding? Self-centred? Perhaps you're trying to say I'm immature? Live in cloud-cuckoo-land? Which is it, then? Or does it happen to be the whole lot?"

"Perhaps I'm trying to say you're taking it out on me, what Sharma's done. Perhaps I'm trying to say it seems an easier alternative to do that than think positively about the future. Perhaps I'm trying to say you've got no trust, since it obviously hasn't occurred to you that just maybe there's a purpose to all of this and just maybe we're not getting this house because there's an even better one waiting for us someplace else."

"Oh – *please* – don't give me that shit!"

"I thought I was giving you hope. I thought I was giving you love. It must be you who turn things into shit."

"You make me sick," he said. "Thank you for your sympathy. It's always nice to know you've got a sympathetic wife when times are hard." Flushed, ashamed, disconsolate, he pushed back his chair.

"Where're you going?"

"Out."

"Good riddance! Thank God for a moment's peace, a moment's freedom from self-pity. Go out and have another breakdown!"

It was a Saturday, one of those in every three he got off. Ginny was no longer working; complications had developed to do with her pregnancy. If she didn't rest at home, her doctor had warned, she would have to be taken into hospital. Normally, therefore, during the week she spent the whole morning in bed...unwillingly. But today they had been planning to go down to the house and if the weather was fine – as it was – to eat a picnic lunch in the garden.

At the door he stopped.

"Funnily enough, it isn't just myself I'm thinking of. What about those dozen or so names Miss Calthrop had earmarked for us? What about my mother? What about Jenny? For Mother it was more or less a lifeline, this chance to start anew, have other people to work for, other people to live with and to care about."

She answered: "I notice that you don't spare much thought as to where I'm going to have my baby."

Her elbow had been resting on the table. Now she put her head down on her forearm and began to sob.

He watched her for a moment in exasperation. Exasperation cooled to helplessness. He went to stand behind her and put his hand on her shoulder, wordlessly squeezing.

"No, go away!" she said.

"Ginny, I'm sorry. Of course I hadn't forgotten about you and the baby."

"Go away!"

"God knows why I act like this. Forgive me. He's *my* baby as well, you know."

"No, he isn't."

"What!"

At last she raised her head. "Sometimes I feel he's just mine. Nobody else's. I'm the one who really cares. You only pretend to."

"That isn't true. Darling, it's not true."

"Would you lay down your life for him?"

"Do you mean now or after he's born?"

"Either."

"I don't know."

"There you are, then."

"There you are then, nothing! It would be so easy for me to say yes – of course it would – but to really mean it..."

169

"I'd say yes and there wouldn't be the slightest question of my not meaning it."

"All right, if so. Perhaps you love him more than I do. In any case I won't deprive him of somewhere to be born. We'll find another house."

"What?" she said. "In ten weeks?"

"Yes."

"Rush us in there just the day before, you mean? You may not realize this but a woman likes to get things ready in advance, have a moment or two to *gloat* before the start of her contractions. Not merely the nappies and the bootees and the jackets and the vests. She even likes to have a room to put them in, with clean curtains at the windows and a scrubbed and polished floor and pretty lining paper in the drawers. Me, when I come out of hospital, I'll be lucky to have a Pickford's removal van to bring my baby home to!"

He shook his head, frowningly.

"Pickford's aren't always the cheapest. We'll need to get estimates."

"I will not bring my baby back to *this*!"

Suddenly she caught his hand, which still rested on her shoulder.

"Oh, Simeon, there was just the sweetest little room for Joel in that damned house! Do you remember how we pictured the cot against one wall and a little chest of drawers with a vase of flowers on it, and for some reason it was practically the only room without carpet but the way the sunlight fell across the floor it made us think of richly stained wood, golden and glossy, and of warm-looking Scandinavian rugs? I'm sorry I was bitchy to you. I'm not unsympathetic, I'm truly not. We'll be all right. But whatever happens we must find somewhere for the baby. We must. That's the only thing that truly frightens me."

He did his best to reassure her.

"I wonder if we could appeal in any way?" he asked, finally.

"This house at Lee Green? Haven't we already wasted enough time over it?"

170

"I suppose we have." He added vehemently: "You're right, of course; there has to be some purpose. It couldn't just be so...so *arbitrary*. You couldn't face life feeling it's got no point – the wicked prosper, the unfortunate suffer, and that it's all for nothing, without hope of any rhyme or reason or redress. No balance to it whatsoever. Nothing beyond the present pleasure or the present pain, the odd humanitarian impulse, the meaningless ambition to improve, achieve, create. The urge to make your mark, to leave a memory. Life without point is just so..."

"Pointless?"

"Let's take a walk."

They strolled gently on the Heath, had coffee at the cafeteria in Kenwood House. But though the day was warm and springlike and everyone seemed happy and everything looked good – ducks on sparkling lakes, primroses and crocuses, a few early daffodils – they couldn't wholeheartedly enjoy it, not even in their more frenetic moments. Finally they called on the two estate agents who'd been most helpful to them during the previous September. There was a house they could go to see that very afternoon. They got as far as the first landing and for the second time that day Ginny was suddenly crying.

They ate a Chinese meal out, saw a film at the Playhouse, made love when they got home, but the only thing that could effectively ease their disappointment for more than fifteen minutes at a time was sleep; and even then it happened to be one of those Saturday nights when their landlady downstairs got drunk and had a long series of battles with her black lover, younger than she was, and doors were slamming and murderous threats being screamed until sometime after two when Simon telephoned the police. Not out of any real fear for anybody's safety but out of sheer, bloody-minded, suicidal vindictiveness.

33

On returning to his sermon Simon found it difficult to concentrate; eventually decided that he needed exercise. At first he intended to take a brisk walk to Flixborough, go down through the woods and into the warren, then along the track where pheasants flew up out of the trees and where the mauve-tinted hills against a bright skyline reminded him of the smoky blue landscapes in American westerns. Yet as soon as he reached the foot of his driveway he turned in the opposite direction, barely aware that he was heading for Tiffany's. He might have thought it absurd if he didn't always try to act upon his instincts. Absurd because, after all, the church would surely have been a better place to pray, as would the warren, the wood, the track between the copses. Why did he feel impelled towards the disco?

Indeed, when he got there he found that any of those other settings would have been preferable, almost beyond doubt. He hadn't expected serenity, not precisely, but he certainly hadn't expected to find men and machines so busily at work. Not merely had the place been cleared of debris, they were putting down a whole new surface: the smell of fresh tar lay sweetly on the air.

A short and heavily built man in a grey suit was standing to one side surveying the nearly finished work. He recognized Simon – although they'd never met – and walked cheerfully towards him.

"Afternoon, vicar! This is going to look pretty good, eh? We've been meaning to do it for years. Disgusting, the state it had got itself into!"

There were about twenty bystanders observing the activity. One of them was using his movie camera.

"Howdy do, by the way? My name's Champney. No need to tell me yours!"

A puffy hand was offered for a clammy handshake.

172

"And we're going to tart it up in other ways, too. Great wooden tubs of flowers all round the perimeter, big ones I mean, too heavy for anyone to steal. That'll add a nice bit of colour, make it almost like a park!" He laughed at his own little joke.

Simon, who was anxious only to make his getaway, gave a nod but said nothing.

"You know, thanks to you a lot of people are going to want to take a gander. Or largely thanks to you. Well, let me put it this way. I've never been a one for going to church, I make no bones about that, yet there are plenty who still get comfort out of being religious and I can understand them feeling drawn here. Of course I can. They'll come in their coach parties from all over. May even have to make appointments!"

An intolerable suspicion entered Simon's mind. "Surely you're not thinking of charging an entrance fee?"

"What? Just to take a dekko at an old car park? Oh, if only you could show me how!" The burly fellow slapped himself on the thigh. "No, of course not, vicar, and you wouldn't want it that way, I can tell. But at the same time you've got to admit how they'd be disappointed if they couldn't get a nice cup of tea or a hot dog or a burger to perk them up after a hot and dusty journey, or ice cream and toffee apples for the kids. And ditto if they couldn't get themselves a little souvenir to remind them of their visit? We're going to have a big van here from Saturday and there's going to be T-shirts you can buy (tell you what, vicar, we'll be proud to present you with one, that'll be *our* pleasure) and peak caps and enamel badges – yes and painted mugs and tea towels too – it's all going to be great, a real crowd-pleaser. To be honest, it hadn't occurred to me but if you're not busy on Saturday afternoon around two and could put in an appearance and maybe sign a few autographs...oh, I can tell you, that would go down a proper treat as well. We could have placards printed. We've already got streamers and bunting and raffle tickets."

"I can say one thing. You haven't wasted your time."

His dryness of tone went unperceived. "Well, no one deplores a recession as much as yours truly but at least it does mean you

173

can get things done a bit quicker. Let me put it this way. Every cloud has a silver lining if you're really bent on finding it."

"But don't you need a licence for all this?"

Mr Champney gave a huge, slow-motion wink. He put one stubby forefinger to the side of his nose.

"Well, how about it, then, for Saturday afternoon – eh, vicar? I believe we could promise you a not unacceptable little gift to go in your collection plate. Not to forget about the T-shirt either. You'll be wanting the large size I should think?"

Simon did *not* pray for restraint. "Let me put it this way," he said. "I'll have to consult my diary of course. It will mean my postponing a couple of weddings; that's easy. But I think it may be Saturday I'm down for card tricks and a little bit of magic in front of the public library. They want me to saw a woman in half and make some rabbits disappear – that kind of thing. Then as a climax they'd really like another angel or the Virgin Mary; should I suggest we saw *her* in half? In any case I'll have to keep you posted about the subsequent performance times."

"Remember, though," said Mr Champney, chuckling, "that I'll need to tell the signwriters." Simon didn't even say goodbye. He went striding off towards St Matthew's.

This time he had no instinct; simply felt the church might be the proper place to go.

"*Instinct*!" he exclaimed, bitterly.

Had he thought that he was listening to the voice of God?

St Matthew's was unlocked.

Of course – he'd forgotten what day it was – a meeting of the Mother's Union in the large vestry.

He could imagine the level of excitement showing itself in *there*, the way each member must have been storing for the common pool all her reactions, impressions, speculations. He'd be surprised if attendance this afternoon wasn't setting a St Matthew's record. He decided to go into the Lady Chapel: the part of the church where he was most likely to remain unseen.

Unfortunately, however, before he could reach it Mrs Lorrimer came from the direction of the lavatory and caught sight of him as she teetered through the darkening nave on her way back to the vestry. She put her hand to her heart and gave a cry.

"Oh, Simon! How you startled me!"

"I'm truly sorry. I should have – "

"But thank heaven it's you."

"I really do apologize."

"No, I mean thank heaven you've arrived in the church right now. Thank heaven you're here."

He had to remind himself that an important part of the vicar's role was to be of service, if possible, at any moment he was needed. He turned towards Mrs Lorrimer, with her immaculate blonde hairdo and overpainted face (she was a woman in her late seventies), and waited patiently.

"We have a little crisis on our hands!"

She spread her own scarlet-nailed hands (he had often thought: well, bully for her, at least she does try) in a broad, despairing gesture that one would have believed deliberately comic if Mrs Lorrimer had ever shown much sense of humour. Even allowing for the heels, she stood five-foot-nothing, weighed down by stress and hairdo, and looked every inch a tragedienne.

"Is anybody ill?" he asked quickly.

"It's too bad, it really is."

"Tell me, Mrs Lorrimer."

"We all feel so upset."

"Please tell me what the trouble is." He had half started towards the vestry but thought it better he should go prepared. His forbearance had seldom been so resolute.

"Simon," she said, "I still can't believe this. The unholy cheek of it! The Family Circle has been using the Mother's Union teacups!"

"What!"

She repeated it, with a gratified look at seeing him so aghast; although she had known, of course, he would be.

"Mrs Lorrimer," he said. "Half the world is at war and half the world is starving. There's earthquake, pestilence and flood; man's inhumanity to man is everywhere apparent; we've all been

175

told what we can do about it but no one seems to give a fig. Damn the Mother's Union teacups!"

And he turned abruptly and walked out of the church.

That was on the Thursday afternoon.

34

On the Sunday morning St Matthew's was fuller than it had ever been, whether at Christmas, confirmations, inductions, anything. People were standing four or five deep along the back wall and were also closely crowded into the vestibule, with the doors between this and the church wedged open. The press was there, so was TV. People who hadn't worshipped in years were there, people who had never worshipped, people who didn't live in Scunthorpe. Giving his sermon for once from the pulpit Simon felt a little like an emperor, or a baritone, gazing out across the rippling expanse of the marketplace or else the Coliseum: row upon row of upturned and expectant faces from the chairs and from the pews. Further back a tiptoe impression, of ears and necks and bodies craning out towards him. Hardly any shuffling or clearing of the throat. A long moment of almost incredible stillness before he began.

In fact, he'd thrown away the sermon he had started on the previous Thursday and been working on until Geraldine's call had interrupted him. Afterwards, he had never gone back to it. (In the meantime he had written, partly as a form of escape, three more chapters of his Life of Christ. He thought it was going well; he had even found a title for it – *Firebrand!*) Now, although he had obviously rehearsed all the points he intended to put across in his sermon, he had no notes in front of him, nothing to indicate the proper progression of his argument. He was hoping to rely as far as he could on the inspiration of the Holy Spirit.

He spoke rather slowly and with many pauses.

*

176

In the eleventh century (he said) a woman called Richeldis thought that the mother of Jesus appeared to her, asking her to build in Norfolk a replica of the holy home in Nazareth, so that the replica might become a place of pilgrimage. This miracle was never authenticated: Richeldis was the wife of a squire: in those days you didn't doubt the lady of the manor. But most people have probably heard about Our Lady of Walsingham.

Yet that happened nearly a thousand years ago. Ask anyone to tell you about any more recent manifestation in this country, authenticated or not, and the chances are they're going to be stumped. I know I should be.

I wonder if in years to come, when we've all passed into history, many will have heard about what happened here in Scunthorpe, eleven days ago.

Of course, I wonder if that question isn't purely academic. Because...will there be anyone left at that time either to have heard of it or not to have heard of it? Impossible to speculate about a point so far in the future, the point at which we've all passed into history, or what at any rate we now speak of as history. After all, I'm talking of a period that could be as much as two whole years away. Or even three.

I take it there's nobody here who doesn't know what happened in Scunthorpe eleven days ago? You notice I don't say "what is alleged to have happened" which seems to be a general favourite with the media? I say simply "what happened".

Right, then, we'll assume there's nobody who hasn't been informed of it, informed of it with varying degrees of wit or impartiality or credence. Some people have been amazed and as a consequence inspired. Some have been uncertain. Some have been entertained. But how many do you know who in the past few days have been talking about that and about nothing else?

Or put it differently. How many do you know who've simply carried on in the same old way with the same old preoccupations: the state of their health, their finances, the weather, the government, sex, diets, football, motorbikes, a new car? The boredom of work, the boredom of leisure. Getting the front room decorated. Anything worth watching on the box?

177

Or – again. How many do you know who in the past few days have actually gone down on their knees and prayed about this thing; or stood at the kitchen sink with their hands deep in soapsuds and prayed about it; or sat on the lavatory and prayed about it; prayed to be shown where the dividing line comes between faith and gullibility?

Come to that, how many of you yourselves have actually asked for guidance, deeply and honestly, with more than just the passing, wistful, intermittent gesture? Have *you*, I wonder? Or *you* – or *you* – or *you*? Is it worth as much as twenty minutes a day, this thing that happened here in Scunthorpe? This miracle? I wonder what proportion of us could say with a clear conscience that it was?

Is it worth as much as ten?

What *is* religious faith? It's the acceptance of a truth which can't be proved by the process of logical thought. We accept it because we have the authority of the Church and of the Scriptures, because we have the experience of God within ourselves and within each other. But there's obviously a world of difference between that and gullibility.

We're gullible, of course, if we're easily deceived or cheated. And no one can deny that there's plenty of that around, the intention to deceive or cheat. We find it in politics, we find it in the press, we find it in the Church. Inevitably, it comes down to the individual: the politician, the journalist, the vicar. So this is the question which you now have to ask yourselves: do you think the present vicar is out to deceive and cheat you? Or do you think, a shade more charitably, he's just a dope, a credulous old duffer who, himself, could be conned into almost anything? And if you do think that – you who belong to St Matthew's – well, how long have you thought it?

Because, *naturally*, there's always the chance I've been bamboozled. And, *naturally*, there's always the chance I'm wanting to bamboozle you. Why? Because maybe I hope to become famous, cause a stir, find myself in a position of some power? You can't ignore it. I could have all the wrong reasons for standing here and saying all the things I'm saying. Of course

178

I could. I could have as little interest in my church and in my parish, not to mention my country or anything beyond it, as...well, as I feel, for instance, that our current MP has in his current constituency. Merely a stepping stone to something better: that's how I may regard St Matthew's and Crosby and all of you now present. And remember, too, you shouldn't automatically trust a man simply because he warns you he may not be trustworthy. You see, you just don't know. You can't be sure. Yes, *naturally*, plausible neurotics can be found in the Church, the same as in any other walk of life.

But...and this is a very big *but*. What exactly is it I'm asking of you? Because whatever you finally decide in this matter it's essential you should be quite clear as to that.

Am I asking you to believe in some sort of celestial messenger sent to Scunthorpe eleven days ago by God? Beamed down, if you will, like Captain Kirk or Mr Spock or Scottie?

No.

Am I asking you to believe that on that day in the car park behind Tiffany's – by means of *any* sort of supernatural agency, benevolent or otherwise – a statement was made to two boys who live in this town?

No.

Am I asking you to believe they didn't invent the whole message themselves, perhaps taking a long time over it and getting a lot of pleasure out of thinking how thoroughly we might all be turned into suckers?

No.

It isn't strictly necessary you should believe any of these things.

Desirable, yes. But not necessary.

Am I asking you to believe the content of that message is good, however it's been come by, and to act as though you believed in it?

Yes.

Yes, I am. Most certainly I am. Most emphatically I am.

For even though you consider the trappings as false as Father Christmas I should still have thought your best course was to

179

play it safe. A gamble. How much do I stand to lose if I act in faith and the angel never happened? How much do I stand to lose if I take no notice and the angel really did happen? How much do I stand to gain, in either eventuality?

The only question not to ask yourself is, what can *I* do about it? Not, I mean, if you ask it in a purely negative way, in that commonly held spirit of helplessness and defeat.

The age-old query, of course. The one, perhaps, that more effectively blocks the path of Good, and stands there signalling the roadway clear for Evil, than any other prevarication on earth. What can *I* do?

Yes, the world is full of apathy. Whether or not it was an angel who said this doesn't alter the truth of it.

The world is also full of kindness. Equally true. All of us in here this morning are probably quite kind. We do good turns for our neighbours. We chat pleasantly to shop assistants. We send off small amounts to charity; we tut-tut at brutality; we're well-intentioned, friendly, *nice*.

But how far does this niceness reach? What sort of effect do we really have on the world, each of us? Who changes matters more: one terrorist, say, or fifty of our kind? And if the answer isn't us, why isn't it?

Our apathy, would you say? Our reluctance to make any kind of *real* personal sacrifice?

To what do we ascribe it, then, this indifference, this basic lack of interest? To laziness? To a dearth of imagination or of courage? To complacency and callousness? To that conviction of helplessness we mentioned just a moment ago? It doesn't matter. What it all boils down to is pretty much the same thing. And that thing *isn't* love – which, whether an angel spoke of it or not, is positive and outward-looking and dynamic and contagious, strides out in strength and beats down devils. Do you believe that? Yes, of course you do. But do you intend to do anything about it?

Do you intend to translate that belief into practical terms, into action and sound, into spectacle and fury? (Yes, *fury*! Fury that this world has been allowed to go so wrong. Fury that we have

180

taken something basically so beautiful, so full of limitless potential, and turned it into something so warped, so ugly and so...*hellish*.) Do you intend to shoulder your responsibility?

And if you don't, if you intend just to leave it to someone else (after all, who'll notice?), how *dare* you call yourself a Christian? Christianity has no room for spongers and stowaways and people who opt out.

Right, then.

What must we do about it? Is it enough merely to sit here in Scunthorpe and spout platitudes at one another? No, obviously it's not. But how in God's name can we make ourselves heard? How in God's name can we influence the thinking of others in the way we believe it ought to be influenced? How can we make those others see just how desperately we *care*? We can't, we simply can't, not unless in the first place we come into contact with them; with as many of them as possible. And how do we accomplish that? There's only one way I can think of – other, of course, than through the media. Only one way! We rise up and march.

We rise up...and we march!

Quite literally, I mean.

We march to London: from Scunthorpe to London, collecting people as we go, collecting signatures, carrying banners, singing battle hymns, chanting slogans, stopping at every town and village for recruitment, a journey such as Christ sent his apostles out on, a journey which Christ *is* sending his apostles out on, over days, over weeks – the period is irrelevant – leaving our jobs, begging our food, throwing ourselves on people's hospitality, expecting their kindness, expecting all that's best in them, showing that one thing is important to us above all others, making our opinions known...known and accepted and *acted in accordance with*. This is the one solution. Take it or leave it – I hope to heaven that you'll take it; or are you indeed one of those parasitic types we've just been speaking of, sheltering among vast numbers? Naturally there are going to be those who, for completely valid reasons, won't be able to come: young children, the infirm, people who look after young children or the infirm,

181

people whose absence from their place of work would genuinely put at risk the safety of the community; in the last resort it's a matter for your own conscience. But as for the rest, those of us who have no genuine excuse to hold us back and who are neither wicked nor simply weak (and I can see that by the time we get to Downing Street there are going to be *millions* of us, many, many millions), as for us, we meet here, outside St Matthew's, at nine o'clock on Tuesday morning. Bring sensible footwear, plenty of changes of socks et cetera, adequate protection against the weather, plasters for blisters, soap, towels, toothbrushes, toilet paper, TCP, as many provisions as you can comfortably carry in a knapsack, as much money as you can afford (but not to worry if you can't bring either money or any of those other things) and a lot of positive thinking and love and prayer and reliance. Tuesday morning. We shall hope to move off at a quarter-past-nine. In the name of the Father, the Son and the Holy Spirit. Amen.

*

Having spoken these last words and crossed himself Simon descended the pulpit stairs. He wiped his forehead and walked back to his position before the altar and between two servers in a silence that still wasn't eased by any whispering or coughing or shifting of limbs. Eventually, though, the coughing did break out, along with those other customary signs of relaxation, and then the congregation started to straggle to its feet, that part of it which had been seated. At first the Creed sounded ragged and automatic but gradually gained in cohesion as well as in volume. The atmosphere returned more to normal, allowing for the size of the congregation and its largely foreign content. During the Peace, however, a partial exodus occurred. When Simon again returned to his place he laughed and said to those remaining, "It's at times like this you find out who your friends are!" and then, with the doors now closed upon the empty vestibule and the heavy curtain pulled across, he continued with what little was left of the service.

182

35

In May they returned to Eastbourne. Ginny hadn't been well and Simon thought that sea air and a change of scenery might help. It was an impromptu decision, made at breakfast, because the Friday was warm and the sunshine was expected to last. But they went only for the weekend, going down in the evening, since of course he had to be back at his job on Monday – and on Mondays, too, Ginny had a regular checkup at the hospital.

They chose Eastbourne mainly because they knew the hotel was comfortable and because Miss Bryanston had promised a small discount in the event of their return.

They also chose it out of sentiment.

"But I hope we're not being foolish," said Ginny, on the train. "Granny went back to Venice after fifty years and claims it was the greatest mistake of her life."

"Yet that's completely different."

"I know it is."

"I think you're round the twist."

"Simeon, don't say that. I'm half scared it could be true!"

She spoke humorously yet with a certain underlying seriousness. He knew what she was thinking of: her morbid fears that she was either going to lose the baby or else give birth to one whose brain was damaged – "I've had to take so many drugs!" ("But, Ginny," he would say, "it must be the same for nearly all expectant mothers, even if their pregnancy is easy. Most of them must think they're heading for the loonybin!" In this context he didn't ever speak of expectant fathers, feeling it would hardly help to mention they were sometimes subject to the same fears. "You're such a tower of strength!" she kept on telling him.) But now he didn't comment on her last remark. There was nothing new he could advance.

183

"Well, Venice is still a place I'd very much like to see," he said. *"Despite* Granny. We'll have an assignation there one of these days if ever we get tired of coming back to Eastbourne."

"Oh, did I tell you? I promised we'd stay in Surrey for a week of your fortnight off."

"That won't be any hardship." Ginny's grandmother lived with two of her sisters in a cottage fronting the village green, where, the previous September, as a last-minute replacement on account of illness, Simon had scored seventy-six runs for the local cricket club. While waiting to go in he'd lounged with Ginny on the dry grass beside the old ladies' deckchairs, and all the hackneyed, idealized ingredients – like the click of the knitting needles, the chock of the cricket ball, the players in their white flannels, even the church spire rising obligingly above the trees – all those Miniver-type props redolent of the spirit and tradition that had once made Britain great: *those* plus the thought, never a long way from his mind, of all the pleasures which that night could be relied upon to bring, suddenly made him say, "I think I've never been so happy! Surely this is how the world was meant to be!" Certainly the relationship which he and Ginny enjoyed with that trio of spry octogenarians contrasted hugely with the one which they did not enjoy with Ginny's parents. Although Ginny and her mother had managed to make up and were again on friendly and affectionate terms – their closeness expressed mainly in phone calls and during occasional, clandestine meetings – Ginny's father was far less conciliatory. Simon had met him only once. Despite Mrs Plummer's efforts the meeting had not been a success.

As the train reached the coast and they caught their first smell of the sea they felt again all the excitement of childhood. Ginny cried out, "Oh, darling, let's go back there!"

"Where? To London?"

"No, you lunk. To the spot where you first held my hand and kissed me." She stopped. "But I'd forgotten: I suppose I'm not in a condition to go clambering over Beachy Head. Besides..." There was a slyness in her look. "Perhaps it would be a mistake. Like going back to Venice."

184

"A magic now beyond recapture?"

"Well, what do *you* think?"

"I think you're growing tired of me." He put the back of his hand up to his forehead; adopted an air of tragedy that, many years later, would have made him the perfect soulmate for Mrs Lorrimer. "Love for sale!" he announced, looking around the compartment for a potential purchaser.

"Stop it!" she rebuked him softly, with a smile. "Making an exhibition of yourself."

He hung his head. "*Simon the Show-Off Strikes Again*! I'm sorry. I do keep trying to reform."

"Oh, *that*? The unending Madison quest for self-improvement! But can a leopard change its spots?"

"Or can a lover give up sex?"

"You see! You can't stop! And I'm not sure at the moment I think it's anything so very much to brag about. I may feel different in another month."

He was immediately contrite, honestly contrite, as if her scolding had been wholly in earnest, instead of only partly so.

The next day was his birthday. Ginny had brought his present with her: the book of Arthurian legend he'd become so engrossed by in a Hampstead bookshop that he'd at once gone to order it from the public library, for he had always found fascinating the idea that Arthur would come riding back from Avalon in Britain's hour of need. ("Mind you, I'd have thought that thirty years ago things were getting pretty desperate! Or do you suppose Mr Churchill could have been one of his reincarnations?") As a child, his three greatest heroes had been Galahad and Jason and Robin Hood. During the afternoon, while Ginny rested in a deckchair in the garden of *Sea View*, Simon lay in trunks beside her and read thirty pages of his book; then he dozed and Sir Galahad cantered through a Sherwood Forest where sunlight slanted through the trees and where in a dappled glade he found the Holy Grail being guarded by a dragon. The dragon belched out smoke and fire and Simon's dominant image upon wakening was of the undimmed chalice gleaming through

185

the black, vermilion shroud. Sir Galahad had shrunk from the flames as Simon himself would have shrunk from them.

Later they had dinner at the type of restaurant befitting a birthday celebration. Ginny said, "I do hope your cousin wasn't at all put out – your cousin seventeen times removed – but then of course it's not as though she were actually the cook, is it?"

Simon accorded this his full consideration.

"I imagine Mr Butcher will be *quite* put out and it isn't as though he were actually the cook, either."

"My God! Are you *wanting* to bring back my indigestion?"

The state of their finances was certainly no topic for a gourmet meal. They hadn't found a house to match the one in Lee Green and about a month before had finally decided to postpone the whole project and to take a furnished flat in Muswell Hill, where they had been lucky enough to discover a landlady sympathetic to babies. So for the time being Simon continued unambitiously in menswear – unambitiously, though not without some pleasure. Already there were customers who returned to him regularly because he gave, as one ex-colonel put it, "the sort of service, young feller, that these days one very seldom comes across!" (Simon laughed at this but still he treasured it.)

"It's been such a nice day," said Ginny, as they lingered over coffee and liqueur. "Although I'm sorry for your sake that it couldn't have been a little more exciting."

"It's been perfect."

"No, not for you, not as exciting as your first married-life birthday ought to have been. Not as exciting as mine was. But in other years your timing may be better."

"You're very *young*," he told her. "All this emphasis on excitement! Of course, it may not have been a day to compete with that other, that idyllic one, whose magic now lies way beyond recall. I realize that."

"Not way beyond recall. Earlier you said recapture. I can remember very well for instance you ate nearly all the picnic and I thought oh dear he's not as much in love as I am."

"At that point you didn't know I was in love at all."

"I hoped."

"I know we talked about the moon landing."

"And I said you ought to be a vicar."

"You *didn't*? Why on earth should you have said anything so extraordinary?"

"I can't remember. But it was less than a year ago. I think you must have blocked it out."

"You're dreaming."

"No. I know I said it and that you didn't like it. You were cross."

"Nonsense. When have you ever seen me cross?"

"I still think you'd make a good one."

"What, because Colonel Blimp said to me he liked the service I gave? And even *he* might have thought it preferable a vicar should believe."

She stared at him.

"Ginny, what's the matter?"

"But you do believe!"

"I mean, wholeheartedly."

She continued to gaze at him. "Darling, I think I ought to warn you. You might be about to bring on the baby."

"No, I mightn't. When did *you* last set foot inside a church?"

"But that's irrelevant."

"Why is it? You're as indeterminate as I am."

"Yet you always gave me the impression...I always had the distinct impression... Why, I remember how you took my period pain away...and your Aunt Madge's migraine. And I remember... " She paused.

"Oh, okay. I admit. Intermittently I may try to convince myself, and anybody else around, that things aren't all haphazard. But what belief I have is really so feeble that it strikes me as shameful and debasing even to call it that. What do I ever do about it? Tell me."

"What do you have to do about it? You lead a good life. You try to help people. Isn't that enough?"

"No. Anyone with a true conviction wouldn't be content to coast along like me."

187

She smiled. "Of course! I should have understood. With you, it's all or nothing. Always. You can't exist in the centre. You thrive upon extremes."

"Let's leave this boring subject."

"All right. But first let me say that *I* believe. I couldn't bear to feel my life had been quite pointless."

"Oh, my love! You'd never have to. Pointless? Why, if there'd been poison in your coffee and you were struck down right this very instant..."

"Yes?"

"Do you think they'd overlook the bill?"

She gave him a look of strained indulgence.

"I'm sorry. No, what I was going to say was that even if you were struck down right this very instant you'd still have left the world a fine example."

"Of what?"

"Of how to influence your man."

"Yes. Exactly what I wanted! And anyway, what would he do, my man?"

"Commit suicide."

"Apart from that?"

"Well, I don't know. Something wonderful."

"All right, I'd haunt you every minute, be with you night and day, just to make sure you did. I wouldn't leave you for a second. I'd clank my chains at you and demand some magnificent memorial, some golden piece of evidence. To demonstrate that, in the end, my life *hadn't* been pointless."

"What a dopy girl you are! And how strenuous you make it sound."

"For myself as much as you, please note!"

"You know what? I'm not certain that in the long run it wouldn't be easier if I simply paid the bill."

"Oh, Simeon! Where's your spirit of adventure?"

36

On the Tuesday morning it was raining. Mrs Madison, after a night in which she'd hardly slept, drove Simon to the church.

"Darling," she'd said at breakfast, "I wish I wasn't such a coward. But you know me: if I walk to the end of the road I feel I've been on a good hike. After the first half-hour you'd all have to take turns to carry me." She'd produced a piece of paper from her pocket. On one side it said, 'Infirm' and, further down, 'Remarkably infirm'. On the other side: 'And desperately ashamed'. He saw the tears begin to glaze her eyes and wordlessly took her hand. He had known she wouldn't come.

She went and fetched more sugar, glad of the pretext this gave for turning her back a moment.

"But, no, you shouldn't treat me gently. I'm not a special case, you know, because I happen to be your mother. I *am* all those ghastly things you said."

"What ghastly things?"

"Apathetic, lazy, selfish, parasitic. How dare I call myself a Christian?" Having filled the sugar bowl she moved to the refrigerator and opened it to show several large packets wrapped in greaseproof paper. "However, I do make lovely sandwiches."

He smiled. "Blessed are the sandwich-makers. For their children shall be filled. But I hope I'm not being especially gentle with you, even though of course you *are* a special case. Because I don't want to be *un*gentle with anyone."

She was pouring their coffee. "This isn't an excuse," she said, "because I know I'm all the other things, but – *how dare I call myself a Christian*? Quite honestly, I never have. Not in my heart of hearts. Naturally, when your son becomes a vicar, you have a certain front to keep up. You can't go round telling people, 'Oh, gracious, you didn't ever imagine that he caught it from *me*?'"

"I hope you're not expecting this to be a revelation."

189

"No. But I've never actually mentioned it. I thought it might seem like letting the side down."

He said: "Without you there'd have been no side to let down."

"Fiddlesticks!"

"And I don't know why you should think that because *I'd* decided to give my life to God people would somehow expect the same of you. I can assure you I never did." He paused. "However, like it or not, I very much believe you *are* a religious woman. Which doesn't mean – no, not at all – that you've had to accept Christ as your saviour. There are many roads round the mountain. "

She answered cautiously.

"Well, I'm not saying that after spending nearly a quarter of my life with a theological student, and a curate, and a vicar, a little of it mayn't have rubbed off. But Simon. It's really such a relief to be able to talk like this. And while we're at it there's something else I've never quite been able to ask. What *made* you decide to give your life to God like that? Was it Ginny?"

"Yes." The word was delayed; slightly clipped.

"And all along you've believed it was your own fault, haven't you? Oh, you more than foolish child! But you've never let me comfort you."

"Joel would now have been fourteen. Do you realize that?" The child, stillborn, had been a boy.

"Of course I do. There's scarcely a day when I don't think about them both. Him and Ginny."

"In any case," he said, "the guilt I felt, it really doesn't matter whether it was rational or not. Perhaps I should have gone to a psychiatrist. Right now I'm glad I didn't."

His mother put another slice into the toaster.

"If that's for me I couldn't eat it." This morning she had made him a cooked breakfast; insisted he had three eggs, three tomatoes, three rashers of bacon – mercifully, only one piece of fried bread.

"Frank Cooper's Oxford Marmalade," she said. "I got it specially."

"Then Frank Cooper must possess his soul in patience."

190

"But for *how* long? That's the question."

"God knows."

"Oh dear." She stared for an instant towards the window. "And why does it have to be raining? God may know all right but sometimes, it seems to me, God doesn't go out of his way to make things any easier."

"Hey!"

"How do *you* feel about it all?"

"You mean...now that the big day has actually arrived? I feel...well, okay."

"Nervous?"

"Yes. Certainly nervous. *Very* nervous. It would be a little strange if I didn't."

"But you truly did manage to sleep? That wasn't a kind story?"

"No, I truly did manage to sleep. And when I didn't I was resting."

"Praying?"

"If that's what you want to call it. Thinking. Remembering. Feeling grateful."

"Me, I just had a bad night."

"Yes, I know. I'm sorry."

"You didn't mind my talking to you about Ginny?"

"No."

"I only wanted to say..." She looked down at the table.

"What?"

"Well, that while you're walking to London, whatever the problems, however great the discouragement – "

"You don't need to finish. I know that. Wherever I happen to be. Whatever I happen to be doing. I know that."

She smiled, waveringly. "More of it must have rubbed off than I'd thought! Who would have guessed it: I'm a religious woman!"

He laughed – also a little waveringly. Bit his lip. Got up from the table.

She said more practically, "Have you remembered to pack plenty of these things?"

191

"Mother, I'm travelling down to London, not into the wilderness. In the wilderness, I grant, there aren't too many corner shops. On the road to London you can certainly buy tissues."

"Darling," she said, with a sudden sharp and urgent note of warning. "Please. Please don't hold out too much hope."

"What? Of corner shops, or tissues?"

"Of there being lots of people waiting at the church."

"My love, I'm not naive. My words from the pulpit may have made me seem so, but – in this rain? *Especially* in this rain, I ought to say. Twenty? Even if there are only twelve, that wouldn't be too bad. In fact, tolerably auspicious." He thought it must have helped prepare him that having sent off a score of letters to his and Ginny's friends he hadn't received one reply that had basically done more than wish *him* luck and his whole *fantastic* enterprise success. (Or *mind-blowing* or *worthy* or *admirable*, whatever.) "Anyway, give me a few minutes and we'll go to find out," he smiled. "Thank you for the breakfast. And once again – thank you for the money."

The previous afternoon she had withdrawn five hundred pounds. He had accepted it, gratefully.

Now he went to the lavatory, cleaned his teeth and put some final items into his haversack – including the sandwiches and a large vacuum flask which made the straps almost impossible to fasten. And through all of this he prayed, as he did, too, during their brief car journey. It was all going to be all right. Even the fact of his mother not coming was providential: with Alison and Dulcie gone she'd be able to keep a watchful eye both on Sharon Turner and on others. Not so long ago he'd wondered if he could really leave these people; but now things had changed and although of course he recognized an element of rationalization it was in fact perfectly true that nobody was indispensable. While he was absent his duties would be covered by the vicar and the curate of St Lawrence's, also by the vicar of All Saints. These were willing, sympathetic men, and he was pleased it hadn't been necessary to foist additional problems onto the rural dean.

192

But praise the Lord: it was still as well his mother would be staying.

The first people he saw when he got out of the car were Alison and Dulcie. They stood beneath the same umbrella.

"Simon," said Alison, without preamble. "We've just heard something unfortunate. About Tony."

"What about Tony?"

"Well, as it was raining he went to pick up the Heaths. Skidded on the way back. All that's happened is that he and Bill have mild concussion plus a few cuts and bruises: they hit a lamppost. Dawn and Mick were sitting in the back and luckily weren't hurt – just a little shaken up."

"Are Tony and Bill at the hospital?"

"The ambulance took them all. Dawn's husband went as well."

"Was *he* in the car?"

"No. But I don't know why not. There'd have been room."

"What about April?"

It was Dulcie who answered this.

"Jack's run her up to the hospital. Her and the babies."

"Well, at least then it could have been worse." He looked about him, dully. "Not what you'd call a *massive* turnout." Apart from the two women in front of him and his mother at his side there were four. "Still, it isn't yet nine."

"Simon," said Dulcie. "Jack and me aren't coming."

"What?"

"I only turned up so that I could let you know. We talked and we talked about it – and – well, you see, it's like this, sort of..." She glanced at Alison for assistance.

"I'm afraid I'm not, either," said Alison.

His eyes moved slowly from one to the other. With his lips, however, he said nothing.

"Simon, don't look at us like that. At least we've had the guts to come and tell you. On Sunday you made it sound so simple. It isn't simple. We've got homes and we've got families. We've got jobs. And once you lose a job these days – "

"Jobs," said Simon.

193

"Yes. You don't know what it means – "

Again he interrupted her. "Also, it's raining."

"Darling," said Mrs Madison, reaching out to touch his arm and then holding onto it lightly. "Not ungentle – you remember?"

"Yes, and also it's raining," went on Alison, better able to cope with aggression than with pathos. "Simon, we all think the world of you, we really do, you're the best thing that ever happened to this parish. And we'd like to be fully behind you, every one of us, but *this*, Simon, dear" – she briefly laid a hand on the other sleeve of his oilskin – "this really isn't the way to do it. It's a gallant gesture, it's a marvellous gesture, it shows how very, *very* much you care. But it's just quixotic, it won't accomplish anything, and as Robert says..."

"Oh, yes? And what does Robert say?"

"He says it's better to leave it to the proper ecclesiastical channels – quietly, correctly, without the rabble-raising element – to do that and...and to put all one's trust into the good sense of the Church...and into...well, obviously, he says, the power of prayer."

"Oh, has Robert suddenly become a believer, then? Great! But supposing you tell him that as a matter of fact I *have* been putting all my trust into the power of prayer? And at the same time you could try asking if he's acquainted with that little phrase about a person's stepping out in faith...? Excuse me, though, I'd like a quick word with the others."

Easily pulling free of his mother's restraining grip and leaving the three women standing at the kerbside he hurried to the church porch. He'd been surprised to see that Paula was one of those hanging back out of the rain – and at first even she had difficulty about meeting his gaze.

She appeared more breathless than ever. The problem was: she had an arthritic mother who said she couldn't cope on her own and that, no, she didn't want to have Cousin Rosie in the house, much less any stranger. Paula knew that – if she had to – her mother could have managed perfectly well.

194

"What do you say, Simon? If you tell me it's my duty to come along, support *you*, that's all I need to hear. I would come with you anywhere; yes, to the ends of the earth if you'd let me. I'd even..." But then she recollected herself and he suddenly saw she was Pitiful, not Pious, this podgy woman with the porous, over-pancaked complexion that looked about to crack up – crumble in the wet weather – and he half lifted a hand towards her in a vague gesture of comfort.

He said, "Paula, I told you from the pulpit that anyone who had to take care of the elderly or the sick was automatically exempt." But he wasn't sure whether it was gratitude or disappointment he noticed in her eyes or whether it was rainwater or tears he witnessed on her cheeks.

"What time do you make it, Paula?"

He'd long since realized that the three others in the porch were made up of a photographer and two journalists. It struck him with faint irony that there weren't any TV cameras or radio microphones. The media had shrunk a bit since Sunday.

"It's after nine," she said. "It's really quite surprising that your *Saints Alive* group isn't out in force."

"I imagine you've heard about Tony?"

"Yes. Poor Simon. You mustn't take it as a sign."

"I don't."

"Myself, I just don't see how people could have stayed away. It was the best sermon I've ever heard. I told you that, didn't I? And afterwards over coffee everyone was talking about it. Your mother said she felt like clapping at the end. And I agreed with her. How *is* Mrs Madison this morning?" Paula's voice had grown a bit unsteady.

"She's standing over there. I suggest you go and ask her."

"I think she's so courageous." She was taking a thickly folded wad of papers out of her handbag. "I took the liberty of preparing a few hymn sheets, Simon. I only did about three hundred. I thought that everyone could share them."

He transferred them to an inside pocket of his waterproof. "Thank you, Paula."

195

She took out something else, which was wrapped in gold paper and tied with red ribbon. "Simon, I hope you won't be offended: I bought you six bars of fruit-and-nut. The large ones. I believe they ought to be sustaining and in none of the shops – not even Binn's – could I find any Kendal Mintcake, like I've read all the mountaineers take on their expeditions."

Simon – sincerely appreciative of such thoughtfulness and generosity, albeit a little embarrassed – caught a whiff of Bluebell as he accepted the heavy gift. The smile he summoned up felt as though that, too, were made of plaster and starting to crack beneath the pressure of the infiltrating damp.

"And you're really determined to go ahead with it?" she asked. "Just you and your dear mother?"

"My mother isn't coming, Paula. I'm sorry – I think these men are waiting to speak to me."

"Well, yes, sir, if we *could* trouble you with one or two more questions...?" Both the reporters were local: one from the *Telegraph*, the other from the *Star*.

While he was answering them as civilly as he felt able and while the photographer was energetically lining up a shot of Paula and his mother and Alison and Dulcie, another journalist, this time a woman, and this time, he knew, from one of the national dailies – well, formerly so at any rate – stepped out of a taxi that had just pulled up; and, having settled with the driver, lifted her brand new knapsack off the back seat.

*

Yes. *Formerly so at any rate.* Geraldine had both handed in her notice to the *Chronicle* (and it wasn't *everybody* who could resign upon a Sunday afternoon!) and then had to say she didn't intend to work it out, either. Her notice.

Geoff had told her not to be a bloody fool. This was hardly unexpected. She had held the receiver some distance from her ear and even at one point put it in her lap (she was sitting on the hotel bed) and smiled at it benignly.

If she wanted to join in this demonstration he had said...well, that was entirely all right; just to phone in her copy in the usual way; she was back on the assignment. He had apparently found it incomprehensible that she should wish to take part in the march completely free of professional commitment.

And then she had rung up Alex, not caring much whether his wife answered the telephone or not. He also had called her every kind of fool, not simply because she had given up a good job ("Don't you realize yet that there are four million people out of work?"), not simply because she intended to "roam the country like some half-witted gipsy," but because she had told him she was pulling the plug on their affair, there was nothing to discuss, neither owed the other anything, she didn't want to meet him again. Alex was as incredulous as Geoff – more so. "Then are you in love with this preacher boy, this mountebank? It sounds as though he's got you just where he wants you, twisted around his no doubt highly inadequate little cock?"

"Yes to the first – though I don't quite recognize your description. No to the second – though as you're speaking from experience you clearly think yourself the better judge."

"Listen, I can't talk now," he'd told her, urgently. "Come back to London, we'll thresh this thing out properly, you've had these crazy whims before. Perhaps they're even, I shouldn't say this, in some way a part of your appeal." Why did this remind her of *the endearing charm of Fleet Street*? "And as to our never seeing each other again – not merely absurd but patently out of the question: what about my bathrobe, my dinner suit, my electric razor?"

She suddenly remembered how she had spoken about this man to Josh Heath.

"Oh, I'll take them to a charity shop," she reassured him. "Don't worry. Hard though it is to imagine, there could even be somebody somewhere who may shortly bless your name. God moves in a mysterious way..." (She thought Dawn would be pleased with her.)

197

"Always the joker!" he said. "Besides. I've been going a little more deeply into this question of divorce and I really think that now – "

"Goodbye, Alex," she said and put down the receiver, uncharitably enjoying the idea of leaving him a little more deeply into this question of divorce. (In fact, it *had* been his wife who had answered the telephone. This was the first time Geraldine had spoken to her. Only a few words, obviously, but actually she'd sounded nice.) Then she began to remember how much she'd loved him at the start and of how kind he had often been. She began to think of some of the silly things they'd enjoyed doing together and of how he had sometimes reduced her to a positive ache of laughter; of how, too, he had occasionally made her body lift to his in a passion of ecstasy which – although she could now recall it only intellectually – she knew at the time had seemed utterly unsurpassable...and she abruptly regretted the affair should have had to end so bitterly. She felt a sense of loss along with liberation.

The sense of loss extended itself. She had spent almost ten years working on the *Chronicle* and as she'd said to Josh they had been pleasant years. She owed a lot both to Geoff and to several others on the staff including Graeme. She would write to Geoff, she decided – at the first opportunity call in, as well, and further make her peace.

Peace... She stretched out on the bed, luxuriously, and told herself she didn't for one moment regret the fact of having terminated those ten years: only the fact that, perhaps, she had handled the phone call too lightly. Both phone calls, possibly. Never mind. That slightly unstable but basically underlying awareness of happiness was returning to her. Earlier, during Simon's sermon and for at least twenty minutes afterwards, it had felt overwhelming. Intoxicating. She could have hugged herself with the enormity of it.

Yet then she'd had an encounter in the church hall and that elation had faded. To be truthful, it must have been fading a little beforehand (and, of course, she knew why), otherwise she

198

couldn't have conducted herself in the way she had. Return of the demon, possibly?

She had said a short prayer, however, and – beginner's luck? – things had righted themselves: Mrs Madison had come over to invite her to the vicarage that evening for a light supper; and clearly she wouldn't have done this without consulting her son.

Euphoria returned.

But... *Always the joker*? No, that wasn't true, except maybe in one respect. The fifty-third card... The outsider... Used only in certain games; and often employed as a substitute.

Too late, she thought of what might have been an appropriate exit line. "This joker," she could have snapped, "is wild!"

But from now on, she vowed, she was going to be one of the pack. More than that. One of the court cards.

She smiled. Simon would say, of course, that every card in the pack was of equal value. (She couldn't imagine Josh Heath ever saying such a thing!) But she wasn't thinking of celestial parity. She wanted to be (for once) the highest in value. Or at any rate, remembering that photograph on his desk, she wanted to be *currently* the highest.

With the chance and the challenge, she knew, of eventually taking over!

She dreamt a little...then after some half-hour reached out lazily for one of the books on her bedside table. Her hand first encountered the Gideon bible which she'd put there on the Friday evening out of a vague sense of obligation but so far done nothing about. She supposed that really...*really*...

Having acknowledged this much, however, she instead picked up the paperback of *Jules and Jim* which had come as a free gift with a copy of *Options* and which she found that she was very much enjoying.

*

She said: "Has everybody gone? Am I really that late?"

"No, you're not really that late. And it isn't that everybody's gone; it's more that nobody's arrived. It seems as if the two of us are on our own."

"But...? But, Simon...?" She looked at the group of women sheltering from the rain. Out of the four of them the only one she knew was Mrs Madison.

"They're here to see us off," said Simon.

"Then where's Dawn? And William and Michael? Why, I'd have bet a thousand pounds..."

He told her about the accident.

"*You* don't want to back out, do you?" he asked.

"No!"

She added a little less explosively: "Besides. I wouldn't dare."

"Good." She could tell that he was doing his best to be upbeat. "So how many banners do you reckon you can carry?"

In fact, she and Tony and Mrs Madison had spent most of the previous day preparing them.

"Fully spread?" she checked.

"Well, naturally. What on earth would be the use if people couldn't read them?"

"Then I'm sorry," she answered. "I know this must sound pretty feeble. No more than half a dozen."

37

Josh awoke on that Tuesday morning having spent like Mrs Madison and many others a further sleepless night. He'd been having a lot of them lately. Dawn had said he should go to the doctor and get some tablets, either that or sleep on the sofa in the lounge. On Monday night he had slept on the sofa in the lounge. The principal benefit, for him, had been that he could lie there and masturbate without any fear of detection: slowly and with intense enjoyment: although it hadn't helped him to relax. He'd been chiefly in a wood with Geraldine Coe, the warm sun filtering through the branches, and had lain on the leaf-strewn, perfumed earth and watched her perform a tantalizing striptease. Then, naked, she had come to him and freed him of the little clothing he himself had worn.

He had seen her at St Matthew's on Sunday. (They had both been fully clothed.) It was the single time he'd been there since the confirmation of Dawn and the children. In the church hall, after the service, she had tried to avoid him.

But when it had proved impossible to do so she gave in to what had been a very strong temptation.

"You shit!" she said. "You complete and utter shit!"

Josh had been more than a little disconcerted – although it was true that he'd expected difficulties.

"People will hear you." He couldn't give it quite the levity he'd aimed for.

"You knew how much it meant to him."

"Whom?" he asked, teasingly.

"How could you do it? For just a bit of rotten money."

"I told you. I was mercenary. In *The Buccaneer* you seemed more understanding."

"In *The Buccaneer* I didn't know what was involved."

"Four-and-a-half years of unemployment. *That* hasn't changed."

"My God! *Still* he offers me a sob story!"

"I'm sorry." He tried to indicate that the apology covered more than merely the offering of a sob story.

"May I go now?"

"I can't hold you here against your will."

He watched her starting to walk off, between small crowded tables and animated groups of people holding Pyrex cups of tea. A minute or two earlier (it was laughable) he had been feeling somewhat uplifted. By lots of cheap emotion, by the thrill of mass involvement, by the thought of seeing her. But now he felt tired. All he wanted was to get away.

She turned.

201

"And something else while we're about it. Purely personal yet it still rankles."

"I know what it is."

"'Part of the endearing charm of Fleet Street...' If I hadn't actually heard that with my own ears – "

"What else could I have said?"

"*What else could you have said*!"

"In such a situation? It really wasn't done without a twinge of conscience."

"Oh? *Thank* you for that twinge. Well, that makes it all all right, then."

She was again on the point of leaving.

"But do you remember what you said yourself?" he added. "How sometimes you come out with things just to impress or to amuse: things which you later feel ashamed of?"

"Yes," she said. "I do remember that." But her tone remained cool.

"And you were wanting (I mean, I know it was only at *that* stage, don't think that I've forgotten), you were wanting to amuse or impress merely one person – or maybe two. But I was wanting to amuse and impress...millions."

"And from the sound of it, oh by hook or by crook, you most certainly succeeded."

"That's nothing to accuse me of. You succeeded, too."

"Yes. Well..."

"And I know that I do get carried away by things. I show off. I exaggerate. You see, I have this real need to impress, which you... You don't have the same excuse. I imagine you know what people say about small men?"

She muttered: "I told you, I'm not in the mood for sob stories. *Everybody* has a need to impress."

"Did it cause you lots of hassle, then – that remark of mine?"

"You know, Mr Heath, this isn't the way to get on the right side of me."

"It must be, a little. Because I don't know any other and because I'm trying very hard to be sincere."

"In fact, for you there isn't any way at all. I'm sorry. None whatsoever."

"I should have asked about your parents; I realized that afterwards. I should have asked you how they'd died, how old you were, how it felt, who brought you up. There were so many things I should have asked. That night, after I'd gone to bed, you don't know how much I wished I could have acted differently during that afternoon and evening."

"Yes. Well, it seems to me you should have wished you'd acted differently during the morning. Which is the whole crux of this matter. The rest is purely vanity: yours – mine – who cares?"

"I care. Care very much."

She shrugged.

"But, listen," he said, "don't you see? You heard our noble vicar's sermon. Maybe alternative routes can conceivably be better ones? Like getting there faster or more safely on a detour, because you could have encountered trouble on the main road."

"Josh, spare me the theology."

He was heartened by the use of his first name, however unconscious its utterance.

"Yet I'm here in church. I've actually come to church. What better place for theology? And the very fact of my presence...doesn't that say anything?"

"Yes. That you were hoping the television cameras would be here." Indeed they had now gone. Without being of any use to him at all.

He smiled. He felt persuaded she was softening towards him. "I agree. That was definitely a part of it."

"It was all of it."

"Nine-tenths."

"I'm not convinced."

"Can't an agnostic give an atheist the benefit of the doubt?"

"In fact you're out of date."

"Geraldine," he said. He waved a hand before her eyes. "This is *not* the Russell Harty Show."

It was a small laugh, quickly stifled, but it had happened.

"Since last Monday?" He was both pleased and not pleased. "That was fast."

"Does there need to be a time factor?"

"It must be the Simon Madison Show."

"Yes," she answered, candidly. "I think it must."

He hesitated.

"But doesn't it occur to you this was a show I also might have caught – just briefly?"

"No. Or *so* briefly that if you did you switched off almost at once."

And here she had to remind herself not only of what he had done to Simon but of what he had done to his own family. Judas called Joshua. The man without scruple. The man with one eye invariably alive to the main chance. She reminded herself about his talk of bandwagons.

Or to be absolutely fair, she supposed, *her* talk of bandwagons.

"Will you excuse me now? I'd like to speak to Mrs Madison. And to be perfectly frank with you – "

"In *that* tone? Brutally frank is the expression. *Perfectly*'s a long way from anything that's going on here at the moment. And if I, too, may be brutally frank for just an instant: it doesn't say much for the Simon Madison Show. Does it now? 'By their fruits shall ye know them.' Perhaps I'm better off with Harty."

"Oh, you – !"

"Shit? Don't be afraid to say it. It's utterly in keeping." This time it was he who turned away.

It was he, though, who came back about fifteen seconds later. It would have been hard to tell which of them looked the more defeated.

"But I was under the impression," he said, "that to start out on the road to Christianity, or of course the road to any properly based religion, one had to put other things in one's knapsack than toilet paper and toothpaste. I would have sworn that absolution and charity, though less immediately useful in a British public convenience, were just as indispensable. I don't suppose the father of the prodigal son had all that much toilet paper or toothpaste knocking about the house. But there," he said. "If that's the way you want it."

"No. Hold on."

She couldn't deny that if only on the lowest level he evoked in her a powerful response. She recalled how she had shied away from him in the car, as though from something electric, something dangerous.

"Suppose," she asked, "that you could put the clock back? To last Monday?"

"I don't know."

She waited.

"I simply don't know."

"Is that an honest answer?"

"As you suggest, I may have switched off almost at once. But the sound waves or the emanations could still have been getting through to me."

A child approached them shyly, asked if Geraldine had finished with her cup, then bore it off importantly in the centre of his small round tray.

"The other evening (don't get me wrong when I say this, it's not one of my more lurid revelations) I had an experience in the lavatory."

"What happened?"

"Nothing. That's the whole point." He elaborated.

"Then do you mean to say he hasn't come looking for you?"

"If he has, he must be rather better as a vicar than a tracking scout."

"Listen. You asked just now how you could get back on the right side of me."

"Okay? What of it?" He didn't even question the 'back'. He was learning.

"Well, he's standing over there. And for the moment there's nobody speaking to him."

"Poor lonely soul! Why don't *you* go to speak to him?"

Privately, there was an answer to this, too. Up to now it was she who'd made all the running and she wanted to know whether or not Simon was going to follow it up. Last night she had taken him out to dinner but this morning he had done little more than respond politely to her congratulation, before hurrying off to speak to the youth leader and the church secretary.

"I mean it, Josh. Remember how you told me you believed in making a grab for what you wanted? Or was that just a lot of talk?" She paused. "And don't you even realize this could be your last chance?"

*

She didn't know that a little more than thirty-six hours later, in a sunlit forest somewhere in the south of France, she would be taking off her clothes for him.

As a matter of fact, a short while earlier, in marginally less exotic climes, merely her bedroom on the third floor of the Royal Hotel in Scunthorpe, she'd had him perform a similar service for herself – reciprocally – her clothes, his clothes...although she'd been less wakeful at the time. She didn't even know how it had turned out to be Josh. It had begun as Simon. But, like the handover in some kind of not-quite-conventional relay race, the torch must have passed from one contender to another without her being fully aware.

Or perhaps not even passed. The details had become blurred. Jointly carried? Might such a thing be possible?

And where would that leave Dawn?

Thank God, she thought, you couldn't be held accountable for your dreams!

*

Yes. Josh woke on the Tuesday morning having spent another largely sleepless night. He gave up all further attempt to doze when it finally penetrated his consciousness that, in the bathroom, Mickey was singing.

> "No more Latin, no more French,
> No more sitting on the old school bench..."

206

It was Dawn who knocked on the bathroom door: not because she wanted to go in there: she herself had been up since half-past-five getting things ready.

"Michael, I'm glad you're happy. It's nice to hear you singing. But not *that*. There's something more to this important day than that."

"*Onward Christian Soldiers*, please," called out Josh, severely. "Or, *When They Begin the Beguine*."

But by the time they were ready to depart his good humour had diminished. Should he go? Shouldn't he? This year, next year? Sometime, never? There didn't seem to be much point: he might do better on his own, even here in Scunthorpe: a free agent with his own flat who might find somebody to share it with him for a short while. For instance, there was this young woman behind the cheese counter in Littlewood's, whom last week he had chatted up a couple of times and who had appeared to him...receptive. She wasn't Geraldine Coe, of course, but Geraldine Coe would have other company upon that march. Tall and blond and handsome: literally the blue-eyed boy, or man. Josh had few illusions as to why Miss Geraldine Coe had suddenly found religion. (Though in all fairness he thought she herself didn't have many illusions about that, either.) And since he realized that there wasn't a chance in hell of his being able successfully to compete, why not simply wish them luck and proceed upon his way? Old Jericho and Moses. They deserved one another. They were both pleasant people.

So if *he* went on this march, that would leave him, essentially, with Dawn and the children. And certainly they, too, were pleasant people, but...well, they were just Dawn and the children, and call him any name you liked – immature, irresponsible, utterly self-centred, king of all the shits – that was simply not enough. And maybe never had been.

He shouldn't have been a father. That was the trouble.

(No, it wasn't. How in all honesty could he regret fatherhood? No matter, of course, how his children might well regret him being the father they'd been saddled with.)

207

He should never have been a husband. Now *that* was the trouble. Certainly not Dawnie's. Perhaps not anyone's.

Also, if he did go on this march he would have to be a witness to the strengthening of the bond between Simon and Geraldine. It was one thing to wish them luck. It was another to be there and be forced to see that wish bear fruit.

38

There was a ring at the doorbell.

A young man stood outside who said he'd come to fetch them in his car. "At least try and keep you dry until we start!"

It was the rain as much as anything that had got on Josh's nerves...his wife's reaction to the rain.

"What we can't help we must endure!" She would have made a far better teacher than ever he did; especially good with six-year-olds. (He couldn't imagine her trying to seduce them, either.) "Swearing at the weather is just the same as swearing at our Lord." (He'd only said, "Oh, blast this rain!") "We should wrap up well and walk out singing."

"If Gene Kelly were dead," he said bitterly, although he personally wished Gene Kelly not the least harm in the world, "I would now swear he'd come back to haunt us... Except that you can't dance as well as he can."

And then it occurred to him that he would possibly have preferred – oh dear – living with Gene Kelly than with Dawn.

He hadn't thought of that before.

This man who'd come to get them was likewise your submissive and cheerful philosopher. Even when Josh said that, speaking for himself, he always liked to have a really good grumble, this Tony-person humoured him with the same brand of patient jollity; told him just to go ahead and grumble. Why not?

Hell.

Besides being artificial they were cliquey. And clearly very pleased with themselves.

208

"I don't think I'm coming," he said. "I've decided not to come."

They humoured him in that, too. "Oh, Josh," Dawn repeated twice, without much variation. "I wish you would. Won't you? It would be so much nicer if you did." But that was it, more or less.

"In that case," she said, "I'm sorry I gave the milk and margarine to Mrs Newton."

"I'll go and get them back."

"You can't do that!"

"Why not?"

"Because you just *can't*!" Maybe not such a very good teacher, after all. But she might have got on okay with the inspectors: judging from the harried smile she flashed at Tony, trying on the one hand to apologize, dissociate herself, and on the other to pretend it was all just part of the day's fun, thoroughly structured and perfectly healthy. "You'll have to leave another note for the milkman then and – for today – get whatever you need at Presto's."

As soon as they were gone, however, he couldn't face the thought of leaving another note for the milkman or of getting whatever he needed at Presto's. (Cream, please. Butter. A female with a sense of humour. How about a fairly witty cow?) Nor even at Littlewood's. He *could* go back to bed, he supposed, induce sweet dreams. Though where was the point? The only dreams worth having were those which had at least a fighting chance of coming true.

Fighting...chance: an adjective and noun he'd always thought made stimulating bedfellows.

Five minutes after the four of them had gone he closed the door behind himself as well. Locked it. Put the key under the mat; he needed no extraneous luggage. From now on anything he wanted he would buy new. Colourful socks. Sexy underwear. Toothbrush. Nail clippers. Razor. In London he'd get a job – eventually – no big rush. (Labourer? Dishwasher? Something would turn up. Kept man? Male escort? TV personality?) In the meantime Cashpoint would keep him ticking over fairly nicely. (He'd given Dawnie her share of the loot in cash – an envelope

209

containing seventy-five twenty-pound notes – he hoped she wouldn't give most of it away. But just in case she did he'd left a hundred pounds on the kitchen table.)

There was bound to be a London train quite frequently.

He could have got to the station in several ways, the station being nearly next door to the employment office. Generally he cut through the side roads: past the auctioneers, the magistrates' court, the Civic Theatre.

Generally? No, always.

This morning he went up the High Street.

Afterwards he tried to work out why – since it was undeniably a longer route, busier, less attractive. This way, of course, there were the men's outfitters and the travel agent's and the shop that sold Walkmans...but what kind of idiot would buy anything in Scunthorpe when three hours later he could be in London? Here, indeed, he had wandered a lot more often with his family yet he was in no frame of mind for nostalgic recollections nor for journeys of farewell. There was no reason on earth why he should have chosen to walk up the High Street on his way to the railway station.

But it was near the top of the High Street that he came across the car and all the people standing round it. He wouldn't have stopped. He wasn't interested in accidents or the possibility of blood – not unless there were no helpers on the scene, naturally. And because of the crowd he didn't see his wife sitting sideways in the front seat with both feet on the ground and Billy's head resting against her shoulder – she had him on her lap and was crooning to him, massaging his brow. Nor did he see, next to the open door of the driver's seat, his younger son leaning in and trying to give support to Tony. All that alerted him was the whimpering.

Josh had no idea when he'd last heard Mickey whimper. Quite possibly, never. And furthermore he'd have sworn he wouldn't be able to distinguish, even for money, his own child's whimpering from the whimpering of anyone else's. But now, as soon as he heard it, an image of Mickey rushed into his mind.

210

Josh pushed through the spectators with an impetuosity bordering on violence.

His first thought was that Billy was dead. "No?" he cried. "*No*!" It struck him later it was almost like a prayer.

Dawn didn't question his prompt arrival. She clutched his hand, held the back of it to her cheek, instantly allayed his fears. "The young gentleman says there's nothing to worry about. Not for either of them." The 'young gentleman' was a doctor and had hurried off to phone the hospital.

"Thank God! Thank God!" Josh transferred his hand to Billy's forehead, then brought it back to his wife's cheek. It didn't stay there long. Mickey had realized he'd arrived and had hurried round the car to throw his arms around his father's legs, hugging them tightly. Josh's hand had fallen to the top of Mickey's head. "It's all right, my love; it's all right."

"You need to get yourself an umbrella," Dawn remarked inconsequentially – and then began to cry.

"Dawnie, don't! Please don't. Think how bad it might have been."

"I know," she said. "I know. But if it had to happen – why *today*? Why did Tony have to remember he'd gone and left something at home?"

It hadn't occurred to Josh to wonder about the accident's location. St Matthew's lay in the opposite direction.

"Why did he so much want us to let Simon down?" For a moment Josh thought the pronoun referred to Tony. Then he realized that in Dawnie's mind it began with a capital.

She was still crying.

"It doesn't make a difference," he said. "He'll have hundreds going with him to London."

"We can't be sure of that. We can't be sure! And every single person counts – every one!" Her voice held a note of vehemence.

He said: "I'll let Simon know what's happened."

"The young gentleman said he'd try to catch Dulcie Owen before she left the house; luckily I knew her number. But not one of us, Josh – not one of us! It doesn't seem right."

"You mean, not one of us, the Heaths? Not one of us going to London?"

"And walking in step with Simon and the Lord."

"Well, if you like..." He'd had no notion he was going to say that.

Her eyes widened. "You, Josh?"

"Me, Dawnie."

"Oh, *would* you?" Not simply had she stopped crying. She was suddenly laughing. "Oh, I can't believe it!"

"Got to do something for the Lord," remarked Josh – joshing. "I mean, after everything he's done for us!"

He didn't specify. But if he had (and done so honestly) he'd have said: "Spared Billy's life! Put three thousand smackers in our pockets! Given me this chance to get away – and to do it, furthermore, without hurting either you or the kids!"

The real irony was that at this moment he no longer cared so much about getting away. But he knew himself. Very soon he'd be feeling every bit as frantic as ever. Of course he would.

Yet at least the question of timing now seemed less important. Three hours by train or three weeks on foot? What did it matter? He had his whole future ahead of him. And once in London he'd be able to find a good enough reason to stay. Good God, yes. *At last! I've been given a decent job!*

Nor was it as if he wouldn't be able to come home from time to time or as if Dawnie and the boys mightn't occasionally travel down to London. It *could* be worked. It could.

"Yes, I'll go on that march – certainly I will – if it means so very much to you." He smiled. "*I'll* walk to London with the Lord."

Dawn looked at him not merely with respect but even with wonder. There were renewed tears glimmering.

"Oh, Josh! Do you realize that all my dearest prayers have just been answered?"

He accompanied them in the ambulance. Later she came with him to the main door of the hospital and even a few yards down the road, despite the rain and the fact she carried one of Tony and April's siren-suited babies. Mickey came, too. Thank heaven

212

it was Dawnie who'd refused Mickey permission to go on the march without her. Refused him categorically. Thank heaven, thought Josh, because if it hadn't been for that, he himself would probably have let the boy come. His memory of that quietly unrestrained grief had affected him deeply, especially the fact that it had only been unrestrained until Josh himself had got there. And it would continue to affect him, he believed, whenever he allowed himself to think of it.

Yet Mickey would have been an encumbrance.

"Besides," said Josh, "you don't want to miss the wedding, do you?"

"But you'll be back by then? Surely you will?" protested Dawn.

"Who knows? And if not, you mustn't let them postpone it. For it's now *my* turn to testify to the miracle in which our own two sons were chosen to play so pivotal a role; my turn to bear witness to the enormity of the privilege conferred on them – conferred on us, as well. And you've often said it yourself, Dawnie: that when you're engaged in the Lord's work you simply can't tell how long it's going to take."

"Oh, Joshua!"

"Now don't go all soft on me, you great big silly! You've no reason to start crying again."

"You'll take good care of yourself, won't you? Really take good care?"

He laughed. "Ever known me not to?"

"Perhaps I feel I don't know this new Josh at all. Perhaps I feel he's more like the old one I *used* to know. During the early years."

Carrying the baby, it was difficult for her to get at her handkerchief. He handed her his. This reminded him of practicalities. "I've left the key under the doormat. You should be okay for most things while I'm gone. The boys can see to fuses, washers, jobs like that. In any real emergency go to Ted Wilson. And as for money...whatever you do, don't wait until you've nearly run out before you reapply – "

213

"Run out?" she exclaimed. "What, run out of fifteen hundred pounds?"

He gave them both a hug – it was a little awkward with the baby – handed Mickey two ten-pound notes, one for himself and one for his brother; then broke away and instantly began to run.

"Come back safe," Dawn called. "And may God be with you!"

He glanced back several times to wave but then Mickey came racing after him to tell him about all the stuff for the journey – its still being at the hospital – and he had to return for it...which was anticlimactic. The delay, however, was only short. On his second departure Mickey accompanied him to the first corner, the end of Highfield Avenue. When Josh looked back Dawn was still standing at the roadside near the entrance, waiting to wave to him. Perhaps it was only because of her own recent words but he suddenly remembered the girl behind the counter shyly passing him his cigarettes. "Look after her," he said, "you and Billy. Look after yourselves too. I'll send more money when I can."

"And a postcard?"

"Yes."

"And we'll write as well. Care of places. You can do that, can't you?"

"Yes."

Again he had to pull away.

"I love you, Dad."

"I love you too. I'm glad that Billy's all right. I'm glad that neither you nor your mum got hurt."

"Oh, Dad, do you really have to go?" And Mickey's voice quavered. His hand reached out for his father's. "Do you *really* have to go?"

In short, the departure of Josh Heath from Scunthorpe was a lot more difficult than – only an hour or so earlier – he had ever imagined it could be.

"Remember," his mother had said, crisply – almost her last words to him – "Take pity on Frank Cooper!"

"I will. I promise you. At any rate I'll do my best."

"Take care of one another."

Paula, disliking herself but unable to help what was happening, had looked with hostility upon this woman who came from London, this intruder with her city airs. Even while offering wishes that she tried to make sincere, her voice, to herself, had sounded sulky and resentful.

Simon asked if they would gather around him in a circle: Geraldine, Alison, Dulcie, Paula, his mother, even the three men from the press: a small group under black umbrellas.

"Lord," he said, after a long moment in which they all stood quietly, with their heads bowed, "we humbly ask you to bless this venture and to be with us through every single minute of it, both those of us who are going and those of us who are staying..."

When he had finished they said the Lord's Prayer together: which in the open air, even with the background noise of swishing traffic on the nearby busy road, made Geraldine think of a crowd of fishermen standing on the shores of Lake Galilee. Once, she would have warned herself against sentimentality. Now, she saw no harm in the reflection.

"The grace of our Lord Jesus Christ and the love of God and the fellowship of the Holy Spirit be with us all, evermore. Amen."

They set out along Frodingham Road. In spite of their boldly stated resolves, Simon and Geraldine carried only one banner between them: *Our angel says act now!* (The photographer and reporters had fixed the remainder across Simon's haversack.) At Britannia Corner – since Simon had naturally notified the police of his intention to process, possibly with fifty or a hundred

215

others, more likely, he had said, with only twenty – a constable waited to hold up the traffic while they made the ninety-degree turn into Doncaster Road. At first they felt abashed, yet were glad to have him there, less for his upraised arm than for his friendly grin. "Good luck," he said. "Really. We're all of us behind you."

"Then why not join us?"

"The sergeant wouldn't like it!"

"Blow the sergeant."

"Funny you should say that." He called out after them: "Hope *our angel* comes up trumps! A bit of better weather would be a good beginning."

Others wished them luck, as well. Without the rain they might have had a larger send-off but small knots of pedestrians stood and watched as they went by, people waved, drivers hooted in encouragement. A bus driver shouted, "Give Maggie our love!" but his conductress cried, "Not mine! No bloody fear!" An old man with a beer can in his hand raised it unsteadily and said something of which only the last few words became intelligible: "...were always fucking crazy." ("Who were?" asked Simon. "I think," said Geraldine, "the British.") They both kept shouting back, "Why don't you come with us?" or "Don't you want to save the world?" But it seemed that nobody did. Not enough.

Further from the shops, pedestrians were shyer about bandying opinions, even to the point sometimes of pretending, despite exhortatory hails, not really to have noticed the two marchers.

Then an odd thing occurred while they were walking down the steep hill towards Berkeley Circle. Or, rather, a couple of odd things occurred.

First, noticing a bin attached to a lamppost, Simon disposed of Paula's hymn sheets. "Should you really be doing that?" asked Geraldine.

"Well, what the eye doesn't see..."

"No, I just meant that in your sermon – though you didn't happen to mention throat lozenges in that exhaustive list of

216

yours, surely something of an oversight – you *did* happen to mention singing hymns."

"I know. I think at that point I must have gone a bit over the top."

"Yet you told me you hoped you were being inspired."

"So?"

"So what do you suppose went wrong at that particular moment?"

He retrieved the hymn sheets.

"You know," he said, "I believe it's reasonably possible that you could turn out to be a reasonably good influence."

The smile she gave conveyed hardly anything of the pleasure she experienced.

"But on the other hand," he added, "if you would simply like to take a *look* at Paula's hymn selection...!"

"Well, they may not be your own all-time favourites but even so... You never quite know what unlikely thing is maybe going to touch somebody somehow – and perhaps you're not the only person round here who can sometimes feel inspired."

"Now I think it must be *you* who's gone a bit over the top."

"Anyway, shouldn't we just wait and see if at any time...? After all, we're not committed to using those sheets merely because we've decided to keep them. I'll even offer to carry them for you if you like."

"Why for me? Why not for us? But in any case it's generous of you."

"I'm glad you noticed. Especially as Paula was glaring at me the whole time as if she thought I was related to Lucrezia Borgia."

"Nonsense."

"It's not."

"Utter nonsense."

"No."

"Of course it is. Why just *related*?"

And the second thing which occurred was that they heard a shout and – when they turned – saw someone running down the hill.

217

It was not only that he was out of breath and sweaty (he'd gone first to the church, then had to double back); he also seemed a little shy.

"Where is everyone?"

"Here."

"Everyone is you and Geraldine?"

"Looks like it."

Josh hesitated. "Then," he said. "then...? Then would you mind...?"

Simon said: "*Mind*? I tell you, Josh, there's nothing that could give us greater pleasure."

"*Really*?"

"Really."

There followed a moment's silence. Geraldine broke it by asking after Billy.

"And I've got some money with me," added Josh quickly, as though this were a natural consequence of his son having got off so very lightly (despite the damage inflicted on the car's bonnet) and as though this *too* might make his presence more acceptable. "Or at any rate a cashpoint card. Ill-gotten gains, as of course you'd both agree. And I ought to say this, as well – make it clear from the beginning. I'm probably not here for any of the right reasons."

"Oh, *reasons*!" shrugged Simon. "Who's qualified to talk of reasons?"

"You are, I'd have said."

"Listen. Who knows but that even Peter didn't really tag along in the first place because his mother-in-law was driving him crazier than mosquito-bites? Yet look at what happened to Peter. So maybe the mother-in-law was purely a put-up job."

"I thought you people believed in free will?"

"We do. He could have bashed her."

*

218

There was a rider attached to this. "In fact, I'm inclined to think of *you* as a bit of a put-up job," said Simon.

Josh had by now taken over Geraldine's end of the banner. "Oh, *good*!" he exclaimed. "How *very* lovely!"

"No. You don't realize. It's an honour."

"My alter ego: Simon-Peter's mother-in-law. Do I merely revel in that accolade or am I permitted to ask why?"

"Well, yes. Sometime ago – I think it was during my first few months in Scunthorpe – I heard a bit of gossip which *obviously* I shouldn't have listened to and which *obviously* I'm not condoning. Yet I believe that if it hadn't been for that bit of gossip – or, rather, the incident that underlay it – then Scunthorpe might never have been chosen for this recent revelation, for the miracle which is driving us forward this morning."

"Cryptic allusions...," murmured Geraldine a little drily. "No key, I suppose, to be handed round to the uninitiated?"

"I don't know. That's up to Josh."

"Oh hell!" said Josh. "You simply don't care what you come out with, do you?"

There followed a minute of indecision.

Josh gave Geraldine a quick look.

"I didn't go to Germany," he said brusquely. "I fucked one of my older pupils. Obviously I got the sack."

Simon said: "And Dawn got religion. So did her sons."

"Incidentally, there's no book, either. That was just a story." In spite of that small, irresistible joke, he still sounded brusque. "Where were you," he said to Simon, "four-and-a-half years ago?"

"Bournemouth."

"But contemplating making a move." It wasn't a question.

"*Madison for Pope*? Yes – as a matter of fact."

"I suppose that's the wording you've got on one of the other banners?"

"Look, Josh. Even for you it would be dangerous to underestimate me. *All* of the other banners."

Geraldine was scarcely listening.

"I wonder what's happened to the girl?" she said. "And I wonder what effect it had on the girl's family, come to that, and on everybody else who knew about it?" She felt appalled.

But neither of them answered. Indeed, for at least a minute, possibly longer, all of them stayed quiet. But then:

"Good God!" said Josh. "Am I imagining things?"

"No," said Simon. "No, you're not. Here comes the sun!"

"Is it a sign?" asked Geraldine. "And look...! Over there! Isn't that the start of a rainbow?"

*

The power of association.

As a child, Ginny had been taken to see *Where the Rainbow Ends*.

"I'd never been to the theatre before, not even to a pantomime. Simeon, you've no idea what a revelation it was!"

He could still see the expression in her eyes.

"And never again," she said, "have I felt more utterly convinced of anything."

He remembered, even, the apologetic American accent, along with the joyful confidence of her smile: "I guess you kinda know things at the age of six!"

"Well, out of the mouth of very babes and sucklings," he'd agreed. "Convinced of what, though?"

"No, you mustn't laugh at me. You see, it was the first time I knew, really *knew*, that the world was magical – and good – and that dragons would always be slain," she said.

220

<u>40</u>

But it seemed that the dragon-slayers weren't living in Doncaster. Nor in Newark, Grantham, Peterborough, Stevenage, Milton Keynes, nor anywhere. And the three of them didn't merely keep to any straight line: they made literally dozens of small diversions. Stamford, Leicester, Bishops Stortford, Cambridge. You might at least have expected to find dragon-slayers in an old, much venerated university. Yet it wasn't to be. The term had started by the time they arrived in Cambridge and although there were certainly any number of undergraduates who came to wish them luck and offer them not only encouragement but even overnight accommodation (blankets to provide extra cushioning for their sleeping bags) as well as food and beer and often fairly heated debate – and opportunities to wash – at the same time they'd gradually been made to realize they were now regarded, if not precisely as freaks, then perhaps as performers in a type of travelling show which was undoubtedly topical and shouldn't be missed but couldn't in fact be taken *that* seriously. And this wasn't because the remedies they advocated were disagreed with – they weren't, not in *theory* – but somehow, even before the handing out of the prescriptions, these indispensable cures seemed to have garnered a certain air of quackery. The angel Gabriel had turned into a sort of superior Billy Smart. The travellers were only vaguely aware of this and for a long time they fought against believing it but Simon in particular flared up at the facetious comments regularly and persistently made, especially when he considered them disparaging of God.

He spoke to his mother every second day, and at more specific times Josh did the same to Dawn and the boys, gathered in a neighbour's flat, but it was hard for either of them to sound continuously positive. Admittedly, they minimized the hardships and the failure to recruit followers, other than weirdoes and

221

winos, who almost invariably dropped out after little more than a mile. Yet it would have required practically superhuman strength to remain constantly, persuasively, upbeat. Naturally, Dawn was always easier to convince of the rightness of things than Sally Madison.

Simon sometimes remembered those pages he had written about the apostles' return from a journey lasting several weeks, but he was wondering increasingly if such pages would ever form a chapter in his Life of Jesus or whether indeed that whole project hadn't reached a dismayingly untimely end; he was no longer so sure of where his duty lay. He realized he was tired and confused and subject to a lot of strain. But he was frightened, too, that his duty now lay in an utterly different direction and might indeed prove inescapable. Over the years, he had suffered three nervous breakdowns – the second being after Ginny had died and he thought that he must surely then have drawn close to madness. Although he often wondered if a fourth could now be imminent, he felt determined if such were the case he would this time say what he hadn't said on either of those previous occasions.

Our Father which art in heaven, thy will be done... Dear Lord, not my will, but thine.

*

The month of Nisan came, none too quickly for some. The apostles, stragglingly, returned. Simon-Peter, who had been paired with Lebbaeus ("I hadn't even liked him before; now I grew to love him!") gave a lengthy account of what had happened.

"It was fine to begin with. The two of us were just so eager, stopped almost everyone we passed, planned to win a thousand converts." He gave a rueful and apologetic smile. "Almost on the first day! We couldn't quite decide, though, where to start. I was all for going into the hills. *My* territory, of course. Zealot country. Lebbaeus demurred at first but then agreed. It seemed such a wonderful challenge, taking pacifism to the terrorists. And

222

I was so sure they'd listen to me – at least *listen*. I used to be quite a key figure: nationalism personified!

"But they only laughed at us. 'Tell those Romans to repent,' they said, 'tell *them* about your Kingdom! And if *they* come to us with messages of love and friendship – *and* messages of farewell – then we might really sit up and take notice.'

"Well, we tried. We truly did persevere. But so unavailingly. We were hooted and jeered down that mountain track as though we were, I don't know, jugglers from Tiberias. Indeed, I think we were lucky to escape a roughing-up. 'Might knock a little sense into 'em,' they said. We scarpered. But we weren't too downhearted, not for long – we could still laugh about it. 'They'll eat their words! Let's just press on.'

"Lebbaeus wanted to return to his own village, which was where he'd wanted to go in the first place before I overruled him. It wasn't till some five weeks later, though, that we arrived. And in the meanwhile our success had been patchy to say the least. It was incredible how seldom people wanted to listen. I think, Master, as you said to Thomas, we must have been doing the job badly, even when it seemed to us we were being quite powerful and inspired: we went hungry for days at a time and more often than not, *far* more often than not, had to sleep rough. Even when villagers brought their sick to be healed, initially as an experiment, almost as a joke, but then a sure-fire thing; even when we drove out demons and anointed people with olive oil and thought, 'This is it, brother, there's no stopping us now, tonight we eat!': even after all of that...well, it's hard to credit people's ingratitude. They'd got from us what they wanted and, oh yes, they'd feed us all right and slap us on the back, but that was absolutely it: the talk-part was just a nuisance and as for giving us shelter for more than one night...well, we began to think it something of a myth, the reputation we Jews enjoy for hospitality. Oh, it's true that twice we were offered a roof for as long as we wanted, and in fact found it hard to get away, yet in each case it wasn't for what *we* had to say but for what *they* had to say, our hosts. In each case they were lonely and neurotic and...leechlike. Naturally, we prayed for them and laid hands on

223

them but they seemed oddly resistant and perhaps we didn't have enough faith. Then another time, when we were welcomed into a home with so much warmth and cordiality that we looked at one another and said, 'At last! We've cracked it! This is what it's all about!' we were woken in the middle of the night and the woman of the household smiled at us and lowered her lamp and she was naked. And yet another time, when once more we supposed we might be making headway, in a house where the only woman was very old and wrinkled, her two sons, who were themselves in middle age, came to us shortly after we'd retired and... That night we again slept beneath the stars.

"In short, we sometimes felt, both Lebbaeus and I, it was a tougher assignment than anyone could possibly have imagined ...this business of changing the world..."

41

They reached London on the last day of November. The closer they'd got to it, the slower had become their progress: the more detours Simon had suggested. Also, Josh thought, he spent a lot more time in prayer, even apart from those occasions when he was actually down on his knees. But his praying didn't seem to refresh him. He was clearly very tired despite the fact that they were frequently in their sleeping bags by nine and often spent the night in some seedy guesthouse or other and he looked haggard; sometimes appeared to have aged enormously. He didn't make jokes any longer. Added to which, Geraldine or Josh would regularly address some remark to him – it might be as they were walking or it might be as they were sitting over supper, maybe in a Macdonald's or a Kentucky Fried Chicken – and Simon simply wouldn't hear; at such moments he was preternaturally withdrawn. He'd lost his appetite as well, and Josh – reminded of when his children were young – had to try to coax him into eating...he was better at this than Geraldine. Simon was either ill or shortly about to be.

And, possibly most telling of all, he had to be nagged into telephoning his mother. On one occasion it was a long time before he came out of the box although the others had seen him terminate the call some minutes earlier. They had assumed he'd been praying but whether this was so or not it soon became clear he'd been crying. Geraldine had taken him in her arms and Simon had seemed to welcome it. Josh had looked on with exceedingly mixed feelings.

That same evening they'd come across a little inn so utterly unlike the cheap and soulless places at which they normally put up that Geraldine hadn't given it any proper attention. Josh, however, saw the initial wistfulness of her expression and correctly interpreted it as a longing for hot water and soft pillows and the sort of comfort pilgrims had no right to expect – saw such an investment, moreover, as something which didn't need to be paid for by lengthy hours of conversation, either serious and challenging or, at the very least, entertaining. "Yes, we can! We *can* afford it!" Josh was in charge of their finances. "There are times when we all have a need to *splurge*!"

Geraldine looked at him gratefully but Simon, who had seemed strangely disorientated by his surroundings even before Josh had made this statement and hadn't up till then appeared to concern himself greatly with their expenses, was at first inexplicably resistant. The inn overlooked a village green and was indeed – after Simon had finally, but suddenly, caved in – found to be an oasis of comfort.

Now they were each drinking a late-night whisky in its chintzy, inglenooked lounge, at present its sole occupants and sitting in a companionable if sleepy silence. Had she been able Geraldine would have stopped Josh from ending that silence, although she couldn't feel in any way hostile to what he was saying, only worried about its effect on someone she had grown to love.

"Look, Simon," Josh said, "we've got to face facts. This has been going on for *weeks*!" In fact, it had been going on for only about five, yet because of the unremitting pressure it had seemed more like twice that figure, not simply to Josh but to all of them.

225

"And we're just not getting anywhere, are we? We're all utterly worn out. Wouldn't this be a good time, maybe, to admit defeat?"

"*Defeat*?" It might have been theft – murder – betrayal that Josh was wanting to admit to. And in Simon's eyes, of course, that's precisely what it was. Betrayal. "When Gabriel himself pointed us the way to victory?"

"Simon, perhaps he didn't. Perhaps my sons *were* hallucinating."

"That's nonsense and you know it."

"Then why is God now making it so difficult? I'm aware you'll probably talk about free will but free will hasn't stopped his intervention in the past."

"What intervention?"

"Miracles."

"In other words you're hoping he'll suddenly create a great tidal wave of humanity" – Simon clearly liked that metaphor, he used it fairly often – "to crash against the walls of No 10 and whip away all opposition? Beat it to smithereens?"

"Well, yes, if that's on offer. It would help."

"A tidal wave composed of puppets?"

They had up to now collected over nine thousand signatures but relatively few actual marchers: at the period of their greatest success (numerically) they had had a hundred-and-eighty-seven walking with them – men, women, children – yet all of them had eventually fallen away; even the record-holder had lasted only thirteen days. Nevertheless, there'd been a moment when Simon had grown practically euphoric. "A hundred-and-eighty-seven!" he'd declared. "My God, we really *are* going to end up with a million!" Josh, touched by what he'd thought of as appealingly delusional, had merely said, "These country lanes are going to get a mite congested in that case but no doubt we'll be happy to keep to the motorways."

He thought it might have been the last time he'd seen Simon laugh. Simon's optimism was by then at its zenith and he was possibly visualizing a small army, even a large one, bringing gridlock, mayhem and salvation, with every few minutes *another* driver cheerfully getting out of his vehicle to fall into step with the marchers.

"All right, forget the tidal wave," said Josh. He leaned back and tried to derive inspiration from a watercolour which most likely dated from the nineteen-twenties and had a caption *Trust the Umpire!* "How about this? Why not let Gabriel put in a second appearance? To you and Geraldine and me; if he came now he could join us in a nightcap. All he'd have to say is, 'Cheers, you brilliant little trio, well done, here's to your continuing success!' Which, may I submit, is hardly going to tinker with *anyone's* free will?"

"Except ours."

"No, I don't see it."

"Josh, you're asking for authentication. God wants *faith* to be our touchstone. Life would be very easy if there were little dollops of proof awaiting us at every turn."

"But a small sign of his approval, a bit of skywriting or another rainbow, would that really be *too* much to ask?"

"Yes, if his purpose is to test us."

"I thought his present purpose, his *overriding* purpose, was to make the world a better place."

"Yet he doesn't lose sight of the individual even in his concern for the mass."

"Then perhaps he ought," grumbled Josh. "He doesn't have to impress *me* with all that multi-tasking."

"Josh, do you want to go home?"

"Well, since you ask..." His tone was still light, although he remembered his dream of getting away from Scunthorpe, of finding a life far more fulfilling. He couldn't really understand why but this dream had now lost a lot of its drawing power.

"Then go."

"You mean, without you? No. I was talking about the three of us. The three of us! Geraldine, you haven't said a word. Have we sent you to sleep?"

"No, no, I've been listening and trying to work out exactly what..."

"Geraldine, do *you* want to go home?" asked Simon, when she paused.

She said slowly, "Like Josh, I certainly wouldn't be happy to do so on my own."

"We're still a fair distance from London and – if you remember – I announced publicly my intention of walking to London."

"Then announce publicly," broke in Josh, "that you have now – through experience – judged it wiser to change your mind. It's not a sin to change your mind."

"No, in this case it would be. I suggest, Josh, you have a good night's rest and then you'll be fresh to return to Scunthorpe in the morning."

"There's no way I would leave you both."

"Why?"

"Because I respect you too much, respect the pair of you, although I'm not addressing this next bit to Geraldine. I just wish you weren't so pigheaded and could see that there are other ways to achieve what you want to achieve; and that I and lots of others would do everything we could to help you... Eh, Jericho?" Absent-mindedly he had slipped back into using a name he was fond of but nowadays realized would be tactless. He didn't even know he'd said it.

Simon, however, didn't appear to have heard any of that last part. "*Want* to achieve?" he repeated. "That's only part of it. What I have been *asked* to achieve, given the *duty* to achieve... And, no, there are no other ways."

"Wouldn't you think that's a hell of a duty to place on the shoulders of any one individual?"

"Yes. I would." But there was neither rancour nor pride in the utterance of that statement, it sounded purely matter-of-fact. "And, indeed, I wish that were all," he added.

Geraldine asked sharply: "Why? What's the rest?"

But Simon only shook his head.

"I think it's a duty more than *anyone* could bear," she said quietly.

"Hear, hear," agreed Josh.

228

"Nobody is given more to bear than he's capable of bearing. And as I say, it's a test." Simon's voice suddenly acquired a tremor. "I feel honoured."

"Honoured?" exclaimed Josh. "The very fact you can use that word! Doesn't it strike you it could be a form of arrogance?"

"Oh, Josh, Josh...," said Geraldine. She stood up. "Excuse me, gentlemen. I'm shattered. I think I have to go to bed."

"I can well see why you'd say that," replied Simon, after she had gone.

"*Is* it a form of arrogance?"

"Possibly – and, if it is, God would certainly be counting on it. I'm sure he uses all the traits in somebody's character, good or bad, to help him achieve his purpose."

Josh laughed. "And is that, then, your definition of free will?"

Simon said wearily: "Josh, go home. You've been wonderful – a tower of strength – and I appreciate everything you've done for us. But now it's time for you to go back to Dawn and the children."

"No. Not without you. Whether you realize it or not, you plainly aren't yourself any longer. You've changed, and in some ways, I'd say, not for the better. I'm sure God never intended that. I remember the man who tried – and tried again – to get me to have a pint with him and who laughed about our handbook, *How to be the Perfect Clergyman*. Would he laugh now? Where have you gone, Simon? The essential *you*? What's the number of that paragraph which deals with arrogance?"

"I'm really sorry if the essential *me* has disappeared, rather than – on the contrary – risen to the surface. But people have to develop, Josh, in accordance with the times. In accordance with a duty that's finally been revealed to them."

"Oh – and you keep on talking about duty! Duty, duty, duty! Stuff duty! I hate it."

"But you yourself, Josh, have developed in accordance with the times. I called you a tower of strength just now. I didn't do so lightly. It's a term which Ginny would sometimes... What I mean is, it's a phrase I always associate with her."

"Your wife?" Josh knew she'd been his wife but couldn't think what else to say.

"Yes. And tonight she happens to be especially on my mind. It's this place...the way it overlooks a village green. Also that picture I saw you looking at. Reminds me of a cricket game I once took part in. While I waited to bat, the two of us were lounging on the grass, her grandmother and great-aunts were sitting in their deckchairs..." He stopped, his expression more relaxed. "But, then, she's always on my mind. Literally not an hour goes by when I don't remember her and talk to her and draw comfort from her presence. It was she who wanted me to be a vicar."

Josh said nothing.

"I truly feel she walks beside us and that if anything hurtful were ever to happen to me she'd be right there to hold my hand. Basically, it's the thought of Ginny that provides me with the strength to carry on."

"Would you consider marrying again?"

"No. I shall never do that."

"I think Geraldine might be rather sorry to hear it. I suppose you realize she's in love with you?"

"In other circumstances, who knows what might have happened? But, no, I've been shown that I shall never get married again." Yet, despite the repetition, his words sounded hesitant and once more his voice revealed the hint of a tremor.

"Shown?"

Simon ignored this but now said much more lightly, "It's pretty clear she's fond of you, as well."

"There was a time when she was *anything* but that!"

"Though – as I must have told you in a dozen different ways – you too, Josh, are a changed man. And, in your case, most *definitely* for the better!"

"Thank you. I hope so. However, I trust you're not encouraging me to think of Geraldine romantically!"

"Of course not."

They went to their rooms soon afterwards. Josh slept well. Simon didn't, but anyway he had more or less given up the idea of being able to sleep. Or even of wanting to. Although for much of the day he felt so tired there were moments when it was hard to keep his eyes open he nonetheless had no wish to squander his nights mainly in a state of unconsciousness. It would have been an escape, yes, but it would also have meant a reawakening. He wondered how a person felt awakening on the day of execution. And, besides that, time was much too precious. Although he wanted to *rest* and be recharged as fully as was humanly possible he also wanted to spend each hour in preparation: in thinking, remembering, coming to accept the things that had to be: in communing with his God as peaceably and as submissively as he could.

42

The next day was November 5th. In the evening there was to be a firework display, together with a bonfire: a bonfire visualized as being so large – their landlady had mentioned whilst serving them breakfast – that locals had spent over twelve hours building it. Both Geraldine and Josh had persuaded Simon of the great opportunity awaiting them here; they felt surprised that persuasion should have been necessary and that Simon's objections should have seemed not simply atypical but even feeble – chiefly to do with people being in the sort of festive mood non-conducive to any consideration of serious issues.

In the end, though, Simon relented and gave them the real reason. "I don't like fire; I never have liked fire." Other, he meant, than in a proper fireplace or, better still, confined to something like a matchstick or a gas ring or even an Olympic torch.

"Has it always been like that?" asked Geraldine.

Apparently it had.

"You poor devil," sympathized Josh. "Mightn't counselling help? Haven't you ever had any?"

231

"Why? Up till now it's never been a major issue in my life. And if you don't mind, the pair of you, I'd prefer we changed the subject."

Geraldine shrugged. "Okay. But may I just say this? I wish there were some way I could make it better."

"Thank you. Yet it's not important."

"And, I promise, not another word, except to say that we do have the megaphone, you wouldn't need to go within a dozen yards of the bonfire – and, yes, people in a jolly mood mightn't want to listen to a preacher, not to any old common or garden preacher but, Simon, you're different, a celebrity – "

"I'm a charlatan."

"No, not at all. Yet even if that were true you'd still be a very handsome charlatan, so don't underestimate the difference sex appeal can make. In other words," she said, "a charlatan with charisma. Lots of pull at the box-office!"

Yesterday, Josh might have felt a lot more jealous than today.

"Oh, yes?" said Simon. "No doubt they'll be queuing up for autographs?"

"Or else queuing up to give *theirs*," she answered. "On the petitions."

And in the end she prevailed; and it turned out roughly as she'd foretold. Far from being resentful of any interruption to its enjoyment the crowd showed itself by and large to be good-natured – with scores of its members ready to furnish their signatures. Even some of the initial excitement appeared to have returned.

Otherwise it was the old story. Their signatures would have to stand proxy for the signatories. Next morning the original three were still on their own.

Simon seemed more than usually disappointed.

He eventually explained why. In part.

"A vow is a vow and I've made an unbreakable one."

"One needn't ask to whom," observed Josh.

"Directly to God, yes, but indirectly to the world itself. A vow that will show how very much we *care*! Somebody has to show his appreciation of God's message. Somebody has to show the

232

lengths he'll go to, to express his acceptance of its truth. It's really now or never and there's got to be *some* effective way in which to make the government give us its full attention."

"We ought to make contact with the women of Greenham Common!" declared Geraldine. This wasn't wholly in response to Simon's last comment but was certainly an offshoot.

"The women of Greenham Common ought to make contact with *us*!"

"Yes. True."

"There's absolutely no alternative. It's utterly crucial we renounce Trident! Then with all those billions we shall save we have to get rid of starvation in the Third World, eliminate poverty over here. That'll be a start. Obviously, we shan't get Utopia in the first week."

If Margaret Thatcher stayed in charge, reflected Josh, we shouldn't get it in the first decade, or century.

Simon must have guessed what he was thinking. "If, in the face of everything we do, the government remains obdurate (although I can hardly believe it will: despite all outside differences and discontents it *is* made up of well-intentioned people, many of them religious) but, if it *does*, then the way forward will clearly be to work on basic popular opinion. We're a democracy, remember. And what's more, unless angels have indeed appeared in other countries, Britain will clearly have been chosen to lead the way." Simon smiled, a little twistedly. "That is an honour, you understand."

Josh returned the smile. "Arrogant, I know, but other visitations...well, I'm sure we'd be aware of them in the same way that Gabriel's visit to *Scunthorpe* – so one hears – has been reported all across the globe."

"In that case, leading the way will plainly mean leading the world. Leading through example."

Neither Josh nor Geraldine could help remembering that old and well-known argument: that if Britain relinquished her nuclear deterrents, and even managed to get America and the West to follow suit, where would that leave them then if

233

countries like Russia, say, or Iran or Iraq, decided to retain (or in some cases *develop*) their own weapons of war.

But they had long since realized something. Simon was intractable in matters such as this. He had the idealist's viewpoint, the fanatic's viewpoint, and such viewpoints were invariably and inevitably blinkered.

(They also realized, though, that they themselves – at least to some degree – had now come to share this viewpoint, even if the renunciations in question should prove flagrantly unilateral. How extraordinary was that!)

"Anyway, this vow of yours?" asked Josh. "What does it entail?"

"That, I can't go into."

"I suppose you're not thinking you might kill yourself as a way to point a moral?" Though the question was put playfully it proceeded from a serious foundation. "'Vicar in Angel Controversy Leaves Poignant Suicide Note...to Show How Very Much He Cared'?"

"Stop it, you're breaking my heart," said Simon.

"I'm relieved to hear you say so!"

"All I can tell you is this. I've given my word. And it's a promise there's to be no going back on. Well, I mean, apart from one – now rather unlikely – eventuality."

"Which is?"

"That when we present ourselves in Downing Street on November 30th it has to be with five hundred sympathizers. At the very least."

"Specifics laid down by God or offered by yourself?"

Again Josh was speaking playfully but over the days that followed he and Geraldine conferred increasingly about the true meaning of Simon's words. *Could* it be an intent to kill himself which he'd implied? At moments when they felt rested they managed to shrug off such an idea, almost to laugh at it, but when they felt tired they couldn't see what else he could have had in mind. And Simon's condition seemed unstable enough to warrant such concern. He kept referring to his 'duty', which now seemed to comprehend far more than it had done merely a week before. Perhaps he'd always been a zealot. But now the zealotry was undisguised and unmistakable. He had become a different person.

Therefore the two of them, Geraldine and Josh, each immensely grateful to have the backup of the other, made it their mission to be vigilant – especially when they went into a chemist's for their TCP or soap or plasters, or into corner stores and supermarkets, anywhere, indeed, that might sell aspirin or the like. Thinking of such solidarity, Geraldine had once half-humorously suggested that this was why a lamppost had been placed before a skidding car, "so as, please understand, not to mess around with anyone's free will!"

"Oh, that all-important free will! Yes, thank you, Lord!"

Josh could now use that word without a trace of mockery. It seemed that miracles could still occur.

"And talking of miracles..." (he could now use *that* word as well) "...would it honestly require a miracle to raise just five hundred supporters? Isn't there a company called Rent-a-Crowd? Haven't I read that film studios sometimes use it?"

Geraldine wasn't sure. She'd imagined, maybe wrongly, that even humble extras had to belong to Equity.

But anyhow, as November 30th approached, they were now only forty, thirty, twenty miles from London. Twelve! Ten! Surely people could be persuaded to walk a mere ten miles? Bribed, even – Josh still had money. And a distance that short could easily be covered in a morning: with everyone home again that very afternoon: nobody's job at risk! And apart from the thought of bringing good to the world there'd be company and exercise – something to talk about for weeks – maybe a picture in the papers! Altruism *and* adventure. Any bribes considered, said Josh, should be coming in the opposite direction.

Five hundred supporters?

Five hundred was *nothing*!

But what in God's name was the matter with everyone? By November 29th Josh was going into pubs on his own, into shops and cafés on his own – Geraldine was doing the same – as well as continuing to knock on doors on his own. Geraldine and he

235

would usually canvass opposite sides of the street, these days more and more frequently leaving Simon to himself, to his prayers and meditation. By now they were offering an inducement of twenty pounds to almost anyone they met. Yet nobody at this point was taking either of them very seriously.

And whenever Simon had indeed been coaxed into being a little less 'shut down' as Geraldine had termed it (although certainly not to him) and into resuming his interaction with strangers, Josh kept suggesting he should please get his hair cut as he himself had done (by Geraldine) – or, at the very least, *washed* – and that he should also begin to shave again; but he couldn't suggest he put some weight back on or get rid of that frequently rather scary look in his eye. Simon had developed into what Josh had started to think of as a John-the-Baptist figure, gaunt and staring and unkempt, even to the extent that his two disciples sometimes did their best to keep him in the background, telling him to take time off, rest and recoup his strength. Or, at any rate, his equilibrium...although, again, they didn't call it that.

Yet apparently to no avail, so far as concerned a healthy emotional balance. And the closer had approached the last day of November, then the more strenuously had both those disciples been striving to improve the situation – Josh especially, spurred on by the thought of his own duplicity. He couldn't come to terms with it. If only he had paid heed to Simon's early prognostications! If only money had never entered into it and Simon had been left to proceed along the proper channels! If only he had never made that phone call!

But then, of course, Geraldine wouldn't have been here to share the burden with him and he rather doubted he could have borne it long without her.

Now, however, he made other, far less selfish phone calls. He phoned Sally Madison and was sorry he hadn't thought of doing this earlier. She naturally agreed to travel south immediately. He phoned Elsie, the St Matthew's church secretary. He phoned the vicar of St Lawrence's, and then Tony, Dulcie, Alison and Paula; even Mr Dane at High Ridge (Josh suggested that perhaps he could hold a special assembly, bring all his staff and pupils down

236

to London). He phoned everyone he could think of, including job centre employees, librarians, shop assistants, post office staff, officials on the town council, his doctor and his dentist. And of course he phoned Dawn – whom in any case he was communicating with on a regular basis, his sons as well – but now with a lot more urgency than normal. With every conversation he was proposing the hire of several charabancs – obviously at his own expense – and a mass exodus from Scunthorpe on the following morning, arriving in Westminster by midday.

"Dawnie, I wouldn't say this to anyone else but Simon's really in a bad way."

"Then how very blest he is, how very blest we all are, that he's got *you* there to look after him."

"Sometimes I even begin to fear for his sanity."

She laughed. "Oh, Josh, dear! Don't be so absurd!"

"All right but just you wait until you see him."

"I will! And I won't tell him what you said! Probably all he needs is a good long sleep, the same as you do, and Geraldine! We're so grateful up here for what you've all been doing."

"Only trying to keep the show on the road!" he said.

It was a light, even a modest comment, not in any way self-conscious.

"So, then," she continued, "we'll leave here bright and early, shall we, and make sure we're at the Abbey by twelve? Do you realize, Josh, that all the time we've lived in Scunthorpe I've never once been down to London? It's Mum and Dad who've always made the trip. Won't they get a surprise when we pop our heads round the door and cry out Boo!"

"Dawnie, this isn't about giving your mum and dad a surprise, it's about saving Simon's sanity, maybe his life."

He felt mean about saying that, because he knew full well she'd place her responsibility to Simon and the Church far above any wish to cry out boo to her parents. (Not so long ago he'd have encouraged her in the latter rather than the former, welcoming a happy touch of levity amid all the psalmody and frequent quotes from scripture.)

237

"On second thoughts," he said, "eleven o'clock might be better. Then there'd be time to go into the Abbey, first, to pray." And the walkers, too, so long as they left early enough, could very comfortably reach Westminster by then.

"Oh, Josh..."

For years now she had never told him that she loved him, any more than he had ever said it to her, and the tone in which she spoke his name was perhaps as close to expressing it as these days she could come.

"And while you're in London," he declared, jokingly but not entirely so, "maybe we'll buy you a smart new dress and a hat for the wedding and some really elegant new shoes – Dawnie, how would you feel about wearing high heels again?"

While talking to her like this, he realized it was the first time he'd felt halfway optimistic about anything since...well, possibly since the start of the pilgrimage. He could even feel happy his earlier advice had been ignored and that Dawnie and Janice had refused to contemplate a wedding during his own absence. (Naturally, Simon's absence would also have been a consideration but Josh now knew it wouldn't have been the main one.) He even felt it was possible – if he prayed about it hard enough! – that he might *eventually* come to tolerate the husband.

"Then, after we've all got up off our knees," he added lightly, "we'll go to have some lunch somewhere. Before presenting the petitions."

"To Mrs Thatcher?"

"You mean, go there for our lunch?"

She laughed. "No, you silly. For presenting the petitions."

"Indeed to Mrs Thatcher – whom else?"

She now spoke half-jokingly. "I ought to get a hairdo, then, to make way for that posh new hat!" For she really did wonder whether Sandra could possibly fit her in that afternoon without an appointment. "Will you be coming back on the coach with us, dear – you and Simon?"

"Yes, on one of the coaches – the one you and the boys are in! Can't see why not! Grief, it will be good to be home again."

"Good for us, too. We've missed you, Josh."

238

Again, he thought, it didn't need to be the actual words.

Not on either side. "And I've missed *you*, Dawnie. Things haven't always been that good between us, have they? But now we can make a brand new start. Yes?"

He could imagine the softness of her smile. "Absence makes the heart grow fonder," she said.

"Not for everyone," he laughed. "What about – out of sight, out of mind?"

"Oh, I hadn't thought of that one! Which reminds me, Josh: while you've been away I've been planning something! After Christmas I might enrol for an evening class, maybe a couple, to catch up on some education. If it isn't too late, I mean."

She added quickly and on a clear note of victory, "And it isn't, is it? Because – here's another old quotation for you! – *it's never too late to mend*. There! And I want to be the sort of bright one you deserve."

"I want to be the sort of bright one *you* deserve."

"Easier for you than me," she said.

"That's bullshit," he replied, and perhaps it was a sign of the times to come she didn't reproach him for it. In fact, he'd sent up a little prayer asking that she wouldn't. Perhaps she'd even be less churchy? "Anyhow, old thing, getting back to our muttons... Shall we have lunch in some big and busy place if we can actually *find* one big enough – then we could sweep up all the other customers and get them to accompany us round the corner? A lot of 'em will be tourists and they'll probably see it as something typically British and on no account to be missed."

"And we could also go back in the Abbey and sweep up all the people who we find in there!"

"Not to mention everyone on the pavements, all the sightseers and office-workers!"

"I'll stop the traffic in my smart new hat. We'll get all the cars to turn right round and follow us."

"Some of them may not even have to turn round so long as they follow us! I can see we'll end up with five *thousand* not just the measly five hundred Simon's been asking for. He's going to

239

be let off the hook in *triumph*, to the swelling accompaniment of a vast celestial choir and a multicoloured sunset."

And he almost believed it.

43

So it hardly seemed to matter that on the following morning, November 30th, on the very last leg of their journey, the final ten miles or so, Simon and Geraldine and he had no more than a baker's dozen marching alongside. Josh had explained to Simon how – if he'd *really* feel satisfied with just a paltry five hundred beside him in Downing Street – then he'd have to get the remaining four-and-a-half thousand either to drop out voluntarily or else arrange for everyone to draw lots; and he must have sounded fairly convincing (well, rightly so) since the atmosphere was far lighter than a short time ago he would have considered possible. Admittedly, Simon wasn't *initiating* any conversations but he answered fully enough when any member of the party put some question to him and he even, to some extent, joined in the game of spotting the Christmas decorations already displayed in windows and on rooftops. The game was short-lived but provided a few bursts of laughter.

There was only one coach from Scunthorpe. Thirty-seven travellers in all including the driver. But added to the sixteen who'd been on foot the total was already over fifty and would barely need to be multiplied by ten. And good heavens, exclaimed Dawn, all the hundreds of people they'd seen here practically fighting one another for space! She meant: seen here during the ultimate stage of their journey, in Baker Street and around Marble Arch and along Park Lane. In *London* – Geraldine agreed, immediately catching on – in London, not just Westminster. What about Trafalgar Square, the Strand, Fleet Street, Ludgate Hill? Add the worshippers at St Paul's to the worshippers in the Abbey (the Cathedral, too), add the shoppers in Oxford Street to the shoppers at the Army & Navy Stores, add

240

the rail passengers at Waterloo to those at Victoria; not to forget the cavernous, bustling coach station only half a mile up the road? And so on and so forth. All right, that whole prodigious catch might take a little longer to land than anyone had allowed for, but what was so special, what was so sacrosanct, about November 30th? The Scunthorpe contingent would doubtless be able to sleep in the coach while everyone else, if necessary, could look for modest accommodation funded by the common purse. And, in all honesty, the first day of December would actually make a better date. Dawn reminded everyone that December was the month in which our Saviour had been born and nobody, not even Josh, who in times gone by would certainly have come up with some fairly crushing response, did anything but nod in acquiescence.

They had their lunch. The restaurant was large and it definitely became busy following its sudden influx of fifty-three. At the last moment there were those who said it might be better if they split up, eating at five or six other places, but no one apart from Josh seemed to greet this plan with enthusiasm – Simon appeared wholly indifferent – and by then several of the staff had gone to a lot of trouble to get all fifty-three seated; the suggestion was abandoned. Besides, what with the National Gallery and the British Museum and the Victoria and Albert, what with all the other spots where people congregated in their thousands – department stores, train termini, Madame Tussaud's, the Tower – who really needed the few displaced customers from Wendy's Homemade Lunches, Teas and Suppers? The fifty-three mostly ate pasta, followed by ice cream with chocolate sauce, then made a choice between coffee and tea. Josh footed the bill.

While everyone was awaiting the arrival of these hot drinks Simon got up and went to stand behind Josh's chair, lowering his head and speaking to him softly. "I want to go to check out what it's like in Downing Street at this time of day and to discover, if I can, when Mrs Thatcher is most likely to be around. So you won't mind if I leave you here to keep an eye on things?"

"No, of course not but – "

"In fact I don't know why I ask. It's *you* who've been keeping an eye on things, anyway, almost from the start – you even more than Geraldine. Don't imagine I've not been aware of it or that I haven't felt incessantly grateful. As well as astonished!"

Josh wasn't sure how to answer but in any case it wouldn't have been easy to say much, not with Simon's hands pressing down on his shoulders (Josh noticed he hadn't cut his fingernails for some time – which was *not* an appropriate thing to become aware of at such a moment) and presumably with no one else being meant to overhear. He replied fatuously:

"But even if she's there – Mrs Thatcher – it's not she who'll be coming to the door."

"No but I shall tell the policeman on duty there'll be petitions to hand in and of course I'll give my name and confirm it's God's messenger I represent and I would think that out of pure courtesy...I don't mean towards me but towards God..." In spite of the fact he was talking quietly Simon spoke with dignity and his subdued tone suited what he had to say. "If God is doing his work, as obviously we know he is, always has and always will – that should doubtless bring Mrs Thatcher to the door."

Characteristically Josh wondered if even God doing his work could quite accomplish it if the lady weren't willing: surely the Prime Minister was an exponent of free choice if anybody was. But he refrained from making so trivial a comment.

"At any rate," said Simon, "I need to be on my own for a while. It's all been a bit noisy, this, hasn't it?"

"After the relative calm of the wilderness? Yes, indeed it has. We'll meet you back at the coach, then, or look for you in the Abbey."

"Again, Josh, thank you. In the end there could have been nobody better to take charge."

The pressure on his shoulders changed to an affectionate squeeze. Momentarily Josh laid his own right hand over Simon's. Then unhurriedly Simon moved across to the other side of the table, where Dawn and William and Michael were sitting. The pride on Dawn's face was unmistakable. Her air of happiness and perhaps also the different way in which her hair

242

was styled made her look surprisingly good – youthful, pretty. "Obviously," Simon said, "if it hadn't been for you three, none of us would be sitting here today."

He spoke to them for less than a minute. But it was enough. When he'd moved off, Dawn glanced at Josh as if to tell him life could scarcely be more wonderful.

Simon then walked across to Geraldine and thanked her, as well, for everything she'd done and for everything she'd wanted to do.

"Oh, any time!" she replied, swivelling round in her seat and smiling up into his face. "I hope I'll be given lots more opportunity!"

He hesitated. "If only we could have met five years ago..."

"Yes, that would have been good. But you, better than most, should realize God usually gets his timings right!"

"Usually?"

She laughed; she had decided to be brave. "And at present he's saying it's absolutely the right time for you to get rid of that beard – it really doesn't suit you! He's wondering whether there isn't a barber nearby whom you can patronize before you pluck up the courage to invite me on a date."

He smiled but didn't answer. Pleased with the effect of her daring, Geraldine felt that things were going to turn out as she wanted, although she knew she would have to be patient. She watched as he made his way back to the spot where he'd begun his wanderings. There was a vacant chair beside Mrs Madison, the chair on which he himself had been sitting, but now, almost as if scared of having to make too much eye contact, he again stood behind the person he spoke to. This final conversation was as brief as the previous two and ended with Simon putting his arms around his mother's neck and kissing her on the cheek. When he left she turned her head to watch, with ill-concealed anxiety, as he walked out of the restaurant – his having nodded a thank-you to the man and woman who had chiefly served them. In addition to seeing her anxiety Josh thought he saw the sheen of tears.

Because he had to make two stops along the way, one at a hardware store, the other at a public convenience (and the former being in a side street he found it difficult to get directions), it took nearly an hour for Simon to reach his destination. But God *was* doing his work. This afternoon, Mrs Thatcher was indeed at No 10 – in Simon's mind it had never been relevant, that talk about tomorrow – and when eventually she was summoned by her staff she did graciously consent to come to the front door.

Regal. Soignée. Smiling.

In a way, he felt sorry for her...and for everyone else who'd be a witness. But it had to be done. These next minutes had to be got through. He hoped he wouldn't scream. Naturally he prayed that he wouldn't, that somehow it wouldn't even be necessary, but as he struck the match before applying it to his wet, still dripping, underwear (quantities of methylated spirit having been poured down both its back and front and onto his jumper and socks as well but not elsewhere, since he'd had to reduce the risk of its being either seen or smelt)...as he struck the match before applying it, his thoughts were as much with Ginny as they were with God – for the moment the two were indivisible. In his heart, he was reaching out his hand to Ginny.

Swimming with William

The action of the play is set during an evening in February 1985. It takes place in the sitting room of the Freemans' house in Scunthorpe.

Characters:

William Freeman	middle-forties.
Norah Freeman	similar.
Tom Freeman	seventeen.
Linda Freeman	nineteen.
Trevor Lomax	twenty-one.

Act One

The time is about 8pm, on a Friday in February. A sitting room.
Lamps are lit, the curtains drawn. Some five or six armchairs.

TOM   (Loose-leaf file on knee) Hey. You know
               you're always looking for a chance to shine?

WILLIAM   (Reading) Is it me you're addressing? Have I
               changed into the light switch?

TOM   I thought you were supposed to be observant.
               Light switches don't shine. They like it best
               when someone turns them on.

WILLIAM   What did you want?

TOM   It's interesting, though, the way that people see
               themselves... I'll put you down as some sort of
               hybrid.

WILLIAM   Please, Tom. I'm feeling tired.

TOM   It's your own fault. If you didn't make so much
               fuss about the heating, I'd be working upstairs.
               What are the Seven Deadly Sins? Apart from
               pride?

WILLIAM   The deadliest of all: getting upon the wick of
               thy father.

TOM   Thanks. And I'd better get down all the
               subdivisions. (Pretends to write) Thou shalt not
               play thy music too loud, nor too late. Thou
               shalt not stay out beyond the witching hour
               of midnight. Thou shalt not –

WILLIAM	Be fair. Without first saying where you are – or at what time you'll be home.
TOM	In other words…the third degree.
WILLIAM	If you but knew it there are fewer commandments in this house than in most. Thou shalt always admit the truth ought to be one of them.
TOM	Careful, though. Tricky one, that. It could redound.
WILLIAM	Why do you need to know the Seven Deadly Sins? I'm surprised you don't already – a sophisticate like you.
TOM	A crappy essay. "What makes the Seven Deadly Sins so deadly?" Having to write a crappy essay on them for a start.
WILLIAM	The crappiness is mandatory? They insist on it, do they?
TOM	I like to hold the mirror up to life. That's where my essays differ from your novels.
WILLIAM	Oh, what a tease you are! All right now. Gluttony…lust…sloth. We've mentioned pride. Envy…
TOM	Two more.
WILLIAM	Why don't you look in the dictionary?
TOM	Defeated, eh?

He puts down file and crosses to bookcase. NORAH comes in, carrying cups of coffee on a tray. WILLIAM takes his; she sets one down for TOM.

NORAH   (To TOM) Goodness! So you really are doing your homework?

TOM   Of course, Short Wobbly Mum.

NORAH   I thought it was a Pretext to avoid the washing up. I mean – homework just after supper on a Friday evening instead of last thing on a Sunday night! It isn't natural.

TOM   And people call me ironic. Besides, I don't need any pretext. All he's doing is reading Georgette Heyer.

NORAH   Your father happens to be the breadwinner, my darling. He is also feeling a little under the weather.

TOM   The breadwinner! And how can he be feeling under the weather on a night when his little Goody Two Shoes is trotting home as fast as her ten little toes can carry her? And nobody ever cares whether I'm feeling under the weather or not.

NORAH   Are you?

TOM   Yes. Always and ever. It's a condition of my life. I have the Bomb hanging over me – and it's driving me *mad*! Also I can't find this bloody… Oh, yes I can. Anger and covetousness: the two we're missing.

255

WILLIAM	(To NORAH) Deadly Sins. Essay on.
NORAH	Oh. Well. No one better qualified.
TOM	(To WILLIAM) Interesting that gluttony was the first one which came into *your* mind. I said you took the biggest helping of stew.
NORAH	Oh, Tom, don't start on that again. Your father never takes –
TOM	Only joking, Wobbly Mum.
NORAH	Well, you weren't joking at suppertime. You should know by now that he develops indigestion the very instant he thinks he may have taken a fraction more than anybody else.
TOM	"Quick! Help! Fetch my Rennies!"
NORAH	(To WILLIAM) Darling, it isn't indigestion you need help with. It's insanity. Are Rennies any good for that?
WILLIAM	You're not suggesting that I'm neurotic or something?
NORAH	And the awful thing is…people who don't know you think you're the easiest-going man on earth. Sometimes I could cry.
WILLIAM	No doubt you disillusion them.
NORAH	No. I think you wouldn't like it.
WILLIAM	These days I honestly wouldn't care. At forty-five I've grown mature; I'm no longer

ashamed of my neuroses. Indeed, I pay them
tribute. They've made of me a deeper and far
lovelier person.

TOM   Plus a real pain to live with.

WILLIAM   So disillusion them all you like.

NORAH   Right. I'll go and telephone.

WILLIAM   In fact in some ways I think I'm rather less of a
             hypocrite than you.

NORAH   That's very sweet.

WILLIAM   When I feel depressed I let everybody see it,
             outsiders as well as family. I don't parade it –
             but nor do I hide it. In my view it's wrong to
             behave one way in the home and another in the
             street. You, on the other hand, can mope about
             all day feeling unfulfilled, frumpish, fading, *fat*;
             and then as soon as the doorbell rings sparkle
             like a girl who's just fallen in love.

NORAH   Well, I must say I think that's a bit unfair. I was
             always taught that your first duty to any visitor
             was hospitality, not self-indulgence. (Looks at
             TOM) And I didn't realize we were talking in
             earnest.

TOM   That's okay, Wobbles. I'm not listening.
             Besides, you always claim you're progressive
             parents. If I see you two putting in the knife, it
             helps me deal with any guilt arising out of my
             own...very occasional...lapses from patience.

NORAH   I was not putting in the knife.

257

WILLIAM	Oh, you...fibber.
NORAH	Well, not very far, anyway. Not half as far as you deserved. Would you like some more coffee?
TOM	Yes, please.
NORAH	I was speaking to your father; showing my forgiving nature. My sparkling and forgiving nature.
WILLIAM	No, thanks. I imagine we'll be having some more when Linda arrives?
NORAH	My forgiving nature may not last that long. You told me I was fat.
WILLIAM	No, I didn't.
NORAH	It was in your mind. I shall now sit here and refine on it; the way that you refine on things.
WILLIAM	Shall I tell you what's in my mind at present? Despite everything? I think you're a pretty good wife to me, and a pretty good mother to your children. I'm very fond of you, at heart.
NORAH	That's nice. I'm also very fond of you, at heart. Despite everything.
TOM	And then some.

WILLIAM goes over and kisses NORAH; remains standing behind her chair for a while, with his arms around her neck. TOM pulls a face and jots down a few more notes.

TOM   I wonder why murder isn't included?

WILLIAM   Superfluous, maybe? I mean, it may always
                 arise out of anger – or envy – or covetousness?

TOM   And suicide? Despair? Why aren't they there?

WILLIAM   Let's hope...because the compilers were imbued
                 with humanity. Otherwise – I agree – they did a
                 remarkably sloppy job.

NORAH   Perhaps the sin of sloth – sloth is one of them,
                 isn't it? – is a nod in that direction? And it seems
                 to me that with every day and in every way I
                 grow a little bit more slothful – (Sparkles and
                 caresses her cheeks) – with beautiful pink
                 Camay.

TOM   Poor old Wobbles. I think you're next in line for
                 the Rennies.

Front door slams. LINDA is heard.

LINDA   Hi, everyone! I'm home!

WILLIAM   There she is!

He rushes into the hall. "Hello, my love. Here, give us a hug."
Pause. "Now come in and get warm. But first let me look at you.
You've grown even more beautiful than when we saw you last."
"Thanks, Dad. And you've grown even more youthful-looking
and handsome." "The difference is, though: *I* haven't grown
insincere." "Nor have I. You see, I meet the fathers of so many
girls that every time I come home it really does hit me just how
young you look. Most of them are bald and have tums."

TOM   (To NORAH) And that's only the girls. You
               should see the fathers!

Linda: "And I bet there's not one of them can do more than a
hundred press-ups non-stop." "Oh, currently it's about two
hundred and fifty." "Seriously?" "More, on my good days." "On
my good days I might manage...three?" William and Linda come
in.

NORAH   Hello, darling.

LINDA   Hello, Mum. (They embrace)

TOM   Hi, Freak!

LINDA   Hi, young brother! Hey, Mum, is that a new
               dress?

NORAH   Oxfam. Like it?

LINDA   I might borrow it.

NORAH   Oh, Linda's home all right! Sweetheart, come
               and stand by the fire. What kind of journey?

LINDA   (Taking off coat, scarf, gloves and woolly hat;
               shaking out her curls) Excellent. Somebody
               gave me a lift.

NORAH   Oh, that's good. Somebody nice?

LINDA   Somebody very nice. And as a matter of fact –

NORAH   But, darling, before you go into that, may I just
               ask...? Have you eaten?

LINDA   At an Indian place in Doncaster. Delicious.

NORAH   Well, that was sensible. But it's a good job, you
             wretch, we didn't wait supper for you. We had
             no idea what time you'd be coming.

TOM   I've always said so: she treats this place like a
             hotel. Don't you, Freaky?

LINDA   Creep!

NORAH   Oh, Linda. Clear up the mystery for us! Why a
             telegram? In a way it was thrilling. In a way it
             was frightening: I thought I'd reached a hundred.

LINDA   I'd never sent a telegram before. I felt it would
             be fun.

TOM   All of life should be experienced. Even its more
             seamy and disgusting side. You need to plumb
             the depths.

LINDA   Exactly.

TOM   I think she's probably been at the booze. Shall
             we dance?

LINDA   It's just so good to be home.

TOM   Oh, what a freak!

WILLIAM   There is absolutely nothing wrong, my lad, with
             being a home-loving girl – (Turning back to
             LINDA) – even though university life very
             obviously agrees with you. You've got all the
             sparkle of your mother. (To NORAH, unable
             to resist it) I mean, of course, only on one of
             your off-days, love.

261

NORAH	(To LINDA) Yes, when we came for that weekend last term he looked quite green for about the next fortnight.
TOM	Remember now: that terrible sin of envy and all that it can lead to.
LINDA	(Slightly baffled – after a pause) You two are looking very good.
NORAH	Thank you, darling. And some of us even manage it without going to the solarium twice a week.
WILLIAM	There's nothing wrong with going to the solarium.
NORAH	No. Did I say there was? Except that it dries out the skin.
TOM	And all that money you're chucking away could go to Ethiopia. Or – better still – to me.
WILLIAM	Oh, for heaven's sake! All that money! In any case, from now on it'll probably be only once a week. Perhaps not even that.
LINDA	I think they're both quite rotten: the way they pick on you. Let me state here and now that I intend to stick up for you this weekend. Come hell or high water.
NORAH	No matter how you have to perjure yourself.
TOM	Do you think it makes you look sexy? At your age?

WILLIAM   Oh, you'd be surprised.

NORAH   Certainly some of the more elderly shop
              assistants seem to give him the eye.

TOM   And not just the female ones, either.

LINDA   Oh, no! Tiny Tom isn't still going through that
              phase, is he – calling everyone a poofter?

TOM   No. Only your father.

WILLIAM   In a moment he's going to say – sorry, just
              joking.

TOM   Well, I don't really mind his being a poofter.

LINDA   (To WILLIAM) Oh, do you remember that time
              on the station – just the two of us – you were
              seeing me off somewhere and while we were
              waiting you did a series of dance steps – or
              maybe sang, I can't remember?

WILLIAM   A rather fancy piece of footwork.

LINDA   And I said, "Stop it, you look like a poof!" and
              you turned to this haughty-looking woman
              standing near us and said, "Madam, I don't look
              like a poof, do I?"

WILLIAM   And she smiled very pleasantly and answered,
              "Not in the slightest."

LINDA   I wanted to die.

WILLIAM   No, you didn't. You laughed. And it *was* rather
              a fancy piece of footwork, wasn't it? It went

something like this, I seem to remember... Drum roll, Maestro, please. (TOM shrugs and then enters into the spirit of the thing: produces a drum roll) No – wait. Where's my cane? (LINDA laughingly throws him his cane) And top hat? (Now he powders the ground with French chalk) Okay. Spotlight. Come on now, Norah, please be ready with that spotlight. Has anyone got a staircase with a hundred lovely girls? (NORAH now runs towards him, sparkling, and offering herself) All right, here's a staircase; we'll have to do without the girls.

NORAH   Oh, wouldn't you have guessed I'd be cast as Staircase?

TOM   You always get these walk-on parts.

NORAH   Well, I'm glad that someone realizes it, at long last. Electrician, staircase *and* admiring audience. Life holds no surprises. (She weeps theatrically and LINDA comforts her)

WILLIAM   She's only wanting to upstage me. She has this sadly competitive nature. (To TOM) Now if you'd be so good as to give me that intro once again... (Goes into his dance, which he performs well, with undoubted talent) Pick out a pleasant outlook. Stick out that noble chin. Wipe off that full-of-doubt look. Slap on a cheerful grin. And let there be sunshine...all over the place. Put on a happy face. (Takes a bow, blows kisses in acknowledgment of all the cheers and applause, and sinks back into his chair wiping his forehead) Not a bad house, I suppose. The reception wasn't all it might have been.

NORAH   Was it ever?

LINDA   You were always so embarrassing. (TOM nods
               enthusiastically)

WILLIAM   At least you're alive when you're embarrassed.

NORAH   Well, that's certainly one point of view. Can
               anyone deny it?

LINDA   (To WILLIAM) And you saw it as your mission
               to give life?

WILLIAM   Yes! Oh, yes! I did – and do – and shall. Indeed,
               I'd like to think that one day they might inscribe
               that on my tombstone.

TOM   I'll take a note. (Pretends) Otherwise – with any
               luck – we might end up hating ourselves for
               having forgotten it so quickly.

NORAH   And, children, you wouldn't believe: his parents
               – God rest their souls – were always so *very*
               respectable and self-effacing! Not to mention
               dull.

WILLIAM   You leave my parents out of this. (More lightly)
               Well, anyway, my mother. You can say what
               you like about my father.

TOM   How history repeats itself!

NORAH   All I was meaning was...they might have been a
               bit surprised. You were such a very polite
               young man – so quiet – you even seemed a little
               shy.

LINDA	Shy! Do you know, I was always quite terrified of your meeting my friends? I could never be certain of what you'd say next. With 'shy' I would have been in heaven.
WILLIAM	I'm glad you decided that this weekend you were going to stick up for me.
LINDA	And from now on I shall, I promise you. Besides – sometimes, even while squirming, I remember – there was still a part of me that used to feel a bit proud. (To NORAH) But was he very much the gentleman?
NORAH	Oh, yes, when I first knew him I could take him anywhere and feel no apprehension. He wasn't at all unpredictable. So where did I go wrong?
WILLIAM	I thought you were complaining that life holds no surprises.
NORAH	Yes, but I meant pleasant ones.
LINDA	Well, anyway, let's say it may still hold a few pleasant ones… You see, I've asked someone to come round to meet you all in roughly ten minutes.
NORAH	The friend who drove you up?
LINDA	Yes.
WILLIAM	Is she blonde, long-legged and half as beautiful as you?
LINDA	Long-legged and beautiful but not a she.

TOM   Ah-ha. Sex enters the equation!

NORAH   Undergraduate?

LINDA   Yes. Same year as me – but only because he
             took time off to explore America; his parents
             have a home in San Francisco, you see.
             (Casually) As well as two others. In London and
             the Isle of Wight.

TOM   Jesus Christ.

NORAH   Tom!

TOM   No wonder she sends us telemessages!

LINDA   Well, I knew if I spoke to you on the phone
             you'd start to guess at some of it and then I
             wouldn't be able to hold back…when what I
             really wanted was to be here to see your faces.

NORAH   You're engaged!

LINDA   Yes!

NORAH   (Jumps up and kisses her) Oh, darling, darling!
             My congratulations! This is marvellous. This
             is *so* marvellous! (Wipes her eyes) Aren't you
             impressed by my restraint?

LINDA   Aren't you impressed by mine? I've been home
             all of ten minutes…and have only now spoken
             his name.

NORAH   But darling! You haven't!

LINDA   No, so I haven't. It's Trevor. Trevor Lomax.

NORAH   Trevor Lomax... Oh, that's nice. It's got
          something.

LINDA   It's got everything. Well, almost everything.
          Dad? You're being very quiet.

WILLIAM   I... Am I? I think I've only just got back the
          power of speech. I thought you meant to
          wait...at least another six years...no earlier than
          twenty-five, you said. (Pulls himself together
          and kisses her) But what the hell. You know
          your happiness is all I care about.

LINDA   Thanks, Dad.

WILLIAM   And you really want to marry him: this long-
          legged paragon? (She nods) You said...you said
          just now...*almost* everything. What
          reservations?

LINDA   Oh. none. None at all. Nothing worth the
          mention.

WILLIAM   You're sure?

LINDA   Quite sure. (WILLIAM paces restlessly) Mum, I
          told him he could spend the night here. Is that
          all right? I said you'd probably ask him for the
          weekend.

NORAH   Of course, darling. Later, we must put a duster
          over the spare room. I hope he enjoys quite
          ordinary, simple things.

LINDA   Brother mine, I haven't yet received *your*
          congratulation – nor your kiss.

TOM   You can have the first, I suppose; I'm damned if
               you'll get the second.

LINDA   All right, then, a compromise. We'll shake
               hands.

They shake hands and LINDA exuberantly pecks him on the
cheek.

TOM   Oh – what a freak! But of course I should have
               known. What else but low cunning could have
               landed you a rich man? Or any man at all?...
               Hey, do you think much of it will ever come our
               way?

NORAH   Tom!

LINDA   No, Mum, don't worry. Anyone can say
               anything tonight. *Carte blanche.* Or at least
               until Trevor gets here.

NORAH   Oh! Talking about him I'd forgotten he was
               actually coming. Linda, how do I look? I wish
               you'd given us some warning. (Indicating
               Linda's coat and things) Tom, run and hang
               those in the hall, please.

TOM   Why me? They're not mine.

NORAH   And then take these coffee cups into the
               kitchen... William, do be helpful or else sit
               down again.

WILLIAM   How long have you known this boy?

LINDA   A little over two weeks.

269

WILLIAM   Two weeks!

LINDA   And, Dad, he isn't 'this boy'. He's Trevor.

WILLIAM   Norah, did you hear that? Two weeks. I'm really
            not at all sure about this.

LINDA   Why? What is there for *you* to be sure about?

TOM returns.

WILLIAM   What can you know of anyone in just a little
            over two weeks? Except, perhaps, you want to
            go to bed with them. And when do you plan on
            getting married? Monday?

TOM   Or don't you care for long engagements?

LINDA   We don't know yet. We thought perhaps at
            Easter.

WILLIAM   This Easter?

LINDA   Yes, we realize it doesn't give us long. But we
            don't want a large wedding. And don't worry,
            by the way: his parents will be paying.

WILLIAM   Do they know about this yet?

LINDA   Of course.

WILLIAM   Why of course? We've only just found out.
            Aren't we as important as they are?

NORAH   William, you know Linda didn't mean that. Oh,
            heavens, I must go to have a wee – but how can

270

I, when I'm so afraid of what you two... I mean, things that you'll forget to tell me? Will you promise me, all of you, to sit here in complete silence?

LINDA   Yes, Mum. We won't say another word.

WILLIAM   Have you *met* his family yet?

LINDA   That's happening next weekend.

NORAH   Oh, please! I don't want him to find me in the loo.

Doorbell rings.

LINDA   I'll go! I know you're going to like him. Please – you've got to make him like you. (Exits)

WILLIAM   Oh, that's nice. *He* doesn't have to work at it. We do.

NORAH   My goodness! Don't be so touchy!

TOM   Who was the silly girl, then, who left it too late? Nothing for it now but to keep your legs crossed. Or do I mean your fingers?

NORAH   Anyway, it's only nerves. As soon as he comes in, I'll be fine. Tom, do I look reasonably okay?

TOM holds up his hand, with his forefinger and thumb making an O of high approval. WILLIAM, standing before the mirror, quickly pats his hair into place, smoothes both eyebrows with his middle finger. He turns away from the mirror, pulls his sweater down, sticks out his chest; is annoyed to find TOM watching him.

271

TOM	Smashing. You'll outshine us all. The light switch doesn't stand a chance.

LINDA enters with TREVOR. TREVOR is blond, attractive and expensively, although not showily, dressed.

LINDA	Well, everybody, here he is! Mum, this is Trevor.
NORAH	Hello, Trevor. Are you feeling half as nervous as I am?
TREVOR	Petrified. Those must be my teeth you hear. Or possibly my knees.
NORAH	(About to shake hands) Or are we allowed to kiss? This is the first time. I don't yet know the form.
TREVOR	Well, I haven't been through it all that often myself. Let's make up our own rules. (They kiss)
LINDA	And this is my father.
WILLIAM	Trevor Lomax – the man of contradictions!
TREVOR	Sir?
WILLIAM	Petrified; turned to stone. And yet your knees knock. (They shake hands)
LINDA	I think that's a joke. You soon get used to Dad. You don't need to pay him much attention.

WILLIAM	You might have concealed that for at least a minute.
LINDA	You bring these things upon yourself. And this is my little brother: that *enfant terrible* I warned you about. You don't have to pay him much attention, either.
TREVOR	(They shake hands) Hello, Tom.
TOM	Hi, Trev.
LINDA	Trev! (Pulls a face)
TOM	Is that really a nice, normal, healthy reaction to the man you say you want to marry? Oh – who expects 'normal' in this household?
NORAH	Trevor, never mind any of them – you come and talk to me. You must be frozen; perhaps it wasn't just nerves making your teeth chatter. Warm yourself first at the fire.
TREVOR	Thank you – but I'm fine. (TREVOR sits, having looked round to check all the family is seated. LINDA is sitting on the floor)
NORAH	Well, do I need to say this has been one of the biggest surprises of my life – and definitely one of the happiest? But what have you been doing for the past twenty minutes while Linda was giving us all such pleasure? Not just sitting in your car shaking?
TREVOR	Oh, no. Driving round the town a little. Shaking.

273

NORAH	Poor Trevor. And you couldn't have seen much of it at this time of night, anyway. Come to that, there isn't much of it to see, not even at high noon.
TREVOR	No shoot-outs?
NORAH	I almost wish there were. Anything, I sometimes feel, to mitigate the dullness.
WILLIAM	Except unpredictability.
NORAH	At the moment all we've got is slush on the roads.
WILLIAM	Darling, won't you please make up your mind what it is you really want out of life.
NORAH	Oh, that man! He makes it sound so simple.
WILLIAM	Of course it's simple.
NORAH	No, for shoot-outs, Trevor, you have to step inside this house. But had I known you were just sitting in the car I'd have come and sat next to you. Held your hand.
TOM	Oy, oy! Oy, oy! Oy, oy!
LINDA	He's mine. Not on loan to anyone. Even you.
NORAH	That's not fair. I shan't let you borrow my dress.
WILLIAM	Oh, your mother drives a hard bargain! What kind of car is it?

TREVOR	A Lambourghini.
TOM	Lambourghini! Is it yours or...or your dad's?
TREVOR	It was my birthday present last year – when I was twenty-one.
TOM	Did you hear that, folks? Only another four years to go; you can start saving. Did you have any car before that?
TREVOR	Oh, just an old beat-up banger of my sister's. Do you drive?
TOM	No, worse luck. People round here are too mean to cough up for lessons. And on the pocket money I get –
NORAH	Trevor, how many brothers and sisters do you have?
TREVOR	I've two sisters, Mrs Freeman – no brothers. They're older than I am: Vanessa's twenty-three, Sally twenty-four.
WILLIAM	Just wait until you've got a job and can pay for your own lessons.
TOM	And when will that be?
NORAH	Are either of them married?
TREVOR	They both are. I've a niece and two nephews.
WILLIAM	In the meantime use your bike.

NORAH	That's enough! If it's not one pair of them, then it's the other. When you were younger did you and your brothers, I mean sisters, squabble all the time?
TREVOR	Oh, I'm sure we did. Or would have. You see, we weren't together all that much. Went to different schools.
NORAH	Ah, yes. You mean boarding schools?
WILLIAM	He means public schools.
TREVOR	Yes, I'm afraid so.
WILLIAM	Now that's interesting. Why afraid so?
TREVOR	Well, I suppose I'm a little ashamed of the privileges money can buy.
WILLIAM	How ashamed?
TREVOR	Sir?
WILLIAM	Let's put it this way. How much, for instance, have you given to Ethiopia?
NORAH	Oh, William!
LINDA	Dad!
TREVOR	No, it's a perfectly fair question. I've given a...well, a reasonable amount. Nowhere near as much as I should have done, naturally, but...
WILLIAM	Twenty pounds?

LINDA	Don't answer that. He's got no right to ask.
TREVOR	A thousand.
WILLIAM	A thousand pounds! But I wasn't talking about your parents' contribution. I was talking about your own quite independently of theirs.
TREVOR	Yes, so was I. I don't know what my parents gave; we didn't discuss it. But I'm sure, of course, that they gave something.
WILLIAM	How do you know, then, if you didn't discuss it?
TREVOR	We discuss the *situations*; I know their attitudes. But nobody says, "Look at me: I'm now going off to be charitable!" And nobody asks.
WILLIAM	(Pause) I feel I owe you an apology. Linda was right. I was entirely out of line.
TREVOR	I don't see why, sir. But thank you, anyway. I never turn down a good apology.
TOM	And especially you shouldn't in this house. They're extremely rare.
NORAH	You speak for yourself. And even for your sister. Your father is always very quick with an apology, if he considers he's been in the wrong.
WILLIAM	Mother likewise. And she does it more often – since she's more often in the wrong. (NORAH sticks out her tongue at him)

277

TREVOR	(Laughs) I really hope I didn't give the wrong impression just now. We're a very ordinary sort of family. The only difference is...that we've been lucky. Yes, we try to be decent, but so do most people.
WILLIAM	Do they?
TREVOR	I think so.
WILLIAM	Yes, I suppose I think so too, on the whole.
NORAH	Of course you do. You're an out-and-out optimist by nature.
TOM	Except when he's an out-and-out pessimist by nature.
NORAH	No, if you're talking about that slightly cynical air which he –
TOM	I'm talking about the days when all he does is mooch around with the mask of tragedy upon his face, not eating anything, not speaking to anyone...
WILLIAM	All right, I get depressed; we've already been through that once this evening – although I concede, not in front of Trevor. But you get moody too. You're not exactly Nature's Own and Best-Loved Little Sunbeam, may I point out?
TOM	(Jumps up and feigns a tantrum) I am, I am, I am! Mummy, how can he say otherwise? (Runs to her for protection) Beat off that naughty man! (To WILLIAM) But even if that's true...I

have a special dispensation. It's my age. It's the Bomb. It's my inheritance from you. (Sings) "My sister wears a muss-tach, my brother wears a dress. Golly – gee – no wonder I'm a mess!"

WILLIAM   But I have a special dispensation as well: God's attempt at consolation for saddling me with you. It was inadequate but at least it showed willing.

TOM   Now that could be your epitaph! We'd hardly have to change the pronoun.

WILLIAM   Well, one could end up with worse. (To TREVOR) You may have noticed by now: we have a love-hate relationship, my son and I.

TOM   Only half of that is true.

WILLIAM   Rubbish. Sometimes you think I'm okay.

TOM   Sez who? And even if that were so, it doesn't seem to work in the opposite direction.

NORAH   Honestly, I've seldom heard you two talk so much nonsense. No, that *isn't* honest: I've often heard it. But poor Trevor, what must he be thinking? They're really very nice. Both of them. And basically, too, they're really very fond of one another.

LINDA   Look, if Trevor wants nothing more to do with me after this weekend…!

TOM   Do you really think, then, that he's going to last the weekend? The kid must have stamina.

LINDA   Very funny.

279

NORAH	You seem to have caught us on a particularly bad day.
TREVOR	But at least – whatever you may say – you don't really need Gary Cooper round here to liven things up. Whereas... Well, next weekend, when Linda comes to meet *my* parents, I know exactly what the first half-hour will be: all talk about the weather, and how pretty Linda is, and how are you getting on with your studies, dear – and, why, what a charming dress that is and, oh, do you take sugar in your tea? The only bit with any intrinsic interest will be how pretty Linda is. I shan't mind them spending the first half-hour talking about that.
LINDA	Oh! Sugar in the tea! Would anybody like some coffee?
TOM	Do you always stand up when she does?
LINDA	Yes, and he opens doors for me as well, and even pulls out my chair at table.
TOM	You mean – in *private*?
LINDA	Yes. I'm trying to cure him of it but it isn't easy.
NORAH	Oh, I wouldn't try too hard if I were you. It may be old-fashioned but it's very nice.
WILLIAM	In any case I don't suppose you'll have to. Time usually takes care of things like that. Time unassisted.
NORAH	He's speaking from experience. At the start *he* used to practise all those little courtesies.

280

TOM	(To WILLIAM) And when you said that time would take care of it...is that the optimistic or the pessimistic side? No, it's a serious question. I really don't know.
WILLIAM	No, nor do I. I'll tell you what, though: let's all forget about the coffee and get out the alcohol instead. Trevor, are you wedded to the thought of coffee – or would you rather have a whisky?
TREVOR	Thank you, I'd rather have a whisky.
NORAH	No doubt his shattered nerves require it.
WILLIAM	I was a little afraid you might turn out to be tee-total.
TREVOR	Now that's interesting. Why afraid, sir?
NORAH	Well done, Trevor! One can see you'll be able to give as good as you get.
WILLIAM	All right: *touché*. Vengeance is mine, saith the Lord. 'Afraid' – because it would have made you altogether too wholesome, too healthy, too square. I think that none of us could have stood it.
NORAH	Speak for yourself.
TREVOR	Vengeance is mine, I will repay, saith the Lord. Sir, isn't *that* the line you were quoting?
LINDA	Give up. I think you might have met your match, Dad.
WILLIAM	Rubbish. The devil, too, can quote scripture.

281

TOM	Did he really say 'too'?
TREVOR	In any case, I'm aware I was being priggish. I apologize.
WILLIAM	And please don't call me 'sir'. It makes me feel ancient.
TOM	You are ancient. And a line like that's not going to put him in his place.
TREVOR	(Starts very purposefully, then breaks off) Well, as a matter of fact... Oh, may I give you a hand with that?
WILLIAM	No, you sit down. Tom can profit from your example. Tom, come and take these round. Norah, you're going to have one, aren't you?
NORAH	Certainly!
TOM	Do I get one? My nerves are shattered too.
WILLIAM	If you come clean: admit how much you really love me.
TOM	Does the size of my drink increase with the depth of my devotion?
WILLIAM	Remember, I can sniff out the least taint of insincerity.
TOM	Dad, I love you enormously.
WILLIAM	And didn't we always know it? (Gives TOM a drink)

TOM   Ta, Pa.

WILLIAM   You're welcome.

NORAH   (Looks at Tom's glass) I think I would prefer he
               had loved you a little less. (Looks at her own) I
               think I'd prefer *I* had loved you a little less.
               You're going to be our ruination.

WILLIAM   That figures. I sometimes feel everything I
               touch has a tendency to crumble into ashes. You
               always hurt the one you love, the one you never
               meant to hurt at all. Trevor, you'll no doubt tell
               me if I got that right?

NORAH   How can Trevor possibly tell you? That song
               came out of the ark.

WILLIAM   Oh, I hoped it might have come out of St Paul's
               Epistle to the Romans. Well, never mind. At
               least the ark is still scripture.

NORAH   And yours came to rest in the nineteen-forties or
               thereabout. Got stuck there.Grounded not so
               much on Ararat as Annabella. You forget that
               some of us weren't even around until the middle
               sixties… And, by the way, I have absolutely no
               intention, thank you very much, of sitting here
               disintegrating into ashes just to fulfil some
               heart-rending little theory which happens to
               appeal to your feelings of self-pity. Not this
               evening, anyway.

TOM   (Pause) Hey, Wobbles, what is all this?

NORAH   You know, truthfully, I'm none too sure.

TOM	Then please don't quash his generous instincts. They already find it hard enough getting by. Who was Annabella?
NORAH	What? Oh...she was the film-star wife of Tyrone Power.
TOM	And did Tyrone Power mind Dad's ark being grounded on his wife?
WILLIAM	I tell you, I never even saw her. She was well before my time; though plainly not before your mother's.
TOM	Oh God! Imagine! Painful enough having somebody's ark grounded on you to some real purpose. But...*I never even saw her*... Poor, poor benighted lady. Mum, I think he's right: he does seem to have this unfortunate effect on people.
NORAH	My son's a lunatic. But since it may appear I'm going that way myself, I hope he'll think he's in good company.
TREVOR	Well, anyway, I know that I am. And may I drink a toast to that? To good company!
NORAH	Oh, it's not fair! I've been wanting to propose a toast for the past five minutes. I wanted to be the first to do so. (Nevertheless, they drink)
WILLIAM	We can see that as a dummy run. Now this will be the proper thing.
TOM	I trust it's going to be to Annabella. That's the very least we can do. You know, it's going to be

a long time before I shall forget the fate of that innocent, once-lovely creature. I shall dream of it for ages.

NORAH   No, it's *not* going to be to Annabella. (Raises her glass) Now this ought to be champagne; but we'll have to see what we can do tomorrow. To Linda and Trevor! To Trevor and Linda! May they always be as happy as they are tonight! Happier. You look like figures from a fairy tale.

WILLIAM   To Linda and Trevor.

TOM   To Freaky and Trev.

LINDA   Thank you, Mum. That was sweet of you.

TREVOR   And here's to all of you. I feel very blessed to be here. Thank you for taking me in.

TOM   'Taking me in' is not a happy phrase.

TREVOR and LINDA drink a silent toast to one another. Everybody sips. A short silence.

WILLIAM   Trevor, you started to say something earlier and then appeared to think better of it. "Well, as a matter of fact...," you said; and I felt sure something of significance was about to emerge.

NORAH   Darling, if he thought better of it, then obviously he'd rather not tell us what it was.

WILLIAM   It's just that he started out so decisively. "Well, as a matter of fact..." And people's first thoughts are always the ones I find most interesting.

285

NORAH	That's only because you yourself launch into things without a moment's hesitation, not caring what you say or even whom you say it to. Until afterwards, I mean, when inevitably you wriggle around in paroxysms of remorse, wondering whether so-and-so will have been hurt or so-and-so will consider you a fool or so-and-so will repeat what you've just said – or in extreme cases, of course, all three possibilities at once. I don't think it's the novelist in him, I think it's more the Aries. Trevor, when's your birthday; what's your star sign?
TREVOR	I'm Sagittarius.
NORAH	Oh dear. Linda is Scorpio... Anyway, who believes in all that nonsense?
WILLIAM	My wife is supremely skilled in the art of drawing red herrings.
NORAH	She has to be.
TREVOR	I stopped saying what I was going to, because I was scared it might sound counterfeit – which, honestly, cross my heart, it wasn't. You asked me not to call you sir since it made you feel so ancient. Well, my first thought on seeing you – *as a matter of fact!* – was that you couldn't possibly be Linda's father; you looked far too young. I still can't quite believe it.
TOM	Forget about Scorpio and Sagittarius! Trev and Freaky – clearly, the two of you are soulmates!
LINDA	(Ignoring this) There, what did I tell you about Dad? Peter Pan himself.

286

WILLIAM	Trevor, that's very kind of you.
NORAH	You've made yourself a friend for life.
TREVOR	Good. If that's true nothing could please me more.
TOM	Are you really only twenty-one?
TREVOR	Why? Do I seem ancient?
TOM	Where do you get all the right words?
NORAH	Oh, *yes*. Please tell him.
TREVOR	Well, I think I'm just in luck tonight. You should hear me sometimes. It depends on whom I'm with – and here I feel very much at home.
TOM	Oh God. He's done it again.
NORAH	And you notice he doesn't blaspheme. That's certainly a large part of it.
TREVOR	But any moment now I'm bound to take a fall. It's dangerous to tempt providence.
TOM	By saying which, folks, he's shown that – against all expectation – he's fallible. He appears to have taken that fall.
TREVOR	How come?
TOM	Because if taking a fall is a direct reflection on the company you're in…why at any moment were you expecting to take one?

WILLIAM	Convoluted, but I see your point.
TOM	Do I get another drink?
WILLIAM	No. Trevor, are you ready for some more?
TREVOR	No thanks. Not yet.
TOM	I'm obviously employing the wrong tactics. Wait…let me rack my brains. Dad, you must be the youngest-looking man ever to have a daughter about to be spliced. Honey chile, I jus' carn believe it, it plum defies belief!
WILLIAM	Thank you. No go.
TOM	Yes, sir, the very youngest. Not to mention the most suntanned.
TREVOR	Yes…I was going to ask. Have you just come back from abroad?
TOM	Was it winter sports, Dad, or the Caribbean or was it something a little more exotic? Like the Leisure Centre? You know, Trev, they have almost real palms down at the Leisure Centre in this town. Dad rents a sunbed beneath them.
WILLIAM	And I go twice weekly. Weekly total: half an hour. It makes me feel good. I know it must sound very sinful.
TOM	Does your father look as madly sexy as ours?
TREVOR	My father's getting on for sixty. Silver-haired, handsome and distinguished…although he could do with losing a bit of weight.

288

NORAH   My heart warms to him already. Can't you tell
                   that Trevor would never talk about his father the
                   way you talk about yours?

TOM   Wobbles, surely you know my one concern is
                   that it might dry out his skin?

LINDA   Anyway, if Dad's still taking his cod liver oil,
                   you can relax; that should help to keep it from
                   getting all shrivelled and loose.

TOM   Phew! I was afraid it might simply fall off at an
                   inconvenient moment – undoubtedly when one
                   of my friends was present.

WILLIAM   (Pinching the skin on his wrist) Perhaps if I
                   took lessons from a yogi I could learn to slough
                   it off at will. (To NORAH) Now that would be
                   something to control him with.

TOM   God, yes! Imagine having Dad's baggy old skin
                   held over you. Worse than the Bomb. I'd reform
                   upon the instant. But may I have another drink
                   before I do?

WILLIAM   Only if you go round beforehand refilling
                   glasses. And don't forget the soda water. Here, I
                   think I'll see to me first.

TREVOR   (To NORAH) Actually, in spite of what you
                   said about my father and me, I can't let you
                   think we have an easy relationship. I do respect
                   him, yes...but, though we both try, we can't
                   really talk to one another. There's a distance
                   between us which seems impossible to bridge.
                   What goes on here – with these two – has
                   infinitely more vitality. (To WILLIAM) Is it

                                   289

	true you can actually bring yourself to take cod liver oil?... Now that's what I call courage.
WILLIAM	Even if you begin by hating it, you very quickly reach the point where you wouldn't be without it.
NORAH	I take it as well, if you're handing out the plaudits. (To TOM) I take that, too, if you're handing out the whisky.
TREVOR	No wonder you both look so fit.
TOM	You should see the vitamins they have beside their breakfast plates!
NORAH	*Minerals* and vitamins. Not so many. You make us sound like cranks.
TOM	Or hypochondriacs. (Looking at WILLIAM)
WILLIAM	I am not a hypochondriac.
TOM	Oh no? Who keeps thinking there might be something wrong with his heart, then? Who keeps testing his pulse rate when he believes there's nobody looking? Who can't bear to hear of anyone in their forties who suddenly drops dead?
WILLIAM	Whereas we all know it's *your* favourite news item.
TOM	Yeah, I'd have it on my own personal Pick of the Week. Probably take it to my desert island.

LINDA	Honestly, listening to you, Tom, anyone who didn't know Dad would think he was the most terrible wimp. Well, let's finally see which of you is the real wimp. How many press-ups can *you* do?
TOM	You freak! Probably a great many more than you.
LINDA	(To TREVOR) Do you know how many Dad does? Two hundred and fifty! At one go!
TREVOR	You're joking. (To WILLIAM) Tell me she's joking... At one go? Crumbs. If I could get up to fifty I should be amazed.
TOM	It doesn't have much to do with strength. It's far more a matter of practice. Like swimming.
WILLIAM	Swimming? Is that a matter of practice over strength? Why at eighty, then, can't you swim so far as you did at forty?
TOM	Well, that's stupid; it isn't the same thing.
LINDA	There speaks the fellow who probably can't manage even ten press-ups.
TOM	Anyway, have you ever seen Dad do two hundred and fifty? Go on, Dad, get down on the floor and do two hundred and fifty.
NORAH	This is an exceedingly boring subject. Can we drop it, please?
TOM	And if it truly is a matter of strength...well, if Trevor and Dad were to have an arm wrestle, I

know which *I'd* lay my money on.

NORAH   Did you hear what I said?

WILLIAM   Yes, stop it, Tom! I'll come and hold my skin
over you.

LINDA   Oh, Dad, you went and spoilt it. If there *is*
anything wimpish about you, it's the way you
don't keep that boy in order.

TOM   You cow! There are times when you make me
positively sick!

NORAH   Oh ye gods, ye gods, ye gods! Why, *why*, can't
we be like other families? Why can't we, for
instance, be a little more like Trevor's? Here a
much loved daughter – *and* sister! – comes
home one night and says she's getting married.
It's never happened to us before. Yet how do we
behave? Do we ask this happy couple where
they met or if they live in the same college? Do
we ask how long it took before suddenly they
knew? Do we discuss weddings and plans and
where they mean to live? Trevor, I've not even
learnt if you take sugar in your tea! It's all very
well being a family with – what did you call it?
– *vitality*, and trying to show that at least
superficially we're alive; but this... all this...!
Do forgive us. I know that – being you – you
almost certainly will, but just the same it seems
to me...it really does seem to me...

She is very close to tears. Again, there is a short, stunned silence.
LINDA jumps up and puts an arm round her shoulders. Everyone
looks concerned – in the case of WILLIAM and TOM, actually
a bit contrite.

292

TOM   Well, anyway, isn't it more important, Wobbles,
             to have found out that sort of thing about him? I
             mean, you know now that he has a forgiving
             heart; does it matter so much if he has a sweet
             tooth? After all you've got two whole days to
             winkle that one out.

All look at TOM in disbelief. He shrugs.

WILLIAM   Has there just been a sign? A miracle? A
             message of encouragement? Should we sink
             down on our knees and praise the Lord?

TOM   May I have another drink?

WILLIAM   Everyone may have another drink. From now on
             we shall raise you exclusively on whisky.

TOM gulps his glass empty for a refill. WILLIAM goes round
pouring drinks. Only LINDA declines.

TREVOR   (To NORAH) So yes, as Tom said, we have two
             whole days to start learning about one another.
             All of us.

NORAH   I'm sorry I made an exhibition of myself.

TREVOR   If that's what you term making an exhibition of
             yourself I wish my own mum would sometimes
             follow suit. And believe me, Mrs Freeman, I do
             mean that.

NORAH   I suppose you couldn't see your way to calling
             me just Norah?

TREVOR   Thank you. I'd like to.

WILLIAM	So long as you don't call me just William.
TREVOR	But he was always one of my very best friends! William the Bold, William the Showman, William the Pirate. Other people may have had James Bond as their hero. Never me… What should I call you, then?
WILLIAM	Why not simply William?
TREVOR	Are you ever Bill?
WILLIAM	No – for some reason. Nobody ever calls me Bill. I don't feel like a Bill.
TOM	You see, we can't present him. On the other hand, you could say he's something we shall never stop having to pay for. Of course, it could be Bill of Health. Even *Clean* Bill of Health.
WILLIAM	You simply hate to let things go.
TOM	Funny...I thought that was you.
WILLIAM	Anyway, I suppose I should feel grateful for 'clean'.
TOM	Yes, let's be fair. One never quite knows where you've been but you do at least give the *impression* of cleanliness.
WILLIAM	Thank you. Only one step away from godliness.
TOM	I say the impression. Of course that might be partly all the after-shave you splash on yourself: in the pitiful hope that it will drive the women crazy.

294

LINDA   (To everyone except TOM) Wait for it.

TOM keeps quiet; the others look at her inquiringly; she shrugs, with slightly awkward air.

LINDA   (Cont) Some crack about the men as well.

TOM   Why should I say that? Now, honestly...!

NORAH   (To TREVOR: indulgently) Such silly children. What were we talking about?

LINDA   (Shade sullenly) Wedding plans and how we met and all that sort of nonsense. You didn't give me any whisky.

WILLIAM   I didn't think you wanted any.

LINDA   I've changed my mind.

WILLIAM   Attagirl! (Gets up to give her some)

TREVOR   (To NORAH) But in fact there are some other things I'd like to talk about first. I've made no reference to your husband's writing. That strikes me as rude: to come into the house of an acclaimed and well-known novelist and not show any interest in his work.

WILLIAM   Acclaimed, you say? Well, yes, thank God – to some extent. Well-known? Unhappily not very. But it was nice of you to pretend otherwise.

NORAH   You will be, darling. Oh, you will. One of these days. I promise.

295

TREVOR	About a week ago Linda made me a present of *The Swimmer* and I don't know when any novel has affected me so much. I started it, I have to say, more out of a sense of duty than anything else – but now I'm telling all my friends about it; making them buy their own copies, of course. I can't wait to read the other two. I felt such sympathy for Mark. I swear by the time I was a quarter of the way through I knew it would become one of my all-time favourites.
TOM	You mean, along with *Just William*?
WILLIAM	I feel...quite overwhelmed. I must give you copies of the earlier ones.
TREVOR	I've already bought them. Blackwell's had them both. I'd like you to sign them for me, though.
WILLIAM	On every page if you request it.
TREVOR	And Linda tells me there's a new one with your publishers.
WILLIAM	Not any more there isn't. The bloody fools don't want it.
LINDA	(Sullenness forgotten) What! You're not saying they sent it back?
WILLIAM	They told me it was...non-commercial.
TREVOR	They must have had a brainstorm.
WILLIAM	That's what I said, too. I spoke to my editor direct. She said they still had faith in me. That was nice. And that I mustn't look upon it just as

296

three years' wasted effort. That was nice as well. And when I felt I had a new idea, perhaps I'd like to go to talk it over with them. I had a new idea right then, but apparently it wasn't the kind she'd been hoping for; she slammed down the telephone. Severance of connection.But if she really thinks I'm going to fall to my knees to apologize... Besides, their marketing was crap.

LINDA   But some other publisher will take it – won't they?

WILLIAM   Ask me another. No, don't; not at the moment. It's been a slightly discouraging two days.

LINDA   (Pause) You're very quiet, Tom. Are you all right?

TOM   What?

LINDA   I said – are you okay?

TOM   Sort of. Bit sleepy, maybe.

WILLIAM   Do you want to go to bed?

TOM   I just want to sit here quietly. Leave me alone.

NORAH   He's had too much to drink. I told you not to let him have it.

WILLIAM   No, you didn't.

NORAH   Well, I meant to.

LINDA	I think the time may now have come for coffee. I'll go and see to it.
NORAH	You know...I remember when Willie used to stand like that for me. He used to open doors, as well.
WILLIAM	Yes. Where have all the flowers gone? Long time passing. I used to open doors for people.
NORAH	And especially for me.
TOM	I think maybe I will go to bed.

At this, LINDA pauses on her way out; returns for a moment; TREVOR remains standing at the door.

WILLIAM	You don't feel sick? (Moves across to TOM)
TOM	No, Dad, I do not feel sick. After just a couple of measly drinks?
WILLIAM	Three. And they were pretty far from measly.
TOM	Well – I can tell you – I get through a lot more than that when I go to the pub.

As he begins to get up, WILLIAM tries to help; TREVOR also moves forward. TOM immediately sits down again, shaking off his father's hand with some violence.

TOM	(Cont) I promise you: I'm not going to stand till you've moved right away. I hate it when you fuss. Don't be more of a prat than necessary. (WILLIAM backs away. TOM stands – a bit unsteadily) There. You see. I'm perfectly all right. (Going towards the door) Good night.

WILLIAM	
LINDA	Good night, Tom.
TREVOR	

TOM half turns to raise his hand in farewell; gives a slight lurch.

NORAH	I'll come with you, darling. Tuck you in. Just like the old days.
TOM	Oh, Mum!
NORAH	Lean on my arm.
WILLIAM	Talk about the blind leading the blind! I'll take him, Norah.
TOM	I told you: I can manage.
NORAH	What do you mean: the blind leading the blind?
WILLIAM	Stop it, Tom. No nonsense. Don't be a fool.
NORAH	Anyway, I'm perfectly capable of taking him.
LINDA	Mum, it's much better for Dad to do it.
TREVOR	Can I help, perhaps?
TOM	(To WILLIAM) Listen. I don't want you to come.
WILLIAM	That can't be helped. I'm coming.
TOM	Oh, for God's sake! Fuck off!

BLACK OUT

299

Act Two

A few moments later. TREVOR and WILLIAM wander about the sitting room.

TREVOR   He'll be all right.

WILLIAM   Yes, I suppose he will. Tom will be all right. What – do you mean in the sense that tomorrow morning he'll treat that little incident as though it simply never happened, and perhaps be extra cheerful for a bit in his attempt to re-establish the status quo? Or do you mean in the sense that he may not fiddle on his income tax, push drugs, plant bombs, molest old ladies? Hmm. Tom will be all right... Perhaps you were meaning in his closest relationships: inside his skin – inside his home? Because that's at the base of it all, isn't it? There have to be solid foundations in the skin and in the home before you can begin to build elsewhere. How are your own foundations, Trevor? The edifice looks fine.

TREVOR   I have my hang-ups – the same as Tom. The same as anybody.

WILLIAM   What! Sloth? Anger? Small misunderstanding here. I'm talking about Trevor Lomax. Who can you be talking about? Would you like another drink? (TREVOR shakes his head)

WILLIAM   You don't think a drink might help you...if ever you should feel like it...to tell me to fuck off? (He pours himself one)

TREVOR   I'm really sorry about this trouble with your book. Surely it can only be a very temporary sort of hiccup?

303

WILLIAM	I heard of a hiccup once that turned into a choking fit, that turned into a death.
TREVOR	Oh, no! How ghastly!
WILLIAM	Well, don't look quite so stricken. I only made that up. It was an allegory. I don't go much on allegories. Do you?
TREVOR	Half the time I'm not even sure I get them.
WILLIAM	An honest man – obviously. It's good to meet an honest man. (Holds out his hand; TREVOR shakes it; doesn't at once relinquish it)
TREVOR	I was under the impression you thought me pseudo.
WILLIAM	Too good to be true. It's not the same thing. Which was the public school?
TREVOR	What? Oh, yes – sorry. Eton.
WILLIAM	I somehow imagined it would be. I'd have liked to go to Eton.
TREVOR	Why?
WILLIAM	I like the Eton Boating Song. Also...to win the Battle of Waterloo.
TREVOR	If I could choose, I'd have chosen to write *The Swimmer* – rather than go to Eton.
WILLIAM	Life's hell, isn't it?
TREVOR	No, I was being serious.

304

WILLIAM   So was I. I should think you're pretty serious about most things.

TREVOR   That makes me sound extremely dull.

WILLIAM   No. No. *I'm* the dullest thing since Bisto. If only you knew! Inside. There's this thick sludgy brown gravy wrapped around my heart. Oh – do you think we could maybe set that to music? (Singing – to the tune of the Eton Boating Song) Thick sludgy brown gravy, wrapped all about my heart, I fancy boys from the navy, I yearn to make a fresh start. (Stops singing) Don't follow the sense, just follow the spirit. When you're looking for a rhyme you really have to prostitute yourself. But when you're looking for a reason ... Well, that's more difficult.

TREVOR   Yes. Well. I...

WILLIAM   Yes. (He wanders over to the window; pulls back the curtain; stands in silence for a moment, staring out. TREVOR comes to stand beside him) I hate February. The worst things always happen in February. It was the month when my mother died. And when I die it will be on just such a day as this. Or on just such a night. Wet; windy; filled with snow. Snow on the ground and snow in the air. Seeping into your bones. Penetrating your soul. Cutting you off from all those around you – any who may still be around you – just as surely as it will cut you off from life itself. I'm afraid of snow. I'm afraid of being alone. I am very much afraid of dying.

TREVOR   I think you're feeling a bit low, aren't you? A bit tired.

305

WILLIAM   A bit drunk?

TREVOR   You don't need to think about dying for another thirty years yet.

WILLIAM   You're wrong. You should think about dying every day of your adult life. It helps you get things into perspective. You should wander through country churchyards; visit art galleries; watch old films. You should... Don't you admire the way that I've got things into perspective? In another thirty years you won't be much older than I am now.

TREVOR   Yes, I shall. Besides, it could just as easily be forty.

WILLIAM   Why not forty-five? Yippee! I'm only halfway there. Will you hold my hand when I'm dying? (Turns to TREVOR, takes his hand and studies it, but with apparent detachment) A strong young hand like this. The thought would give me comfort.

TREVOR   It won't be such a strong young hand in forty years.

WILLIAM   Forty-five.

TREVOR   Liver spots and things.

WILLIAM   I don't suppose I shall much mind liver spots, once I have my own... Tell me something, what are your views on God?

TREVOR   That he exists.

WILLIAM	Oh, very good. I can see you're going to pass with flying colours. Is he benevolent?
TREVOR	To me – yes – very. Always.
WILLIAM	Excellent. The Bomb?
TREVOR	One wishes that it didn't exist. And it's not at all benevolent.
WILLIAM	Our present government?
TREVOR	Same answer.
WILLIAM	People with dark compulsions?
TREVOR	They need sympathy and treatment – obviously.
WILLIAM	Sex before marriage?
TREVOR	Oh, for God's sake! Is that what all this was leading up to? Why didn't you ask me outright, if you so much wanted to know?
WILLIAM	I didn't. I don't. But do you realize that you swore? You actually swore. So why won't you carry it one step further? Be like Tom, tell me to fuck off. We would all respect you enormously for that.
TREVOR	Because I was brought up in a home which wasn't like this one!... For better or worse.
WILLIAM	For richer, for poorer. In sickness and in health... I'm sorry: I just keep on needling you, don't I? I don't mean to do it. Well, yes, I do. Well, no, I don't. No I don't, more than yes I

307

do. Or vice versa. You see, in some former
existence I must have been a lemming – and bits
of it still stick, no matter how I try to put them
to flight… Now that would make a good title,
wouldn't it? *The Flight of the Lemming*. Or do I
mean *The Fight of the Lemming*? Have you ever
heard of that Hitchcock film, *Strangers on a
Train*? Well, as a child of about ten I was
intrigued by the way they advertised it. They
made it look as if a letter had been left out.
Strangers became stranglers. Now flight
becomes fight – well, in reverse, if you see what
I mean. Where was I? Oh, yes. Apologizing for
needling you. My whole life has been a constant
battle against lemming-like instincts.

TREVOR   In fact – if it will ease your mind at all – I might
as well tell you we haven't. Not yet.

WILLIAM   Enormously. Haven't what, though?

TREVOR   Had sex.

WILLIAM   No, I promise you, I should have noticed.

TREVOR   (Tolerant) Linda and I haven't. I mean, we've
talked about it and Linda understands – agrees it
would be better to wait. Not that it's any
business of yours. But, still, if you're going to
find it of the least comfort...

WILLIAM   Comfort? Comfort? No, I find it of no bloody
comfort at all.

TREVOR   In this house – it seems to me – you just can't
win.

WILLIAM	Oh, brother, you have said a mouthful. (Pause) Brother, can you spare a dime? No, not brother. Buddy.
TREVOR	I wish you wouldn't drink any more.
WILLIAM	Oh, but you're not your buddy's keeper. And it's of no bloody comfort at all.
TREVOR	I'm sorry
WILLIAM	If you really want to know, I'd rather think you'd had it off a hundred times already. Two hundred... You know, one gets so tired. I don't think I'd want to live to be ninety. I really don't. I mean, of course, if I wasn't so shit scared of dying, and of my being on my own, and of nothing coming after... No. I would rather think it was all over. In the past. The wonder of it – well, the reported wonder of it – well and truly gone.
TREVOR	William, you're wrong. I know there's something that comes after. That's what it's all about. That's when the wonder begins.
WILLIAM	I've always felt more comfortable in the past. Even when I was quite young – at school – on Mondays I would look back at the weekend as if at some halcyon time; regretfully; knowing that I really hadn't made the most of it. That's why I'm grounded in the Forties. Or the Fifties. Or even last week. The past is all soft – and secure – and I know that I got through it. But the future ...well, that's a completely different matter. Although she covers it up quite well – as I myself do, regarding my equal lack of basic

309

contentment – I sometimes feel that Norah only barely tolerates me. You can't blame her. In her place, I wouldn't do that much. I'm mean and small-minded and devoid of charity. No love – no wisdom – no charity. What shall I do?

TREVOR   No love, no wisdom? That's not what *The Swimmer* shows.

WILLIAM   *The Swimmer* is only a novel.

TREVOR   But based on experience. Without charity in your heart, you simply couldn't have written it.

LINDA re-enters with a tray. As she does so TREVOR moves – almost guiltily – from his position on the arm of WILLIAM'S chair; and forgets to take the tray from her.

LINDA   Trevor, would you please move those magazines? Also the ashtray.

TREVOR   Oh, yes, of course. Sorry.

LINDA   Have you two been getting to know each other?

TREVOR   Yes, we've been...talking of this and that.

LINDA   Me, I hope, principally.

TREVOR   Of course.

LINDA   What else?

TREVOR   Oh, I don't know. A bit about God. A bit about the Bomb. A bit about Eton.

310

LINDA   Has Dad been going all pretentious on you?
                 What's he been saying about Eton? He can be
                 such a snob.

WILLIAM   It may be true I'm a snob but is it *only*
                 snobbery? I used to be so envious of the kind
                 who went to Eton, or Roedean. I always felt
                 their lives must be such wholly charmed affairs,
                 so civilized, smooth-running, so filled with
                 pleasure and content. I still do...emotionally.
                 Emotionally I feel there are millions of people
                 who drift serenely on from one occasion to the
                 next, exquisite in their top hats, always saying
                 the wise and witty thing. No hang-ups, no
                 migraines...no piles.

LINDA   (Pouring coffee) Dad, please don't feel you have
                 to entertain us.

WILLIAM   (Sings – from *Gypsy*) "Let me entertain you, let
                 me make you smile…" I'm sorry. I was merely
                 making small talk.

LINDA   Then concentrate on drinking this, instead.

WILLIAM   It's a little sad if you don't appreciate my
                 conversation. There was another point I was
                 hoping to make, sort of arising out of the last, if I
                 wasn't boring you too terrifically. I was going to
                 say it's exactly the same with sex. I always think
                 that sex will be magical for other people – I
                 mean, of course, so long as they're young, or
                 youngish, and physically attractive. No lack of
                 responsiveness, passion or invention. And no
                 problems whatever about staying the course.
                 Lasting a good fifty minutes.

311

LINDA   Oh my God! Have you ever heard anything like
                 it?

TREVOR   Well... In places, some of our vicar's sermons
                 get a trifle spicy.

LINDA   But why does he pick on fifty? I'd have thought
                 sixty would have been a much rounder figure.
                 And forty would have been more biblical. In the
                 Bible they were always doing things for forty
                 days and forty nights.

WILLIAM   They had staying power in those days. Trevor,
                 can you last a good fifty minutes?

LINDA   Dad...

WILLIAM   But at least you can do fifty press-ups. You can
                 do fifty press-ups?

TREVOR   I'll tell you one thing: I certainly couldn't do
                 two-hundred-and-fifty.

WILLIAM   You know, Tom didn't believe that. The young
                 whatsit called me a liar.

LINDA   No, he didn't.

WILLIAM   As good as.

TREVOR   Well...between father and son... It's natural
                 he should feel this need to belittle you.

WILLIAM   And vice versa?

TREVOR   Perhaps. But I suppose that depends on the
                 father.

WILLIAM   You're absolutely right – yes, I'm a rotten
               father. But why am I drinking this? I want
               another whisky. Trevor, old fellow, will you
               join me in another whisky? Keep me company?
               Please?

TREVOR   All right, I will. Thank you.

WILLIAM   Lindy?

LINDA   A very small one – in my coffee.

TREVOR   By the way, you know, I didn't say you were a
               rotten father.

WILLIAM   Shall I tell you something pathetic? Twenty
               years ago I wanted to be the very best father and
               the very best husband. Believe it or not, there
               was even a time when I wanted to be the very
               best human being. But that came earlier: I must
               have been somewhere near your own age. I went
               through a phase when I used to distribute
               largesse to old people on street benches if they
               looked as though they needed it: two or three
               pounds: I must have been insufferable.

TREVOR   Loving.

WILLIAM   Smug. Then something put an end to it. An old
               man stopped me in Baker Street and started
               some hard-luck story; he wanted the price of a
               cup of tea. I was delighted; this was almost what
               I lived for. I gave him everything I had. It was
               only about thirty shillings but he thought he'd
               won the jackpot. He could hardly speak. I
               remember his eyes, his old rheumy eyes. "God
               bless you," he said, "I swear you'll go to

313

'eaven." It was a lovely moment for the pair of us. And then he stepped off the pavement – and was knocked down by a bus.

LINDA   Killed?

WILLIAM   Smashed and squashed and bloody. There was a ten-bob note that looked like crêpe paper at Christmas. I had nightmares about it for weeks. Occasionally still do.

TREVOR   At least he died a happy man. Perhaps there couldn't have been a better moment for him to go.

WILLIAM   There was a child that I remember screaming. A woman threw up just behind me. I don't know whether the vomit I found on my trousers was hers or mine. I was responsible for all of that.

LINDA   Nobody could possibly – ever – have said it was your fault.

WILLIAM   I saw it as a message straight from God; a punishment for my complacency. And then I was so disgusted – disgusted that I could seriously view the death of a human being, not to mention what it could have done to everyone who saw it, as just another step in my own education.

LINDA   Daddy, why have you never told us this?

WILLIAM   What does anyone ever tell anyone about the things which have helped shape him?

LINDA   The big things? Normally a lot.

314

WILLIAM	I suppose I didn't want to pretend to a goodness I no longer possessed – even if I'd ever got close to it in the first place. And I didn't want to lay myself open to the kind of sympathetic banalities for which I might have seemed to be asking. In fact, I just can't think why I'm telling you tonight. Oh, yes, I can. (Holds up his whisky glass) But I don't mean you to pass it on to your mother – or to Tom – or indeed to anyone.
LINDA	Obviously your...your parents knew?
WILLIAM	My mother had been dead for almost precisely a year. And I hadn't seen my father for about ten.
TREVOR	Of course! There was that episode in *The Swimmer*, wasn't there? Where Mark causes the neighbour's death – Mrs Wolfit's death – because he doesn't do anything about the fault in the wiring; he's dog-tired and intends to take care of it the following day. And then that spoilt and sulky six-year-old sees her mother being electrocuted and runs out of the house gibbering...
WILLIAM	(Almost accusingly) You're very perceptive, aren't you?
TREVOR	I loved that book. If I had written it, I think that whatever else I had done or had not done with my life...
WILLIAM	No. That's the sort of thing I used to think: one book I could feel really proud of...! But of course it never stops there. How could it? You always want more.

TREVOR   Like what?

WILLIAM   Like recognition. Fame. Money. Friendship.
                The next book to be something more than 'just a
                played-out repetition'.

TREVOR   Nonsense. I know that both the others also had
                very favourable reviews. Mainly.

WILLIAM   Mainly. But it's always the one cruelly
                negative review you pay attention to. And –
                besides. There weren't any film offers.

TREVOR   (Laughs) Oh, I'm sure those will turn up – in
                time! But to get back to *The Swimmer*, if I may
                ...although I don't want to become a bore on the
                subject...

WILLIAM   Possibly Lindy could find you boring. I assure
                you I never could.

TREVOR   Well, I so identified with Mark. There was that
                theme of friendship in the book. I remember the
                two quotes – both from Byron, weren't they? –
                'Friendship is Love without his wings!' and that
                other one – wait a moment, on the surface not at
                all connected – yes! – 'A solitary shriek, the
                bubbling cry of some strong swimmer in his
                agony.' I know that I'm repeating myself but I
                found it almost unbearably moving. That's why
                I didn't want to talk about it too soon after I got
                here. I wanted the moment to be absolutely
                right. It was a marvellous piece of writing.
                Horribly disturbing. The whole book was
                disturbing…but as for the electrocution of poor
                Mrs Wolfit…! I didn't realize, though, that it
                was quite so central.

316

WILLIAM	Central? I don't know that it was. I almost didn't put it in. But I wasn't strong enough to leave it out – not when it came to it.
TREVOR	Leave it out? But why should you have wanted to?
WILLIAM	I felt badly about it. I felt shifty.
TREVOR	I don't understand.
WILLIAM	Because you write about things – transmute them – and almost they become all right, as though they've now fulfilled some higher purpose, justified their awfulness, through being developed into 'art'. No tragedy that can't be utilized! I can respect a lemming. But no one can respect a leech.
LINDA	Oh! You! You could manage to feel guilty over anything.
TREVOR	Couldn't you say it was a form of exorcism?
WILLIAM	Is purging yourself more important than profiteering?
TREVOR	You were alive; the old man was dead. He wasn't going to care. (WILLIAM gives a shrug) Did you yourself ever have ambitions of entering the Olympics as a swimmer?
WILLIAM	You mean, as opposed to the old man?
TREVOR	Stop it, you're needling me.

317

WILLIAM   (Laughs) Lindy, I like this golden boy you've brought home. I really do like him.

LINDA   Needling? Is there something here I'm missing?

TREVOR   (To WILLIAM) *Did* you have such ambitions?

WILLIAM   Of course. I do a pretty mean dog paddle.

TREVOR   No, be serious.

WILLIAM   Yes, I had ambitions. I used to love swimming. But it was only a dream. In reality, I was far too lazy. All that training… Also, I used to love writing. And for *that* – well, between friends – you never had to leave your armchair.

TREVOR   'Between friends'. And returning to that theme of friendship, I always hate it, too, that these days one man can't show any deep affection for another without everybody instantly supposing … Even my mother, who's normally one of the least cynical of people. I think that was the thing that really drew me to Mark in the first place: his constant hope that somehow, someday, there would materialize from somewhere this fellow who would turn out to be the sort of friend he'd always been longing for; the only proper friend he'd ever need. Somebody with whom he could make natural physical contact which wasn't all tied up with...oh, I don't know...

LINDA   All tied up with what?

TREVOR   Does one really have to spell it out?,,, Anyway, enough of being so earnest! Shall I go and fetch my bag out of the car?

WILLIAM   I'll come with you. Give you a hand.

TREVOR   Thanks. Although it's not that large a bag.

WILLIAM and TREVOR go. LINDA gathers up the coffee
things and takes them out. NORAH enters, surprised to find the
room empty. Sees the whisky and the soda water and goes to put
them away. While doing so, suddenly breaks down. LINDA
returns.

LINDA   Mum! What's the matter?

NORAH   Oh, nothing. Nothing, darling. I'm just so very
               happy. Where is everybody?

LINDA   Getting Trevor's not-very-large bag out of the
                 car. How's Tom?

NORAH   A bit better. A good night's sleep should do the
               trick.

LINDA   Anyway, at the moment it's not Tom I'm
                 worried about... Is that really on the level: tears
                 of joy?

NORAH   Yes – of course. What else? Don't you know I
               always cry at weddings? And because this will
               be the biggest wedding of my life I'm getting
               into practice.

LINDA   The second biggest – one should hope?

NORAH   What? Oh, yes – naturally. But I didn't cry at
               my own wedding. In fact, I blush to say it, I got
               the giggles. We all did. Standing right there at
               the altar. Daddy – his best man – finally myself.
               It was dreadful. But then, you see, I had nothing

319

to cry about at my own wedding. I wasn't losing
a beloved daughter.

LINDA   Who was the best man?

NORAH   Oh, heavens, do you know I can't even
remember his name? Isn't that awful? Some
teaching colleague of Daddy's: a nice enough
man; he made me laugh a lot... Brian something
or other... Why?

LINDA   Just wondered. Did you laugh a lot afterwards?
After the wedding?

NORAH   What do you mean?

LINDA   I don't know, really. I don't know what I mean
... Well, you weren't losing a daughter but you
were certainly losing other things. Like freedom;
like... Mummy, do you ever regret having got
married?

NORAH   Oh, darling, what a question!... I know there've
been times – many, many times – when I've said
I wanted to run away...and if I'd had anywhere
to run to...

LINDA   Well, yes, but there was always Granny's,
wasn't there?

NORAH   There would have been, obviously, but half the
time I didn't have the train fare. Nor the heart, I
suppose, when it really came down to it. For
how could I ever honestly have regretted it, you
great foolish lump – with you and Tom, and
everything like that?

LINDA	What was 'everything like that'?
NORAH	Why, Dad, of course.
LINDA	At the start were you very much in love with him?
NORAH	At the start? Oh dear. That does sound ominous. But...no; no, I wasn't. In fact I married on the rebound. It was the same for him. The more *exciting* loves of our lives were both behind us; and for both of us probably, even if those loves had been reciprocated, they would have proved disastrous. Oh, darling, you must have heard me talk about Rory, the James Dean lookalike, with the tight jeans and the motorbike and the disapproving mum; I must have told you how I went bananas over *him*. I don't suppose we truly had a single thing in common...other than sex... but he was definitely a bit of a dish; especially in those tight jeans.
LINDA	And what about him? Who was his great love?
NORAH	Rory's?
LINDA	No, not Rory's. Dad's.
NORAH	Oh, you remember. She was a woman some ten years older than him; already married, divorced, three young children. *Very* suitable. I imagine he must have fancied the idea of a readymade family. Hermione... But I can tell you all this – it's nothing that we need to hide – because on the whole it's been a good marriage. And I'm not sure that the things we had – our mutual respect, enjoying one another's company,

sharing many of the same interests – don't in
the long run make a better foundation for
getting married than just being giddily in love.
Though I'm not saying that what you and
Trevor have... No, I envy you the excitement. It
will be something wonderful to look back on; so
much more wonderful than...than the rather
prosaic beginning your father and I had.

TOM has come downstairs and is now standing at the door to the
sitting room. LINDA and NORAH are unaware of his presence.

LINDA   But it won't last, will it? It will come to much
             the same in the end.

NORAH   And is that really such a horrifying prospect?
             Darling, your father and I are happy. By and
             large. We both made the right decision. We
             clearly don't always give the right impression...
             No, it won't last. Your pulse won't accelerate
             each time you see him, or talk of him, or think
             of him... Indeed at the moment you scarcely
             ever stop thinking of him, do you – almost, he
             underlies your every thought? But in place of
             that there'll be an accumulation of little
             everyday entwining things, a million pleasant
             memories that no one in this world other than
             your two selves knows anything about; half-
             submerged memories it will need only one
             of you to reach out a groping hand towards...

LINDA   Hey, Mum. I think you're being a little
             sentimental.

NORAH   Sentimental? Let me just tell you this –
             sentimental or otherwise. If suddenly your dad
             weren't to be here for any reason – I mean dead

322

rather than gone away – there would be a vital part of me that wasn't here either. Terrifying… And I can never understand how people can actually choose to break up for no particularly good reason, after they've been together ten, twenty, thirty years or more. I really can't.

LINDA   Perhaps you could say...stuck it out? Two out of three marriages, these days, end in divorce.

NORAH   What is this? Why are we talking of divorce; tonight of all nights?

LINDA   You know, I never planned to marry this young. I thought I'd travel round the world a bit, see something of life, have a good time. Sow my wild oats. I vaguely thought of twenty-five or six or seven.

NORAH   I know you did, darling, and that's the sort of thing we hoped you'd do, Daddy and I. But this is different. You've got a truly exceptional boy out there, the likes of whom – I can tell you! – only come along once in a lifetime…and not usually that. And he won't stop you travelling round the world, seeing something of life, having a good time. In fact he'll make it all the more possible because he's financially in a position to do so, and you'll be getting twice the fun out of it because you'll be doing it with somebody you love and stocking up that storehouse of memories together. Just so long as you don't start on a baby it will be... Darling, you haven't, have you?

LINDA   Oh, no, nothing like that. Trevor's very proper. Very proper indeed.

323

NORAH   Well, from all one hears nowadays that sounds
            remarkably refreshing. Where does the money
            come from, by the way?

LINDA   His father's the Lomax of Lomax Foods.

NORAH   Good gracious!

LINDA   Yes. Not bad, eh? Haven't I done well?

NORAH   Is it really Easter you're thinking of? My word
            but we'll have to get things moving! Eight
            weeks – do we have as much as eight weeks? Or
            won't we be holding it here...since his parents
            have offered to pay for it, I mean?

LINDA   Trevor was saying they'd want to get together
            with you – as soon as they've met me.

NORAH   Great heavens. Whatever shall I wear? Do you
            suppose the DHSS will cough up?

LINDA   Oh, hell. Is it really back to that?

NORAH   A few days ago. You see, we were holding on
            by the skin of our teeth, counting on Daddy's
            new advance... As a gesture of defiance he spent
            our last twenty pounds on three bottles of
            whisky. He just went out – didn't tell me – I was
            furious. He said I wasn't the one who had to fill
            in all those bloody forms; sit there while they
            pried and patronized and prevaricated; he
            thought he'd got away from all of that for ever;
            and then he started to cry... Obviously you'll
            never mention it to Trevor – I mean, our being
            on supplementary benefit – you'll promise me
            that, won't you? I think I'd die of shame.

324

LINDA	I wish we had money. I really do wish we had money. I wish Daddy was a success. I wish it hadn't always loomed so large: our poverty, our having to make do.
NORAH	Linda! That's not like you! At least, I hope it isn't. I wish it hadn't always loomed so large as well – of course I do – but Daddy is a success, and anyway we're not poor, not by so many people's standards. And what we do have – which thousands of others don't these days – is hope. We're the lucky ones; we're going to get out of it. Imagine knowing that you're stuck forever...imagine the sheer helplessness of feeling –
LINDA	How? How are we going to get out of it?
NORAH	Why, because Daddy will get better and better known with every novel he writes; because maybe at this very moment – or next week – or next year – some film producer somewhere –
LINDA	You sound like him. You're sounding just like him.
NORAH	Perhaps I am. But a little faith is never such a bad thing.
LINDA	Again! I remember he said something very similar – was it five years ago? – that evening he told us he'd been fired. "Perhaps it's just to test our faith!" he said. "And so long as you can only keep your faith in me...everyone...I promise you it's going to be fine! It will all be absolutely fine!"

325

NORAH	He was not fired.
LINDA	All right. Gave in his notice. Which is worse, far worse. Consigning us to all of this...and simply over some really stupid question of offended pride. What a piddling little thing to sacrifice a job for!
NORAH	It wasn't a piddling little thing: to be accused of teaching an examination paper. When both the headmaster and the head of your department imply that you're a liar and a cheat – and when you're the type of person who always sets such store by the truth; always tries to behave honourably; and won't even show one sort of face outside the house and a different one inside it...
LINDA	I just can't see why you and I and Tom also had to give up so much on account of his honour. Anyway, how do you know he resigned? How do you know he wasn't sacked?
NORAH	How do I know? Because that's what your father told me – that's how. How do I know you haven't gone crazy? I don't. Besides, there isn't much that teachers can be sacked for any longer.
LINDA	What can they be sacked for?
NORAH	Oh, I don't know. Sexual offences – political indoctrination – running berserk with a shotgun? What difference does it make?
LINDA	Well, supposing he had been sacked? That would account for his difficulties in finding another job, wouldn't it? And supposing it was for something

different to what he'd told us? There's no way
we'd have known.

NORAH   Why are we discussing this? Why are we
         discussing this?... They seem to be a long time
         out there. I'm sorry – I didn't mean to scream at
         you; but I just don't understand what's going on.
         When you came home a couple of hours ago you
         were radiant – bubbling. And now look at you.
         What on earth has happened in the meantime?

LINDA   Nothing. Nothing has happened.

NORAH   Something must have. Don't you want to marry
         Trevor any longer?

LINDA   I certainly don't want to feel I have to. Just
         because he has money and we haven't.

NORAH   Darling, no one's asked you to restore the family
         fortunes. That can't be what it's all about. Please
         tell me what's upset you.

LINDA   I can't.

NORAH   Yes, you can. Come on; you can tell your old
         mum anything.

LINDA   I mean I can't, because I don't know. I think I'm
         suddenly frightened of handing over my life to
         another person, that's all.

NORAH   Handing over your life! This isn't Victorian
         England.

LINDA   It's the first time I've ever been in love. Perhaps
         I'm scared it's not the real thing. I'd rather

	simply live with him to begin with. But he won't. Why won't he?
NORAH	Because he has principles.
LINDA	You know, he's never done anything more than kiss me. And even that – very chastely.
NORAH	Darling, you've got your whole life before you – why are you in such a hurry? When did you actually become engaged?
LINDA	On Wednesday evening, after a dance. And after he'd been going on and on about Dad's book. In fact I was beginning to think I might be getting increasingly tired of him – when he found this rather novel way of recapturing my interest.
NORAH	And after you'd known each other for a fortnight? Yes, I'm starting to see what you mean about his taking things so slowly. That… combined with his insistence on wanting a full eight weeks before the wedding. By the way, did his parents have any scruples, do you know? Or did they wholeheartedly give it their blessing?
LINDA	Oh, apparently they're tickled pink. They're very keen to have him married.
NORAH	But you're not suggesting that's the only reason why he's doing it…because presumably they feel impatient for more grandchildren? I do wish Tom could learn these habits of obedience. I wonder what their secret is… (Some movement makes her suddenly aware of TOM) How long have you been standing there?

TOM	About a minute. Less than a minute.
LINDA	No, of course I'm not suggesting that. Oh, I don't know what it is I'm suggesting. Should you really be down here? You still look groggy.
TOM	I feel okay. What *were* you suggesting, Linda?
NORAH	It seems to me the sensible thing all round is just to ask him to wait. Have a six-month engagement. If he's the man I think he is, he won't make any protest.
LINDA	If he's the man I'm beginning to think he is, he won't make any protest.
NORAH	Since tonight?
LINDA	Oh, I don't suppose so. Maybe it's just that things have come more into focus.
TOM	It's Dad who's upset you, isn't it? Well, you know Dad...all that need to be the centre of attention, the funniest person in the room – or, at any rate, the least conventional. Somehow it makes me think of that poem: not waving but drowning.
NORAH	And you know how he'd hate to hurt you in any way. Remember those paroxysms of remorse I mentioned earlier. He's probably going through one of them right now.
TOM	And, Freaky, you are his little Goody-Two-Shoes.

NORAH	So it was a bit mean, wasn't it, darling, to hit out like that at his notions of truthfulness and decency?
LINDA	Decency!
NORAH	Yes, haven't you always thought him decent?
TOM	Especially when he walks through the house in his underpants!
NORAH	Essential decency. Honour.
LINDA	Oh, I suppose so. Yes... Yes.
NORAH	What?
LINDA	Yes! But he's certainly been acting quite oddly.
TOM	I'll drink to that!
NORAH	Tom thinks he's jealous – that's what he said upstairs. Daddy's little girl and all that.
TOM	Of course he's jealous.
NORAH	But, my loves, jealousy isn't a sin. It can't be helped any more than...well, uncharitable thoughts, for example. Which, so long as you do your very best to push them from you... And I feel sure he *has* been doing his very best. Because I feel sure he always does.
TOM	And Trevor is really nice. So whatever you do don't get all silly.

WILLIAM and TREVOR return.

WILLIAM	We heard that. Why is she getting silly?
TOM	Because she's a girl. And because she's my sister.
WILLIAM	In any case, I thought you went to bed, young man.
TOM	I suddenly felt better – grew afraid of what I could be missing.
WILLIAM	Well, as long as you do feel better.
LINDA	Where have you two been?
WILLIAM	Down to the end of the road and back. Actually we did it twice. It was good to have some fresh air. Cold but invigorating.
LINDA	I'll go and get the fresh coffee. I set it going a while back.
TREVOR	Can I help you?
LINDA	No, you stay there. Won't take a minute.
NORAH	(Calling after her) Oh and bring in the biscuit tin, darling. Or – Trevor – are you hungry? Would you like a sandwich, or some scrambled egg or something?
TREVOR	That's kind – but we ate very well in Doncaster. (TOM removes the ashtray which Trevor had earlier, absent-mindedly, put down on a chair) I don't think I've yet seen anyone smoke, have I?

331

TOM	It depends what you mean by smoke. Maybe smoulder?
WILLIAM	I see he's beginning to feel far more like his usual self.
TOM	The thing is, Trev, there's something here you should always be prepared for. Spontaneous combustion. If people anywhere can suddenly burst into flame – then someday it's got to happen in this house. We keep an ashtray to collect the cinders. Less showy than an urn – and you know how it is: they'd only run through the holes in the wicker basket. Irritating, when you have a father who...well, when you know that everything he touches turns to ash.
WILLIAM	Especially if you haven't got the Hoover handy.
NORAH	Or the Rennies!... But I think we'll let that pass.
TREVOR	One query gets solved; another arises. But, Tom, there was a Dickens novel, wasn't there? And I believe it *has* happened. Grief, though... (Gives a shudder) Imagine actually seeing it!
TOM	*Bleak House*... That was the name of the book, I mean, in case you thought I was merely glancing about me.

LINDA re-enters with coffee; pours it and hands it round.

NORAH	Thank you, darling. Trevor, do have a biscuit. They're homemade.
TREVOR	And look very good.

332

NORAH	A special American recipe. But ignorance is bliss. If I'd known you were coming they would probably have gone all wrong.
TREVOR	(Having taken a bite, raises his coffee cup) In that case, let's drink to ignorance.
NORAH	No, you're always preempting me. *I* shall drink to bliss!
LINDA	What about American recipes?
NORAH	Yes – all right – but after that I want to drink to Paul Newman, The perfect American dish! Actually, to be completely frank, I would rather drink *with* Paul Newman but I suppose one can't have everything.
TOM	I think at this point we should remember Annabella. To you, Annabella!
NORAH	And to you, Paul Newman! Indeed, to Paul Newmans everywhere! (Raises her cup towards WILLIAM) Upholders of decency. Upholders of truth. And incredibly sexy with it.
WILLIAM	Well, if we're drinking to the world of make-believe – (Returns NORAH'S gesture, lifting his cup chiefly towards her, but also including LINDA) – perhaps we shouldn't leave out the Cinderellas.
TOM	I think he means the Annabellas. Well done, Dad. *I'm* thinking of you, Mrs Tyrone Power.
WILLIAM	For, once upon a time… Yes, once upon a time…

TOM   Oh, good! A story.

WILLIAM   …those were the two fair hands that held the
             beautiful glass slipper. Before ever they knew of
             beautiful pink Camay.

NORAH   Why, my darling, how very sweet of you! My
             own Prince Charming!

TOM   That's jumping to conclusions. Why not your
             own fairy godmother?

LINDA   Your own ugly sister?

TOM   Your own other ugly sister?

NORAH   But more to the point, I am proud and happy to
             say, this was the foot that fitted the glass slipper.
             (Another toast to WILLIAM) They don't make
             slippers like it any more. (Toast to LINDA and
             TREVOR) Except on very rare occasions.

WILLIAM   Nor feet.

TOM   Of course, the whole thing was a con trick from
             start to finish.

NORAH   What was?

TOM   The glass slipper. After midnight. It didn't exist.
             It couldn't have. If all the other finery vanished
             or turned back into rags –

WILLIAM   It was clearly a most superior product. Gucci,
             not Dolcis.

TOM	I say if everything else vanished where was the logic, where was the integrity? And please don't waffle on about poetic licence. What I demand from my stories is the truth.
NORAH	It might have been a miracle. Have you ever considered that?
WILLIAM	Hear, hear! Hear, hear!
LINDA	I said you were getting more and more like him. It's almost indecent.
NORAH	Then does no one today believe in miracles? Other than Daddy and me?
TOM	Mother, you're not treating this with the seriousness it deserves. And in any case there was only the one slipper. Does Gucci *often* go in for half-price sales?
NORAH	But, darling, you can't say I wasn't being serious. Relative to the context.
TREVOR	Yes, Norah, I believe in miracles.
TOM	What, Trev – outside of fairy tales and the waving about of wands? Perhaps you mean on the level of bending spoons and forks; producing white rabbits; doing two-hundred-and-fifty press-ups?
TREVOR	No, I mean I believe – or want to believe – that there are certain times when God does intervene. And yes I do believe, quite definitely, in two-hundred-and-fifty press-ups.

TOM	Or want to believe?
TREVOR	In this case, both.
TOM	Personally I don't see how anyone could want to believe in God's intervention. If you believe he intervenes you've immediately got to work out why he's so damned particular. "All right – let's part the Red Sea; that would be fun and provide a bit of spectacle...someday I know they'll put it into a movie. But no – sorry – application turned down for saving all those Jews again and Ethiopians and Father Popieluszko. And right – okay – so there's a baby in the microwave and eighteen bandsmen in the burning bus and God knows what's happening right this moment in Northern Ireland – excuse me, I sometimes talk about me in the third person – but go away: I'm just not in the mood."
NORAH	Tom...Tom, love...Tom...
WILLIAM	Darling, it's a valid point he's making…
TOM	So what person with any scrap of intelligence would ever want to believe in God's intervention? Present company excepted, of course.
WILLIAM	…but I wish that I was seventeen again and could feel so utterly cocksure.
NORAH	No, you don't.
TREVOR	No, you don't.

TOM	I bet you anything he does. Then he'd have been the swimmer that he's always bleating on about, or the actor, or the politician. The totally incorruptible and all-reforming politician. Naturally!
WILLIAM	Naturally.
TOM	You approve of that word, do you? I suppose you don't so often hear it, in connection with yourself?
WILLIAM	The sad thing is. you were born a disbeliever. I wouldn't wish to be seventeen again if it took away my trust. *Naturally* I don't expect you to believe that.
TOM	All I'm saying is: if you had the chance to be seventeen again in someone else's shoes...
WILLIAM	Oh, I still don't know.
TOM	...and more especially, perhaps, in someone else's glass slippers...
WILLIAM	I'm not sure what you mean by that. I believe in miracles, not fairy tales. I don't believe life is a fairy tale. I don't think I'd even want to believe it. People wouldn't have the opportunity – or would they? – of making any real progress. I'd rather opt for free will.
TOM	Oh, yes: so now you're harking back to those old neuroses of yours, which you're so happy to have picked up along life's way.
TREVOR	What neuroses?

337

WILLIAM   Well – this won't be easy – but let one example
                 stand for all. I'm posting a letter, right? Unless I
                 hear it go plop inside the pillar box – a nice, fat,
                 unmistakable plop – I think at once it must be
                 lost: held fast for all time in some unsuspected
                 crevice. Okay, I tell myself – while wiping a
                 suppliant palm back and forth across the
                 opening – a passing car or bus has camouflaged
                 the plop. But...oh God: did I remember to put
                 the stamp on? And if so did I lick it sufficiently?
                 And what about the flap? On some buoyantly
                 reckless impulse I didn't reinforce it with my
                 usual strip – or strips – of Selotape... So will the
                 letter at length work its way out, leaving only an
                 envelope to reach its destination? Most likely
                 not: it's now my writing I'm aware of: my
                 threes and my capital S's so often look like
                 fives; my r's are interchangeable with n's. Oh
                 hell. I know there's absolutely no chance at all
                 of delivery! That is, until I suddenly remember
                 the wording of my final paragraph: perhaps the
                 humour of it wasn't clear – couldn't it suggest
                 something callous, even deeply hurtful, the very
                 opposite of what I meant?... Oh God, there was
                 never anything more certain: that letter *will*
                 arrive. The British postman is wonderful – I
                 recall a card I once received from Tokyo,
                 addressed to Willing Peeman, with only the
                 name of the town beneath. Oh, yes, beyond
                 question it will get there. And I didn't even read
                 it through: all part of that liberating, devil-may-
                 care attitude I sometimes get as a reaction to my
                 customary old-maidishness – but which, despite
                 my every hope, seldom outlives a single day...
                 So now I really am in agony. What shall I do?
                 Swiftly send a second letter to try to put things
                 right? Difficult. If there's even the faintest

chance of my witticism *not* having misfired,
then all I'm doing is suggesting the possibility
that, after all, the other meaning was the one I
had in mind. Besides, of course…that first letter
will get there but what guarantee have I that the
second ever will; because unless I hear it go
plop inside the pillar box – a nice, fat,
unmistakable plop... Trevor, I don't know if that
answers your question quite fully enough or
gives you any flavour at all of the one or two
small –

TOM   – of the one or two *thousand* small neuroses
which so much broaden and enrich his life...and
of course the lives of all of us.

NORAH   And that was merely the abridged version, praise
the Lord! Which meant I had to wait no more
than half an hour to express the one poor thing *I*
now wish to say… You see, my darling, it just
isn't true that Tom was born untrusting. He used
to think you were the fastest runner in the world.

TOM   When I was six years old and actually had faith
in all the things that people told me. All right – I
accept – I was a backward six-year-old.

NORAH   Darling, I so well remember that afternoon when
you ran out of school all hot and flushed and no
hello's or anything. "Jonathan is the silliest little
boy in all of England!" you cried. "He says that
Daddy *isn't* the fastest runner in the world! I
tried to pull his hair and push him in the mud.
And I told him that his stupid sister has buck
teeth." And I could still see the little runnels
down your cheeks. You weren't a boy who cried
often.

339

TOM	I'd forgotten all of that. I'd forgotten Jonathan.
NORAH	Jonathan for me went down in history. Oh, Tommy was the sweetest little boy. Tomorrow I must show you photographs. And he can try to pull the wool over everyone's eyes as much as he likes; but underneath he still is – no parents ever had two sweeter children, more openhearted and loving. And, Tom Freeman, you can scowl at me till Doomsday: I don't believe you've really lost that trust; or at the very least – if you have – I think you'd like so very much to retrieve it.
TOM	Who wouldn't like to have trust? In peace on earth and goodwill toward all men? In Gary Cooper beating back the baddies? In Superman and all that crap?
WILLIAM	I wish I could have been the fastest runner in the world – in the face of all those Jonathans.
TREVOR	Well, there are Jonathans and Jonathans. My middle name is Jonathan. I'd have put my money on you. (To TOM) We'd have had no need to push each other in the mud.
TOM	But one of us, I'm glad to say, has developed a bit since then. You've gone on listening to the same old stories...even if you've turned a remarkably deaf ear to all those parts which didn't suit you.
TREVOR	Such as?

340

TOM   Such as? Well – for instance – how about old
              Christopher Reeves or Sean Connery or
              whoever it was saying to the rich young man,
              "Come back, sonny, when you've disposed of
              all your dough"? Now for me to claim it's all
              camels and needles and moonshine is no copout.
              But for you...you clearly need to be selective;
              like so many of your kind.

TREVOR   What kind is that?

TOM   The dishonest kind...with all due respect.

WILLIAM   Now watch it, my young Thomas – my young
              doubting Thomas. Trevor looks as though he
              wants to hit you, for one thing; and for another,
              it may be according to the rules for you to strike
              out at us, you family, but it is very much against
              them to treat a guest in the same way. I ask you
              to apologize.

TOM   I thought you were the one who always said you
              should treat guests and family alike!

WILLIAM   I never said you took advantage of a guest's
              politeness and his inability to answer back. Or
              at the very least, if you're offering hospitality to
              someone, you acquaint him with the house rules
              at the same time that you're showing him where
              the lavatory is or where you keep the milk.

NORAH   Oh Lord. Trevor, have we shown you where the
              lavatory is?

TREVOR   Yes, William did.

341

WILLIAM   Besides, Tom, Jesus himself was selective. "For many are called, but few are chosen." So, you see, it isn't such an insult. And what about Orwell, whom you like so much – and Tolstoy – and Dickens?

TREVOR   And Freeman?

WILLIAM   All selective in our own small way.

TOM   And you more than most. (Looks significantly towards LINDA and TREVOR) But, anyway, I'm sure you're well aware you're fudging the issue. Once again.

WILLIAM   You're such a great big dope in some ways. Even if you do think up some rather good titles. *Camels and Needles and Moonshine*. May I use that for my next book? I'll credit you, of course.

TOM   What next book?

WILLIAM   I suppose you don't believe there'll be one. In your eyes I'm all washed up? A has-been?

TOM   Albeit a suntanned has-been. But I can see why a title like that would excite you. A story of humps and pricks in the waning light. Who's got the hump, because who's doing the humping and so who's got – ?

NORAH   Enough! Oh, this is too much! Now you've really gone too far!

TREVOR   Tell me, is he just going to get away with it?

342

NORAH   Remember what happened upstairs? I've already
               slapped your face once tonight! Do you want me
               to slap it again?

WILLIAM   It's a story of one so sharp that someday, if he
               doesn't learn, he's going to cut himself off
               beyond all hope of reparation.

TOM   Learn what? What is it that you've learned –
               after your long, frustrated, cocked-up life?

WILLIAM   Norah. Trevor. Let me tell him what I've
               learned. I don't know what I've learned... That
               when people are unhappy they very often don't
               mean one word of what they say? That, for
               instance, "Go away, I won't discuss it!" usually
               means, "Please stay with me and can't we talk?"
               That, "I'm not hungry, I shan't eat!" is far more
               likely, "Don't give up on me, I just need you to
               be patient."

TOM   And is that the grand sum total?

WILLIAM   Well, at least it's something. Better than nowt.

TOM   No, it isn't. Others may find that wonderfully
               affecting; I find it simply part of the facade – an
               offshoot of all those awful Forties tearjerkers
               that you love to sit and cry over. Didn't Mum
               herself say as much earlier on – before she
               sobered up or changed sides or buried her head
               again, whatever?

He overrides reactions: "I never said that – when did I say
that?"..."Your mother didn't...!"..."Fine, so now it's your
mother's turn?" – this last from TREVOR)

343

TOM   (Cont) Because the thing is, you see, it's all
               about you. I wish I were the fastest runner in
               the world. I wish I were an actor – one of the
               company, all of us pulling together, intent on
               the common cause. I wish I were a swimmer;
               I wish I were a skier; I wish I were Fred Astaire.
               All you, you, you! Nothing but you!

WILLIAM   I was only saying that I don't like to see anyone
               unhappy.

TOM   And that makes you so different, does it, to
               everybody else?

WILLIAM   I didn't suggest that.

TREVOR   It's no good. I'm sorry but I've simply got to
               say it. I think you're such a bastard. Snide and
               bitter and vindictive. Ungrateful, too. You'd
               never get away with it in most families.

LINDA   Yours?

TREVOR   Not in mine, certainly. Never in a hundred years.
               (To WILLIAM and NORAH) Would you rather
               I left?

WILLIAM   Just when you're beginning to learn the house
               rules – and play by them? Never!

NORAH   Trevor, we wouldn't hear of it.

TREVOR   (To LINDA) Would you?

LINDA   Oh, sit down – don't be a wally – even if you do
               seem to think your own family so much better
               than mine!

344

NORAH   Linda, stop it! This instant! Stop it! Do you
             hear?

WILLIAM   Turn on me if you like but don't you dare turn
             on Trevor. None of this is Trevor's fault.

TREVOR   Not better. Better behaved, perhaps. Though I
             don't mean your mother. And I don't mean
             'perhaps'. And I don't mean, either, that it's
             necessarily a plus. (Directed at TOM, with a
             wry grin) Only sometimes.

TOM   But you still think I'm a bastard?

TREVOR   A lot of the time – yes.

TOM   And shall I tell you what I think of you?

NORAH makes a gesture of being about to tear her hair.
WILLIAM slides down in his chair and covers his eyes with one
hand.

TREVOR   By all means.

TOM   I think you're more honest than I believed.

After a moment WILLIAM uncovers his eyes. NORAH looks up
in disbelief. Even so, during the continuing pause, they await the
punchline.

TREVOR   But?

TOM   No buts. I've remembered, too, about that
             thousand pounds.

TREVOR   (With conscious irony) And that makes me so
             different, does it, to everybody else?

345

TOM   (With a smile) It certainly makes you richer.
             (Smile goes) And it means that at least you
             don't just sit and gab.

WILLIAM   All right, then, Tom. You want actions? You
             shall have actions.

TOM   Crikey! Is he going to kiss me or kill me? And
             tell me quickly, someone: which would I prefer?

WILLIAM   I'm going to do neither. (Bends to take
             something off the floor)

TOM   Oh, God, he's offering me his bottom.

WILLIAM   You should be so lucky! I happen, you mutt, to
             be picking up that gauntlet you've thrown
             down.

TOM   Oh? A duel? To the death? Yippee! Rapiers or
             pistols?

WILLIAM   Press-ups.

TOM   Oh, no! You fiendish brute! Anything but that!
             Anything but that! (To LINDA) I suppose you
             wouldn't care to take my place?

WILLIAM   Don't worry: it's only a one-way duel. Duet for
             one. All you need do is witness. And eat crow.
TOM   Two-hundred-and-fifty?

WILLIAM   Yes.

TOM   Non-stop?

WILLIAM   Yes.

346

TOM   Supposing I lose? What, then? What do I have
               to do?

WILLIAM   So far as you can – soften your attitude. Try not
               to be such a clever clogs.

TOM   I have to admit: it *is* rather tempting.

WILLIAM   A deal?

NORAH   You're not serious?

WILLIAM   Et tu, Norah? Don't you have any faith left,
               either?

NORAH   Oh, William, don't be so foolish. You'd have a
               heart attack. You'd kill yourself. No. What I
               think you'd better do – something a *lot* more
               useful – is accompany me upstairs, to make up
               the spare bed.

WILLIAM   After I've killed myself. I'll be with you in
               spirit. Turning the mattress, tucking in the sheet.

NORAH   No, actually I forbid it… Trevor, would you try
               to stop him. You're the only one, I think, whom
               he might listen to.

TREVOR   Mrs Freeman – I mean Norah – it's not as if he
               doesn't put in lots of practice. It's not as if he'd
               be doing it after a long period of…well, of not
               doing it.

NORAH   But you aren't making any allowances for...

TREVOR   What?

NORAH	Braggadocio.
TOM	Oy, oy, oy! Now who's the clever clogs?
NORAH	(Still to TREVOR) Perhaps a little harmless exaggeration, which suddenly mayn't be quite so harmless.
TREVOR	William, you're not being forced into anything – and certainly no one's going to consider you've lost face if you decide against it, or if you find you just can't manage it… But on the other hand I think that somehow it might do us all a spot of good if you did feel like carrying on.
WILLIAM	And afterwards I'll give you an arm wrestle.
TREVOR	Done! But don't kid yourself you'll find it such a pushover. I'm quite a cool hand at arm wrestling.
WILLIAM	We'll move back this chair here.
TOM	And this one. Let's give the fellow room.
NORAH	Well, if you suppose I'm going to stop and witness this... (Kisses WILLIAM on the cheek) I think you're an awful fool but I do love you. Good luck, my darling. Linda, why don't you come and keep me company; let's leave these little boys to their games.
LINDA	No, Mum, don't go. This is important.
NORAH	Important! Why?
LINDA	I'm not sure. Just something inside tells me so.

348

NORAH   Oh, very well. Never let it be said that I'm as stubborn as…some others I could mention.

WILLIAM   Good. Full house. (Rubs his hands in preparation) Right. Right, then. Right.

Limbers up a bit, gets down on the floor, positions himself, does one press-up. Jumps up.

NORAH   Oh, was that it, darling? Very nice. Well then, everyone, good night. It's been quite a day.

WILLIAM   I want to wipe my nose first. (He does so, then takes off sweater) Ah, that's better. Trevor, hold this. You can keep it if I don't come back.

TREVOR   Thanks. I should certainly treasure it. But you've got to come back. You haven't signed my books yet. And that's only for starters.

WILLIAM gets down on his knees again, as a first move towards taking up the proper position.

TOM   Hush! Christopher Robin is saying his prayers! And while you're about it, Dad, throw in one for me.

WILLIAM   My son, you mustn't mock. Isn't that the whole object of the exercise?

TOM   I'm not mocking – merely hedging my bets. You can see it as the first step towards my *not* being a Mister Know-It-All.

NORAH   Hallelujah!

TOM	(To WILLIAM) And don't forget, at the same time, to throw in one about your heart!
NORAH	There is nothing wrong with your father's heart. Neither physically nor...nor in any other way.
WILLIAM	Bless you. Now, who's going to count – apart from me?
TREVOR	I will.
NORAH LINDA TOM.	We all will.
WILLIAM	Yes, you all count – every one of you! Right, then. Here goes. Final take.
SPECTATORS	One!...two!...three!...four...five...six...

Then the lights fade. We hear them counting in the darkness, their voices gradually receding, until eventually – say, at the count of twelve – everything is silent and the play is over.